Published by Ambrosia R. Harris

Edited by
Cover art and design by Marcus Pallas

Authorambrosiarharris@gmail.com

Paperback ISBN 9798349478703

Printed in the United States of America

First Edition December 2021
Edition 3

The Taking of Persephone Series in its entirety is heavily based on the original Greek myths of ancient times. The series takes place between the original Iliad and the Odyssey by Homer. Consequently, the events, discussions, topics, cultures, Religion, and the general way of life reflect the beliefs of that time and do not, in any way, represent the author's own beliefs aside from modern Hellenism (religion based in Greek mythology).

KORE

AMBROSIA R. HARRIS

To: The Bringer
of Destruction

DEDICATION

To my dear children who will not see this until they are 18 years old, and my loving husband.

For without all of you, I would not have had the motivation and support to complete this tale.

BOOKS IN THIS SERIES:

KORE
HADES
DEMETER
THREE YEARS WITH ARES *(Novella)*
WAR & ROSES *(Novella)*
PERSEPHONE

PLAYLIST

Devil's Backbone – **THE CIVIL WARS**

Castle* – **HALSEY

Youth – **DAUGHTER**

Baby – **BISHOP BRIGGS**

Force of Nature* – **BEA MILLER

Haunting – **HALSEY**

River – **BISHOP BRIGGS**

Ghost* – **HALSEY

Dark Side – **BISHOP BRIGGS**

Dead Man's Arms – **BISHOP BRIGGS**

Dream – **BISHOP BRIGGS**

Goddess – **BANKS**

Young God – **HALSEY**

Smother – **DAUGHTER**

Demons (Cover) – **JASMINE THOMPSON**

I Will Follow You into the Dark – **DEATH CAB FOR CUTIE**

Fall Asleep – **JARS OF CLAY**

Plant Life – **OWL CITY**

My Garden – **KAT DAHLIA**

My Oh My* – **CAMILA CABELLO

Tennessee Whiskey – **CHRIS STAPLETON**

Graveyard – **HALSEY**

Fire N Gold – **BEA MILLER**

GLOSSARY

ITEMS

Amphora – Vessels were used to carry wines and drinks (no lip)

Amphori is Plural

Cella – *(or naos)* The main chamber of a Greek or Roman Temple, built to house the cult statue

Coffer – Ceilings in Ancient Greek Temples

Chiton – Rectangular piece of linen was draped around the body in many ways.

Kylix – Shallow bowl

Kantharos – Goblet/cup

Kantharoi is Plural

Kline – Bed

Kleidí – Key

Lekythos – Vessel to store oils

Lekythoi is Plural

Oinochoe – Wine jug (lip)

Polis – City-state was the community structure of ancient Greece

Peplos – A long, tubular cloth with the top edge folded down about halfway, so that the top of the tube was now draped below the waist and the bottom of the tube was at the ankle

Skyphos – Bowl

Strigil – Tool used to scrape off dirt and oil during baths

WORDS/PHRASES

Aischrourgòs – A pervert

Agora – Shops for trading goods.

Bdelyròs – Bastard

Chairetísmata – Greetings

Enthousiasmos – Intense and eager enjoyment, interest, or approval.

Ergastírio keramikís – Pottery Workshop

Es Kòrakas – Fuck off

Eirini meta ti zoi – Peace

Hetaira – Female Companion "Prostitute"

Ichor – Divine blood, Immortal blood. Has a golden color.

Xenos – Stranger

Kuna – Bitch

Kalimera sta archaia – Good Morning.

Moon – 1 moon cycle / month

Miasma – Stain or pollution. Spiritual contamination

Metrokoites – "Mother-bedder" Motherfucker

Proavlio tis Kolaseos – Limbo

Perimene – Wait

Penemorfi – Beautiful

Syncharitíria – Congratulations

Theamatikos – Spectacular

Theos – Gods

Vasilissa – Queen

Vasílissa Mou – My Queen

Vasilias – King

O Vasiliás Mou – My King

Yperochos – Gorgeous

DAYS OF THE WEEK

Theftera – Monday

Triti – Tuesday

Tetarti – Wednesday

Pemti – Thursday

Paraskevi – Friday

Sabato – Saturday

Kiriaki – Sunday

TYPES OF NYMPHS

Lampades – The torch-bearing nymphs of the Underworld

Naiads – The spring and river nymphs

Hamadryads – The nymphs of the orchard trees and grapevines

PREFACE

They say she was taken.

They say she was stolen to rule over the dead.

But these tales are folly.

For Lady Persephone had ventured to the Underworld to flee the agreement made between her mother and Zeus.

They do not speak of her journey with the shades across the river, or how she pulled a Cyclops from its feet with her vines. They do not speak of how she ran through the caverns of Tartarus, barefoot and free. Or how she, the sweet daughter of spring, brought even Hades to his knees.

—Ambrosia R. Harris

She wore linen dresses and flower crowns. She was loved, and she was soft.

Then she was stolen.

And this is the story they tell.

They do not speak of her rage when she would pull rain from the clouds and the flowers beneath her feet turned black. They do not speak of how she laughed when Icarus fell from the sky in a golden plume. They do not speak of how she grew flowers because she enjoyed watching them fade and die. They do not speak of how she pounded at the gates of Hell until they opened or how she let the pomegranate juice drip from her smiling lips. Or how even Hades trembled under her gaze.

—Author unknown

CHAPTER I

THE FLYING CREATURE, THE YOUNGEST GODDESS, AND THE KING

1192 BC: EIGHT YEARS OLD

Helios toted his great sun behind him as he rode through the sky, joyous in the cloudless heavens. Making for a perfect day to explore. Kore tilted her head back and closed her eyes, letting his rays soak into her skin as she perched peacefully on the highest branch atop one of her mother's tallest cypress trees.

Demeter was very fond and cautious of her only daughter. It was because of this that she decided it would be safest to raise the young goddess in the mortal realm, where they would be closer to their work with the harvest and vegetation, tucking them away in a meadow just at the base of Mt. Olympus, on the skirts of Doliche. She surrounded them with her most favored cypress trees, twisting the trunks around into a labyrinth that stretched on for miles.

This did not stop young Kore from adventuring to the very edges of the forest. She knew it better than the back of her hand and had created hidden coves and passageways over the last few years—her way of escaping the constant eye of her mother and her mother's handmaids, the hamadryad nymph sisters.

Kore inhaled deeply, letting the earthy pine air consume her. With a gentle and kind pat against the trunk of the cypress tree, she sent her positive energy through it.

"Such a nice day," she sang.

The tree vibrated back in response to her touch, eliciting a soft smile that pulled at the corners of her lips. She enjoyed days like this, clear skies and fresh air. It had been quite some time since the last clear day was to be enjoyed. The mortals raged war almost constantly, and this one had left a lot of Kore's childhood filled with black smoke and the smell of ash and death. The sound of clashing swords and screams rang through the air daily.

Mortals did not understand the beauty of the world they were gifted. The beauty of life worth living. Instead, they caused destruction and war. There was no balance for her to understand. No give and take. The mortals only knew how to take things, and she feared they would continue to do so until their realm was no more.

She took another deep breath and pushed such thoughts from her mind. Her mother always told her she need not worry, for it was beyond her years—but Kore knew better. War could start between the mortals at any moment. One clear day never meant they were through.

Kore searched the sky's horizon for any signs of doubt that this day was a good one, but she saw nothing. Only clear blue skies stretched on for miles in all their bright, blinding glory.

She did not mind the clear skies, but it was the brightness she could do without. She always had to squint and she hated that.

The young Goddess of Spring closed her eyes once more and let the sweet, earthy air fill her lungs. She was content. It would be some time before Demeter returned from her trades in the village. The rare days Kore was free from her lessons and practices. A day free to be herself. Nothing to worry about and nothing to do but enjoy her time alone.

She was resting her head back against the tree when the silent air was suddenly sliced with distant cries for help. Kore's eyes shot open as she searched the horizon for the source, and it was not long before she spotted a shiny, winged creature flapping wildly in the distance. It flipped and twisted in such ways that captivated her in its bizarre movements, and the tree beneath her vibrated with worry.

"Nonsense, silly tree! 'Tis but a winged creature. Mama said all winged creatures must learn to fly." She giggled, keeping her eyes on the creature as it drew closer and closer to the furthest part of her mother's forest.

Kore wrapped her hands around the clear quartz her mother had given her for protection. She did not feel it often worked, but it had become a symbol to her, letting her know she was awake—that what she was experiencing was real. Allowing her to differentiate between her night terrors and reality.

The closer the creature came to the trees, the faster the young goddess's heart thundered in her chest. The cypress beneath her vibrated again as the creature broke the surface of the upper canopy.

"It must have needed more practice." She sighed, and her eyes locked on the spot where the creature broke through. The tree continued to vibrate wildly, urging her to investigate the intruder.

"Fine, fine, I will go and see!" she shot, almost irritated that the tree would not stop.

Placing her hands at her sides, she pushed off, landing softly on a branch that had been a few offshoots below her. She did this until her bare feet touched the damp grass. To her surprise, the blades were just as anxious, begging her to find the creature as quickly as she could. Kore knew the direction, and it was still early in the day. Her mother and the nymphs would not be back until dark. She had time for a small adventure.

"All right! I am going!" she snapped.

In truth, she was not looking for the creature to see if it had survived. She was more interested in what kind of creature it was. Demeter did not often let her daughter venture from the meadow. She *never* let her venture from the meadow, leaving a lot of the outside world a wonderous mystery to the curious child.

Kore had never even been to Mt. Olympus, though her mother went almost every week. The only other god she had seen was her older half-brother, Hermes, who visited often to chat with Demeter and bring gifts to Kore from her father, Zeus.

The young goddess made her way into the woods, following the flowers' vibrations to where they knew the creature to be. She tried to use them to get a better look at it, but all they could show her was what looked to be a big, golden mess.

Not useful, she thought as she jumped and ducked over twisted, fallen tree trunks. She came across one of her trails that she had lined with lavender plants. The only trail she had that passed by clearings that would lead her to the creature quicker than the one she was currently on. She grazed her fingers over the small petals as she passed, and their vibrations indicated that she was growing closer.

She hurried along the trail until she came up to the first clearing—small in size and lined with a bed of colorful flowers that vibrated in unison upon her arrival. Their energy radiated to her in waves of worry, fear, and urgency. The energy shook her body, rattled her head, and fogged her mind. The flowers' voices grew louder, and she cupped her hands to her ears in hopes it would stop, but their cries to her only intensified.

"You keep saying I am getting closer, then yelling at me when I pause for but a moment!" she barked.

But the flowers, trees, and grass did not let up. Their cries rang wild in her head as if they were speaking to her, yelling at her.

"Ugh, stop! Please stop!" she cried, falling to her knees, her hands pushing hard against her ears. The grass grabbed at her legs, urging her to get up and continue.

The volume of their cries and vibrations grew in Kore's head, and the pressure made her feel as if it her head would explode.

"Stupid flowers! I said stop it!" she hissed, shoving her hands into the ground.

Her eyes fogged over as the earth around her began to glow. The air grew silent with a deep chill, and as the light faded from the grass, so did the vibrant colors. The bright green blades, the colorful petals from the small flowers all faded to an eerie black and wilted from her touch. The soil grew dull, dry, and barren while hideous dark and shriveled vines crawled from it.

They looked of death but moved with such life and spoke to her in a whisper as they snaked around her ankle. She was not fearful, as the vines were not something new to her, but they were not something that would be accepted by her mother. They were her secret, something she tried desperately to keep away from Demeter, which proved difficult at times when they seemed to have a mind of their own. Another thing her mother would not approve of.

The vines continued to creep around her legs and arms gently. Their whispers began low but quickly grew for her to understand.

An invisible man.

She spun around, using the plants' sight to see what was hidden from her, and found herself facing a large, clouded figure; she could hardly make out the horse's mane helm atop the figure's head, a distorted image from whatever magic it used to cloak itself with.

The goddess's vines rushed to protect her, swiftly

snaking around the figure's legs and ripping it into the air. The hasty movement sent the helm flying across the cove, and the figure's head smacked against a nearby fallen cypress tree, knocking him unconscious. The vines lowered him until the top of his head rested on the earth, allowing Kore a moment to investigate what she had captured.

Before her hung a man who looked no older than Hermes. His jet-black waves sprawled out along the grass.

She circled him, her vines still holding him aloft while she inspected his head to make sure he was not injured from the hit but found no wound or welt. She had not often seen men and found this one to be a bit more battle-worn than she found Hermes. A deep crease set between his brows, and the corners of his lips pulled down in a hard scowl.

Where Hermes's youthful glow was soft and warm, this man's face was not.

"'Tis a man," she breathed.

His face twitched for a moment before his eyes slowly opened. With a few blinks, his focus came to and his eyes landed on Kore. He gave her a questioning look before his attention turned to the vines around him. Jerking from one side to the next, he tried to pull free, but this only caused them to tighten their grip.

"I wouldn't." Kore giggled.

She knew her vines were a deadly trap when need be, and struggle only made them more dangerous.

"What is this?" the man spat as he continued to wiggle, ignoring her warning.

"Mama said I should be wary of men, and you are a stranger." Kore got to her feet and examined the man a bit more. He was beautiful, if a man could be such a thing, and though she was young, pretty things were not lost on her.

It was rare for a mortal to obtain such beauty, and no mortal may enter Demeter's meadow. Which only meant that she had caught a god.

"Your mother is not wrong," the man said flatly. "Can

you put me down, young one?"

"How do I know you will not steal me away?" Kore countered.

The man lifted a brow to her and glared.

"I am not here for you," he hissed.

"Well, my mama is—"

"Demeter?" he questioned.

Kore stared at him quietly without response as if she were allowing him time to realize his mistake. Interrupting her.

"Well," she began again, "Mama is not here."

The man continued to glare at her through narrowed eyes. "Hasn't your mother informed you it is not safe to talk to strangers?" he finally asked.

"You are a god." Kore ignored him and it was clear that was not something this god was used to. His face twisted until it held a quizzical expression.

"Yes?"

"How do I know you are not here for me?"

"How do I know you will not end me like you did the flowers, there? You seem to be more of the threat," he snipped.

Kore looked back at the black, barren spot she had created. Her lips pressed flat together.

"Fine, fine. Just know, the plants are with me," she warned, snapping her fingers. The vines released the god, and he fell to the ground with a loud thump.

He groaned, shuffled to his feet, and rubbed his head.

"Sorry," Kore said sheepishly as she ducked down.

Now that he was upright, the young goddess could get a better view of him. His dark hair flowed down to his shoulders like a calm, dark river, making his already bright blue eyes even brighter against his light skin. He was possibly the tallest thing Kore had ever seen, but still, his face was youthful and beardless.

The man looked at her briefly, and without a word, he turned to the forest and headed off in the direction Kore was going. She watched quietly as he disappeared into the trees and wondered what he was in search of.

Her attention fell to her feet as something hard and cold tapped against her leg. She looked down to find one of her vines wrapped around the man's silver helmet.

"That was not nice." She giggled as she took it and trailed behind the man into the darkness.

He had not gone far and looked to be trying to figure out where he needed to go.

"*Perimene!*" she called as she skipped to his side and held out his helmet.

The man froze and looked over the young girl with furrowed brows and downturned lips. He hesitantly took the helmet from her, tucking it under his arm.

"Thank you," he offered coldly. Kore smiled in return, but the man continued to look confused as if she were missing something important.

"So, what is your name?" she asked innocently.

The man lifted a brow to her, taken aback by the question.

"I thought your mother informed you to be wary of men," he said in response.

She scrunched her nose, ignoring his words. "I am Kore," she informed, but the man gave no name. Instead, he continued forward. "You know, you are not the first visitor to my mother's meadow this day!" She ran to catch up with the man. "In fact, I was headed this way in search of a fallen winged creature!"

The man paused and looked over the child again, his expression a bit softer. "A winged creature?"

"Yes, it was very sparkly. I was on my way to see what it was."

"You know of his location?"

Kore nodded with a smile and took the man by the hand before leading him off again. "This way!"

They walked for what seemed like hours. The trees and

plants continued to guide them and seemed to change vibrations the closer they got. The man remained silent most of the time. Only sighing a few times here and there.

"You never told me your name." Kore finally broke the silence as they came up to an old fallen tree. It was one of the thickest trees that had sadly dropped not too long back, and it took up a lot of space, lying across Kore's path.

The man tossed his helm up before lifting himself with ease and turned to offer his hand to the child, but Kore simply closed her eyes and allowed her vines to lift her up and over the trunk. He watched with raised brows before he jumped down to her side.

"You do not know of me?" he asked in a voice less reserved, but deep.

"Nope!"

"*You* may call me Aidoneus," he offered.

"I have never heard of you. Are you sure you are a god?"

"I am."

She was not sure what he was the god of but felt that that was the only answer she would get. She went over all the gods her mother had told her of, how they looked, how they spoke. Yet her mother had never mentioned an *Aidoneus*. Kore thought maybe he was the son of Aphrodite, being that he was so beautiful. Or son to Ares, being that he was so big. A question to ask the hamadryad sisters during one of their lessons.

"Kore!" Aidoneus shouted as he snatched the child from the ground, holding her high in the air.

Kore was confused and the movement was too fast for her to track. Her eyes fell to the ground where she once stood to find a large gray serpent, coiled and ready to strike.

Without a second thought, Kore's vines quickly wrapped around the serpent. Some crawled from its mouth as the ones around it squeezed. The snake wriggled and writhed before them until its movements slowed to a stop.

Aidoneus watched quietly, but concern etched his face.

"Did you do that?" he asked as he set Kore on her feet.

"My vines are very protective," she said, unbothered by the event.

She bent down and ran her hand through the grass; their vibrations indicated the creature was just overhead in the next clearing.

"This way!" Kore cheered as she sprinted off, Aidoneus close behind. They pushed through more brush before they made it into a large clearing shaded by trees that curved inward to make a dome shape. Kore loved this part of the forest because it was open like the meadow, but the sun filtered through the branches and leaves, creating dancing lights across the ground. With lush grass and very few flowers to worry about, it still smelled of peonies.

However, Kore noticed something new, and it was not her mother's fragrant peonies and cypress.

Kore began to scan the field around them when suddenly everything went dark, and she could feel something heavy on her head.

She lifted her arms to remove the object that blinded her.

"Leave the helmet, child," the man ordered, but Kore's curiosity had the best of her.

She turned the helmet so that one eye could see from the opening and watched as the man stepped up to what looked like a glob of liquid gold. He circled it a few times before bowing his head and speaking a few soft words.

Kore was amazed by how kind the man seemed to care for the mass as if it were a loss to him of some sort. She took one slow step forward, and then another, and another, until she was only a few feet away from what she could now see was no glob. The smell that radiated from it was that of rot that she had never encountered; it turned her stomach but still, she stayed.

She lifted the helmet to get a better view of the mass before her and quickly wished she had not. Now she was able to see clearly what had fallen into her mother's meadow. It was not a winged creature; it was not a creature at all, but a boy. His wings were made of nothing more than wood, feathers, and a sticky gold substance that dripped slowly down his bubbling skin, leaving a golden streak in its wake.

Skin peeled with the sticky solution as it dripped down into a liquid mess at her feet. The colors of blood, the substance, and mud mixed before her and brought forth a sour, rotten odor, causing Kore's stomach to twist into a knot. She could not control the involuntary gagging that consumed her as she clutched her belly.

"Gods!" the man, Aidoneus, hissed as he ran and spun Kore around to face the opening of the clearing from which they came.

"Do not look," he ordered, returning to the mess.

She could hear him whispering a brief prayer that she remembered her mother saying only the gods of the Underworld used. A welcoming prayer, to welcome them to their new life, the afterlife. Kore turned her head just slightly so that she could get a glimpse from the corner of her eye. She could see the man bow once more and place his hand over the mass.

She watched as it slowly sank into the earth and was quickly replaced with a patch of white asphodels.

Kore turned around completely to face the man. She looked over him a bit harder this time, taking note of his dark chiton and the pin that held it together at his side. She had been too focused on his reason for being in her mother's meadow and looking for the boy that she had overlooked the most identifying symbol for gods. Their pins. The golden pin symbolized Olympians and Mt. Olympus, while Kore's mother spoke of a dark pin that only the gods of the Underworld wore.

The same dark pin *this* god wore.

She stared at him, confused. Her mother had said the Death Gods were cruel and mean. But Kore had spent much of her day with one, and he had been mostly quiet—a bit cold, but quiet. He did save her from the serpent, after all. That did not seem the act of a cruel person.

"Are you—are you the God *of* Death?" Kore knew that god to be Thanatos, but she also knew that two divines managed the sun and two for the moon. She figured collecting souls could not be a one-god job.

Aidoneus tilted his head with a smile teasing the corner of his lips, but he did not answer. He stepped to her side and guided her from the clearing toward the way they entered.

They walked in silence for a while before Kore finally spoke. "You do not say much, do you?"

But the man stayed silent.

"Mama says when mortals are quiet, it is because they are either shy or scared," Kore added after a while.

"I am no mortal," he finally scoffed.

"Me either," Kore shrugged, "but we do not differ from them much, do we? At times, I do not think we differ much from them at all."

"That is an interesting view." His voice was smooth again as he thought on her words.

"So, are you shy, or are you scared?" she probed.

"Neither."

"Then why do you not speak?"

"I haven't much to say." The man turned to her with a soft smile.

"If you do not have much to say, I hope you do not mind that I do. I am not shy," she sang, placing her hand over her chest with a smile.

"That, I can see." He sighed.

"How do you expect to make friends if you haven't much to say?"

"I do not need friends," the man said coldly.

"Sure you do! Everyone needs a friend—even gods! Here, look!" Kore hopped in front of Aidoneus, stopping him. "I can be your friend!" she cheered happily. The man studied her with confusion etched on his stone-like face. "I do not have many friends either," she added.

He tilted his head, and for a moment Kore thought she saw a hint of sadness cross his face. "May I ask you something, Kore?"

"Of course!"

"Does your mother know you are capable of that? With those vines and with the plants?"

"She does not. If she knew I caused flowers to wilt and die, she would not be too happy."

"You can take life?"

"I can make it—and take it. From the plants, of course." She sighed.

"Of course."

"Mama would think it be the work of Hades himself." She pouted. "I do not know much about him. Mama does not speak of him often."

"Oh, and what has she said about the Lord of Darkness?" he inquired in a more relaxed tone.

"Not much—just that he's cruel, and travels with hounds, and—" She paused.

"And?"

"Well, she said the sound of screams can be heard when he is near. But that one I am not too sure she was being honest about." She thought back to the tales her mother had cautiously told her.

"And that would just be horribly annoying for him—I would guess." There was a hint of joy in his voice as he spoke, and a large smile spread across his face.

"Do you know him? Hades?" Kore looked to Aidoneus's dark pin that held his robes up. He took notice of what she was eyeing, and his face hardened again.

"Have you no fear in speaking his name?"

"Should I?" Kore stopped walking.

She had always been confused by the fear that surrounded the God of the Dead. The fear around death in general. It was a necessary event for mortal life, for all life that was not divine. Death helped the world continue and grow, but even the Deathless Gods feared it as much as they feared its ruler.

"Besides, I think he and I have something in common," she sang as she reached down and grazed a small patch of chamomile.

The petals and stalks recoiled from her, wilting and turning black until the spread of death took the whole flower patch. "We both have something to do with the process of death." She pulled her hands up to her face and gazed at the tips of her fingers for a moment before smiling back to Aidoneus. "So, do you know him?" she pushed again with a wicked smile.

"You could say that," he said as he started back on the trail.

Kore kept close behind. "Where are you going?"

"Taking you back to where I found you."

"Oh, well, we went the wrong way for that. We passed that not too long ago. But we are close to the spring!" She placed her hand on a nearby trunk and allowed its vibrations to lead her to the exact spot. "This way!" Her voice rang.

She grabbed Aidoneus by the hand and tugged him in the direction advised. Pulling him through the trees, up and under fallen trunks, and taking aid from him when needed. When they finally made it into the clearing and the branches no longer obscured the sky, Kore could see the sun was near setting.

"Oh!" she gasped. It would not be long before her mother would be returning to the main meadow.

"It was fun meeting with you, Aidoneus—God of whatever you are the god of!" Her angelic face lit up from the ichor that flushed her cheeks.

"As with you, young goddess." He bowed to her and she lifted her hand and waved it over his head, bringing forth a crown of black asphodel flowers that clung to a dark, creeping vine. The petals were weak and soft, falling limp against the vines.

"Please tell your king hello for me," she cooed, attempting to hide the small frustration of the flowers from her face.

"I will be sure to do—"

"Lady Kore!" a soft voice cried from the bushes.

"Lotus!" the goddess cheered as she skipped to her friend's side.

She turned to introduce them, but Aidoneus was gone with only a dark cloud of smoke left in his place and the faint smell of burning cypress and ash.

"Oh." She sighed.

"Kore! What are you doing?" The small creature frantically looked over her friend.

Lotus, a naiad nymph who Demeter had adopted not long after Kore's fifth year. Unlike her adopted tree nymph sisters, Lotus was a river nymph and spent most of her days in the small pond Demeter had constructed for her.

Her skin was a faint tint of blue that appeared dull compared to her seafoam eyes. Her ears were also what set her apart from the sisters. Where the hamadryad nymphs had branch-like ears, Lotus had pointed ears that matched that of a spiked fin.

"Lotus, you will not believe my day!" Kore shot happily. "First this creature fell from the sky!"

"Kore—"

"Then, this invisible man comes by looking for the creature! Turns out he was not a creature but a boy!"

"Kore—"

"So Aidoneus—the invisible man—did some prayer, and the boy was gone!"

"Kore!" Lotus shouted, clapping her hands together. "Do you not know who that was?" she questioned with wide, fear-filled eyes.

"Um, Aidoneus?" Kore said curiously, watching Lotus for a moment. She had never seen such fear in the young nymph's face.

"No. Kore, that was—" Lotus cast her eyes to the ground, and in a voice just below a whisper, she breathed, "Hades."

CHAPTER II

THE YOUNG GODDESS, THE YOUNG NYMPH, AND THE SECRET

The young girls looked over the now empty spot the mysterious god had stood. The divine Kore had spent the afternoon with was nothing close to the tales Demeter had shared with her daughter.

"No." Kore giggled, looking back to where the man had stood. "You heard Mama's stories. Aidoneus is nothing like Hades. I do believe he knows him, though!"

"Yes, because he *is* him," the nymph urged.

"Mama said Hades—"

"Shh! Stop saying his name!" Lotus cried desperately.

"Mama said Hades was followed by vicious hounds from Hell and screams of the tortured souls! Did you see any hounds, Lotus?"

"No. But—"

"And did you hear any screams from the tormented?"

"Well, no, but—"

"Then how are you so sure it was him? Besides, isn't Hades—*old*?" Kore quizzed.

"Because I have seen him before! My cousin is a nymph

of the river in his realm. I did stay with her for some time," Lotus reminded.

Kore looked over her nymph friend for a moment, the realization washing through her. The pin, the prayer, the helmet.

Kore's heart raced as she thought back on her evening with Aidoneus, with *Hades*. Her mind flooded with questions. Questions she was sure Lotus could not answer, not at this moment anyway. That did not mean she could not help her find the answers. Kore reached up and grasped her crystal; the vibrations that pulsed through it reminded her that her day was just as real as she thought.

"Lotus, I have a favor I must ask of you," she breathed.

"Yes?" Lotus's voice was wary, and she knew that whatever Kore was about to ask, she wouldn't like it.

"I need you to keep this whole day from Mama. She must not know."

The nymphs had been ordered to tell Demeter of any unknown guests, specifically the gods. However, Lotus was Kore's handmaid—so long as Demeter did not specifically ask if anyone visited, the young nymph had to follow the young goddess's word.

Lotus nodded as she accepted the request and turned to leave the clearing, waiting for Kore just at the edge.

"Kore?" Lotus called and the goddess skipped to her side. "What was he like?"

Kore filled her in on the day's events as they made their way back to the meadow. She skipped over the part where she wilted a few patches of flowers. Even Lotus did not know of the power, and Kore preferred to keep it that way for the time being. Lotus was good at keeping secrets; it was just that Kore could not bear to hear her mother's words leave her friend's lips.

They laughed and giggled about the things she had said to him without thought. How she had questioned the man on his knowledge of the king and how he had acted indifferent in his responses.

"But why would he give you a different name?" Lotus probed.

"I do not know. I'll have to ask him the next time I see him."

"You plan to see him again?" Lotus shot in surprise.

"You never know." Kore shrugged. "I did not think I would see him today, but I did. So, who knows? I am just saying, *next time*, I will ask him."

They made their way into the meadow—a spacious and open field with a small cottage in the center of a flourishing garden filled with flowers and vegetables, fruit trees, and bushes that held all of Demeter's magic. It was the fruit used to make the ambrosia the gods consumed. Being the Goddess of Harvest and Grain, Demeter was tasked with producing food and nectar for all the divine.

Next to the garden stood four simple beehives that had been crafted of twigs and mud. Kore felt they could be better, but Demeter always said, *They have worked fine all these years; no need to fix what is not broken.* But still, Kore felt the amount of nectar would be more rewarding if the bees' homes were nicer. For this, too, had to be taken up to Mt. Olympus weekly, and Demeter constantly complained that the nectar harvest was slightly short. Clearly, it was not working.

It was at the beehives that Kore saw her mother tending to the small creatures. A tall, slim woman with hair as red as fire that twisted in unified curls down her back, Demeter leaned over the hives, her long fingers dancing around the opening as she drew forth the nectar before she looked up and met eyes with her daughter.

"My precious daisy!" Demeter's voice sang through the trees. She righted herself and made her way toward Kore and Lotus. "How was your day? What did you spend your time on?" She happily embraced the child.

"I just spent the day at the spring, Mama! I am happy you are home!" Kore lied; she shot a glance at Lotus before

Demeter pulled away.

"You only spent the day at the spring? No practice? My dear, you know how—"

"Oh, but I did practice." Kore ducked her head; again, this was not a lie but not the whole truth.

She did practice this day, but Demeter would not consider her vines a proper practice. Kore adored her mother; she just did not like that her mother would not be able to accept her powers for what they were. Being the Goddess of Harvest, she must ensure vegetation success.

Success Kore could rip away in seconds.

Demeter smiled softly at her young daughter. "Go get cleaned up, dear. I have something for you." She bent down and pressed her lips gently against Kore's forehead, then fluffed the child's hair. With a soft smile, she turned and returned to her hives.

Kore and Lotus raced to the cottage, laughing and screaming with joy when Lotus reached the stone steps first.

"Lady Kore, please!" Ampelos pleaded, the youngest of the hamadryad sisters and Kore's handmaid, but the goddess always considered her more of a spy for her mother. She was kind, but Kore would rather not speak with her about her personal matters.

The hamadryad sisters were orchard nymphs and thus spent their time helping Demeter in the garden and with the hives. But Ampelos more specifically was the nymph of the grapevine, and she was just as delicate and lovely as one.

She pulled her thick, dark hair back, ready for the work ahead.

"Do not look so serious, Ampelos." Kore laughed, noting the fold between the nymph's brows.

"If you behave this time." She sighed. Her angled jaw set tight as she exhaled deeply through her nose in irritation.

"She is not so bad!" Lotus giggled.

The three entered the cabin. Though small from the outside, Demeter had cast upon it a spell that caused the inside to be much larger once entered, with several large halls and a dining area with columns made of white marble. Giving Kore a small taste of life on Mt. Olympus.

"The bath hall, ladies," Ampelos ordered as the girls hurried in front of her, constructing another race to see who could get there first. Their laughs and giggles bounced off the marble, echoing through the chamber like music. Ampelos sighed.

"I win this time!" Kore cheered, jumping up and down before turning into the small chamber with a marble-carved basin set in the center. The far wall had a narrow opening that led out to a stream of fresh water. To the right sat a table lined with oils, herbs, and rags.

"Yes, yes. Undress," Ampelos ordered. "Lotus, please grab the rosemarinus and Lavandula oil. Oh, and the rags."

She began filling an amphora of herb water to add to the bath and set it beside the basin before turning back to the fresh stream, handing off the mix to Lotus.

Kore climbed in as the nymphs collected and readied the space. Ampelos grabbed the smaller amphora that sat beside the edge. She filled it and poured it over Kore's head, rinsing the dirt and day away. The chilly water sent bumps across the goddess's skin. "You may plug it now," she ordered as the muddy liquid ran clear.

Kore did as instructed, waiting as they filled the basin to its brim. Ampelos poured the mixture, and Lotus added the oils.

"We shall take our leave now. Call for us when you are done." The nymph bowed.

"Can Lotus stay?" Kore pleaded.

"As always." Ampelos smiled before departing the chamber. The girls waited until she was well from hearing range before they continued their conversation.

"You cannot tell the sisters either," Kore warned, though she had a feeling Lotus knew better.

"I do not know what I would even tell them." Lotus

giggled softly. "Besides, Lady Demeter did not seem to notice, and you are not hurt nor missing. Do you think he will ever return?"

Kore shrugged as she thought the question over. He was only here for the boy, as far as Kore knew.

"I do not think so," she pouted, and Lotus's eyes rounded.

"Somebody has a fancy," the nymph teased.

"I do not! He just has a nice face is all. The nicest I have seen," Kore mused.

"It is kind of the only face you have seen outside of your brother's."

"That does not make him any less pretty. I just thought the Lord of Darkness would be older, like Zeus and Poseidon. He is the oldest of the three after all." Kore moved her hands over the water as she spoke, swirling the oil on top.

"The divine all stop aging at different points. Maybe that's why he is always down there."

Kore thought on that; her mother never said he was old. She only said he was an Old God. Kore drew her own conclusions from that.

The young goddess rinsed her body of the oils and unplugged the basin to drain the cloudy water. Ampelos came without needing to be called for—sometimes it proved useful while other times it was more of an annoyance to Kore.

"Oh good, you are finished. I brought your robes," she sang as she set them on the marble bench just outside the basin.

Kore stood from the bath, and Ampelos wrapped her in the cloths to dry her before helping her into her night robes. The goddess walked over to the reflective metal plate to look herself over, her thick red curls plastered to her face and neck from the water.

She picked up the crystal comb her father had gifted her for her recent birthday and briskly ran it through her hair. Ampelos assisted with braiding it, resting it gently on her left shoulder as she usually did.

"Anything else?"

"My mother?" Kore asked.

"Waiting in your chambers, Lady Kore."

"Thank you. Good night Ampelos, good night, Lotus," Kore cooed before departing the nymphs and meeting her mother where she had been told she would be. It was routine for Demeter to see Kore off to sleep, a way to console the child's fears of her night terrors that were near-nightly events. However, this eve, the goddess had a surprise to share.

Demeter sat at the edge of the bed, waiting patiently. Her bright, electric yellow-blue eyes were piercing, but her voice was soft. "Good evening, my daisy!"

"Good evening, Mama. What gift have you brought for me?" Kore pried.

"Oh, just some new linen robes, dear. I already set them away for you; you seemed to be having quite the time in the chamber with Lotus. I did not want to rush you," Demeter said softly.

Kore climbed into the furs beside her mother, tucking herself into them.

"What story shall I tell tonight?"

"Um." Kore thought. There were a few she wanted to ask for. She could ask about the Three Brothers Draw; she could ask about the heroes who had been freed from the Underworld. There was a wide range, but she needed to ask for one that didn't draw her mother's attention.

"Can you tell me of the Titanomachy, Mama?" Kore pressed.

She would start small so as to not arouse suspicion. The story of how the gods had overthrown the Titans seemed a good start.

"Oh, dear. Have you not grown tired of that history?" Demeter sighed with a smile.

"You do not share it often," the child countered.

"Where would you like me to begin?"

"After Zeus had freed you, Mama." Kore knew the

whole story was hard for her mother, being that she was one of the divine children Cronus had consumed. The story up until that point was hazy, but it was not the part Kore found interest in.

"Well, after your father had freed us, we all hurried to the nearest shelter we could find." Demeter paused as her eyes glazed over, recalling those distant memories.

"It was deep in a cave along the ocean. Zeus had convinced us that it would be for the best that we locked away Cronus so he could not do us harm once more. Something we all quickly agreed to." Her voice fell slightly as if she thought that decision was not a well-placed one. She took a deep breath before she spoke again.

"He allowed us to heal in the cave while he ventured deep into Tartarus to fetch the Hecatonchires and Cyclopes."

"Hecatonchires?" Kore blurted.

"The hundred-handed ones, dear. There was Aegaeon, Cottus, and Gyges. Creatures born of Uranus and Gaia that bore fifty heads and one hundred hands." Demeter raised her hands above her head, animating the size before the child.

Kore gasped. "What did they do?"

"Oh, they and the Cyclopes agreed to fight, and thus Zeus came back for us. Hera, Hestia, Poseidon, Hades, and myself."

Kore noted the slight pause her mother created around Hades's name.

"He took us back to Mt. Olympus and requested the Cyclopes fashion his thunderbolts. The Hecatonchires, well, they only heaved boulders," Demeter continued.

Kore gazed up at her mother with questioning eyes.

"They were strong, dear, not bright." She laughed softly. "But no matter their intelligence, they were mighty and offered much-needed aid. Once Zeus had us settled, he raced down to find Themis and Prometheus, the only Titans that felt our cause—our fight—was just. It kept them out of Tartarus for the time." Demeter ran her hands through Kore's hair and guided her back into the furs.

"Hestia, Hera, and I worked in the palace for aid and supplies. We saw very little of the war. But it was loud. Zeus drew in several times to see Hera while she worked the medical aid. He had a fancy for her. Poseidon fared better, only drifting in a few times for ambrosia and nectar."

"And Hades?" Kore watched her mother's eyes at the question.

"He never entered for aid," the goddess said stiffly.

Kore knew that was the most she would get on that and decided to move on. "You all still won."

"We won," Demeter said with a soft laugh. "It took ten days and ten nights. But we won."

She sighed, drawing her story to an end. Kore had other plans.

"What about after?"

"How do you mean, sweet child?"

"I mean after you won. How did Zeus settle on the draw?"

Demeter's brows folded together as she thought on the question. Her lips pressed flat, and she looked her daughter over with curious eyes.

"Zeus had Hera pluck three twigs from the Olympus Garden, all at different lengths." She paused for a moment. "He drew first, then Poseidon, and then Hades."

"Were Poseidon and Hades happy with their lot?" Kore quizzed.

Demeter looked to Kore with downturned lips. "They did not seem to mind. Why do you ask?"

"I would have just thought one could only stay in the water for so long, and one could only be lonely for so long," Kore said with her mother's eyes still locked on her.

"Poseidon was born for the sea. As for the King of Darkness, I cannot say. He is cold to others; loneliness is what he wants," Demeter said in a hushed tone.

Kore did not feel that was so. He was not so cold to her.

"Nobody wants to be alone, Mama."

Demeter shook her head. "Well, *he* does, my daisy. Sleep now, and dream sweet dreams, my love. I shall see you when you wake," she cooed, pressing her soft lips to Kore's forehead. Hair swept across Kore's cheek, sending out the sweet fragrance of cypress and freshly baked bread. A familiar and comforting scent from her mother.

"I love you, Mama." Kore sighed, closing her eyes.

"I love you too, my daisy," Demeter whispered.

Demeter was off on another trip to the village for trade. She had been in need of a goat for cream and cheeses to take up to Mt. Olympus, and it had been some time since she had last owned one. Demeter did not tend to keep her creatures caged up, but sadly her last set of goats roamed free and met their demise in the thick of the forest. She had spent time since then crafting a fence around the garden and pasture to ensure her flocks stayed where she could watch them more closely.

Kore rid herself of the furs and stretched her arms far above her head. It took her a moment before she sat up, and when she did, she took another deep stretch and dragged herself from the horribly uncomfortable wooden kline.

Demeter only went to trades once a moon with the nymphs. She needed them to have knowledge of the village and mortal life so that they could break off and enjoy trades. Something Kore hoped to be a part of someday.

The hamadryad sisters used to switch off staying behind with Kore, but her mother tended to overtrade with the mortals and began to need the extra set of hands to bring back her goods. This day seemed to be another one in which she would need them.

The nymphs ran through the halls frantically, gathering bread and eggs, fruits that grew wild by the spring, and the sproutlings the nymphs had started to help with the trades.

Lotus stood off to the farthest right of the dining hall, nibbling on a freshly baked bun as she watched the sisters zoom by.

"Lotus! Help!" Syke, the middle sister, cried.

She favored Ampelos with the same deep brown eyes and dark flowing hair, but where Ampelos was timid, Syke was outgoing and animated.

"I haven't finished my breakfast yet." The young nymph shrugged, taking another small bite of bread and chewing it slowly. The sisters groaned in unison as they rushed past her regardless.

Kore stepped into the open hall with a sleepy smile.

"Good morning." She yawned.

"Good morning, Lady Kore," Morea greeted. The oldest of the sisters—sharing their deep freckles and dark hair, the most proper and stern in her ways—made sure everything Demeter requested was not only completed but that it surpassed Demeter's expectations of perfection.

"We have your robes set and ready for you in the bathing chamber," the nymph said in a soft voice.

"And a platter of bread and cheeses on the table," Syke added.

"Thank you," Kore said as she made her way to Lotus's side. The young naiad nymph was still working on her bun.

"Are you doing that on purpose?" Kore whispered and Lotus shot her a mischievous smile.

"Of course not. I am simply enjoying your mother's baking before we venture off." Lotus laughed.

"So, Mama has big plans for today's trades?"

"It would appear so. What are your plans?"

The sky above was cloaked with smog and war, a day not to be enjoyed in the depth of her mother's forest or at the rocky waterside of her spring. Today was a day she would be subject to work in the garden, practicing her sproutlings and cuttings.

"I cannot do much with this sky," she groaned. "I am left to tend the garden."

"Do you think you will get the raspberries right this time?" Lotus joked.

Kore had been having a problem creating proper raspberry bushes. The fruit came out with odd colors and had a pungent taste. It was a plant Demeter wanted her to focus on until she had it perfected.

Kore made a noise in the back of her throat as she shot her eyes to the nymph. "You are welcome to try one when you get back," she taunted as she pushed away from the column they had been leaning on. She made her way to the table, Lotus close by her side, grabbed her platter, and headed to the garden.

"What else do you plan to do?" Lotus pushed as they came to a deep stone gardening bed. Kore placed the platter on the half wall of the bed and turned back to Lotus with a shrug. "Do you think he will return today?" she whispered.

"Who will return today, sweet Lotus?" Demeter called as she stepped from the cabin. Ears like a hawk. Lotus spun around with wide eyes. She was a horrible liar.

"Helios, Mama." Kore looked up to the darkened sky. "Will the village be safe for trading today?"

"Oh yes, my daisy. The mortals rage their war in Delphi now. The trees have insisted we are safe to travel." Demeter smiled. "I would not leave if I felt there was danger for us or you. But please do stay near the cottage, my daisy."

"Yes, Mama." The young goddess bowed to her mother and rested back at her spot by the gardening bed.

"Good day, Lady Kore." The sisters bowed as they took their place at Demeter's side.

Lotus turned her back to them and smiled with cautious eyes before saying her goodbyes and parting ways as well. Kore watched as her mother and the nymphs disappeared into a golden cloud and drifted away, leaving her alone in the garden.

She finished her breakfast and headed to the back where her berry bush grew. The branches hung heavy with light green berries and a raw, sour smell that drifted around the surrounding area. A bush Kore would be more than happy to practice a different skill with.

The leaves brushed lightly against her arm as she passed, aware of what was to come.

"I am sorry, my berry friends. You just are not what raspberries are supposed to be." She shrugged, patting the leaves. The bush rustled in response while the child sat beside it.

"Perhaps we will try something different this go-around. Grapevines maybe? Honeysuckle?" she pondered aloud, placing her palm against a thin, brittle branch.

A warm sensation covered her fingertips and spread over her hand as she drained the plant of its remaining life. The branches snapped and bent away from her as the color faded from a light brown to a chalky white and then ashy gray.

Shriveled black vines crept up alongside her, caressing her arms and legs as she worked. They wrapped around the base of the bush, draining the last of its energy into their stalks and up Kore's arms until there was nothing more before her but dark, rich soil.

"That's better," she whispered, patting the vines as they retreated into the earth. "What to do about you?"

She sighed, working her fingers through the soil. Her mother had taught her to mold the energy in her hand as if she were molding clay, and it seemed a much easier task when the soil was already between her fingers.

The garden had plenty of berries and grapes, a small orchard that left the air full of sweet citrus. She did not want to add another fruit to the collection—more weight for her mother to transport up to Mt. Olympus.

No, she would do something much different. "Honeysuckle it is." She giggled to herself.

It wasn't just about the flowers that grew on the plant, but that it was crafted of creeping vines. Perfect for her to practice controlling hers without making it obvious.

She dug her fingers further into the damp soil, pushing the energy she harnessed from the bush and crafting it anew. Closing her eyes, breathing in through her nose and out through her mouth just as Demeter had shown her. A way to center herself before she crafted. She envisioned the honeysuckle vine, the white and yellow flowers, the sweet honey scent they released. She imagined it twisting upon itself with thick and thin branches. Twirling and folding in a spectacular dance while green and yellow leaves bloomed.

The air around her grew sweet with the smell of honey, and when she opened her eyes, a twisted mess of vines and flowers sat before her. Not exactly what she had envisioned, resembling a bush more than a creeping vine. But the fragrance was there.

Kore leaned in until the petals tickled her nose and the sweet aroma clung to her skin.

"You, my new friends, are absolutely perfect," she whispered.

The vines being twisted would give her a challenge in her practice, and she planned to work on untangling them in the future days. She pulled her hands from the soil and dusted them free before skipping to the next garden bed, where a few strawberry plants sprouted.

She worked her hands in the soil just as she did before, testing and tasting the energy of the plant that crawled around her. Tart and sweet, hints of sour flooded her mouth as she envisioned the small red fruit.

She proceeded to practice this way at each bed, the dark, smoky sky only growing darker as the day carried on. Helios was too far shielded by the smog for her to guess the time, but if she had to, she would say that he was nearing his end for the day as the low chirping of the evening crickets began to set in. A perfect time to head in for the night, as bugs were not her most favorite creatures to roam the meadow.

She made her way down to the bathing hall. Dirt and fallen soot had clung to her hair and skin, mixing with the sweat from her work. The smell of the day and war lay strong upon her. Exhausted from her labors, she sluggishly completed the grueling task of filling the basin with water and mixing in the oils that sat ready for her before climbing in.

The water was soothing, from the heat to the lavender oil, as she rinsed the dirt and ash from her skin. It wasn't long before she heard her mother's return with a loud, gleeful entrance.

The goddess and the nymphs laughed outside the cottage, their symphony carrying into the halls.

"Kore, dear, come here please!" her mother called happily. "We are in the garden!"

Kore jumped from the basin, removing the plug and drying herself. Throwing her sleep robes on, she ignored her slick, wet hair as she ran out to meet her mother and the nymphs.

They gathered in a circle, cooing and giggling at something between them.

"Over here, dear!" Demeter called when she caught sight of her daughter. Kore made her way to them and peeked into the circle, the curiosity burning her chest.

"You can name them, my daisy."

The young goddess looked down to find two baby goats, one with brown fur all over and a white stripe between its eyes. The other with all black fur and a white tail.

"This one is a boy." Lotus pointed to the black one. "And this one is a girl," she added, pointing to the brown one.

"I can name them?" Kore repeated.

"Yes. Anything you want."

Kore did not know many names other than the ones from her mother's tales and history lessons. She thought of a nice matching pair from a recent story, one her mother said was the cause of this meaningless war, but Kore found it to be fitting.

"Helena and Paris," she said.

The nymphs all fell silent and shot their attention to Demeter.

“Are you sure, dear?” she asked between giggles.
“Yes, I think it is fitting.”

CHAPTER III

THE DREAM, THE TREE, AND THE HOUND

1186 BC: FOURTEEN YEARS OLD

The ear-shattering screams jolted her awake to find thick black smoke surrounding her in all directions. It filled the air, choking and blinding her all at once. Kore had only just gone to bed, but now she was someplace unfamiliar.

The sounds of cries continued, stirring a pain in her head as she scanned the space. Her hands pressed down into the soil for assistance. The earth felt warm but silent under her touch. No plant life left to comfort her or even tell her where she was or what they had seen.

She pushed up from the ground to get a better view of this new world around her and reached for her crystal, only to find it missing. Her heart continued to pound against her chest.

'Tis only a dream, she thought and slowly climbed to her feet. She drew in a ragged breath, the smoke and heat burning her lungs instantly.

"H-Hello?" she called out, her throat dry from the air, adding even more difficulty to breathing.

The only sounds that followed were distant screams and

howls.

Kore's night terrors were usually centered in her mother's meadow since that was all she had ever known. They normally involved her mother's great disappointment at learning all that Kore could do. Or worse, losing her mother altogether. Never had they felt so real, nor had they been located anywhere else outside of her home.

Through the echoed cries and screams, Kore could hear the faint crackling of a fire. She scanned the area before her but was unable to make out more than a few steps ahead.

She took one slow step.

The screaming continued.

She took another step and then a third until she was halted by a stone wall. It felt hot to the touch but helped her navigate to an opening of fallen stone. She took another deep breath, ignoring the blistering pain it caused as she stepped over the stone and debris.

In the distance, off to the right, Kore could see the faint flickering of the fire. She figured if she could make it over, maybe she could see what had the mortals in an uproar.

"Hello?" Kore croaked but she received no clear response in return.

The screaming continued.

Kore stepped out, pushing from the building. Her heart pounding against her chest. The sound of rushing ichor filled her ears, muting the screams as she crept through the smoke to the fire. Her eyes locked on the flames until she was standing over them. She caught a glimpse of movement from the corner of her eye and turned to see what it was, only to be met with a black sheet.

She gazed out to the darkness, and the darkness gazed back.

More wailing from the mortals filled the air, but there was no sight of them. The eerie energy that drifted around shook her bones.

The goddess turned back to the flame, her eyes watching

the bright dance it offered.

Look up, a voice whispered. The sound sent chills down her spine, but she did as told. Her heart sank when she was met with a blood-covered mortal. His eyes hungry and his teeth bared. His body shivered as if he were cold. A feral growl rumbled deep within his chest as he studied the goddess, his chest heaving wildly with every breath.

He threw his head back, and the sound that escaped him was guttural. It was not a scream or cry. It was animalistic and hungry. Sending a chill over Kore's body.

He lunged toward her and shouted again, his bloodied face twisted with pain and anguish. But there was an evilness to him, a hunger for something more than food. He did not care about the flames as he scrambled through the fire and cindered logs. Kore took a step back, but before the mortal could reach her, a loud snapping sound filled the air.

The man's feral cries turned to a shrieking scream as he was yanked away into the smoke. There was another deep, rumbling growl as a few more mangled-looking mortals limped into view. Their hate burned on their misshapen faces.

They hated her, she could feel it, but she was unsure why. A wave of energy raced through her arms to the tips of her fingers, the divine power within her building with every cracking of the hidden tree.

She felt hatred for the mortals she had never known. Rage bubbled up from the pit of her stomach, stewing a bitter taste in her mouth. It flooded her head with heat. Her arms pulsed as she took a step closer. The screaming started to fall to whimpers and pleas for help, but Kore did not offer any sanctuary.

"You dare attack a goddess?" The voice that filled the air was not her own. "You mortals know nothing. You care for nothing! Look at this beautiful land Mother Gaia has given you, and you *defiled* it with your war and hate! It is time she takes her revenge. Yes?" the voice raged, clearing the smoke from view. The sight of war and massacre was laid out before

Kore, in a clear and vivid display.

A few yards off from her grew a large cypress tree. Short but wide at the trunk and charred and burned from the fire. Parts of it cindered and expelled a dim red glow as it continued to smolder. It lacked leaves, but its jetting branches were not bare. Bodies of the mortals decorated them from the lowest hanging branch to the highest, their mangled bodies layered upon each other in such a way that Kore could barely see the bark that held them up.

Deep crimson blood rained down into puddles at the roots and mixed with the mud, creating a thick, sticky mess that began to sweep down to Kore's bare feet. She did not move. She just watched as the thick liquid slowly crept closer and closer to her. Her arms ignited from the racing energy.

She snapped her head up to the tree and was face-to-face with a dark, eyeless figure; the one that normally drifted in the darkness of her night terrors. It was silent, at best. Normally useless, until now.

"*Persephone,*" the voice whispered.

The goddess shot up straight in her kline, back in her chamber, in the familiar cottage. Beads of sweat collected at her brow, and her chest heaved wildly.

The bright rays of the sun spilled onto her furs. Indicating Helios had brought it a good distance for the morning.

It was only a dream, she reminded herself.

She struggled free from the furs and slipped from the kline, making her way to the reflective flat metal plate that sat in the far-right corner of her chamber. Her mind still reeling with thoughts on the dream as the memory of heat and energy lingered on her skin.

Her hair was a matted mess, and her sleep robes twisted around her in such a way that it left her exposed on one side. She adjusted the linen and raked her fingers through her hair; sleep still clung to her swollen cheeks and eyes.

Kore could hear faint talking coming from the main hall

and could only assume her mother was already up waiting for her. Over the last few years, Demeter had made it a point to have Kore take daily lessons with her, some of which started from the crack of dawn and ended long after Helios had left and Selene took over the sky.

She sighed deeply before starting her morning and making herself presentable for the day. When she had finished braiding her hair and pinning her robes, she walked out into the hall, where the chatting was more distinguishable.

"Zeus is calling for the council today. There was a development in the mortal war, and he wants everyone in attendance," Hermes informed, his voice like a song.

"Everyone" usually meant all thirteen Olympians, but more specifically, Aidoneus was also meant to attend. Kore paused to listen further in fear her entrance may halt the conversation.

"Is it about the crops?" Demeter pressed in a hushed tone.

"Yes, I am afraid the war has spilled onto the crop fields," he answered.

Kore could feel the heat rise to her face. They had been practicing cloning vegetation to yield double crops. Demeter was better at calling forth the crop from seed, while Kore had been mastering cloning. This was something she could lend assistance with and possibly accompany her mother to Mt. Olympus this day.

She took a deep breath to steady her heart before entering the hall. It was a decent reason for joining them.

"Mama?" she greeted softly.

"Good morning, my daisy!" Demeter cheered.

Hermes turned with a large, welcoming grin. "Good morning, Kore!"

Kore smiled softly at her half-brother before turning back to her mother, who had only one concern this early. The dream would have to wait until Kore could speak with Lotus.

"Mama, I overheard talks of crop loss. I was thinking I

could help." She paused to search her mother's face for any sign of protest; when there was none, she continued, "I was wondering if I could join you today and offer my help."

She cast her eyes down, too nervous to see the look her mother may have created.

"You want to go to Mt. Olympus?" Demeter finally questioned.

"I would like to hear the council and offer aid personally." Kore kept her eyes low. Her mother was silent for a moment more.

"I think it would do her good, Demeter, to listen in. To speak before the other gods," Hermes offered.

Demeter chewed the idea over; the whole purpose of training Kore was so that she could help her mother and take charge of the meadow when the time came. Attending council by Zeus would be of great benefit for her, though it was not the benefit she was interested in.

"Very well. We will not be leaving for some time, my daisy. Please, go eat and enjoy your morning. No lessons for the day." Demeter smiled softly and waved toward the dining hall, where platters of fruits, bread, and cheeses lay scattered.

Kore grabbed a small skyphos of ambrosia and a kantharos of nectar, adding a small bun and a slice of cheese to nibble on later in the morning. She had mastered folding her robes in a way that gave her small pouches where needed. She wrapped the cheese and bread in a cloth and tucked them away.

She sat outside to enjoy her nectar and ambrosia, though the peace was not long-lived. Overhead loomed a dark, smoke-filled sky. The mortals were at it again with their war and burning. The sight flooded her dream back into focus.

Persephone. The word rang in her head. She wasn't sure what it meant, but she remembered her dream vividly. She needed to hurry and find Lotus if she wanted to discuss it before leaving. She gulped down the thick, sweet nectar and practically inhaled the ambrosia. Racing to put the kantharos and skyphos back on the table before running from the hall again. She cut through the right side of the garden, passing Morea and Syke on her way.

"Slow down, Lady Kore, you need not run!" Morea shouted. A phrase heard frequently from the nymphs, and though it was true, most days Kore did not need to hurry away. Today was not one of those days.

"Lotus!" Kore called as she came up to the small dark pond that led deep into the forest. She danced her fingers across the surface and called again, "Lotus!"

From the darkness, two glowing seafoam eyes began to ascend to the surface. Her button nose broke through first, her skin changing from dark murky green to a pale green undertone the moment air hit it.

"Yes, Kore?" she asked, breaking the surface of the water. Her light brown hair clung to her face in a wild dance before she cleared it free.

"I had another one of those night terrors!" Kore began. "But—I am not sure—it was odd. I knew I should have been afraid, but I wasn't. I was angry!" Kore continued to explain the events that took place in the dream, the feeling, the attacking mortals, the tree, the voice, and even the word that Kore had been unfamiliar with.

"I am not sure, Kore. It does not truly sound like you were even yourself in the dream. Where did you say you woke up?" Lotus pried.

"A village, I believe. It was dark." Kore sighed.

"You have never been to any village," Lotus countered, but Kore did not answer; she was not sure it was even a village she had found herself in. The smoke had clouded everything except the tree.

After a few silent moments, the girls pushed it off as just another night terror before the goddess moved on to more exciting news.

"Oh! I am going with Mama and Hermes to Olympus today. I will go to offer my aid."

"That's good!"

"Yes, because Zeus called *all* the gods to meet. So, I am hoping Aidoneus is there," the goddess added.

"Again with that, Kore?" Lotus groaned as she pulled herself from the water, allowing the rest of her body to transform.

"Always, Lotus. I have not seen him in a near six years. He was . . . interesting."

"I think you find too much interest in the Lord of Darkness." Lotus sighed.

Kore could hear the concern, the fear. It was true, Kore did find a great deal of interest around Aidoneus, an interest that only seemed to grow the longer she went without seeing him. She had a number of questions piling up that she could not wait to ask.

"'Tis true. But only—" She was stopped by a sudden snapping of branches in a nearby bush. They waited quietly, searching ahead for a sign of anyone.

"Very funny, Syke!" Lotus called out, but no answer was returned.

They waited a few moments more as the bush twitched here and there. Kore rose to her feet, and vibrations raced down her arms and legs, spreading heat out around her.

"Kore, wait!" Lotus protested, but Kore continued to step forward.

"Come out now!" she demanded. Her arms began to burn as they had in her dream, and she could hear the branches of the surrounding cypress buckle at her call.

"Kore?" Lotus cried. But it was the soft whimper that escaped the bushes that paused Kore. She took another step, calling to her trees to aid her in sight. What they saw was only a black, drifting cloud hovering near the bush. A soft whine sounded again as Kore took a step, raising her arms to prepare an attack.

A black hound stumbled from the bush and crawled to Kore's side. It lopped its head over, rolling to its back, in demand of a belly rub.

Kore looked to Lotus, who looked to the hound and then back to her baffled friend. No creature of the mortal realm could enter without aid from Demeter, who was known to bring a few mortal creatures to roam the forest. Mostly deer and small rodents. Not wolves or any creature she saw as vicious.

"It is a divine hound," Lotus gasped.

"It could only be. But whose?" Kore looked about the trees into the forest but saw nothing.

"Maybe he is Hermes's pet?" Lotus offered.

Kore bent down to rub the hound's belly. She did not think this hound to be Hermes's, for it was too dark and mysterious a creature for his liking. He loved bright and joyful things. This creature was as black as night with bright white eyes.

"Not likely. Hermes would not be seen with such a lovely creature. He likes—more luxurious-looking things. Creatures included," Kore scoffed.

"His favorite creature is a tortoise. Those are not luxurious creatures, Kore," Lotus said with a laugh.

"I meant the hawk!" Kore giggled. "Anyway, he does not seem to be underfed. I wonder who he belongs to."

The hound jumped to attention as if being called, his head pointed straight into the forest. He looked back to Kore, pressed his cold, wet nose to her cheek, and then retreated into the trees as quickly as he had come.

"Well, that was—odd . . . " Lotus said slowly.

"That *was* odd. I have never seen such a creature so close before," Kore mused.

"Kore." Lotus's voice was soft and wary, a tone she usually took when she was nervous. "Do you think maybe your dream was about you?" Her eyes stayed fixated on the trees that had buckled at Kore's command.

"Do you think I have such evil in me?"

Kore could not deny that the question hurt her a bit. The

monster in her dream was vengeful and filled with such hate, something she did not feel.

"Not in you," Lotus paused again, "but I do think you are capable of creating a home for it." She ducked her head quickly, too nervous to see the hurt on her friend's face.

Kore felt a drop in her stomach at the words. "How do you mean?"

There was another long pause as Lotus chewed at her bottom lip, thinking of what to say next. Her eyes scanned the water's surface before she parted her lips. "You know, this river runs throughout the forest," she began. Kore was unsure but nodded. "The water sees everything that happens around it, Kore, and it speaks to me as I do it."

Suddenly Kore realized what her friend was telling her.

She was short-tempered at times and would retreat to the forest to let off steam; she also practiced her wilting and vines near her spring. She felt a tinge of embarrassment. She had not considered the water to release her secret before she could.

She had grown out of her phases of wilting the plants of the forest and had begun creating her very own patch just to watch them wilt before her, her anger and frustration along with it. Perhaps the water saw it no differently.

"Oh."

"I do not think you are evil, Kore. Nor do I think you would slaughter an entire mortal village. But I do think you are capable of it. I do not think you have it in your heart to do something like that. You are a divine, after all. Your powers will grow as you do. So, could you? I think if you wanted to. Do I think you would? No."

Her friend was comforting, though she was giving her a lot to consider about herself. Especially the side of her that she thought she hid so well.

Lotus embraced Kore warmly, as she could see her words cut deep.

"Kore, dear!" Demeter's voice rang through the trees. "We are leaving!"

CHAPTER IV

THE COUNCIL, THE OLYMPIANS, AND THE GARDEN

Hermes and Demeter stood patiently by his white-and-gold chariot. The gold trim on the wings and wheels stood out against the ivory marble. It was a magical accent that sparkled when Helios tilted the sun just right. Before it stood four exceptionally large white chargers. Their manes and tails a golden blonde that fell gracefully to one side.

"Well, Hermes, you even got your chargers to match your bright personality." Kore giggled as she skipped to his side.

He smiled widely at her before glancing back to her mother, who was busy saying her goodbyes to the nymphs, charging them with watching over the meadow in her absence.

"So, tell me. What's the real reason you want to make today's meeting?" he whispered in Kore's ear.

She shot a glance his way; sometimes he was much too observant for her liking.

"What makes you say that?" Kore asked with a shrug, but she could still feel the warmth of the ichor flood her cheeks. Hermes smiled again.

"I do more than just play tricks and deliver messages, young sister. And I can see when one is anxious about something—or someone." He tilted his head with another smile.

Kore ducked to hide the sudden flush of her cheeks. There was no way for Hermes to know of her interests. How could he? She pushed such worries to the back of her head. He was most definitely good at trickery, but Kore was not falling for his tricks. Not this time.

"Don't be silly, Hermes. I have never been to Mt. Olympus, and what better time to go than when the mortals are in need during the war?" she lied.

"Hm." He offered his hand and helped her into the chariot. He took his place on her left and pulled a pair of eye shields from a small, hidden space along the side.

"Are we ready?" Demeter chimed in as Hermes turned to assist her aboard as well.

"Yes, we are," he said.

Demeter raised her arms and closed her eyes in focus. The trees snapped and cracked as they jerked away. Birds flew into the air to flee the commotion, and a few small forest animals could be seen jumping back into the parting brush. She had split the forest and given them a straight path to the base of the great mountain where the gods ruled. With the clear opening, Hermes cracked the reins, setting his steeds off in a full gallop.

Within seconds the meadow around them melted to a blur as shades of green raced by. The wind yanked and pulled at Kore's face and whipped her braid about her back. She looked to see how her mother fared and was amazed to find that Demeter held quite still. With closed eyes, her arms held up and apart, keeping the trees in place. As for Hermes, his hysterical laughter could be heard over the whipping wind.

"Are you well, Kore?" he asked.

"I think," she pushed through clenched teeth.

Her fingers gripped the front rail tightly. The wind began

to ease its pull, and the shades of green shifted to a blur of blues, oranges, and browns. The chargers slowed enough that Kore could have a moment to scan the vast field in front of her. She'd always thought her first time outside of her mother's forest and meadow would be beautiful. But the land that surrounded them fell dead and barren, with mud stained in red, thick and sticky beneath the hooves of the chargers.

"What is this?" Kore gasped.

"This is mortal war." Demeter sniffled, distraught from the sight.

This hurt her, not the mortal war but the war on her plants, her harvest. It was a dreadful waste. She cast her eyes down, unable to bear the destruction of her labor and work.

"Their greed is unquenchable," Demeter hissed in a low whisper.

Kore had never seen her mother so hurt. It was not like Demeter to be vengeful or cruel, so for the mortals to do so, so mindlessly to her gift was a great betrayal. Kore placed her hand atop her mother's on the front rail.

"We shall fix it, Mama," Kore offered softly, and the comfort brought a smile to Demeter's stone sorrow.

"That we shall, my daisy."

They had made it to the base of the mountain, and Kore was surprised to see the entrance to Olympus was nothing more than a narrow trail that ran steeply along the side. A great mountain, large and ancient, that stretched far above the clouds. How much war had it been witness to? Still, it stood strong. Observing the mortals as the gods did at its peak.

"You will want to hang on," Hermes advised, whipping the reins three times. The chargers responded and jolted up the elevation.

Kore dug her fingers into the railing again, but that hardly seemed enough to keep her stable the more they inclined. She wanted to ask her mother how she possibly delivered the fruit and nectar in this fashion, but she feared to even take her eyes from the trail before them. The rushing wind and the sound of the chargers' hooves beating against the earth was all that filled her ears.

Unsure how much longer she could hold on with just her hands, she pulled herself forward to gain better leverage. The clouds above drew closer, and the air became lighter. A sweet citrus and honey smell began to tease her nose with a strange, light feeling that swept her body and left a pleasant chill in its wake. Closing her eyes, she inhaled the sweet aroma that was clear of smoke and rot.

"We are almost there!" Hermes called as the chariot made its way to flatter ground.

Kore risked a glance behind them to see how much of the world she was missing. How beautiful was it? How big? Was the great Oceanus as big as Lotus had described? She thought she would be met with a great sea and a beautiful dance of lights that would reflect after Helios's soon departure, but all she was met with was a foggy cloud that blinded her vision of the world. Nothing to be seen.

She brought her attention forward again, pouting out her bottom lip. There would be no dancing lights for her this night.

It was a disappointment soon forgotten as a large marble statue of what Kore thought to be Poseidon appeared. She thought it Poseidon because of the three-prong scepter the large statue held in its hand. As they drew closer, crossing over a golden bridge, more of the statue came into view, and she could see that it was carved from the mountain itself. A rushing blue waterfall fell free from a spitting hole in the statue's open hand.

The chariot came to a full stop on a plateau just below the whole palace. Another large statue sat opposite Poseidon, bearing a warrior helmet with large goat horns atop and a spike-filled strap slung across its shoulder. A frightening statue, one that encouraged war and sent chills across Kore's skin.

"Ares," Hermes said, taking notice of Kore's curiosity.

He jumped from his chariot and again offered his hand

to assist her down and did the same for Demeter.

The two goddesses stepped over to a small river as they waited. It flowed down from the main palace and spilled over the edge into the clouds below. Beautiful, calm—unlike the mortal realm. But it did little to calm Kore's nerves from the meeting ahead.

Hermes guided his chargers to the stables, which were adorned with beautiful green vines and held lovely red flowers Kore had not seen. He tied the creatures to a white marble post before joining Kore and her mother.

"We have a long walk to the main hall. Would anyone like a little treat?" He snickered as he drew forth three small honey wheat buns from his golden pouch.

"Hermes." Demeter giggled, shaking her head.

She held out her hand, and he dropped one in her palm. Her slim fingers cradled it as if it were a delicate egg. She pulled it to her lips and took a small bite.

"Kore?" He held out the second one, and Kore gladly took it.

Honey wheat buns were one of her favorites, though she would never compare her love for them to that of Hermes. He would do absolutely anything for one and usually made off with a few dozen from Demeter's dining hall during his visits.

Kore took a bite and gazed up to the palace. It was larger than she had imagined, with more than several great halls and chambers that glimmered in the light. Another rushing waterfall splashed down from high above them, reaching to the world below. Long golden pillars and columns balanced high up temples to the right of the great stairway. To the left rested a colosseum on the great peak behind Poseidon's statue.

A beautiful mix of golds and greens, from grass to marble and great white stone sat before her.

She took a deep breath and followed close behind her mother and Hermes as they made their way up the stairs. The walls were lined with paintings depicting the Great Battle between the gods and Titans. After that, the paintings moved to portraits of all the Olympians and gods, all but one.

The air shifted, and a fresh, floral fragrance washed over them, warm and welcoming like all flowers were. The scent grew as they came to an opening between two pillars that led out onto a great garden. Sheet moss climbed up the mountainside and onto another plateau that was just outside of the hall her mother referred to as the council chambers.

Blue and purple aconites and bellflowers lined the path, and Kore spotted accents of basil and parsley tucked in little spots amongst them.

"Come, dear. We haven't the time," Demeter said.

They continued upward until they came to a set of large golden doors. More depictions of the Great Battle were carved into them, but these only showed two divines. Zeus and Cronus.

The God of Thunder held a bolt of lightning in his hand, and he looked to be casting them down one by one on the ancient Titan.

Shouting and roaring laughter could be heard through the thick door, and Kore could tell there were already a few gods present. Her heart thumped heavily against her chest as Hermes pulled at the golden latches. He shot her a quick look with a dazzling smile and tugged open the doors and released the frenzy of loud chatter.

The bright chamber held a thick, electric energy that danced around. White columns flanked the space, leading up to a white-and-gold dome ceiling. In the middle sat a long golden table with thirteen crystal-carved thrones circling it.

Three of the thrones were noticeably larger than the rest. The first, which was gold and by far the biggest, sat at the farthest end of the table. The top of the throne held a golden, sculpted hawk head protruding from it. A very clear indication that was Zeus's throne.

The second-largest throne was made of corals and shells; it was the only one not made of crystal but still had a few encrusted into the seashell armrest. It sat in the center of the table at an even distance from either end. Atop this one sat the heads of an odd-looking creature Kore had never seen—she had seen very few things—but this looked to have been crafted by Dionysus after a night full of wine.

The creatures had long, narrow faces, with big, round eyes that sat on the sides of their heads and no ears. They had one fin that started in between the eyes and ran along their backs into the throne. She was not sure what to make of it, but she was sure the chair was Poseidon's.

The final chair was made of a solid black crystal Kore was also unfamiliar with. Jagged and hard, it looked most uncomfortable. This chair was closest to the entrance and sat across from Zeus. With three black hound heads carved from the top, Kore was positive it was Aidoneus's throne.

"He will be along," Hermes whispered into her ear.

Kore felt her breath catch in her chest. "I know not of whom you speak."

"Save it, Kore. I *hang* with the sun gods. They see all, and *gossip* just as much," he teased softly.

"You *hang*?" Kore made a face, though she didn't mean for her tone to come out as harsh as it did.

"Yeah, like, *hang* out. In 'company with.' The mortals are going to love it!" he insisted with a wave of his hand. But she did not fall for the switch of topics. "Anyway, Hades had some small business to tend to. But he will be here. I know you've been waiting," he continued.

"How would you —" she began but Hermes just pointed up and mouthed the words *sun gods.*

Demeter, who had wandered to greet the other divines, returned with a bright smile.

"Are you ready to meet everyone, Kore?" she asked.

Kore felt a rock harden in her stomach. She hadn't considered meeting everyone, though that was silly not to consider since she was going to offer aid in the war. She gave a hesitant nod and took her mother's hand as they made their way around the table to greet the already seated gods.

"Artemis, this is my daughter, Kore," Demeter introduced.

Artemis jumped to her feet and quickly embraced the young divine. Her long, dark hair swept across Kore's nose, sending a musky yet sweet smell into the air. She knew Artemis as the Goddess of the Hunt and that she was an eternal maiden. Which she only knew because her mother made mention of it almost constantly, hoping Kore would follow in those footsteps one day.

"It is so lovely to finally meet you!" Artemis gushed, pulling away to look Kore over. "You are quite lovely!"

Kore looked over the goddess as well. Her ocean-blue eyes were circled with a black ring that helped the color stand out. A splash of freckles crossed her nose and cheeks. Kore thought her eyebrows were very distinctive and thick, but they shaped the goddess's face in such a lovely way and allowed her to stand out amongst the rest.

"As are you! It was lovely to meet with you as well." Kore bowed as her mother shuffled her along.

Next to Artemis sat a mammoth of a man. The muscles in his arms flexed in such an unnerving way, Kore felt too nervous to move. An unsteady knot formed in her stomach. It was the god from the statue, the one with the helmet.

Ares.

"Ares," Demeter said flatly, almost as if she was forcing herself to move forward with the introduction. The man stood, towering over Demeter and Kore. The young goddess shivered, and her mother's grip tighten around her hands. The energy around them too thick to breathe.

"This is my daughter. Kore." Her flat voice a near hiss.

"Hello," the giant man thundered frighteningly. Kore pushed back into her mother, searching for her voice, but it was caught in her throat.

"H-Hello," she stuttered.

"I hear we will be seeing a lot of each other in the future," he said with a smile.

Kore was unsure how many more meetings her mother had planned to bring her to. But if Kore expected to follow her mom's place, she would be here more often. She smiled softly before being shuffled away to the next divine.

Demeter moved Kore from one goddess or god to the next until she had met the whole hall. Even young Hebe was introduced. The Goddess of Youth, dubbed so because she had stopped aging so young, usually served the nectar and came and went from the hall frequently, but elsewise was out of sight.

Kore scanned the floor and felt her heart fall when she didn't see who she was looking for. The rest began to take their seats, and Demeter instructed Kore to sit on a marble bench that sat just off to the left near the entrance but, more importantly, faced Aidoneus's chair. Kore also appreciated the fact it was out of sight of Ares.

"Come, come. Take a seat. Who are we missing?" a deep, thunderous voice bellowed from the front.

Zeus made his way to his seat as he searched the chamber. A large man as well, but not so much in height as in width. He wasn't as tall as his mammoth son Ares, but he was wide in the shoulders with thick arms. His gray beard was neatly groomed and his hair pulled back and tied at his neck.

"Poseidon and —" Hermes shot a look to Kore, "Hades."

He flashed her a quick smile before taking a seat in his citrine throne.

Zeus shook his head with a smile and took a seat, turning to Hera. He rose a kantharos, and they began chatting amongst themselves again when the golden doors opened.

Kore froze, holding her breath as she waited for him to enter, too nervous to turn her head. She kept her eyes on Hermes as the sound of footsteps drew near and a heavy energy loomed over her.

"Well, you are new, aren't you, young one?" the bellowing voice said, causing her to look up. Above her stood another large god. His eyes, deep green and hooded by his brows. He wasn't as visually frightening as Ares, but Kore couldn't help but feel slightly more fearful of him.

She craned her neck to meet his gaze with rounded eyes. Her voice, raw and lost again, "Yes."

"And who might you be?"

"K-Kore. My name is Kore," she stumbled.

"Leave her!" Demeter hissed, jumping from her chair.

None of the other divines seemed to notice the outburst, but the god did as she ordered and walked to the seashell throne at the table, his eyes on Kore the entire time.

Poseidon.

Kore began to think her mother's stories were correct. At least about this god.

She rested back in her seat as a black hound ran to her side and placed its head in her lap. A familiar black smoke drifted at its feet. Just like the hound in her mother's meadow earlier that day.

"Oh!" she gasped, running her hand through the hound's fur. "Hello there!"

A high-pitched whistle pulled her attention to the doors. Air felt as fire around her when she saw him. He looked the same as the day they had first met.

His hair fell wildly about his face, and he was covered in ash and soot from head to toe. Beads of sweat collected over his brow and glistened off his shoulders.

Kore's eyes trailed up until they locked with his. He whistled again. This time, the hound ran back to his side with a whimper and joined two others.

"Hades!" Zeus's voice thundered, allowing Kore to break her gaze free of him. Aidoneus looked to his brother before making his way to his throne, the hounds at his side.

"Let us begin," Zeus commanded.

Kore looked to her mother, who was now eyeing Aidoneus. She leaned back with a soft sigh, hoping this didn't make things harder for her than she anticipated. Her mother would never let her leave the cottage if she felt any god was interested. Sometimes, when she spoke of them, she acted as if one would steal Kore away, never to return her.

The meeting went by rather slowly. They discussed matters of war Kore didn't understand and spoke of war heroes she had not heard of—most often a man named Achilles and the tactics the mortals were using to fight.

"That won't work," Ares argued.

The goddess with blonde, shoulder-length hair slammed her fist down. Demeter had introduced her as Athena. "If they do not yield this silly war, innocent Greeks will perish. Not just from battle but from the destruction of harvest and cattle," she urged.

"Yes, the harvest is important for the survival of Greece as well. I fear if they continue this war, there will be a great loss," Demeter added.

"Can you do anything of it?" Hera asked. She sat on a lapis lazuli throne next to her husband, her long, golden-blonde hair a fine river down her back.

"I can replenish what has been lost. I brought my daughter, as she can clone the crop and we can get a jumpstart in the next harvest for more than half of Thessaly," Demeter informed.

Kore couldn't help but notice Ares and Poseidon turn to her with possessive smiles. She shivered under their gaze and looked to Aidoneus; his eyes were not on her like the rest but cast down about the table before him.

"With her under your guidance, Demeter, I see no fault in the plan. Hades, what news do you bring?"

It was here that Kore noticed where these brothers differed.

Zeus and Poseidon both spoke to Aidoneus as if he were a child. He was physically younger than they, and Kore had noted that after learning who he was. She dared not ask her mother of that discovery.

The tone was a noticeable annoyance to the King of the Dead. He sighed deeply as he reluctantly opened his eyes to look to his brother.

"The Greeks seem to be using new war tactics as of yesterday and appear to have quite the success," he informed.

"How do you mean?" Athena blurted out.

Aidoneus looked to her with slight annoyance before continuing.

"In the village just outside Demeter's Forest," he shot a look to Demeter, then Kore before returning his gaze to Zeus, "the Greeks seemed to have managed to capture a group of scouting Trojans and impaled them to a petrified tree."

Kore felt a cold chill run down her back as the words left his lips, his eyes locking with hers once more.

Does he know about my dream? Was *it a dream?* More and more questions flooded her mind.

"They cannot do that!" the redheaded goddess, Aphrodite, shot angrily.

She sat beside Ares and had seemed less than interested to meet Kore when her mother had introduced them.

"It looks like they just did." Hermes laughed, clapping his hands together. He was usually a bright and cheery god, and wartime was no exception. Unless, of course, he favored the losing side.

"What is done is done, Aphrodite. Is that not what you told Hera and Athena when this all started?" Aidoneus said stiffly.

Kore finally understood why her mother said he was cold-hearted and, by her words, cruel. He hadn't seemed cruel to her, but he was cold and distant, not the same god she had met six years ago.

Aidoneus rested back in his chair, his hound whimpering at his side. The pup had been looking to Kore and whining most of the meeting, and this time she assumed he had enough of it. He snapped his fingers and the hound bounded to Kore's side and rested his head atop her lap. His tongue lobbed out, and he appeared to be smiling.

She ran her hand through his thick fur a few times with a giggle before looking up and being met with curious eyes. Her mother's held concern and confusion, Hermes's eyes grew bright with wonder, and Aidoneus looked to her and his hound with no noticeable emotion.

The rest of the meeting went by in a blur, and before she knew it, the gods were up and chatting amongst themselves again. They were loud and formed several groups, none of which included Aidoneus, who sat in his throne unbothered by the rest.

His hound sat contently at her side. This was the best time she would have. Her mother's back to her, the other gods focused on themselves, and a reason to speak with Aidoneus. She rose hesitantly, taking a deep breath before making her way to the god before her.

She stood silently for a moment, just inches from him. The hem of her peplos barely grazing his arm with each breath.

"Hello," she said softly.

His body grew rigid, but he didn't look up.

"I brought your hound back, though I thought he could join me on a walk of the garden?" she added when he did not speak.

He nodded once but kept his focus on his hands.

"You are welcome to join if you'd like," she added again before turning and making her way to the courtyard, the hound close by her side.

A sweet hound, not much like the hellish beast she had been told. She giggled as she thought about all the ways Lotus had described Aidoneus, how her mother described him. But with this pup at his side, Kore could not help but smile.

They walked out into the courtyard. The lush green grass felt softer than even her mother's, back at the meadow. She greeted the blades and nearby flowers kindly before she continued further into the garden. Her nose became overwhelmed with the combination of floral fragrances and herbs, yet everything complemented each other wherever she moved.

She found patches of lavender with echinacea and baby's breath growing in harmony along some paths. Honeysuckle crept and climbed every column along the way, with clematis sweeping across the tops from one column to the other and back again, making a thick canopy of flowers.

The smells danced and twirled around her, and the plants spoke to her in such a sweet and calm way. They had not been burdened by man's war and had nothing but pleasant memories and scandalous secrets they wished to share.

"We will let them keep their secrets. For now." She giggled softly, gently grazing a high-growing coneflower.

The hound let out a soft whimper, and before Kore could ask what was wrong, she heard Aidoneus's voice.

"You do not plan to do to those poor coneflowers what you did to those chamomiles, do you?" His voice was guarded but less cold than it had been in the chamber. Softer now, as she had remembered it. Her body warmed again, and her heart began to race.

"That all depends, *Lord Hades*," she responded without turning.

"You do not have to call me by that name," he said stiffly, and Kore could hear the frown in it.

She turned, locking eyes with his. "That is your name, is it not?"

"That is not the name I gave you." He made his way toward her and his hound, the other two close behind, never leaving his side. His eyes on the bundle of flowers Kore had just spoken with.

"And why not?" she questioned innocently.

It was a question she had been waiting to ask for years.

"You were but a child. I saw no point in frightening you."

"Did I appear frightened?" She rose a brow at him, remembering every bit of the day and how she had spoken of Hades so freely.

"I suppose not." He sighed.

Kore looked up to him and waited. "Do I seem frightened now?"

Aidoneus shook his head. "You do not."

"Does that please you?" she asked, noting his difference in demeanor from the chamber.

He appeared more relaxed and did not hold such a solemn expression. He looked down at her from the corner of his eye. "May I tell you a secret?" A slight smile teased the corners of his lips.

Kore nodded; her breath caught in her lungs.

"I find you more pleasant to speak with."

"How do you mean?"

A large smile spread across his face. "I find your long list of questions invigorating."

The hound tapped his nose against Kore, requesting more pats, and Kore was happy to oblige as she bent to run her hand through the soft fur.

"Your hound is lovely. What is his name?" She straightened to look back up to Aidoneus.

He scoffed, the smile disappearing from his lips. "Pita is a vicious war hound. He is not *lovely*."

"No?" Kore looked down at the hound, who sat with a tilted head and lopped tongue as he gazed up at them. Kore looked back up to Aidoneus with a taunting smile. "He looks bloodthirsty."

"When he is doing his duty, he is," he warned coldly. The tone of his voice sent a shiver down her back. "But it would appear he will listen to you just as well." He paused and side-eyed her once more with a grin. "I do not think you will have to worry."

The space between them grew heavy with an electric pull, and she fought to hold her position facing the flowers.

She had felt the energies around the other gods. Stagnant for some, heavy for others. His was intense and consuming, but in a way that left Kore feeling safe and not overpowered.

He reached up, grazing the petals of the flower Kore had spoken with just moments before. "So, what secrets have the flowers shared with you?"

"Uh—they had not," she admitted.

"Shame. I hear they see a lot." He shrugged with a smile.

Kore opened her mouth to question him, but it was her mother's voice she heard.

"Kore, dear. Please come. We are leaving!" Demeter called in a rushed tone.

She stood with Hermes at the garden entrance. Again, both expressions read something very different from each other. For Demeter, it was fear, concern, and worry. Kore knew that her mother would never let her leave the meadow now. But Hermes looked proud, as if he had waited for a moment such as this. She turned back to the God of the Dead. His eyes still on the flowers.

"It was nice seeing you again, Aidoneus," she whispered.

With a bow, she reached down to say her goodbyes to each hound. The two who didn't seem as friendly were surprisingly welcoming to her touch. She looked up and locked eyes with Aidoneus, who was now looking down to her, before darting back to her mother's side.

Demeter shuffled her from the hall without allowing her to say goodbye to anyone else. She did hope to say goodbye to Artemis, and Hestia, who seemed to be the happiest upon meeting her.

"Dear, what were you speaking with Lord Hades of?" Demeter interrogated as they began their journey down the steps.

"Just his hound, Mama," Kore assured.

The answer did not seem to faze her mother, as Kore could see it only puzzled Demeter that much more.

"It has been centuries since I have last seen a smile grace his face. What did you say to him to stir such a reaction?" she pressed.

Kore had always remembered Aidoneus smiling here and there during their last meeting. It did not seem like such a strange event to her as it did to her mother.

"How do you mean?" Kore stopped, confused by the question, "I only—spoke with him."

Kore could see more questions build up behind her mother's eyes. Demeter tugged her gently to continue down toward the stables. It was quiet for a long moment, and Kore felt her mother was spent for the night by the time they reached the bottom.

Hermes moved forward to untie the chargers and have them at the ready. He assisted Demeter, then Kore on before joining them as he had earlier.

Kore scanned the stable area and near the hill from which they entered.

"He never leaves his chargers up here," Hermes whispered, and Kore felt that her goodbye to the king was the last she would get to say for some time. If ever.

Demeter shifted from one side to the other, and Kore could sense she did, in fact, have more on her mind.

"Is something troubling you, Mama?" she asked with her eyes on her hands.

"I have questions for you, my child," Demeter said in a stern voice.

"Yes?"

"You have no fear of speaking to him? Alone?" she pushed quickly as they began their descent of the mountainside.

Kore thought over the question for a moment. It was the same question Lotus asked her that first day she had met him. She never understood the need to fear him or fear speaking to him. It wasn't as if he was aggressive. Perhaps his coldness was intimidating to others, but it only intrigued Kore that much more.

"I do not understand why that is being asked of me," she said stiffly. "He has been kind, and not at all how you once told me."

Kore cast her eyes down back to her hands and waited. There was a long pause, and she feared glancing up to her mother's disappointment and disapproval.

"Well," Demeter sighed, placing her hand over Kore's, "just be cautious, dear. He is not just a god. He is a king, and they are most unpredictable."

CHAPTER V

THE FIELDS OF THESSALY, THE GODDESS OF SPRING, AND THE HIDDEN BLACK VINES

"Hermes will be here every *Theftera* for nectar and fruit," Demeter informed Morea. "Please do make sure he does not distract dear Ampelos from her work during those visits."

"I am not so much of a bug, Demeter," Hermes chirped, popping his head up from the opposite side of his chariot.

"Of course, Lady Demeter. If I may—do you know how long you two will be away?" Morea asked as she assisted Demeter with loading the last of her and Kore's things onto the chariot.

"It is not certain, dear. We will be moving all over Thessaly, and if the war moves, we will have to follow," Demeter said solemnly.

The extended departure from her meadow was already weighing heavy on her shoulders. She would be away from her plants and trees that connected to so many other lands. Leaving all the worry and care in the hands of the four nymphs who were to stay behind.

Today Kore would see her friend Lotus for some time. She looked at her with a half-smile. The longest they had been apart was no more than a day. Now, she was unsure when she would see her dear friend again. There was no telling when this war would end and when the next could begin.

Venturing from her mother's meadow was everything Kore had wanted. Though, when she had imagined her time then, it had been full of lush green grass and bright, clear skies.

Tilting her head up she was met with a gray, choking cloud. A deep scowl carved on her lips, and she dropped her head to the two goats at her feet.

"Promise me you will care for Helena and Paris," Kore said to Lotus as she bent down to meet the two creatures, patting them between their floppy ears. Helena was near due with her new kid, and Kore was upset to be missing such an event.

"Are we to sell this one?" Lotus inquired about the incoming baby goat.

"Mama would like to keep another dairy goat. If it is a girl, keep her. If it is a boy, sell him at the village."

"Kore, my daisy, it is time," Demeter said joylessly as she stepped onto the back of the chariot.

"Send word through the rivers and ponds," Lotus pushed, throwing her arms around Kore, pulling her in close. "Goodbye, my friend!"

"I shall. I will miss you, but it is not *goodbye*! It is never *goodbye*! I will see you soon." Kore smiled with tear-filled eyes.

It was something easily said, but none of them knew exactly how long they would be away or how far they were to travel. Zeus could have them follow the war until it ended, and not even the gods were sure of when that would be.

Kore gave her final farewells before running to the chariot and standing by her mother. She was happy to leave the confines of the meadow but sad she could not enjoy the freedom with her friend. Nor could she even enjoy the realm's beauty since it had been destroyed.

She had been serious in her offer to assist her mother in aiding the mortals with the harvest. It was the only help Zeus was willing to offer and only to the innocent who were not involved in the war. Kore was young but she was not ignorant of the ways of the gods.

Zeus cared little for innocent mortals or those who stirred up war. What Zeus cared about was the number of them left alive to worship him.

Hermes climbed into the chariot and took hold of the reins with a smile.

"Do not look so glum, little sister. You will be back in no time." He laughed, cracking the reins against his chargers. The chariot began at a slow trot, headed west toward the forest.

Demeter closed her eyes as she had the night before and lifted her arms. The trees parted, filling the air with snapping and creaking branches.

"Where are we headed?" Kore asked.

"Zeus has instructed I leave you at Ithome to start," Hermes informed.

"Ithome? Hermes, that is a distance from my meadow," Demeter advised, her eyes still closed.

"Yes, well, that is where the crops are needed at this time."

Demeter remained quiet as they continued to ride at a slow pace through the forest until they broke clear of the trees. The fresh fragrance of cypress and pine faded and was replaced with the choking smoke from the far-off burning villages.

"Will we be there by night?" Kore asked.

Hermes looked down with a wicked smile. "Would you like us to go faster, dear sister?"

"Perhaps it is best," Demeter answered, placing her hand atop Kore's. She wanted to get settled in and started on their work as soon as possible. The scorn and loss, worn clearly on her face, clouded her eyes with pain.

Hermes cracked his reins again, and this time his chargers responded with heavy whinnies as their hooves began to kick up mud and dirt. His face split from the smile that crossed it, enjoying the speed, the wind in his hair, and the feeling of freedom. His laughter became music over the rushing air.

"Where will we stay?" Kore called to her mother.

"You need not worry, my daisy. I will handle where we will sleep. When we arrive, I only ask that you stay close by my side."

Kore clenched her jaw at her words. As they continued to ride, the sights around them faded from brown to white while they passed, unseen, through a mortal city. The chargers' hooves clicked audibly against the stone streets. They were not in the city long; the chargers' speed made sure of that. No sooner were they in the white city than they were out and back in dirt fields and ash.

The divines rode in silence until the chargers finally came to a slow and steady halt in a dull and barren field. Hermes jumped from the chariot first, holding his hand out to assist both Demeter and Kore down.

The sand and soil felt dry beneath Kore's feet. Rough grass scraped across her heels as she made her way around to view the boundless dry land. The arid air baked her throat, leaving it raw with each breath.

The trees were scorched and charred, their roots lifting and pulling from the earth. No animals to be heard, no birds to be seen in the sky, no furry creatures running along the floor.

Vacant of all that was living.

What was once a flourishing land was now desolate of any life or energy. The only things standing were columns and stone buildings that lay empty and shattered.

"Welcome to the outskirts of Ithome," Hermes began, throwing his hands in the air. "Zeus would like you to start here, with the trees and grass. The creatures of this area must return. So on and so forth. I am sure you can see that one of

Zeus's temples was here. As you can imagine, that is why he chose this location for you two to begin your work." Hermes clapped his hands together joyfully. Unsympathetic to the situation as a whole.

Demeter scrunched her nose at the sight, and her eyes glossed over as she surveyed the carnage of her work.

Kore followed close behind her mother as they walked a few feet from the chariot, looking at the dirt and twigs around. Helios had made it to his highest point in the sky for the day, which meant there was still enough time for her mother to find something for them to complete. No rest from their travels, no time to adventure the area.

"Well," Demeter sighed heavily, raising her arms, "first we will need a place to sleep." The moment the words left her lips, the earth beneath them began to quake.

A deafening crack surrounded them as four sizeable tree trunks emerged from the dirt, climbing high until they passed the divines' heads. Demeter turned her hands over, and the trees quickly folded inward until their canopies clashed. The branches and leaves spread down the trunks, each branch shooting out and connecting to another. The twisting and tucking of the many offshoots and leaves created thick walls on all sides.

"Our new home for now," Demeter said with a soft smile.

"Looks a bit rough for your taste, Demeter." Hermes snickered but Demeter did not turn. A soft smile pulled at her lips.

"For now," she said, taking a step toward the small opening she'd crafted. She waved her hand across the threshold and waited as the inside illuminated with a flickering fire.

"Fire? In a tree? You are living a bit dangerously today!" Hermes teased.

"Have a look for yourself, dear Hermes." Demeter laughed again and the God of Trickery skipped inside. The two goddesses following close behind.

"Oh!" Hermes gasped in surprise.

They stepped into a grand chamber. The marble from the floor to the walls was white with gold veins winding through. Kore noted the lack of windows or openings other than the door they entered from.

Another prison, she thought.

Demeter waved her hand once more, calling forth their trunks and satchels from Hermes's chariot and manifesting them at their feet.

Kore grasped her crystal, the one time she hoped to not find its solid mass in her hand. Sadly, she felt the wild vibrations of energy against her palm. She sighed heavily, dropping her shoulders as the true reality of it all finally crashed down on her.

She looked to the right and found two klines with a small stone firepit across the way. In the center of the chamber sat a small golden table with a round top and two golden chairs. The back of the chamber held several stone tables lined up with different-sized clay skyphos filled with a dark, rich soil Demeter often used.

"This is more suited for goddesses—for the time being." Demeter smiled. "Come, let us survey the area," she added with a soft voice, linking her arm with Kore's, and they made their way back out to the wasteland.

"I must say, Demeter, your magic never ceases to amaze me." Hermes laughed.

Kore could not help but feel a tinge of jealousy. The only magic she had was the growing and wilting of her plants, while the other divines could shapeshift and turn to smoke to move through spaces. They could also create such beautiful things with a flick of their wrist.

Demeter did not often practice such magic, only when she felt the need. Leaving no real lessons to teach Kore. She felt it better for her to focus on the divine powers over luxury magic—as she would say.

"Thank you, Hermes," Demeter said kindly.

"Of course! I will be taking my leave now. I have business to attend in the Underworld." He paused and looked to Kore with a mischievous grin. "Lord Hades needs my attention."

Demeter's body went rigid at the name, but Kore could only feel the heat rush to her face, and she shot her head down.

"Yes, well. Be gone with you then," Demeter instructed, quick to get him on his way.

"Bye now!" he cheered as he hopped onto his chariot. He waved one last time and was off with his chargers, a blur in the sky.

"Come, my daisy. Let us walk," Demeter said.

The two took to the barren fields, stopping at the fallen temple of Zeus and the surrounding building turned to ruin from the passing war. The smell of fire and burning pine still lingered in the air.

Demeter paused in a patch of dry, brittle grass. She unhooked her arm and bent down to run her palm along the frail blades.

"We will work here for now," she said, lowering herself to her knees. Kore joined alongside, sitting on her feet as she watched her mother work. "See how the blades still follow my hand ever so slightly?"

Kore lowered herself a bit more to gain a better view. She watched as her mother's hand hovered a few inches above the grass, gently moving from left to right. The dry, brittle blades leaned mildly with the shift of her hand.

Kore nodded.

"What do you think that means?" her mother quizzed. Kore only knew of one reason the vegetation would follow.

"They—They hold life?"

"Correct. They still hold life. Just enough to feel it. Here." Demeter held out her hand and took Kore's, holding it over the blades. Slight, pulsating energy faintly caressed the softness of Kore's palm. "Can you feel that?" Demeter whispered.

She leaned close to her daughter, sending the dull scent of cypress into the chalky air, giving it just a moment of life.

Kore nodded again. "Yes, Mama."

Demeter released Kore and pressed her hands into the soil. Kore enjoyed watching her mother work her divine power; it gave her insight into what she could create.

Demeter closed her eyes, a bright golden glow emitting from her hands and the soil. Kore rocked back on her heels, watching as the glow spread around them. Stopping just a few feet out from either side. She could feel the energy throb through her arms and legs. When the light faded it left a dull green shade over the blades.

Kore ran her hand across the grass to find it softer than before, but not as soft or lush as the grass in the meadow. It was healing—a process that would take a few days before it looked brighter. She stood and stepped back a few feet from the spot to get a better view. The area covered was small, but it was a start.

"What of the grass around it?" Kore asked.

"Grass connects, my daisy. It has a system to keep it all in line. The surrounding blades will feed from this patch as it continues to grow. Always remember—if it does not answer your call, it lacks a life force completely. Unfortunately, there is no bringing back life to those." Demeter's face fell, the loss of her work a great burden on her shoulders. Pushing them down from the weight.

"What must be done then?" Kore asked.

"I fear it is a lost cause. At least for me. You still can practice that skill." Demeter smiled with much ambition for her daughter. "Come, we shall continue," she added, rising gracefully to her feet.

They were only a few steps away when Demeter froze stiff. Kore could feel a heavy electric energy encase them. It was almost suffocating.

"Lady Demeter, Lady Kore. Pleasant surprise!" a

thundering voice echoed.

The sound sent a deep shudder down Kore's back. She looked to her mother, whose eyes were tightly closed, nostrils flared.

"Ares," Demeter pushed through clenched teeth.

Kore and her mother walked along a small patch of newly sprouted barley, with Ares close behind, trying to squeeze between the two goddesses whenever he could. He had set up a small camp next to Demeter's tree fortress, giving the goddesses little privacy to chat. Kore had questioned her mother on his arrival and stay, but Demeter knew just as little as her daughter.

"Did you make these?" he asked, snaking his rough fingers around Kore's wrist, pulling her into him. Despite her clear attempts to flee, he secured her to his side with one hand and gestured to the row of barley with the other.

A sickening lump formed in her chest, and her skin crawled from his touch. He stunk of war and dirt and musk. It clung to her nose and turned her stomach. Her mother had asked her to be polite and welcoming. But he gave off a frightening energy that unsettled her.

She righted herself, looking to her mother, who gazed back with wide eyes.

"Ares!" Demeter spat, locking eyes with the God of War. A low rumble rattled his chest, and a small smile ghosted his face. He released Kore and turned his attention back to the barley as he cleared his throat.

"Did you make these?" he repeated, his tone remaining the same.

"My mother did. We made them just yesterday. Do you not remember?" Kore pushed.

He looked confused as he thought on her question. He had drunk quite a bit of wine before they had ventured off to do their work. Thinking he had been spent for the evening from the liquid, they took the opportunity to work peacefully, but to no avail.

"I do not," he grumbled.

Kore turned and made her way back to her mother's side.

"Dear, why don't you go practice further down? Clone the barley there, while I share a few words with Ares." Her mother dismissed her.

She snuck her mother a thankful smile and ran down the path away from the overbearing god.

Kore walked until the path of barley sprouts came to an end. Having spent the last week watching her mother call them forth, it was now her turn to attempt to draw forth the sprout before she turned to her cloning. Demeter found a lesson in anything she could and would prefer Kore learn to call upon the plant rather than clone it.

She leaned over the space of moist soil, shoving her hands deep into it as her mother had done. She could feel the life wiggling between her fingers. She closed her eyes just like her mother and called. She called and called, but no seed or sproutling came. It was an odd frustration. She could create life in her palm from nothing, but her ability to grow plants from soil had always seemed faulty.

She could not call for a seed, she could not manifest a seed, and her manifested plants came out wrong. If she wanted it right, she could only clone it. A wave of heat and anger flushed her face.

Why does it matter how the plant came to be? Why does she constantly make everything a moment to learn? Why can't we just have fun?

Waves of energy rippled down her arms, through her fingers into the soil.

Why must everything be her way? There was a gentle tickle at the side of her left thigh, twisting in the fabrics of her chiton. Her eyes opened and shot down to find one of her vines creeping up.

"Hello, friend." She sighed, pulling her hands free from the sprout-less soil, and running it along the vine, letting it twist about her fingers and around her wrist.

"What is that you have there?" Ares pried from her right.

Kore jumped to face him, her vines retreating swiftly into the soil again.

"I'm sorry?" she gasped.

"What was that you created?" he asked again, looking at the spot where the vine had been.

"I have not created anything," she lied, waving her hand to the empty space beside the barley.

She did not plan to share her most private secrets with the God of War. He looked about the space and then back to the patch where her vine had once been. He raised a brow to her and ran his hand over his chin.

"No matter. I was thinking you and I would take a walk," he demanded.

Kore looked him over, tilting her neck back to meet his eyes, then to her mother, who drifted off in the back.

Demeter nodded stiffly and mouthed the word *please*. Kore did not like the way he had demanded her to walk, and she got the feeling she was not the only one he had made the demand to. She swallowed against the lump in her throat.

Before she was able to answer, Ares grabbed her by the wrist and tugged her off.

He found a small trail through the grass that was just starting to mature. Kore was careful to mind it, while Ares walked through the freshly grown blades, flooding Kore with a wave of annoyance. She kept a space between them as they went, her eyes always on her mother, and her mother's always on her.

"War is not generally a place for young goddesses—such as yourself," he said suddenly.

"I am not at war," she replied. "This is the outcome." A sight she felt Ares was all too familiar with.

"This is not bad," he said with a deep chuckle. Demeter and Kore did not feel the same. They saw this as a great loss.

"Is it not? My mother finds this to be quite damaging."

"Plants grow back," he scoffed.

Heat rose in her face, and her nails dug into her palms. She bit back a rebuttal and turned on her heels, headed toward their shelter. Finished with the conversation altogether.

Over the past week, one thing Kore had learned was plants do not grow back after such damage. They needed care and strength, and those that were too far gone needed to be replaced by the hand of Demeter.

"Kore!" Ares shot, following alongside. "I am not done."

"I am!" she barked back.

She spotted her mother kneeling over some barley sprouts, singing her soft songs to them. It was as if she could feel her daughter's emotions, snapping her head up to Kore with concerned eyes.

"Is everything all right, my daisy?" Demeter asked, rising to her feet.

"I think I will get the fire started for the night," Kore huffed, keeping her pace as she marched past. Ares close on her heels.

"Stop!" He grabbed her by the hand and yanked her into his chest again. "Why did you walk away from me?"

"I had no more to say." She pushed against him to break free, but his hand wrapped tightly around her arm, anchoring her in place.

"But we were taking a walk," he pushed.

The heat returned to her face, burning her where his skin touched. Her heart felt like a hard rock thumping wildly against her chest, and she could feel the pressure of tears build behind her eyes. She opened her mouth to protest, but no words broke free.

"Ares!" Demeter thundered, shaking the ground.

The brutish god released Kore and turned to Demeter

with a half-smile.

The young goddess did not waste a second; she turned on her heels and marched back to their shelter. But when she got there, she did not go inside. Instead, she glared at the makeshift tent Ares had constructed for himself.

He had set trunks of weapons and armor alongside it. Atop one of the trunks sat his helmet and cladded wraps, a sword with garnets encased into the handle, and a few more deadly-looking blades.

Heat flooded her body again as she marched over to the trunk. She glanced back and saw Demeter with her finger in Ares's face. Keeping him perfectly distracted.

She turned back to the weapons and armor, kicking her leg out and knocking the sword over. The hilt hooked the helmet, yanking it. Everything crashed down with a shattering clatter as metal crashed upon metal. The noise crafted a ringing that echoed through the field.

Kore ducked her head and swiftly shuffled into the tree shelter. Pressing her back against the door, she hoped Ares had not seen her.

She held her breath as the sound of footsteps came stomping past the door. There was no way to see him, and the door did little to shield noise. Kore held her ear to the wood; she could hear the god thunder about his weapons and helm.

"*Metrokoites*!" he bellowed.

His footsteps fell heavily until they stopped at the door, and he sent three tremorous knocks through the weak wood. "Kore?"

Her heart thundered against her chest, shaking her hand as she placed it on the handle. She drew in a deep breath and pulled, opening the door slightly to peek from the crack at Ares. His face was a deep gold, his chest heaving, and his nostrils flared as his eyes burned into her.

"Yes?" she asked in a shaky voice as she looked at him. He turned a deep golden bronze from the ichor that boiled under his skin.

"Do you happen to know what became of my armor?" His voice loud and rough.

Kore knew little about Ares, like most gods; she only knew stories her mother shared. One, in particular, flashed before her.

"I am not sure. I did see a baby boar run from here as I came up," she lied.

Ares's face twisted into an even deeper scowl. His brows pulled down deep over his eyes.

"A boar you say?" he snarled. "I hate boars!"

He stormed off, grabbing his helmet and sword along the way, and headed out on his invisible hunt. When he was out of view, Kore exited the shelter. Her mother appeared at her side without warning.

"What was that? Are you all right?" Demeter quizzed frantically.

"I am fine, though I cannot say the same for Ares's armor." She sighed.

"Why? What has become of it?"

"Trampled by a boar." Kore shrugged with a soft smile.

Demeter tilted her head. "There are no boars in Ithome, my daisy."

"Ares does not seem to know that." She giggled softly before falling serious. "Mama, I do not understand why he must stay. He is not helping."

"He has informed me he is here on Zeus's word. To ensure you are assisting me and we are proving beneficial. He is also to guard us," Demeter informed.

"Is that what you were speaking of earlier?"

"Yes. I know it is hard now. But do please try to be cordial with him. Who knows—perhaps you will bring out a different side from the God of War."

"I do not think it possible, Mama. He is a brute, and he smells as horrible as the goats. I think they may smell more pleasant," Kore said with a pout.

"Even so, do try. We do not want his presence here being

any more difficult than it needs to be."

That was something Kore could understand after what she had just seen. She had only knocked his sword to the ground; she had not seen any damage. Yet the anger he released was something she would prefer not to unleash again. It would be best to just avoid him altogether. A task easier said than done when he was constantly on her back.

"I will try, Mama." She sighed.

CHAPTER VI

THE FIG TREE, THE CRYSTAL, AND THE GIFT

1182 BC: SEVENTEEN YEARS OLD

"Kore, dear! Can you please go out and pick the wild figs?" Demeter called from the fireplace.

Kore was already in the front garden assisting with the magical fruit harvest. Demeter only needed wild fruit when she was going to the village to trade. It did not grow by their magic and was allowed to grow however it saw fit.

She dusted her hands free of soil and skipped into the cottage and through the halls until she met her mother.

"Planning another trip to the village again, I see," Kore mused.

It being Kore's seventeenth year, Demeter had promised to get her cotton and wool for her spinning, a new hobby she was trying out that took her mind from plants. Over the last three years, Kore and her mother had tended fields all over Greece. Every day and night grew full of plants and crops.

Lending aid as they had promised, despite Ares being in tow, they had managed to complete more than half of the harvest by the first year. Unfortunately, by the second year, the

Trojans and Greeks had made their rounds again, laying waste to half their progress.

It was Hera who pleaded that they continue and so they did. They had finally made it back home after working the last year in Athens before Zeus called for their return, on Ares's word. Ares had been rude, invasive, and drunk most of the time. A constant annoyance to Kore. When she was not cloning and calling her plants, she was fleeing his unwanted touch and advances. But she was grateful for him to have requested their return so he could lend aid to the Trojans. She was happy to be rid of him and the aftermath of war.

"Of course, my daisy. I have a few trades to make. So please make sure to grab a few plump ones," Demeter requested.

"Yes, Mama," Kore turned to walk away when Demeter called to her once more.

"Oh, and Kore!"

"Yes?" She turned on the balls of her feet to meet her mother, who was now facing her.

"Please don't dally!" she pleaded with a warm smile.

Kore nodded quickly before heading back out into the main garden to fetch a basket big enough for figs. On a day such as this, with this task at hand, Kore would call aid from Lotus. But, since returning from the fields, Kore had learned from Syke that Lotus had snuck away for the last moon to be with her secret lover.

Kore was excitedly awaiting Lotus's return to the meadow so they could share stories they so clearly missed.

No matter, Kore thought. She knew she was never alone. The plants were always near. Though she was excited to see Lotus again and it did hurt that she had not been at the meadow when they had returned days ago, she would be content with just herself and the trees at the spring.

Her hands hovered over a wicker-weaved basket her mother had come by during her trades. Its wooden twined handle was wrapped in a thick, discolored cotton cloth. Dry leaves and dirt lay lifeless at the bottom, collected over the windy days that passed.

Kore gripped the handle and flipped the basket to free the leaves and dust, chatting with the hamadryad sisters briefly before making her way to the spring.

She looked to the sky, happy to see a rare bright day after so many days of clouded darkness. She came to a stop at the forest edge, the trunks of the thick cypress lined with sheet moss. Flat white mushrooms sprouted near the base. Kore had missed this spot; three years had seemed like such a long time to her.

Demeter constantly reminded her that soon, years would pass like days, and it would not seem so long. Kore hoped those days would not come as she enjoyed taking things slow and enjoyed her experiences. New or old.

She tilted her head back to allow Helios's rays to paint her skin. Taking a deep breath, she entered the forest, following the open path that led to the cool springs. It was a spot for Kore and the nymphs to relax on such a day as this. It was hot, and it was only getting hotter with each passing minute. Perhaps dallying for but a moment would not hurt.

The path lay clear and straight, not requiring her to hop over or crawl under fallen logs. She hummed a song her mother would hum as they worked, grazing her fingers over the trails of purple wildflowers that lined the path. They had missed her touch, her song. They had feared her on her worst days, but when they loved her on her best, they would shower her with their praise.

Her skin was flushed from the heat as she exited the forest onto a small, rocky opening that led right into a large body of clear water. Around the left, with its branches hanging just over the glistening surface, sat the wild-growing fig trees. A few fruits floated in the water below, and some overly ripe ones sat washed up by the trunks.

Kore wasted no time making her way to the trees and placing the basket in the dry brush behind them, out of reach from the soft, low tide.

She ran her fingers across the water's surface to test the temperature, cool and relaxing against her flesh. Her skin screamed as she withdrew her hand. If she swam for a few moments now, and then picked the figs, she would have enough time to dry in the sun before she returned to her mother. If she wanted to dry quickly, she would have to leave the robes with the basket and figs.

She rid herself of the linens and set them alongside the basket. Her body continued to heat up as if the sun had been brought right to her side, pushing her into the water with its raging blaze.

From her feet to her knees to her hips, then waist. The water climbed slowly up her bare skin until she was submerged from her neck down. She cupped her hands and poured it over her head, allowing it to saturate her thick locks. She groaned at the sensation before dipping her head back with closed eyes.

The cool water soothed her, and her body's buoyancy allowed her to float calmly along the surface. The peaceful chirping of the birds and relaxing calmness of the forest gave her much comfort. She listened to the soft sounds, a peace she had not felt since leaving the meadow.

A peace that was soon disrupted by a gentle tap on her head.

Her heart sank to her stomach and her face grew warm. Her muscles froze, a thousand thoughts racing through her mind. All pointing to one hope. She lifted her head and slowly began to turn.

What if it's somebody more frightening? she thought, pausing for but a moment more. She didn't sense anyone else around, just the burning heat from the day, but not any sinister energy. Sucking in a gust of air, she swung around. To her surprise and disappointment, there were only a few free-fallen figs that landed in the water. A heavy sigh escaped her lips as she grabbed the nearest one. It was a good size and felt rather plump, and she felt it wise to save it in the basket.

On her way to the trees, she collected the remaining floating figs that bobbed in the water. They were all nicely plump and perfectly ripe but not heavy enough to have all fallen free on their own. She figured a deer rubbed against the tree, knocking the fruit loose just a few moments before arriving to the spring.

She placed all she had collected in the basket and plucked a few more figs from the low-hanging branches to tuck away as well, filling it to its brim. Leaving her with more than enough time to spare. She entered the water again for a few more moments of silent relaxation.

Closing her eyes, Kore focused on the sounds around her. The buzzing of nearby bees as they collected the wildflower pollen. The sound of the water washing over the rocks and moss. The birds chirping in the distance.

The most peaceful of moments if she had ever experienced one. The burning against her fair skin became unbearable, causing her to duck under the water until her skin felt cool and her lungs begged for air.

She broke the surface with a gasp. All was quiet except for a nearby deer. Its hooves snapped and crunched twigs as it went about its day. It was an easy sound to ignore.

She continued to float in the clear water until she knew her mother would be expecting her. Reluctantly she climbed free of the cool liquid and slipped back into her robes. The fabric clung to her wet skin like plaster. Her hair dripped water, soaking the linen even further. She hoped it would be dry by the time she made it to the meadow. But with the day being so hot, she figured her mother would understand.

She scooped up her basket and was bidding her farewells to the fig trees when the sound of a nearby rustling bush drew her attention—and caution. Whatever made its way near was large, and her mother did not keep anything larger than a deer in her meadow.

That is not a deer! she thought.

She turned on her heels and swiftly ducked from the opening. Finding the forest path back to the meadow, she held her hand down to the wildflowers for aid, but they saw nothing. Energy pulsed through her arms, calling out to her vines. They snaked their way up, lifting the loose soil but never breaking free. Creeping along her sides like a hidden cage. Ready to strike at any moment.

The rustling of a bush close by stopped as she did, and the forest around her fell silent once more. She scanned the path from which she just came and saw only the sliver of water from the spring. Her body turned back; the thought of investigating the sound crossed her mind. But in search of what? Her foot moved forward, and she was at its mercy, unsure what she was going back for.

She took another step. Her lungs swelled in her chest, feeling as if they were about to burst.

Caw, a low-swooping raven cried, startling the goddess.

"Oh, sweet lilies!" she blurted out, spinning on her heels.

She lunged forward, crashing hard against a strong, solid mass. The collision caused her to fall back, hitting her head against the ground, leaving the world around her spinning.

"Ow!" the goddess groaned, rubbing the back of her head.

"Watch yourself, nymph!" a deep voice grunted over the ringing in her head.

"*Nymph*?" she spat, struggling to her feet and dusting herself free of the dirt that clung to her. "I am no nymph—" she huffed. When her eyes met the man, her chest sank, closing around her lungs and squeezing the air from them.

His blue eyes sat steadily on her, his jaw clenched and his lips pressed together. His beauty was something she felt she would never get used to, especially since she did not see him often.

Kore let her eyes wander the god, noticing different things about him from the last time they had spoken. She felt different things upon these discoveries, and she liked them.

He wore a black chiton, leaving his wide, muscular chest bare and open. His jet-black hair splayed across his shoulders, his face smooth and beardless, showing off the angled shape of his set jaw.

"Aidoneus?" she finally gasped, a thick lump building in her throat.

His eyes swept her face, then body as if trying to recognize who she was, but he said nothing. Kore looked down to see what he was looking at but became quickly distracted by her fallen, scattered figs.

"Oh no!" She dropped to collect the fruit. Aidoneus kneeled as well, grabbing up a few of the deep purple figs and handing them to her without a word.

"What brings you to my mother's forest on this lovely day?" she finally asked, tucking the last fruit into place. She locked eyes with his and waited. His face twisted as he thought of her question.

"I, uh—" he stuttered, pausing to look at Kore once more. His lips pulled up at the corners, flashing his teeth, and little dimples appeared on his cheeks. Kore could feel the heat on her body rise.

"I *fancied* a walk," he offered calmly. His smile still burning in Kore's mind.

"You *fancied* a walk?" she repeated, words that she felt held little truth.

The only reason he had come the first time was on business. Which Kore had intruded on. Perhaps he required her assistance yet again. Assistance Kore would be more than happy to supply if that be the case.

She looked about him and noticed he was missing three of her favorite hounds.

"Where are your hounds?" she probed.

"The Erinyes were in need of them today. I was not in as much need."

"Oh? And what need brings you?" She began looking

through her basket of figs, noticing some were bruised and broken and others had collected dirt. They would not do well for her mother's trades.

"Are you displeased with the fruit?" he asked, ignoring her previous question.

"My mother is taking these to trade in the village, and these broken ones will offer her no success in that." She moved the fruit around. "And these dirty ones just need a bit of water to rinse them." She would have to go back to the spring and pick a few more fresh figs and clean the rest.

Aidoneus reached out and took the basket from her. "We will rinse them then." He offered a soft smile again, and Kore felt her stomach knot. She would watch him smile all day if she could.

"So, what needs are you attending that are not important enough to call aid of your vicious hounds?" she teased as they made their way back to the spring.

"I would not say it is *not* important. Some may say—trivial." His voice was warm and welcoming.

The last time she had seen him, he had been so callous to the other divines. There was a moment in the Olympus Garden when he seemed to have dropped the stone wall—at least for her. Hermes made mention a few times after councils that he was back to his usual distant self.

"And what be so trivial?" Kore pushed, catching sight of another captivating smile.

Her chest warmed. She had never kissed a man before and thought it at times simple, but now, it seemed difficult in practice.

"I came for a particular fruit," he admitted.

"A fruit?"

"It doesn't grow in my realm. Hermes informed me that your mother had a vast variety of fruits. Ones not known to Greece."

It was true, Demeter grew her favorite cultivations from around the lands in her forest and meadow. It was an easy way for her to care for them long distance, being able to mutate and change them from her safe space.

It wasn't a secret, but Demeter wasn't in the habit of letting the divine in for some. Mostly because the forest and meadow were her sanctuaries away from them. However, Kore was in such a habit of letting one god do as he pleased.

"Fruit grows in your realm?" She blinked.

"You'd be surprised what grows in my realm," he said with a wicked grin.

"Which ones do not?"

Aidoneus kept his eyes on the trees that fenced the water. "'Tis an odd-looking fruit with a bright pink flesh, baring green, fleshy leaves as well. The meat of the fruit is white—"

"Does it have tiny black seeds?" Kore interjected.

She knew the exact fruit he sought; it wasn't too far from the fig trees and was a fruit Kore did not care much for. It was not native to Greece—she was unsure where her mother had cultivated it from—but she knew it was of a tropical location.

Aidoneus shared another soft smile, and Kore's eyes lingered on the curve of his lips. Her face flushed gold, and her heart grew heavy at the sight.

She reached up and grasped her crystal. It had been some time since she last held it, but she needed to be sure this was no dream.

"She has such a fruit," she said, guiding him around the edge of the water.

They first stopped at the fig tree to replace the damaged figs. She plucked the smushed ones from the basket and laid them along the base so that when they grew rotten, they would feed it new life.

She apologized to them for the waste, and they reassured her in return. The fruit-bearing trees knew a great deal and held a deep understanding of the process of life and death. Kore felt they better understood it than the other plants in the forest. For when their fruits fell with no one to claim them, they would rot and give back to the earth's nourishment, which would then feed the tree it fell from. A constant cycle.

She turned back to the spring for the fruit that needed rinsing. Leaning over the clear surface, she pulled a muddied fig from the basket and dunked it into the water, watching as the soil created a dirt cloud that slowly drifted as it washed away with the low tide.

Aidoneus leaned down beside her and assisted in the rinsing of fruit.

Kore thought it funny. It was such a mortal thing to do. For her, this was normal. But for a god, a king, this was a sight to be seen.

She remembered her mother's warning about him not only being a god but a king. How they are unpredictable, and though he was very much unpredictable, Kore did not get the feeling he was dangerously so.

Demeter had said many things that had already proven to be false. But still, Kore only knew so much about *this* king. There could still be a slight truth to her mother's words. Zeus wasn't always faithful to Hera, nor Poseidon to Amphitrite. She knew Aphrodite was no faithful divine either. So, was it so much of a king trait as it was a divine trait?

From all the stories her mother told, not one divine seemed faithful, and only one was known to not have taken a wife at any time.

"Why have you never taken a bride?" she suddenly asked. He seemed taken aback by the inquisition. It was an intrusive question, and Kore wasn't sure why she allowed it to slip so freely from her lips.

His face fell back into his set scowl.

"Love is a fleeting feeling," he grumbled.

"I do not think it so," she whispered in an attempt to draw him back to the softness she so longed for.

"What would you know of it?"

Though the question hurt Kore, he was right. What did she know of love? Nothing, but if it were up to her, she would call the feelings she felt for him *love*.

"Not much," she admitted with a shrug.

"Thought not." He sighed. Kore could see the hardness of his face fall.

"Could you explain it to me?"

He looked up to her then, his eyes searching. He did not answer, but he did not need to speak the words for Kore to see.

"You know not of love?" Her voice grew sad, and she leaned in closer to him. He watched her intently but made no motion to move away.

"The Underworld is no place for love," he finally said.

Kore tilted her head and waited for more—but after a few silent moments, she accepted that she would have to push for it. As long as he was willing to answer. "No? Why is that?"

Aidoneus couldn't hide the chuckle that escaped him. "I see your joy of questions has aged as you have." He rose to his feet, the basket in hand, and Kore quickly followed.

"How else am I to get to know you if I do not speak?"

This, too, was a question he had not anticipated. His eyes stayed focused on her as she made her way to the tree that held the fruit he sought.

"Most do not wish to know me."

"Well, luckily, I am not most," she said with a smile. "Do you think love has no place in the Underworld or in you? I have heard many tales of love after life. Tales of mortals venturing to your realm to retrieve a lost love." She plucked a bright pink fruit from the tree's branch and waited.

"Yes, but those do not end well." He sighed. Kore waited for more, knowing he would most likely end the tale there, but he surprised her and took in another deep breath before he continued. "A few centuries back, a mortal woman came to me begging to release her late love. A man whose thread was cut too soon by the Fates. She came to me with an offer. Her soul for his. I allowed this," he paused again, his eyes searching hers as he recalled the moment, "allowing one meeting a moon on the banks of Styx."

His voice drifted once more, and for a moment, she couldn't be sure, but for just a moment, Kore saw a flash of pain cross his eyes.

"The first visit she had with him, he was not there. He never came—not even to thank her for her sacrifice."

He explained the tale so clearly, as if it had just occurred.

"What did she do?" Kore gasped.

Aidoneus's face fell hard once more, pain twisted on it as he thought on the woman and her tale.

"She chose to drink from River Lethe, to forget." He dropped his head; the event clung to him.

Kore was surprised at how pained he was by it. Perhaps he had hopes of love being true.

"That sounds like love lost. Not an absence of it. She truly felt love for him. It was he who did not return that gift. But I would like to think that the mortal woman had felt love—so much she was willing to sacrifice herself so that he could be. That sounds like love to me," Kore mused, partly to herself, but she wanted him to hear the words as well.

His brows pulled to the center, creating a small crease between them.

She held out the fruit he sought and watched as his expression slowly changed once more at her words. Words he had not considered.

"Tell me, *Lord Hades*, is it love you fear or love lost, due to betrayal?" she quizzed, stepping toward him.

"I do not fear love."

She took another step.

"No?"

Another step closer. Close enough to feel the heat that radiated from the flooded ichor that brightened his skin.

"Then, tell me of your fears," she breathed, unsure where her sudden confidence came from, a sort of power that consumed her all at once. Aidoneus inhaled deeply, his eyes scanning over her, from her lips to the hollow of her neck. He opened his mouth as if to speak but then took a step back from her. The heat pulled away with him.

"Apologies," she said softly, dropping her head.

A painful prick to her heart. Her mother would have thought her behavior shameful, but Kore did not feel shame. She felt—hurt, but not ashamed.

"I should not have been so forward." She held out the odd fruit to him once more, and he took it with caution, careful not to touch her hand.

"I fear I would not make a proper husband," he suddenly said, his voice low and smooth again.

Her eyes searched his and saw only sorrow. A truthful answer, one Kore wanted to address again with him, but at a later time. For now, she was happy to have gotten an honest answer at all.

Aidoneus reached around his side and uncovered a small brown leather pouch attached to the thick strap that held his chiton up. He pulled it open and shuffled around the bag before tucking the pink fruit into it.

He moved some trinkets once more to secure the fruit, and as he pulled his hand free, a small black crystal attached to a thin leather strap fell out. It looked near identical to the crystal Kore wore, but this one was a solid dark black, with the likeness of his throne on Mt. Olympus.

"Oh!" She gasped excitedly.

She only knew of a few divines who worked with them. It was a practice, but mostly something they used for decoration. "You work with crystals?"

"Just one." Aidoneus reached down to pick it up. He looked to Kore, whose eyes were wide with amazement at the strange new rock in his hand.

"Would you like it?" he asked, holding it out to her.

"No, I could not!" Heat warmed her face as the ichor flushed her cheeks.

"They are common in my realm. I insist!" He stepped closer.

She hesitated briefly before reaching up and grasping

the crystal. She was not as cautious, allowing her fingertips to graze across his palm, sending a shocking, tingling sensation that caused her to quickly draw back, crystal in hand.

"Thank you," she chirped, hoping he didn't notice the abrupt movement. But he only continued to stare down at her. She could feel the air around her ignite once more, and her breathing became heavy.

"You know," she breathed, "it is my birthday."

Aidoneus lifted his brow, and the urge to trace the arch with her fingers grew heavy. Her foot moved her forward, closing the distance between them again until her chest just barely touched his.

This time, he did not move away. He seemed to allow her to test the limits, either hers or his, Kore did not care. If she was honest, she did not know what she was doing or going to do. She allowed her body to move as it needed, with her no longer in control.

"Thank you," she breathed as she rose on her toes. He did not move to flee, but Kore could feel his chest still as he watched her. She placed her palm against his cheek, warming under her touch. Her nose just barely touching his.

She pressed her lips to his, surprised at how warm and soft they felt as they molded to her. His breath fanned across her face; the smell of spice, cypress, and smoke danced around her and fogged her mind. To her delight, his lips parted against her as he returned the kiss.

The ichor flooded back to Kore's cheeks, and the warmth of it shocked her back to reality. She broke free from him, rocking back on her feet. Her heart began to race as the realization of what she had done flooded her mind. She looked to Aidoneus with wide eyes before quickly looking away, embarrassed by her hasty actions.

"Apologies. Again." With her eyes on her hands, she backed away until she was stopped by the trunk of a tree.

"I fear it is I who must apologize," he said, clearing his throat.

“My—my mother told me not to be long.” She rushed to pick up the basket of figs.

He didn’t speak as she brushed past him; stopping just a few feet away, she turned with a bow. “It was a pleasure seeing you again, Aidoneus.”

In her embarrassment and fear, she turned one last time and raced down the path back to the meadow.

CHAPTER VII

THE REUNION, THE MILK, AND THE OBOLS

"What took you, my dear child?" Demeter called as she caught sight of Kore bounding back to the cottage.

Kore didn't like it when her mother called her "child" since she no longer was one, and she feared Demeter would always see her as a precious young maiden. She no longer felt like the young child she once was, certainly not after what she had just done. The kiss, still burning hot on her lips. The taste of him lingered just as strong. Fire and spice.

"One of your creatures, Mama," Kore lied. "It startled me, and I dropped the basket. Some of the best fruits were ruined, and I had to go back and pick a whole basket full." That part was not a lie, and she hoped Demeter would not catch it, nor would she notice the new flush of Kore's cheeks.

"Oh, dear! I do apologize, my daisy! Are you well?" Demeter pawed at her daughter, checking for any sign of injury. The last thing Kore wanted was her mother inspecting her.

"I am fine," she reassured, but Demeter continued searching.

"I can stay, my dear. I do not have to leave for trades this day."

"No, no, Mama. Go trading in the village," Kore urged.

Demeter pulled away from her daughter with a soft smile. "Are you sure?"

"Yes, I assure you I am well. I am just a bit excited about spinning is all," she lied again.

"Well then. I will not be long. Oh—there is a surprise waiting in your chambers. Now, I must be off," Demeter said, taking the basket from Kore.

Demeter did love to venture into the village; the mortals always had odd and interesting things to barter.

Kore said her final goodbyes to her mother before turning and heading to her chambers. Her mind was in a haze as she thought back to her morning with the god so many said was unkind.

She rounded the column to her chambers and was greeted with a bright, familiar smile. The glowing seafoam eyes popped wide as the goddess entered.

"Kore!" Lotus cried as she threw her arms around her dear friend. "I have missed you!"

Kore thought her heart would burst at the sight. It had been three full years since they had last seen one another. Three years they had missed watching each other grow.

"Lotus!" Kore cried; the tears left watery trails down her cheeks. She hadn't known of happiness such as this.

She missed her dear friend on the late nights that she and Demeter stayed out to clone seedlings and call forth the beginning of the harvest. She had missed her cheerful smile and guarded ways. She had missed her silly frustrations and her sneaky tricks. But most of all, she missed having her friend to talk to and talk her down from her crazy ideas and outbursts.

She held Lotus tight as they both cried tears of happiness into the fabric of their peplos.

"I have so much to share with you," Lotus sniffled with a laugh-mixed cry.

Kore smiled widely. "As do I!"

The two sat on Kore's kline and looked over one

another. Her once long, dark brown hair now was chopped to a length that stopped at her jaw, but other than that, Lotus had not changed much. Tall and slim, with movements so gracefully fit for a nymph.

"Enough of these tears." Kore laughed, wiping her cheeks free of the moisture. "Now, tell me of this new secret lover?"

Lotus dropped her face with a smile, her cheeks flushing a light shade of pink.

"The point of a secret is for it to stay as such." She giggled. "That silly Syke can never keep anything to herself." She took a deep breath and looked back up to Kore. "Well, to start, he is a god." She paused as she searched Kore's eyes. "I was in the village last solstice picking up some parchments, and I came across a man who was wandering around. Not lost, but clearly not sure where he was headed. I could tell he was divine by the ichor glow." She paused again, stuck in the memory of the day.

"What is his name? What is his name?" Kore squealed. The girls laughed at the sound and Kore's impatience.

"Hypnos. The God of Sleep." Lotus searched Kore's eyes once more before she continued. "He—He is from the Underworld."

Kore's eyes grew wide. All the negative things Lotus had said, all the things she had tried to warn Kore of about the gods who lived in the Underworld. Here she was, constructing secret outings to go be with one. Kore could not help but sneak a laugh.

"I should not have spoken ill about the Underworld. Hypnos has always said such lovely things about it." She looked Kore over once more with a sheepish smile. "What of you? How was being out of the meadow?" It was now Lotus's turn to ask the probing questions.

"It would have been better if I were able to move freely from Ares," Kore groaned.

"Ares?" Lotus shot with round eyes. "Why?"

"To stand guard." Kore shrugged. "He hovered mostly." Her mind pulled forward the dreadful evenings Ares had taunted her. She shivered.

"I am just glad to be home," Kore added.

"Hm?" Lotus hummed. "And?" She pushed again, clearly seeking a particular answer.

"And, what?" Kore shrugged innocently.

"Was he the only one to hover?" Her voice fell to a whisper in case the other nymphs were roaming the halls.

"I did not see him *outside* of the field," Kore answered with a smile.

"*Outside*?" Lotus repeated with a raised brow and Kore only smiled. "Tell me all!"

Kore began to tell Lotus about her morning with the god. Of his gift to her, his tale of love and the kiss.

"He kissed you back?" She gasped. "I am shocked you didn't leave with him and run off to the Underworld." Lotus laughed in a high tune.

Kore thought it would be nice to make the trip to see him in his realm. A surprise for him as much as he was to her.

"I—I think I want to," Kore said softly.

Lotus jumped from the kline in shock. "Kore!" she shouted, her voice ringing through the halls.

Kore grabbed the nymph's hand and yanked her back to the kline, pressing a finger to her lips. "Shh," she hissed as she watched the hall for any eavesdropping nymphs. "I do not plan on leaving tonight. But I do plan on leaving to see him, someday. Even if it is for just a day," Kore whispered.

Lotus's brows pinched in the middle. "Kore. It is more than a day's travel to get there."

Kore knew Lotus had to be right if she was visiting a secret lover who lived there. If she planned to go on foot, it would take some time. But that was a minor detail in her mind. With each passing second, the decision to go became more and more solidified.

"Well, I will worry about that when the time comes.

What I want to know is how you get in?"

"Kore—" Lotus paused, her face twisting in a mix of concern and confusion. "I do not go into the Underworld. Hypnos and I meet in a hidden cove. Nobody just goes into the Underworld. Not even the souls." Lotus let out a nervous laugh, but Kore did not understand what was funny. "You have to pay the ferryman," Lotus said quickly after clearing her throat.

"How much?"

"Kore, it is not something you just pay to do. There are rules!" Lotus objected, but Kore knew there had to be a way in.

It wasn't impossible; how could it be? Demeter told of stories about mortal men finding their way into the realm, though none of those ended well. There was still a way, and if a mortal could accomplish it, then it shouldn't be hard for a divine. Besides, Hermes frequented the Underworld often as it was his duty to guide the souls of the dead. He ventured to and from the realm as freely as he did Demeter's meadow.

Hermes. The thought suddenly dawned on her. She had no idea how to get to the Underworld, where the entrance may be, or even how far away it was from her. But Hermes could easily take her there. It was just a matter of persuasion.

"You aren't listening, are you?" Lotus scoffed, pulling Kore back to their conversation. She had been droning on about rules, and how things were to be. But that's all Kore ever heard from the nymphs and her mother. How things should be. As far as Kore had come to realize, that was just not how things were turning out. She turned to Lotus again, her mouth pressed in a tight line.

"Lotus. I am going to the Underworld. Not today, not tomorrow, but someday when I have enough saved. I will be going, and you are not going to convince me otherwise," she said flatly.

She felt her stomach settle and her shoulders relax at the thought. It was a relaxing choice, one that lifted a weight off her that she wasn't even aware of until it left.

Lotus only stared back at her divine friend with wide eyes. She couldn't think of anything to say, but also dare not speak it if she did. For a nymph, the divine's final word was law. Lotus couldn't argue any further on the matter. She could only hope for the best outcome for her friend and be as supportive as she could.

"What do you plan then?" she said nervously, unsure if she should aid Kore or tell Demeter.

Telling Demeter meant she'd lose a friend, but not telling meant she would still lose her friend, and only one outcome came with Kore not being upset with her in the end.

"Well," Kore thought, turning back to face the hall, "I will need to save coins. Do you know how much is needed?"

"I know the souls only need one or two obols for Charon. But you are living, not only that, and you are also a divine. He could charge you nothing at all or a whole fortune," Lotus informed.

"Then a fortune is what I will save." Kore beamed.

"How will you do that?"

"I will have to see if Mama will let me go into town with her to trade and sell goods. She plans to bring back cotton for my spinning and fabrics for robes. We have chickens and my goats—mortals love trading eggs and milk. I shall just take what I can get from that."

"How do you plan to present this idea to your mother? She is going to ask why the sudden interest," Lotus pointed out.

"Hm, I was thinking of telling her I was interested in mortal trade, as she is." Kore thought about several more reasons she could gather for her mother, but she felt just having the same interests would be enough. Demeter always praised Kore extensively when she expressed any interest in the same things.

The girls chatted more about Kore's plan, about their past years apart, and of course about their new secret loves.

They joked and giggled until Helios and his blistering sun were nearing the end of their travels and the shadows grew across Kore's chamber floors.

The sound of greetings and questions of the trip began to fill the hall as Demeter returned from her trading events of the day.

"Welcome back, Lady Demeter," the hamadryad sisters greeted in unison.

"Good evening, my darlings," Demeter greeted back happily. "Where might my dear daughter be?"

"In her chambers," the nymphs answered.

Lotus stood and hugged Kore before leaving the chambers and greeting the Goddess of Harvest. Once Demeter entered it would be a mother-daughter moment as it always was just before bed. It was also the time Kore was able to ask her mother questions and favors without prying eyes and listening ears.

"Good evening, Mama!" Kore cheered, hopping to her feet and greeting her mother with a hug. "How were your trades?"

"They were splendid, dear! Here!" Demeter pulled a bundle from the folds in her wraps. "In celebration of another solstice passed." Her mother smiled softly before placing a gentle kiss upon her forehead.

Kore removed the light wrapping from the bundle and pulled forth black and white wool for her spinning. It was soft and smooth, not like the wool of a sheep, Kore could tell, but she could not name what animal it had come from. She did know it was beautiful.

"'Tis lovely, Mama!"

"The mortals trade finely for that silly goat's milk. They claim it's nectar from the gods." Demeter laughed.

"They are not wrong."

The milk did come from a goat that ate vegetables from the garden. It was milk Demeter took to Olympus on her produce drop-offs. Milk from the gods was a completely accurate statement.

"No, they are not. It is always so interesting venturing down there. There is so much more peace now that the harvest is most plentiful," Demeter thought aloud.

Kore knew the land had fared better since they had last swept through the fields of Greece, as the mortals moved their war on to different lands.

"I would really like to see that one day. The product of our work. Of *my* work. I would love to visit the village for trades." She spoke with a soft, low voice and kept her eyes down on her hands. Too nervous for her mother's response.

"I do not see why not, dear. You surprise me. From your attendance in Council to your work by my side. You have made me proud," Demeter said softly.

Kore looked up to her and was greeted with a soft, warm smile and glistening eyes.

"You may join me on my trip next moon if you would like," Demeter offered.

Kore was hoping she could go sooner, and possibly with only Lotus. But she knew this was a lot to ask of her mother already, and she was grateful to even get a yes from her.

Demeter placed her hand on her daughter's cheek. "You have done great things, my child. I have no doubt you will continue to do so for these mortals."

She placed a kiss on Kore's forehead before wishing the young goddess good night and parting from the chambers.

Kore was overjoyed with happiness and at the same time fear. She knew that with a granted access to the village, it was time for her to start saving. And the closer she got to her goal, the sooner she would leave the only place she had grown to know as home.

Though a prison in many ways, the meadow also gave Kore needed freedom, hidden deep within its forests. She would miss the trees and flowers. But she wanted something greater than what the meadow provided.

She leaned back into her kline and tucked herself under

the thick furs. Finally able to process her morning in the privacy of her own chambers, she allowed the memories to flood her mind.

His smell, his touch, his taste. She placed her fingers gently on her lips, which grew hot with the thought.

He kissed her back and it ignited a need inside Kore, a fire. And she would stop at nothing to ease it.

Chapter VIII

THE SURPRISE, THE ULTIMATUM, AND THE REQUEST

1882 BC: EIGHTEEN YEARS OLD

“Thank you, fair maiden!” The mortal bowed, reaching out his worn, labored hands to drop two obols in Kore’s palm.

“Thank you.” She bowed softly in return, placing the obols in her pouch before turning to Lotus.

“Looks like that is the last of it, Kore!” Lotus laughed. It was not the *last* of the goat milk; it was the *only* goat milk. She only ever brought one amphora full. It was heavy enough and did not keep long.

Kore pulled the hood of her robes over her head as she turned to leave. “We must go.”

“How much do you plan to save, Kore?” Lotus asked, skipping to the goddess’s side.

“I was thinking a hundred pieces would be sufficient enough.”

“How much have you saved so far?”

Kore made a snorting sound at the back of her throat. “After those two pieces? Thirty-eight.”

"By the time you save one hundred pieces, you will be near nineteen!" Lotus gasped but the smile in her voice was apparent.

Kore could not deny trading had proven more difficult than she had originally thought. Some months she and her mother could not go. Other times her mother made the trip without her. Milk had spoiled before being sold on a few trips and spilled on the way to others. Kore sighed heavily.

"I might be Mother's age." The two laughed as they ducked into the trees along the edge of the village that led back into Demeter's Forest.

"Do not fret, Kore. Time isn't an issue for you anymore, right?" Lotus pointed out, and she was right.

Kore had reached a point in her divine maturity where her aging had come to a halt. Forever on the cusp of youth and maidenhood, her body stopped its aging process at only eighteen winters and eight moons. Demeter had confirmed it early one morning a few moons past.

The divine's aging process was slow and would only grow slower the closer it came time for them to reach full maturity in their magic and when their divinity was most powerful.

Her skin began to glow a golden sun-kissed hue, her red hair acquired a fiery glow, and her eyes—a glowing electric blue. It was a new feeling and a new visual she still was not accustomed to. But age was never her issue. It was the wait; it was the not knowing when she would see Aidoneus next. If she would ever see him again, after what they had shared.

She wanted so badly just to be by his side once again, and it was the slow wait and never-ending obstacles that infuriated her.

"It is just lately Mother has been odd about me going to trade. Almost as if it is suddenly an issue again." She paused with a heavy sigh. "I had thought we were past all that."

They struggled through the thick brush and trees of the forest. Helios was taking his leave for the day and making way for Selene. Causing the shadows that greeted her to only grow longer.

They hurried until they could see a dim flicker of light peeking through the trees.

"The cottage!" Lotus shot, quickening her pace.

Kore followed briskly behind. Her legs were sore from the trek, and she wanted to wash the miasma that covered her from her interactions with the mortals. Mortal energy that clung to her like mud and muck. A thick and weighing nuisance to her skin, an invisible filth that was horribly agitating.

The closer they came to the cottage, the brighter the light grew, and with it grew the faint hint of chatter. Demeter had a guest. It was a moment before Kore could make out the sweet song-like voice of Hestia, the Goddess of the Hearth. She was such a lovely divine and had come to frequent the meadow to have evening chats with Demeter since they had returned.

The two crept around and headed toward the back. With Demeter distracted they could easily sneak along to Kore's chambers and change into their average robes.

Demeter never allowed them to stay in the village so late, and they had gotten away with claiming to wander the forest after, but Demeter was no longer allowing for that excuse either.

Kore stopped near an opening between two columns that led into the main meeting hall, where her mother and Hestia gathered. She was getting ready to make a quick dash across the opening when her mother's soft cries gave her pause.

"I do not think Kore will be too happy with me about it." Her mother wept.

"It was by order of Zeus, Demeter. You agreed," Hestia consulted.

"Yes, but it has come time for it to happen, and I just can't—" Demeter's voice broke.

Lotus leaned into Kore's ear. "What's going on?" she whispered.

"Not sure." Kore shrugged, and they continued to listen.

"How would you do it, Hestia? How would you tell your dearest daughter that you agreed to marry her off to a god she despises and fears?" Demeter continued. "What am I asking? You would not know what it means to have a child."

The air around Kore grew cold and tight; everything fell silent except for the sound of her heart pounding in her ears. A tingling heat grew in her palms, shooting up her arms to her head. The sensation fogged her mind, filling her eyes with the stinging pressure of tears.

The trees around her quivered and buckled with her as her anguish sank into the soil at her feet.

"Kore! Stop!" Lotus begged.

Kore jerked away from Lotus's touch, shaking her head to pull her focus back on the conversation between her mother and Hestia. But the trees and bushes continued to snap back as Kore's emotions poured into them.

"I am so sorry, my dear. That was not fair of me. Please forgive me," Demeter begged softly. "I am just . . . upset."

"I am not sore, dear. I understand the fears you face. Though, I cannot share the same amount of understanding. I remember what the gods have done to you, my sister. I understand you wish that not for your precious daughter. She is sweet and quite lovely. Who knows, maybe she will bring out the softness that is hidden deep inside Ares," Hestia soothed.

But no matter how soft her voice, how reassuring her words, Kore could not shake the dread and rage that filled her, turning her stomach until a sour taste coated her mouth like venom.

How could she? Kore's thoughts raged with questions of betrayal. How could her mother agree to such an act? Was it a trade? Had she really agreed to trade her only daughter to Ares? If not a trade, what reason would she have for this?

The trees buckled and branches snapped behind them.

"Kore, we must go!" Lotus urged as she tugged Kore by

her arm.

The vines had begun to creep from the ground, poking free from the surface of the soil.

"Kore, please calm down!" Lotus begged again, tugging the goddess around the cottage to the back entry hall that landed closest to Kore's chambers.

The rustling and crunching of branches fell faint as the sound of her own sobbing flooded her ears. Air left her all at once, and her legs gave way from under her.

"How could she?" Kore cried, falling to her knees.

She buried her face in the moist soil and wet leaves to muffle the clear cry that escaped her. Lotus kneeled beside her, desperate to comfort her friend, but Kore's body shook rapidly as she sobbed into the dirt. Her hands clawed and pounded at the earth in anger and desperation.

She had told her mother every night of her distaste for the god while in the fields of Greece. He was aggressive and rude and drunk most of the time. Now she was to be his, and the very thought twisted her stomach.

If she felt a prisoner in her mother's meadow, she would feel even more so under the eyes of Ares. He hadn't let Kore out of his sight unless she had advised of a boar nearby—he seemed to not learn that the creature did not frequent their sites often, if ever. But it was a great way to rid her of him.

How long would that work when she became his bride?

Lotus wrapped her arm around Kore's and helped her to her feet, taking most of the goddess's weight as they pushed through the hall to the bathing chambers.

The sweet nymph assisted a dazed Kore into the bathing basin and began the long process of pouring in the water.

More thoughts of what Kore would soon lose ran through her mind. Things she hoped for, her power, her independence, all ripped away from her in an instant. The God of War was not known to be kind, and not many of the Olympians even cared for him.

"Kore, let me dry you off." The soft voice brought the

goddess back to reality. Her bath had finished without her noticing, and before she knew it, she was dried off, in her kline, and under furs.

Is this what marriage will be like? The question repeated itself in her head as she sobbed quietly into the furs until she drifted to sleep.

Kore awoke in her chambers. The glow of the moon peeked through the branches and leaves, allowing only minimal light in. She rubbed her groggy, heavy eyes as she slid free from the furs and made her way to the entrance of the chamber, poking her head out into the hall. The candles still burned bright, illuminating the area with an oddly bright light. It couldn't be too late; Demeter always snuffed the lights out before retiring for the night.

"Mama?" Kore called into the halls, but she was met with only silence. She stepped out into the corridor and slowly crept down to the front entry chamber. Though she saw nothing odd, she still felt a sense of dread the closer she came to the hall. A crawling feeling lined her skin, raising bumps with a slight chill.

She rounded a column, stopping just as soon. A few pillars down on the right side of the entry hall hovered a dark black cloud of smoke. It did not appear to notice her entrance as it lingered, facing the meadow, unmoved.

"Hello?" Her voice cracked, startling herself. She reached up to grasp her crystals but found that neither her clear quartz nor the obsidian Aidoneus had gifted were there. An overwhelming sense of relief washed through her.

'Tis only a dream. She sighed as she spun around and headed back to her chambers.

"Kore!" A high voice called to her as she entered.

Her heart caught in her throat while she looked about the space. It appeared empty but Kore could sense a presence nearby. Hot and heavy. Dark energy hidden somewhere in her chambers. She forced her eyes to focus on the darkness but was met with only the faint light of the moon.

"Hello?" she called, her soft voice echoing off the marble around her.

"Over here!" the voice echoed back.

She traced the sound to the left of her, around the reflective plate and storage trunks.

She took a few hesitant steps toward it. At first, she did not see anything out of the ordinary. She wore regular night robes with her kline behind her. It wasn't until she was inches from the plate that she noticed it. Above her kline hovered a tall, dark cloud. The figure, a frequent visitor of her dreams. A spectator who never spoke.

"Hello," Kore whispered again.

Without warning the figure appeared behind her. Only the whites of its eyes were visible as they burned into Kore. Its hands gripped her shoulders, and an intense burning shot down her arms and through each finger, pulling forth a sharp yelp from the goddess.

"It's time."

"Tomorrow."

"Hermes."

The distorted voices echoed around the chamber in a frightening song.

Kore awoke to the bright rays from the sun shining through the trees just outside her window. There was an odd warmth to her chamber, and the morning air smelled faintly of burning cypress. She figured her mother must have begun her day early at the oven.

She looked about the chamber with memories of her dream. Her hand reached up, clutching the two crystals before tucking one away. She had made a habit of hiding the obsidian under her robes so her mother would not see.

My mother, she thought with venom when the memory of the night surged her mind. Demeter planned to tell Kore of the impending engagement soon. She would have to sit and listen to her mother speak the words to her, and that was something she could not bear. The very thought twisted her stomach to knots.

It's time. Tomorrow. Hermes.

The words repeated in her head, and she knew them to be true—two at least. She was unsure about Hermes other than her having to ask him, but it was time to leave and soon. Preferably before her mother could speak the words to her.

Was it not enough of a betrayal for her to have gone behind Kore's back and made such a deal? When? How long had this been in place for her?

She thought back over her last few years with the brutish god. Did Demeter know then?

The sudden realization crashed down on Kore. Of course. Why else did her mother allow him such freedom with her daughter? Why else did she beg her to try to get along with him?

Because she had known all along. Your life was never yours to control and never will be if you stay here. A voice chimed in the back of her mind like a whisper in her ear, but it was not wrong. If she ever wanted her freedom, she could not stay in the meadow any longer. Not to give chance of the secret arrangement between her mother and father.

There was only one place Kore knew her mother would not venture. One place her mother feared to even speak on for too long. A place she had already planned to venture to.

Though she was unsure how likely it was for Hermes to be visiting soon, she still needed to be ready for him so she could ask him the biggest favor she would ever have to ask of the god.

She jumped from the kline and ran to the medium-size chest that sat in front of it and flung open the lid. She began digging through it, pulling forth two robes, a pair of golden sandals she scarcely wore, and a satchel to stuff everything in.

She dug through the folds of her robes from the day before that Lotus had left on the lid of the chest and retrieved her sack of obols and tucked them into the satchel before pushing the sack under her bed.

Jumping to her feet, she quickly changed into her white linen peplos for the day before running out to the dining hall, where her mother sat with her head in her hands, unaware of her daughter's entrance.

Kore wanted to be angry with her, but as she looked upon her hidden face, she could see the heavy pull of her brows, the downward curve of her lips, and the slight perspiration that clung to her cheeks.

This decision was not an easy one, yet still, it was not a decision she should have made without Kore having a say.

"Good morning, Mama," Kore said with a forced smile. "What are the plans for this day?"

She wanted to make sure the day was clear so she could keep an eye out for Hermes, though she knew her mother would announce his arrival as she always did.

Demeter dropped her hands from her face but did not look up. "Oh, well, your father has a gift for you. Something about a big special surprise tomorrow—" Demeter's face fell at the words, and Kore knew what the "surprise" was supposed to entail. "Hermes will be bringing it down as usual."

Demeter sighed once more, her eyes on the nectar at her side. A new pain pulled at Kore's chest as she looked over her mother. This was not a decision or choice her mother had made. This was a demand, an order from Zeus. She wanted no more part of it than Kore did, but Zeus's word was law amongst them all, and whatever he ordered was to be done.

She felt bad for having such negative thoughts about Demeter, but that did not change the fact that she needed to leave. She needed to defy her mother and father on this one thing and live her life how she saw fit.

She would be leaving—tomorrow. If, of course, she could convince Hermes to aid her. He seemed more than delighted to see Kore and Aidoneus that day on Mt. Olympus, and she was sure he would not need too much convincing.

"Will he be here soon?" Kore gathered some fruit and nectar on a platter as she spoke.

"Oh, yes. Yes. He should be here any moment. Please make sure he leaves poor Ampelos to her work. Poor thing can hardly prune a bush with that god around."

Kore could tell her mother was distracted, her mind far away as she spoke. But as much as Kore wanted to comfort her, she had to push on as if she still didn't know of the arranged nuptials or planned to flee. When she had finished loading her platter, she headed out to the garden to eat in peace.

She slowly took down the thick, sweet nectar before nibbling on a few grapes that had been picked from the garden that morning. Once done, she placed the platter on a small wooden barrel that sat by the door of the cottage before running around to the back garden, where Ampelos worked.

Hermes had a fondness for Ampelos, and Kore knew that she had an equal fondness for him, though she would not admit it. Kore could see the way the nymph's cheeks flushed red when he was near and how she watched his every move.

Demeter did not like her nymphs distracted by the god's games and never left them alone with him. But like Kore, Ampelos had a secret place she would escape to that Demeter was unaware of. Kore only knew of it because she and Lotus had followed the nymph one day to play tricks on her when they were young ones.

"Ampelos," Kore sang, skipping to the nymph's side, ready to set her plan into motion.

"Yes, Lady Kore?" Her sweet voice rang. She glanced up with a welcoming smile as she continued to water the bed of dandelions.

"You know Hermes is to stop by today?" Kore tested,

with a quick answer in return as Ampelos's cheeks grew a bright red. She kept her head down, but Kore could see the small smile on her face.

"Would you like a moment with him? Without my mother's gaze?" Kore pushed and Ampelos shot her head up, their eyes locked.

"I could not—Lady Demeter would—"

"My mother does not have to know. She knows not of your small clearing just off to the northern part of the meadow. I could send him to you," Kore offered.

She felt her voice was steady enough, but the lump caught in her throat made it difficult to breathe. Something she hoped the nymph could not see. She took a deep breath as Ampelos looked back to her plants.

"How do you know of my spot?" She sighed softly.

"Worry not about how I know; just know I can send him there. If you would like. I see the way you look at him," Kore pushed further.

A small smile tugged at the corners of the nymph's lips.

"When?" she finally breathed.

As soon as the words left Ampelos's mouth, Kore felt her breath catch up with her again and the knot in her stomach loosened.

"Just after his visit. I will tell Mama he left, but I will send him to your clearing." Kore felt pleased with how her plan had played out. Everything was falling into place as if the Fates had a hand in it. She smiled softly to herself, delighted that she had only one last step left, and that was convincing Hermes to take her.

She skipped back to the front, where she found Lotus saying her morning greetings to Syke and Morea, but Kore's eyes stayed on them for but a moment. She looked up, searching the empty skies, anxious for the God of Messages to land.

"Good morning, Lady Kore!" the three nymphs greeted as they broke off into their morning duties, leaving Kore with nothing more to do but wait with her thoughts. She walked over to Lotus but knew this was not the proper time to tell her of the news. It would be best to wait until after she'd spoken with Hermes and figured out a time to meet. She wanted to have time to talk with her dear friend about the plan and to have a proper goodbye.

She walked around the bed as if inspecting it, just to pass time. Her mother was far too caught up in the next day to give her any tasks and Kore, too anxious to practice anything, already consumed by pretending as if the day was ordinary.

She reached up to grasp her crystal, walked around the beds, and then repeated until her legs grew tired. A small tinge of defeat struck her heart as she began walking back to the stone steps at the entrance of the cottage. She sat and tilted her head back to Helios and his rays and closed her eyes, taking a deep breath of the sweet floral scent that danced around her.

She noted the different scents and categorized them away. She knew from Aidoneus's words that vegetation grew in his realm, but not everything. She would keep up her power by crafting new plants for the god and his realm.

A cloud passed by, blocking the sun's rays from touching her face. She scrunched her nose and began to open her eyes when she heard the smooth laugh of the golden god.

He was there.

Her eyes shot open to be met with his wide, devilish grin.

"Good morning, *sis*!" he greeted.

An odd god, always making up words and phrases that did not seem well thought out to Kore.

"*Sis*?" she spat instantly.

"Yeah. You know. Short for sister, *sis*." He laughed. "Am I interrupting a daydream?"

"Not at all," she lied, jumping to her feet, "but come, let us take a walk before you go in to see my mother. She hasn't been feeling well this morning."

It wasn't a lie; her mother did seem off. But Kore knew

the cause; it was the same cause that turned Kore's stomach and made her want to weep at the very thought. She shoved it to the back of her mind and looped her arm around Hermes as they headed toward the direction of Kore's spring.

"So, to what do I owe the pleasure of this fine walk?" he sang.

Kore made mindless small talk until they were out of earshot of the nymphs and shielded by trees.

"Hermes, I have a favor I need of you. But you cannot tell my mother," she interjected, cutting Hermes off from his banter.

He stared at her wide-eyed for a moment; a mixture of bewilderment and interest etched his face.

"Rude!"

"Let us not act like you do not know of what tomorrow holds for me," she began.

"You mean your betrothal to Ares?" he inquired with a smirk. "Yes, I know of it."

"I do not want to marry him," she hissed.

"Well, who does? Honestly. He's a bit of a brute." Hermes snickered.

"That is why—" she began, but she felt her voice crack. She took a deep breath and tried to center herself before continuing. "That is why I need you to take me to the Underworld. Tonight. Before dawn. Before tomorrow when he comes for me." She kept her eyes on her hands. When she looked up to the god, she was met with a mischievous smile.

"You want me to take you to the Underworld?"

"Yes, and nobody can know."

Hermes was quiet for a moment as he thought over her request. A wicked smile spread his lips.

"Why do you want to go to the Underworld of all places?"

"I desire to see—a friend," she fibbed.

Hermes lowered his eyes. "A friend? Is this—friend—no longer one of the living?" His smile grew wider.

"He is living," she said softly. Why must he torment her so?

"You know," he began, "if you want to be with the King of the Dead, you need just say so."

"How—"

"As I have said before, sweet sister, Helios is quite nosy." He flashed her another mischievous smile. "I am afraid the god is also dangerously loose-lipped when it comes to things he sees."

His smile grew as he continued. "Can you guess what he saw you and Hades—King of the Underworld—doing but two springs ago?" he taunted as he circled her. "How does a young, sweet goddess such as yourself find the courage to plant one on the all-feared God of the Dead? Helios claims it was the most scandalous thing he had ever seen. I wish I had been there!" His gaze drifted off as if he was imagining the scene for himself.

"So, you will take me?" Kore asked sheepishly.

The god drew his attention back to her, a playful smile etched on his lips.

"I take you down to your *love*. In the Underworld. Risk your mother's wrath? What will I be gaining out of this—*favor*?" he mused. He wasn't one to miss an opportunity to help himself, but Kore was more than prepared.

"I have a way for you to gain audience with Ampelos without my mother knowing," she offered, not positive how much that would get her or if it was even enough to cover what she was asking. But still, his face turned bright, and his eyes lit up from his smile.

"Really? I was just going to ask for some of your mother's sweet honey wheat bread, but I like your offer far more!"

Kore looked at him for a moment, a bit shocked at his response. What a simple offer to request. He really did love her mother's honey wheat bread beyond anything else.

"When can I see her?" he asked anxiously as he turned,

ready to head back. "Where is she waiting?"

"First, let us discuss when I need you to take me."

Hermes happily plopped down in the soft grass, resting his back against a boulder, waiting for further instructions. Like a child waiting for a lesson from a mentor.

"When would you like to leave?"

"I need to be out of the meadow by dawn. I was thinking late in the night. I can meet you back here," Kore offered.

He nodded in response and swiftly hopped to his feet.

"Sounds like a plan. I will be here once the moon reaches the highest point in the sky. Do not be late," he warned. "Now, if you do not mind, point me in the direction of sweet Ampelos!"

"Please treat my nymph with kindness, Hermes. She is a gentle creature," Kore warned. "She has a clearing in the northern part of the meadow. You cannot miss it if you are in the sky. Go now. I will tell her you are waiting there."

She embraced her brother, thankful for him in more ways than he would ever know.

He took to the sky and off toward where Ampelos would soon be. It was not until he was out of view that Kore realized he hadn't left Zeus's gift to her. Whatever it was, Kore did not care for it, but she needed to walk into the cottage with something to show her mother.

She dropped her gaze to the ground when a shiny object caught her attention. It sat propped up against the boulder Hermes had leaned on. She picked up a heavy metal dagger with a large, raw rose quartz encrusted in the hilt, which resembled that of the hilt on Ares's sword.

A wedding gift, she thought; her face melted from happiness to disgust as she looked over the brutish object.

"A symbol of war," she hissed, curling her fingers around the handle. A blade of war was the last thing Kore wanted on this day when she had accomplished all that she needed for the night's escape.

She made her way back to the garden, where Ampelos was busy weeding around some vegetable beds.

"Ampelos! I bring great news," Kore whispered, rounding the bed to where Ampelos stood. The nymph shot up in her spot and waited.

"He will be waiting in the clearing. I will keep Mother busy. I have a feeling she has a few things to say to me." Kore sighed. "Go, now. Meet him!"

It was the least she could do, not only for Hermes but for her dear handmaid who had done so much for her.

The nymph dropped the tools at her feet and skipped to the forest's edge. She turned back to Kore and offered one last smile before disappearing into the shadows.

"Goodbye, dear friend. I will miss you," Kore whispered after her.

It would be the last time she would see Ampelos, Syke, Morea, and even Lotus, her dearest and oldest friend. She would miss her the most, but now it was time to gather a few last-minute things and say her final goodbyes.

She turned and headed into the cottage through the back entrance. As she crossed the threshold, she could smell the sweet wheat of fresh bread cooking in the brick oven.

She walked to the long table, which was lined with dough ready to be baked and bread that sat cooling after baking. She saw a nice assortment of honey wheat bread, wheat bread, pita, and some things Kore loved most of all. Her mother's honey-cheese *plakous* and sesame honey milk plakous.

It was rare her mother made fancy bread, and Kore knew she could not leave without having one last taste of the sweet treats.

Looking around, she saw no sign of Demeter. She took the opportunity to grab a cloth from the table and pile a few small loaves of bread in it. She grabbed another cloth and wrapped up both plakous and headed off to her chambers to pack them and the dagger away in her satchel.

She had the rest of the day to pass, and she felt there to be no better way to spend it than with her friend, on their last evening.

"Lotus?" she called as she passed a few of the garden beds.

"Kore?" the nymph sang back in the same musical tone. Her head popped up from behind a high stone bed wall. Soil was smeared across her forehead from tilling and weeding the beds.

"Come, let us walk." Kore made sure to keep her voice even as she looped her arm around the nymph and tugged her off.

"Kore. I must finish my work for the day," she protested.

"Shh. Just walk with me for a moment," Kore pleaded. This time her voice was less controlled, and Lotus understood.

They walked quietly until they were at Lotus's pond and out of earshot of the sisters and her mother, whom Kore was still unsure the location of.

"He agreed?" Lotus guessed, sorrow coating her voice.

"He did. I leave tonight," Kore said flatly. She was more than happy to leave, but she would miss her friend dearly. However, she could not live her life for her friend just as she could not live her life for her mother.

"Do you think you will ever return?"

"When my mother is no longer angry with me." Kore knew her mother would be upset, angry even, but she knew her mother could not stay sore with her for too long.

"She will search for you, you know."

"She will. But all I need is the head start." Kore turned a soft smile to her friend, and Lotus only replied with a faint turn of her lips, the hurt clear on her face, but she understood what Kore had to do.

"I will miss you," Lotus finally said with tear-filled eyes. Kore felt the pressure of tears build behind her own.

"As I will miss you, my dearest friend. I will find no one like you again in this world. So please, do not change in my absence."

"This is not a *goodbye*, remember? It is never a *goodbye*!" Lotus sobbed, repeating the words Kore had spoken to her years ago when she first left the meadow.

The girls fell into a fit of sobbing as they held on to each other for what could be the last time. Crying until their tears ran dry and their sobbing turned to laughter, they began to reminisce on all their glorious adventures in the forest and the crazy secrets they kept. None crazier than what Kore was about to do.

When the sky shifted to beautiful swirls of orange and shades of pink, they headed back to the cottage.

"I must see my mother for the night, then to sleep and be up before the moon reaches its highest point," Kore informed as the two friends embraced for the last time and separated for the evening. Lotus took leave into her pond, while Kore went searching for her mother.

CHAPTER IX

THE MOON, THE GOGGLES, AND THE LYRE

Demeter sat at the edge of Kore's kline, her face stained with pain. The toll it took burned on her usually delightful face. Kore reached her hand out and placed it atop Demeter's to comfort her.

"Are you well, Mama?" Kore knew the answer, but she need not let it be known to her mother.

Demeter scrunched her nose as she thought how to respond. Her eyes were dull and cloudy, and her lips pinched with her face swollen and damp from tears.

"Oh, nothing for you to worry about this eve, dear," she finally said, patting Kore's hand. "I am well spent for the day. You rest well tonight, my daisy. I have big news for you tomorrow," she added with a forced smile. Kore nodded, knowing she would not be there when her mother woke with such news, and she knew that would hurt her more than the arrangement.

I would not have to run away so soon if she had not agreed. She could have suggested someone else. Anyone else, Kore thought as she, too, forced a smile before watching her mother rise and leave her chambers. She waited until the lights were snuffed out and the sound of her mother's chamber doors closed with an echoing click.

Kore had not been able to sleep; instead, she stared into the sky. Watching for Selene, thinking about her journey ahead, waiting until the moon was peeking over the treetops of the forest outside her window. If she had to guess, she figured she had just about an hour before it reached its highest point.

She slowly slid her legs from the furs and onto the cool marble floor before lowering herself to reach under the kline and retrieve the satchel she had prepared earlier. She freed the dagger she had shoved away with it and looked through the remaining contents of the bag. There was more room without it, and she figured she had some room for a few more buns. After all, Hermes would need a treat as well.

She dressed as quickly and as quietly as she could before slowly creeping through the halls until she reached the dining area. The freshly baked assortment of bread and pastries still lay scattered across the table, waiting for the *celebration* ahead.

She grabbed three more small honey loaves that sat together in the center and replaced them with the dagger. She would not be needing it on this trip, and what better way to let her mother know that she did not plan to marry Ares.

Wrapping the bread in another cloth, she tucked it away before stepping out of the cottage, into the cool, dark night. The moon was closer now to its highest point, and Kore knew she had less than thirty minutes to meet Hermes in the spot they agreed on. She walked around to the small, fenced patch that housed her goats, to offer her final farewells.

"Goodbye, you silly goats. I shall miss you," she whispered, holding her hand out to them. Both Helena and

Paris sniffed her palm and gave her a soft nuzzle. Thankfully, they were quiet, only half aware of her presence. With a few more pats, she rose back to her feet and turned to the sky once more.

She reached up and grasped her crystals in one hand, and with the other, she reached into her satchel to make sure she had the small sack of obols. The weight was reassuring enough, but she did fear it would not be sufficient for the ferryman.

Pushing the worries behind her, she took a deep breath and began heading toward the forest where she had taken Hermes.

The meadow was dark with long shadows that reached from one end to the other. The wind blew through the trees, causing the shadows to dance and fight across the earth.

Kore inhaled deeply, taking in the sweet, floral fragrance for the last time. The grass caressed her bare feet as she walked, begging her to stay. She reassured them her departure had to be done. This they understood was for her happiness, but they would miss her while she was gone, and she offered little to console them.

She neared the forest's edge, where the darkness was more still and silent. Less moonlight reached the thick of it. Making it harder for Kore to be detected if her mother just happened to wake up before dawn, before they could leave the forest. But it also made it hard for Kore to navigate, and she stumbled over lifeless, fallen logs and stumps.

She scraped her palms and knees, ripped the bottom of her robes, and tangled her hair into a matted mess by the time she located the spot where she was to meet Hermes. Which she only realized she had reached when she heard him snicker from high in a tree.

"Took you long enough, *short stuff*," his voice sang. Kore jumped up and brushed herself free of dirt and twigs.

"I cannot see!" she hissed at the stinging pain in her palm.

"The plants couldn't assist you?" He jumped from the tree and landed gracefully by her side.

"It was the *dead* ones that were the problem," she groaned. "Are you ready? I really want to be as far away from the meadow before dawn as possible."

"Yeah, yeah. I know. Trust me, we will be far gone before dawn. I hope you do not mind, but I have stops to make. Souls to guide, you know. My duties," he informed as he dug through his own sack at his side. "Here, you are going to need these." He pulled forth a pair of golden winged goggles and assisted Kore in securing them to her eyes and around her ears. His fingers moved lightly, like feathers brushing against her skin as he worked to latch them in place.

"These will help with the wind," he said.

He stood back and looked over her with a smile, his eyes trailing from head to toe and back up again until stopping at the sack at her waist. A playful smile peeling his lips.

"Now, is that honey bread I smell?"

"Yes." Kore sighed as she pulled the top bun out and handed it to him. He took it quickly and placed it in his sack, clearly a treat for later.

He spun and landed in a crouching stance in one swift motion.

"Climb on!" he instructed, slapping the top of his thigh.

"How do you mean?"

"Wrap your legs around here," he pointed to his waist, "your arms around my neck, and hold on tight!"

Kore did as told, pulling her chiton up to her knees and struggling to climb on. Once she managed, she locked her legs together around his waist and her arms around his neck. Being sure not to hold too tight to allow him to breathe.

The God of Mischief shifted his body so that he was lunging forward, hooking his arms around Kore's thighs for support.

"Ready?" he called.

Before Kore could even think of an answer, cool wind

smacked against her face, whipping her hair about her and snagging it on the twigs and branches that flew past them.

She closed her eyes. Despite the goggles, the flash of trees, shadows, and bits of moonlight were enough to make her stomach turn in circles.

Hermes ducked and jumped over the vegetation with such ease and movements so gracefully smooth, Kore was unsure if he was still running or flying.

The air around her changed, and the sweet, floral fragrance transformed to a cleaner, more earthy musk. The rustling of trees and leaves faded and was soon replaced by whistling from the clear air.

Her body felt light, tingly, and cold as wind blew against her cheeks, sending a slight shiver down her spine. She tucked her face in Hermes's neck to hide from the cool mist against her skin.

He was warm and smelled of honey and wine. Sweet with a hint of tartness.

How fitting.

"Are you all right, *sis*?" he called over the wind.

"Please do not call me that!" she cried back. She was not in the mood for his antics and riddles.

"You can open your eyes!"

"Are we still in the forest?"

There was a moment of silence before Hermes's body shook with laughter. "Gods no! Have your eyes been closed this entire time?"

"No! Not the entire time." The wind around them slowed and, to Kore's surprise, became even lighter.

"Just look! You are acting like a mortal," he urged with an irritated groan.

Kore was not sure what there would be to look at. It was still dark when they left the forest, and she knew it was too cold for Helios to be out and about. She pulled her face free from the crook of his neck and peeled her eyes open. The balmy, moist air clung to her hair and thickened the strands, weighing them down to her skin.

Even with the goggles, Kore could see a clear night sky with vivid colors painted across the black canvas and a sprinkle of stars. She drew her gaze down on a sparkling blanket of dark blue below them moving back and forth in unison as waves washed over soft sand. The bright white illumination from Selene and the moon shimmered across the top of the liquid sheet. Creating a scene Kore could only have dreamed of.

The faint smell of salt and sand drifted around her nose. It was sweet in a way but not in the familiar floral way. It was cleaner, thinner, and easier to breathe in.

Hermes began their descent to the sandy floor with his grip loosening around Kore's legs. The lower they got, the thicker the air became with moisture and a sour rot.

"Hermes?" Kore gasped.

"First stop I mentioned. No fear, just do not interact with them and stay close to me. We walk from here." He glanced down at Kore's bare feet. "Did you bring—"

"I move faster without them," she assured, removing the goggles from her face and tucking them into her sack.

"Okay. Do tie up the bottom of your robes, though. I am afraid they will be in the way. Besides, the shades will not be impressed with your attire."

Kore grabbed a handful of cloth in each fist, one over the other, and pulled, ripping the fabric around until the bottom half of her peplos fell to the ground and landed about her feet. The rest of the chiton fell just above her knees, giving her more mobility.

"Gods," she breathed as the two divines walked along the shoreline.

"What? The ocean or the freeing breeze from your new chiton?"

"The ocean." She sighed. "How long are we going to be walking alongside it?" She reached down and grazed her fingers across its surface.

"Until we find the shades. They should be around here . . ." Hermes's voice trailed off as he looked around them. "It's hard to see anything in this low light," he growled to himself.

"Do you know how they perished?"

"Uh. Warship. Crashed—somewhere around here . . ." He looked from one end of the shore to the other and began to pace.

"Maybe the water?" she offered, peering into the darkness of the chilling sea.

Poseidon wasn't known for his kindness to seamen. Greek or not. Her mother said he did it for sport, and Kore could sense from his presence that her mother's tales couldn't be too far from the truth, in his case.

Hermes stopped pacing and looked out onto the open sea. Its waves calm and welcoming. Not something you'd think would gobble up a war boat and its men.

"That is a possibility." He snapped his fingers. "You stay here. Try not to cause any trouble."

He laughed before taking flight into the dark sky. His golden talaria caught the light of the moon and signaled his location. Kore watched as he darted across the sky in a sporadic and ill-coordinated pattern.

The cool mist blew past Kore, sending chills down her legs as a murky fog began to drift around the shore. It grew thick and robbed her sight of Hermes and filled her nose with a thick salt scent. The chill that began in her legs crept up her spine and caused the hair on her neck to stand straight.

There was an energy that lofted around her and pulled her stomach to her feet. A cold energy; one she did not find welcoming or kind.

"Her-Hermes?"

A loud flutter echoed in the wind, and Kore could not put a name to the sound. She thought it a bird at first, but birds don't often travel at night.

She spun around in the sand, searching the beach up to where the cliffs began. The fog masked almost everything, but she could still make out the jagged cliff face peeking out. The moon came just over the ridge, casting the large silhouette of a dark figure at the ledge.

"Hello?" she called to it, but it did not move. "Hermes?" she called again, hoping it was the God of Trickery just trying to scare her.

She took a few steps forward, tilting her head back to see if a different angle would reveal the figure. But the whole while, it did not move, and Kore saw no more features than before. She turned back to the sky above the sea, in hopes Hermes would reappear with his moonlight-catching talaria.

"Hermes? Hermes, have you found anything?" she cried out desperately, but the only sound that returned to her was the sound of waves washing against the sand. She hoped he had not left her. A horrible mistake on his end if Demeter ever learned that he not only helped Kore leave the meadow, but then left her alone to find her way back.

She shuddered at the thought of what her mother might do, and that frightened her more than the thought of Hermes leaving her.

The loud flutter filled the air again, this time coming from the direction of the mysterious mass. Kore could hear her heart race in her ears as the feeling pulled down on her stomach. As much as she did not want to turn, she feared the creature coming near. She called out to her vines but was unable to reach them through the thick, damp sand that surrounded her.

She took a deep breath and held it in her chest as she slowly peeked around. Her thick, damp curls created a shield with just enough opening for her to search for the dark figure. Her eyes scaled the cliff face until they reached the top, tightening her stomach in knots when she realized the spot sat empty with just a thick fog over it.

"What are we looking at?" His voice was close, and the sudden sound startled her enough that she let out a high-pitched scream.

"Okay. Keep your secrets then," Hermes said, throwing his hands up in defense.

Kore looked over the god, his blond hair a dark gold that was plastered to his face. His chiton was soaking wet from the mist and ocean spray.

"Did you see that? Up there?" Kore questioned, pointing to the cliff's edge.

"See what?" He shrugged, following her finger and searching the emptiness. "The fog?"

"No, not the fog. There was a—" She stopped as she tried to find the words.

In truth she did not know what it was she saw. She could not even be sure if it was real or a creature to be concerned with. It did not appear to notice her and did not bother her.

"Never mind." She sighed, shaking her head, remembering the lost shades. "Did you find them?"

"Oh, yeah!" He reached into his pouch and pulled out a dark lyre; it was not the normal golden one he toted around and played while back at the meadow. The body looked to be made of the same dark crystal Kore had seen several times in association with Aidoneus. The top of each arm held small skulls with blue crystals for eyes and strings made of bright, glowing gold.

"What is that?" The words fell from her mouth before she had time to think them. Hermes smiled and strummed the strings one slow time. The sounds that came from them were more beautiful than that of his own lyre.

"Hades's lyre. Not Lord Hades—he does not care for it. But the place Hades, the Underworld," he explained.

He strummed the strings again, and this time the sound was opaque. Soon they were surrounded by translucent-looking mortals who still wore the wounds that caused their end. Their features looked to be melting away with only their dark, sunken eyes being visibly clear.

Hermes struck the lyre once more, and this time the sound that came gave Kore a calming feeling that washed over her like waves. He squatted down, shoving the lyre back into his sack, ready to proceed with the adventure.

Kore quickly climbed on; this time it was a bit easier to wrap her legs around him with the shorter fabrics. She pulled the goggles out of her satchel and back over her head before securing herself to his back.

"Ready," she announced.

Soon he was in the air and off over the sea, the shades close behind.

"I have one more stop to make and gather shades. Then we will head to your *love*."

CHAPTER X

THE SHADES, THE FERRYMAN, AND THE THREE-HEADED BEAST

Kore stood quiet amongst the fallen, bloodied bodies while Hermes circled the carnage. He strummed the lyre as he worked, skipping and prancing about in an odd dance, collecting each shade as he passed. The bodies around her were mangled, some with large slice wounds she could only assume came from an equally large blade. Different limbs lay scattered around the bodies with blankets of red, thick mud coating every inch of the field.

A wet, gargled cough caught her attention, and she turned her gaze, scanning the mess before her.

"H-Hermes?" she called softly. "There are living amongst them!" She took a step forward, reaching out to the roots and grass for assistance, but they were far too weighed down by blood, sweat, and mud to be of any help.

"Kore!" Hermes shouted as he dashed to her side. "We cannot help here. Not for those whose fate has yet to be decided," he said coldly, a carelessness Kore had not known Hermes capable of. "I will be back later for these if the Fates so choose. If not, they must find their own way. We do not interfere."

"Why?"

Hermes looked at her as if he did not understand her question.

"We mustn't interfere with the Fates. They do not like it much." His eyes grew dim as he repeated himself. "They do not like it."

The thoughts of a distant memory seemed to infiltrate the god's mind, and he fell silent. His eyes unfocused. Kore tapped his arm, pulling him back to the present. The God of Trickery blinked a few moments before looking back to the Goddess of Spring.

"We must leave now." He crouched down, allowing Kore to climb on his back again, and strummed the lyre, allowing the last tune to carry in the wind before lifting from the ground and flying off.

Helios had finally made his way well into the day, and Kore knew her mother was aware of her absence by now. She would be looking for her daughter, calling to all the gods in search. They had to hurry, and she could sense that Hermes felt the same.

"How much further?" she called over the wind.

"Not much! Trust me, I do not want to get caught by your mother any more than you do! She will have my head!" he shouted back.

He flew high in the clouds, leaving Kore blind to the world below her. The sky shifted—growing dim as Helios tucked himself behind gray cover—thick and cold, like the air over the ocean, but it was not the smell of salt and sea that filled her nose.

Kore couldn't put a name to it, but she knew it to be bad, and the smell reminded her of the rotten eggs some chickens laid back at her mother's cottage. The ones that had been hidden for weeks before one of the hens would squish it, leaving a horrid surprise for the nymphs in the morning.

The wind became steady as Hermes slowed and

descended back to earth, kicking his feet out in front of him to brace for the landing. The clouds shifted to a light fog, and Kore was able to make out shapes and colors more easily.

The sky grew gray and murky, but the land surrounding them was lush with moss-covered cypress that peeked through the fog.

Kore stepped free from Hermes, the round river rocks crunching beneath her feet. The sound of light waves washing over the stones fell as background to the low chirping of crickets.

"Are we here?" Kore asked softly.

Hermes grabbed her hand and led her a few feet from his landing spot.

"Yes." He chuckled.

The fog cleared a bit more, and Kore could see that they had stopped near a river. The dark, tepid water appeared still from the surface, mimicking a black mirror with a clear reflection of the sky above.

Hermes bent over and tapped the surface with one finger. Sending ripple after ripple through the water and causing the slowly growing trickles to stretch out as far as Kore could see.

"What was that?" she inquired.

"An announcement." He smiled, looking down the river into the smog.

They waited patiently with the shades looming close behind. Their grim faces watched aimlessly in any direction, lost and confused.

A long, thin boat appeared from the mist, headed their way in a slow drift. The closer it got the more Kore could see that the boat was adorned with skulls, mortal skulls, and the sight sent a hard shiver down her spine.

Her eyes drifted to the creature manning the skiff, pushing it leisurely through the water. Its tall stature surpassed the top of the stern, even with a severe curve in its upper back. A thick and tattered hooded robe lay draped over its ghoulish frame.

"Charon?" she breathed.

"Correct!"

Kore quickly shuffled through her sack and pulled the small pouch out that held her obols.

"What is that?" Hermes inquired with a lifted brow, his eyes on the pouch.

"Obols for Charon."

Hermes tried to suppress a laugh. "How did you come by that?"

"Selling Helena's milk," Kore said stiffly, not understanding what he found funny.

"How much did you save?" he pushed again, his face growing a deep gold from his efforts not to laugh.

"Thirty-eight pieces." She sighed.

Hermes threw his head back, clutching his side as he fell into a roaring fit of laughter. His face turned even more golden, and tears collected at the corners of his eyes. His laugh was like music, but still—Kore was unsure what he found comical.

"Is that not enough?"

"It's more—than—enough! Trust—me," he pushed between giggles as he wiped his eyes and righted himself, taking a few moments to catch his breath. Kore lifted her brow and watched him. "You were determined," he finally said after clearing his throat.

"I had planned to leave when I saved one hundred pieces, but the Fates had other plans."

Hermes gazed at her with cautious eyes. "Not the Fates. Just Demeter and Zeus."

The boat finally drifted to a stop in front of them, giving Kore a better view of the hooded creature, Charon. The hood of his robes hung low to shield his face from view. The only thing Kore could make out was his hand. If you could call it as much. It was more bones with black, rotting flesh dangling by threads. The bony hands curled around a long, dark pole that he had used to push the boat.

Kore lifted her foot to take a step, but Hermes held his arm out in front of her, stopping her from boarding. She paused and looked up to the golden god.

"We must wait for them to board first," he informed.

Kore turned to face the shades and watched as, one by one, each shade dropped a single obol in the creature's open, boney palm. She watched as they boarded the long skiff and seemingly disappeared when they sat.

"Where did they go?" She gasped.

"You cannot expect Charon to make a hundred trips. Now, can you?" Hermes chuckled.

"I suppose not."

"They will all fit, and once the last is on, we will board."

He smiled, looking back at the rest of the shades. Some wandered mindlessly near the edge of the water, disinterested in Charon and his boat.

"What of those?" Kore inquired again.

"Those were the ones who had no coins. It is an unfortunate mistake—to leave without a coin or two for Charon. Just in case. For whatever reason, those shades there did not think they needed such things. They will *wait* here for some time because of it."

"Wait?"

"It's one coin or one hundred winters. Either way, Charon gets his payment. He says they are quite interesting to watch while they wait. They bore me, really," Hermes said with a smile, his eyes distant as if imagining the shades in some hysterical display.

Kore could tell by the widening of his grin that whatever he was envisioning brought him great joy.

"Anyway! Come now!" He clapped as he guided her to the boat. Kore looked up at the hooded creature who tilted his head to look down at her, then tilted it to Hermes.

"I don't know," Hermes shrugged. "I only bring the messages. I do not ask any questions."

Kore held out the pouch to the creature, and he cocked

his head to the sound of clanking obols. His boney hand rose to accept the offer.

Once she dropped the pouch, the gold bits spilled over his palm, displaying the coins saved. His cadaverous fingers curled around them, and he bowed to her, allowing her passage. Hermes followed behind, muttering something to the creature as he boarded before taking his seat beside Kore.

The sound of rocks scraping against the skiff filled the silent air as Charon pushed off, drifting the boat from the shallow edge to the open center of the river. Thick fog surrounded them in every direction, making the drip eerier than Hermes seemed to take it as he wiggled anxiously in his spot.

"How fun!" he gushed.

"Fun?"

"This is my first time in the boat! I thought I might ride with you, instead of flying over to meet you on the other side. Hades wouldn't be too pleased if he knew I was so careless." He looked down to Kore, his eyes catching the dark crystal Aidoneus had given her. "As for escorting you here, I cannot say."

The boat drifted leisurely along; the only sound to be heard was Hermes fidgeting with excitement. Kore looked over the edge to her reflection, seeing the wear of her journey clung to her hair, frizzing it and tangling it in such wild ways. She had left with it in a neat braid resting across her shoulder, but now it resembled a bird's nest. She undid the tie, pulled the goggles free, and ran her hands through her hair, freeing it of twigs, leaves, and dirt. Without hesitation, Hermes assisted by plucking out anything she missed.

"Thank you." She sighed, tying her thick curls back at her neck.

"Can't have you showing up to the palace looking like you've been through war, can we?" he joked with a musical chuckle.

She swallowed hard at the thought. Trying to keep her

excitement from bubbling to the surface.

She was so close to *him*, to his realm. Crossing the river gave her a sense of relief, under the cover of fog and well on her way to being at the gates of the Underworld. She would be well within the realm by the time her mother learned of her location.

Rocks scraped against the bottom of the skiff, bringing it to a slow and steady halt. Hermes jumped from the boat, swiftly landing on his feet; he held his hand out to assist Kore as she wobbled free. The fog was not as thick, allowing her to make out the land a bit easier.

Behind them sat the river that stretched out on either side; in front of them stood tall, thick pines, their trunks covered with sheet moss and yellow, flat mushrooms. Kore felt the energy pulse through her arms and legs as she reached out to the trees. Their language was new to her, and she could tell it was an older language. An ancient language.

They shook and swayed in return, sending black ravens scattering from their canopies. Their leaves rustled together, and their branches popped and cracked as they welcomed her happily.

"I recommend you put on your sandals. You will need them," Hermes suggested.

Kore pulled the pair from her sack, slipped them on, and tied them up.

"It's a fair distance to the gate, and we will want to move quickly," he added in a low tone.

"Quickly?"

"Yes, there are other gods who live deep in these woods, some less friendly than others. You will want to stay close. Once we get to the gates, well, we will just wait until then for the next plan." He snickered.

Kore knew what waited for them at the gate. Her mother had spoken of an enormous three-headed beast born from Typhone and Echidna, said to have the heads of hounds and the tail of a serpent. His mane consisted of venomous snakes and paws with claws like those of a lion. A feared beast said to keep the dead in and everyone else out.

It was something she knew she should be afraid of, but she could not bring herself to fear the stories her mother gave her. After all, so many of them had proven false.

Once all the shades were free of the ferry, they gathered around the two divines and waited.

"Welcome!" Hermes clapped happily to the shades. "We will be touring this here forest, then a cave, fields, and finally the palace. Who's ready?"

But the shades were quiet. They hadn't even looked up when he began talking.

"Did they not hear you?" Kore quizzed.

"Oh, they won't respond *here*. I just think it makes the trip more festive!" He took her by the hand with a bright, comforting smile.

"How do you mean?"

"It is a bit boring walking in silence—so I thought talking along the way—"

"No, Hermes." She sighed, shaking her head. "How do you mean they will not respond here?"

"Oh! They will have to release their mortal world dreams. Once we pass the Oneiroi tree, they will slowly become more vocal."

Kore lifted a brow.

"Come, you will see."

They headed into the trees and mist, stepping over fallen branches that blocked the small, narrow path Hermes followed. He gripped Kore's hand and tugged her along behind him as he led them for a distance. Going up and down hills and winding around trees in the low, drifting mist.

The smell of dirt and rain clung to her skin, her hair, and invaded her nose. It was not as fresh in scent as the meadow. Devoid of flowers and herbs to sweeten the air. This air was not sweet, but bitter.

They arrived in a small grassy clearing, and at the center

sat a sturdy elm tree. As they approached, the deep green leaves fluttered happily, greeting Kore with excitement.

Blue, glowing lights illuminated its branches, and its fronds rustled in the faint breeze. A cool draft surrounded the divines as glowing blue orbs began drifting to the timber.

Kore turned to find the orbs had come from each shade who stood behind them. Their dreams and mortal world attachments clung to the tree and its many offshoots. They wouldn't need them in their afterlife.

Once the last glowing orb found its spot in the branches, Hermes took hold of Kore and shuffled the shades forward, passing the Oneiroi and finding his way to a smaller path that took the group to another clearing.

This clearing was out of place from the rest of the forest. No moss, no trees. No plant life of any kind, just stones and jagged rocks with a cave opening off to the right.

A deep, open wound in the earth.

An entrance.

A gate.

The Gate.

Hermes squeezed her hand and stepped onto the stone. Kore scanned the area, seeing scattered bones and bits about them. Shredded and torn pieces of armor lay sprinkled with the bones, and bent chunks of broken swords reflected what little light they could catch.

The smell grew sour and pungent with decay. Kore shot her hands up to cover her nose. Taking slow, deep breaths—the smell of dirt did little to help.

Hermes whistled softly as he crept closer to the cave opening, holding his hand up to Kore so she did not follow.

"Cerberus? You there, buddy?"

A low rumble of growls echoed through the cave in response.

Kore held her breath when a set of big, yellow, glowing eyes rose from the cave floor. Soon followed by another pair, and then a third peering out from the darkness. The six eyes scanned the stone before the growls grew deeper. Kore could feel the rumbling of it through her feet, rattling up into the pit of her stomach.

"Hermes?" she whispered.

"Shh!" he hushed, his eyes still on the six in the cave. He shifted his weight and glanced back at Kore, gazing at the satchel that rested on her hip. He skipped to her side and began digging through it.

"Excuse you!" Kore shot, snatching her bag free from him, but he had already acquired what he was in search of. A honey bread slice Kore had packed the day prior.

"He loves these just as much as I!" Hermes unwrapped the bread from the cloth and handed it to her. "You must present it to him."

She hesitated for a moment, her hand hovering over the bread and her eyes locked with the six in the cave. She took a deep breath, grabbed the bread from Hermes, and moved forward.

Her movement was met with chest-rattling growls rumbling the stone and bones. She paused and glanced back at Hermes, who was practically jumping up and down with excitement, finding joy in the most dangerous things.

She pulled her attention back to the cave and lifted the bread up for the creature to see, taking another step. This time there was only one snarl that escaped the creature. Two sets of eyes lowered, and soft whimpers followed.

"Toss it! Toss it!" Hermes chanted.

She did as instructed, watching as the creature finally stepped out from the shadows to retrieve the offering. Two of the large heads bent down to enjoy, which soon resulted in them snapping at each other. The middle head kept its eyes locked on Kore.

Cerberus was, no doubt, large, but not in the way her mother had described. Demeter said he was as big as ten men stacked atop one another. But he was no taller than Kore, his six eyes level with hers. He did have three heads of hounds, but he did not have a mane of snakes, nor the tail of a serpent, and his claws and paws were a fitting size for his stature.

If it weren't for the multiple heads and size, he looked like an average hound would.

Kore took another step closer, her hands reaching for another bundle of bread to offer. The middle head continued to keep its gaze locked on her. She tossed the second slice off to the right, allowing both side heads to split and take their share.

Reaching into her sack for the last slice, she closed the distance between her and the creature and held the slice up to the middle head, waving it from left to right.

"Come on now. I promise it is quite delicious!" she insisted, waving the bread around again. He tilted his head to one side; it wasn't much, but it was a start.

"Now, Cerberus, you and I both know you want it. Take a closer look, you big silly creature!" Hermes added as he stepped to their side.

The hound sniffed Kore from head to toe, stopping at the black crystal around her neck. His heavy tail swung from one side to the other with a loud swooshing sound.

Finally, the middle head licked up the bread from her hand and swallowed it in one quick motion. The heads welcomed her by pressing each of their damp noses against her cheek before lying on the cool stone floor. Cerberus acted no different than an average hound.

"Interesting!" Hermes mused as he grabbed Kore by the hand. He turned back to the shades; some seemed to have acknowledged the transaction while some still stared mindlessly into the sky. "On we go!" he called out to them.

CHAPTER XI

THE RIVER, THE NYMPH, AND THE DIRECTIONS

"What is special about this dark crystal?" Kore asked, one hand grasping the stone and the other squeezing Hermes's hand as they walked a narrow slope. The loose dirt caused her to slip with each step. He did not seem to have as much of an issue with it, having traveled the path many times for many years.

"The obsidian is the crystal of the Underworld. It is created here, so nearly everything is made of it. There are very few crafted like the one you carry there," he informed.

"So, 'tis like a *kleidi*?"

"You could say that."

Kore lost her footing once more, sliding forward and almost falling face first. Hermes pulled her hand up and braced her with his arm, a soft laugh escaping him.

"Why can we not fly?" She groaned.

"The Fates have forbidden me from flying through the cave. They say the shades cannot follow me properly," he explained, breathless from laughing.

"How can you see?" Kore inquired again.

“I have been following this same trail for centuries. At first, it was by aid of the lampades nymphs. But after some time, it has become natural for me.” He pulled Kore closer to him to better support her weight, but her feet continued to slide over the rocks. Despite her speed, they proceeded steadily down the rocky slope.

She thought her eyes would have adjusted to the darkness, but there was no light source to even focus on. It was just black all around her. No other sound aside from their footsteps and the low murmur of the shades as their consciousness returned. The trail seemed endless, and without visual aid, Kore felt as if they had been walking for hours. Her legs grew sore and tired from their descent into the unknown.

“How much farther?” She yawned.

“Are you tired, sweet sister?” Hermes chuckled.

“No,” she lied, and the golden god laughed again.

“We should be hitting flat ground right . . . about . . . now!” As the words left his mouth, Kore took a step, her foot falling heavily, crashing down on solid, flat ground.

The air around them became warm with a soft, cool breeze that gave her a sense of ease. A light, sweet scent filled the space, and she could sense they were no longer the only living beings present.

“*Chairetismata,*” he said louder, causing Kore to jump. His body shook against her as he silently laughed.

“*Chairetismata,* Sir Hermes!” a soft voice greeted happily, and a bright orange flame illuminated the space.

Kore had never seen such a strange fire, and the torch was just as fascinating—an ebony-and-gold goblet with finger clasps that fit perfectly over the small, soot-covered fingers that held it. Kore’s eyes followed the arm up until she met the face of a nymph with flickering red eyes. She wore deep crimson robes with the same black clasps at her shoulders. Her wide eyes darted from Hermes to Kore and back again.

“I do not think he will be too pleased by this,” she whispered in a worried tone; her brows pinched as her eyes looked over the goddess once more.

Hermes looked to Kore from the corner of his eye, his lips pulling up into a smile. "For this goddess? I think he will make an exception."

"Very well. How many souls have you collected?" the nymph quizzed.

"One hundred and thirty-six. I counted them this time!"

"Very well. Thanatos collected one hundred and thirty-seven—you just missed him. He already stepped through," she said.

Kore watched as Hermes's body tensed and his face grew brighter from the ichor. His brows pulled down, folding the skin between them. She had never seen him in such a manner. She was not sure if it was anger or if he had been hurt somehow by the news. Hermes was not often known to show anger—at least not in Kore's time of knowing him.

"Has he now?" he growled. "I still have more to collect."

"As does he." The nymph sighed with a soft smile, turned, and pressed her small soot-covered hand against the stone wall behind her. A loud grinding sound filled the cave as flames lit up around them.

With the fire now illuminating the area, Kore could finally see that they were not in a cave but what looked more like an exceptionally large gathering hall. Large, obsidian columns surrounded them on either side, stretching high past the flames.

Kore turned back to the nymph, who stood before a thick, wide door, also carved from obsidian crystal with a battle engraved on it. It reminded her of the golden doors at Mt. Olympus, the one depicting the fight between Zeus and Cronos, but this was not the same battle. This was a battle of gods and souls, fighting for freedom, for life.

The nymph pushed against the door, and with a loud, echoing creak, it opened. Shades of orange and pink flooded in.

Hermes took Kore by the hand again and guided her

through. The hard stone beneath her shifted to soft, cool grass. It took a moment for her eyes to adjust from the darkness, but once they did, she was free to see where they were.

There was a soft tickle against her legs, and when she looked down, she was greeted by the lush green carpet of tall, thick grass that covered the rolling hills ahead of them.

"Oh!" she cheered as she grazed her fingers over the blades, greeting them pleasantly.

"Welcome to the Underworld," Hermes said.

Kore popped her head up and scanned the land in front of her and was surprised, to say the least.

"There *are* plants here! And light!" She smiled, her eyes sweeping the sky and hills.

She turned to find the door they had exited was simply a small black temple from the outside with nothing but a slow-moving river beside it.

"Yes? It's not a desolate wasteland," Hermes scuffed.

"Aidoneus said things grew here, but I never imagined it would be this beautiful. We had been walking down for so long, I figured we were too deep for Helios's sun to reach the plants here," she admitted.

"Well, that's not Helios. The sun gods are not allowed here. That," he pointed to the ball of light that rested just above the distant mountaintops, "is magic placed by Hecate. It gives the shades and the other gods a sense of night and day. Come, let us head to the palace. I am sure you are excited to see the king."

He shot her another smile and began on the small path up a hill. Once they had reached the top, Kore was met with the complete view of the endless realm.

The vast fields were plentiful with white- and purple-petaled asphodels. To the right, in the far distance sat the palace. It favored the one on Mt. Olympus with several differences. To start, it had only one large statue in the front.

She couldn't make out who the statue depicted from where she stood, but she assumed it to be Aidoneus. Several halls led to the main center chamber just like Mt. Olympus, and it even had several waterfalls rushing to the river below. But, unlike its twin, it was much darker.

To the left sat a larger group of several sky-reaching mountains; a number of red, glowing rivers spouted down the sides. The sky that loomed above it was gloomier than that above the fields and palace, with dim-colored clouds and smoke lofting above.

"What is this?" Hermes shot as he cut from the path to a large group of newly deposited shades. "Looks like we have stumbled upon Thanatos's collected souls!" His voice grew thick with mischief as he rubbed his hands together.

"What do you plan to do?" Kore raised a brow.

"Isn't it obvious, little sister? It was irresponsible to have left them. Knowing we have such a bet at play. His loss." Hermes shrugged with a smile. "Come, shades, you will follow me to the Judgment Halls!" he announced, walking back to the path. Once the shades were all together, they began down the path once more.

"What bet do you and Thanatos have?" Kore quizzed as they came to another small hill.

"Who collects the most souls, of course. Luckily for me, the number depends on how many we drop off at the halls." He chuckled.

"Why would he have left them?"

"He tends to believe I am slow." A deep cackle rattled at the back of Hermes's throat. "He is probably napping under a tree. Who knows? His hubris is his biggest fault."

Hermes chuckled again as they cleared the top of the hill, giving sight to a slow-flowing river that disappeared behind a jagged cliff edge, with a thick white haze drifting around at the entrance.

"The Acheron River," Hermes began. "It leads right under the palace and out into the ocean." He pointed to the water, then turned to the palace. "As I am sure you can see, that is the palace of Hades. That—" He shifted his gaze to the cluster of mountains that lacked the same vegetation and bright, welcoming feeling. Dirt and rock and smoke.

It was death.

"That is the Field of Mourning; it fences Tartarus. And *we* are walking through Asphodel Fields, as I am sure you could tell," he added.

Kore reached out to the passing flowers, their energy a vibrant tempo of the ancient language. She inhaled their surprisingly sweet scent, allowing it to wash through her, reassuring her even further.

She had made it to the Underworld, and from where she was standing, she could see beautiful, lush hills with clear, bright skies. Her heart skipped a beat as she thought of how close she was and how much she had to go before she could embrace Aidoneus as she wanted to since their last encounter.

"I do not think I can thank you enough, Hermes. This has been the greatest gift you have ever given me." As the words fell free, her hand clasped around her crystals again. She looked up to him, his eyes to the sky as if thinking of a response.

"It was something I had to do," he breathed. The words sunk in but with little understanding of what they meant. He did not have to take her; he had the opportunity to say no. She had not forced or threatened him. Perhaps he knew the marriage would not have been the most fitting.

"Even so, I thank you. Deceiving my mother is no small task." Kore sighed.

Hermes responded with a grimace. "Do not remind me! By now, your mother has probably sent word to Zeus." He dropped his head. Something neither of them wanted to deal with.

"Perhaps he will be too concerned with the war." She shrugged and Hermes tilted his head as he thought on that possibility.

They were interrupted by a loud, gut-curdling roar. It rumbled the ground beneath them and shook the earth.

Accompanying the sound was a vicious hiss. The smell of rotting flesh mixed with a scent that reminded Kore of her goats after it rained began to fill her nose. The floor shook again with the rumbling noise.

"Hermes! What is that?" Kore cried as the sounds grew louder. The shades around them fell into a panic and began breaking away from the group, away from the path, and into the fields.

"It's a chimera!" He gasped.

Kore looked to him, his face as pale as a mortal's. The creature stepped into view from the fields. Its monstrous body was far more massive than she had envisioned. Her muscles locked her in place as she gaped up at the beast. She scarcely remembered holding her breath, but when her lungs cried, she drew in a ragged, burning gust that ripped through her, dry and raw. The creature was one she remembered from her mother's tales. One that was not exaggerated.

It was large, taller than described even. Its lion head and mane were soaked in black grime and dirt. Between its broad shoulders was the head of a sharp-toothed goat, whose horns twisted about its floppy, chewed-up ears. Both sets of teeth dripped a blackish slime that produced a foul odor.

Whipping wildly behind it, with a repeated hissing, this creature, unlike Cerberus, did have a serpent for a tail. Its large fangs bared each time it whipped through the air.

Kore could not find her voice and struggled to pull in air. She could see Hermes from her peripheral as he stood motionless with his eyes locked on the creature's.

"Kore," he whispered.

"Yes?"

"Hide!" He darted from the path into the field to his left, leaving Kore motionless. The creature, the one Hermes called a chimera, looked in the direction he ran, the lion-and-goat head trailing after him while the serpent watched Kore.

Without another sound, the chimera bolted off after Hermes, through the field. Kore took the opportunity to run in the opposite direction, following a few slow shades that took shelter in the fog. She fought the burning pain in her chest as she pushed through the ache in her legs.

Breaking through the mist, digging her heels into the earth, and sliding to a stop. The air grew cold and moist. Smelling of salt and moss and mud. The false sun fell tinted and blocked by the clouds, making it difficult to see.

She continued forward, following a blue, glowing light. A shade. It would be wise to keep them close and pull them back to the path when Hermes called.

The shade's glow drifted forward into the mist, and Kore continued to follow.

"Hello?" she called to it, but it did not pause.

She picked up speed, trailing behind the soul until the ground disappeared from beneath her and she lost her footing, falling hard and hitting her tailbone on a protruding rock as she slid down the cliff edge. The little fabric she had left on her robes caught and tore against the jagged wall and reaching branches.

The sharp edges sliced her skin as her hands dug and clawed at the serrated stone that broke free from the wall. Her attempt to reach out to her plants was far too late, and her body crashed to the ground, landing on a thick patch of pillow moss.

Her hands smoothed across the soft, plush tops, thanking them for the cushioned landing. She winced at the stinging pain in her palms and thighs, the searing burn in her back from her landing. With a soft groan, she glared up into the endless white haze above her. She listened but heard nothing.

"Hermes!" Her weak voice cracked.

She pushed over to her side, coughing as she did, and her eyes fell to the slow-flowing river.

It leads right under the palace, Kore remembered; Hermes was probably busy recollecting the shades to take them to judgment. Leaving the goddess with two options: find her way back to the fields or find her way to the palace. She struggled to push herself up, feeling as though she was being pulled down. Reaching up to her shoulder, her fingers grazed frayed cotton.

Her satchel.

She had forgotten all about it since passing the gates. As she dug through, she found a very smashed and crumbled plakous. She sighed, but it was all she had. She had not thought to pack water to drink or nectar to give her the immortal strength she would need.

The sweetness of the treat dried out her mouth even more. Her gaze fell on the still river, setting a flame to her throat, begging for the liquid. Calling to her until she stood and limped to the edge so she could drink. Positioning herself with her back against the rock, she removed her sandals and set them alongside her.

She leaned over and cupped her hands together, submerging them. Cool and fast, the water raced by her, catching her hands in the strong current and nearly pulling her in with it. With a gasp, she jerked free, rocking back on her heels.

From the outside, the water appeared to be steady and still with nothing visible moving through it. She looked over the surface, her curiosity overwhelming her, and she reached her hand out once more to test the waters again.

"I wouldn't do that," a soft voice warned.

Kore looked up to find a nymph floating in the center of the river. The water raced around her but did not push her as it did the goddess.

She sat still, as still as the water looked from above. Kore knew her to be a nymph by the pointed shape of her ears; this one had the same pattern that Lotus did, indicating her relation to the naiads.

She had never seen such a beautiful nymph, with skin that had been kissed by Helios himself. Her light ringlet curls dripped down her exposed chest. Her deep seafoam eyes locked with Kore's.

"Why not?" Kore finally asked.

The nymph tilted her head and moved forward ever so slightly. "You are not a shade," she guessed.

"No," Kore responded.

"You are not of this realm?"

"No."

The nymph closed the distance between them and rested her arms on the boulder beside her.

"What is wrong with the water?" Kore pushed.

"If you drink from this river, it will wash away your soul if you be not a shade," the nymph warned.

Kore heeded the warning and pushed herself back a few inches from the edge.

"Thank you. I am Kore, by the way."

The nymph's body stiffened, and she pushed away from the boulder. Her brows pinched together as she looked over Kore for a moment more.

"The Goddess of Harvest's daughter?" Her voice wasn't as soft as before, and Kore could sense that this nymph already knew her.

"Yes."

"You must be here to see Hades!"

Kore did not like the way his name came from her mouth. It was not as formal as those who did not fear to say it, as Hermes did. It sounded more personal. As if she were closer with him than she let on. Kore felt a flame of jealousy rise in the pit of her stomach as she gazed at the nymph.

"You must be an oracle!" Kore pushed.

"Not an oracle. I just hear a lot, spending my days in the river and all!" The nymph stretched her arms out and spun around quickly, hooking Kore's sandals with her hand and tossing them into the river, which briskly carried them away and out of sight.

"Oops! Sorry, dear!" The nymph gasped but made no move to grab them.

"No worries." Kore sighed. "I move faster without them."

The nymph moved closer again, a low look of pleasure painted on her face. "Do you mean to meet with Hades?"

"Yes. I was with Hermes, but it would appear we have been separated."

"And he took you through the fields?" the nymph asked in a disgusted tone.

"Well, yes?"

"He is such a mindless god." The nymph shook her head with a smile. "My dear, everyone knows the quickest and safest way to the palace is to follow this river to the Nymph Hall entrance. If you be not a shade, that is."

"The Nymph Hall?"

"Yes, Lord Hades likes to keep his favorite nymphs close. For an easy night," the nymph informed.

Kore felt a sharp pain in her stomach, one that turned her gut in an unpleasing way. She had not thought of Aidoneus's other relationships. From most tales, he had not found a wife, queen, or mistress of any sort. But then again, his realm was also told to be lifeless.

A sour bile grew in her mouth, and she fought back the grimace she felt tease her face. She had made it this far; turning back now meant facing her mother and Ares. Something she would rather avoid if possible.

Kore said nothing as she waited for the nymph to speak again.

"Would you still like to see him?" she asked, her smile growing wide.

"Yes," Kore answered flatly.

The nymph's smile fell for a second but returned when she leaned closer.

"Very well. Just follow the river until you come to a great golden door. Knock three times and someone will let you enter. They are instructed to take anyone to Hades," she assured.

"Is it safe?"

"I wouldn't send you there if it were not."

“I think I should return to Hermes. He—”

“How did you end up falling from that ledge there?” the nymph interjected.

“We were attacked,” the goddess responded slowly.

“Exactly. It is unsafe for you to follow that open trail.”

Kore was still unsure if the nymph was to be trusted. But even Hermes said the river led to the palace, and she did not want to risk backtracking out of the valley in search of the god and running into the chimera again. She stood, walking back to retrieve her satchel, and flung it over her shoulder.

“I do thank you—” Kore said, looking back to the nymph, but found the river empty. “Hello?” she called but heard no reply. With a shrug, she turned back to the path along the river and began to make her way toward the Nymph Hall as instructed.

CHAPTER XII

THE CYCLOPS, THE ASPHODELS, AND THE CHAOS

The stagnant mist and shadows grew darker as the false sun began to set. The path Kore followed was one not often traveled; moss and algae carpeted the ground. She reached for her crystals, this time out of habit and not so much for reassurance. She knew if this were a dream, she would have woken long ago.

She pushed on, watching her footing with each step. The cool, moist air created small droplets that clung to her face and hair. It dampened her robes, plastering them to her skin, which grew stickier with the growing humidity.

She had walked a long distance beside the seemingly calm, quiet waters. The flat surface, a reflection of tricks and dangers. But still, it called to her, burning her from the dry rawness that scratched her throat. Her tongue grew sticky and thick, filling her mouth. She groaned softly to herself, and a louder groan echoed back. Her body froze in place, and her eyes fell to the river of black.

Ripples in the calm surface caught her attention, and she scanned the area around her. At least as far as she could see. Her heart thundered, pounding against her chest so hard, she could hear it in her ears. Her breath caught in her lungs as more ripples spread through the flat surface. A loud, heavy pound accompanied each quake that came.

Thump.

Thump.

Thump.

Kore pressed her back flat against the rocky wall, and her eyes widened when the enormous mass stepped into view, clearing the mist around it with a labored exhale.

"Polyphemus!" the booming voice roared. The rumble threw rocks and stones from the cliff face into the river, casting spouts of water into the air. More mist cleared, bringing sight of the creature in the dim light.

A Cyclops.

Like most of the creatures and monsters outside of the meadow, Kore knew very little of Cyclopes. Hermes had told her stories of when he and Apollo had slain a few. From Demeter's tales, they were at the mercy of the gods, residing here in the Underworld, awaiting their next orders. Leaving Kore with only one question: were they friendly or were they not?

The one before her was wide and tall—tall enough to see over the cliff edge that hung above them. Its one bloodshot eye had been horribly bruised, and puffy skin surrounded it. Fresh blood dripped from open wounds on its face. Scars won from a battle that had ended not too long back.

"Polyphemus! Over here!" the Cyclops shouted again. "I smell it over here!" It sniffed around a few times and searched along the river's edge.

Kore felt a rock in her throat. She was not sure what he could smell, but she wasn't going to wait to find out. She pressed herself against the cliff wall as flat as she could, piercing and scraping her skin against the sharp rock. The shadows made for a perfect cover, as long as she moved slowly and stayed low. She inched her way left until she came to a slight opening that appeared to lead from the valley and back into the fields above.

"Hurry! I'm starving!" another booming voice echoed, sending more rocks into the river.

"It is a strong one! Smells like . . . a divine! A new divine!" the second one bellowed as it came into view.

This one was a bit larger than the first, and its skin bore more scars and marks of battles won. Its face was also bruised—a mix of green, yellow, and purple splashed its leathery skin.

"It's close. I can sense its divine energy," the big one howled.

Kore finally realized it was her they could sense, her energy, her ichor—it all had a distinctive divine scent.

Her heart pounded into her chest, her legs became numb, and her arms began to tingle as the energy pulsated. She peeked around the edge to make sure she had a clear shot, analyzing the distance and the amount of mist cover. There wasn't much left with the two large beasts blowing it away. She could only hope the shadows of the night would help shield her.

Perhaps the nymph was up to something, Kore thought. She would have been better off searching for Hermes for his aid to the palace. Not only was she facing possible capture by two Cyclopes, but the river was cut off by a great wall barrier. If there truly was an entrance to the palace, it was blocked, and for good reason.

She faced the Cyclopes, their heads high enough to catch her movements if she were to run. She searched the plants' sight for another exit, but all she could see was the slope that led to the fields above.

Thump.

Thump.

"Here it is, Poly!" the Cyclops yelled, its booming voice burning in Kore's ears.

Air squeezed from her lungs, her arms and legs pressed to her sides in a tight grip. She gasped with little room to take anything in. Heat raced up her neck to her face and flooded her mind. She struggled as the Cyclops drew her close to his grotesque single eye.

"Hey! You are not one of the Firsts!" it shouted. "Poly, 'tis a strange divine."

"'Tis a child of a First! I can smell it!" Polyphemus said.

Kore felt a tightness in her chest, but not from the squeezing of the Cyclops. The feeling was angry and primal as it ripped through her.

"You put me down!" she barked. The voice that escaped her was an unfamiliar one.

The Cyclops tilted its head to her. "Oh? Why would I do that? You are dinner!"

"Put me in your mouth and see what becomes of you!" She was surprised at the confidence she held, how her voice refused to crack or waver. The tingling in her arms began to feel like pinpricks, her face flushed gold and her eyes hazed over.

"What's that? What's it doing, Poly?" the Cyclops asked.

"Its powers. Eat it!" Polyphemus demanded, and without hesitation, the Cyclops tossed Kore into its mouth.

The dark, moist gullet smelled so foul, she doubled over, gagging, repulsed by the deadly stench. Her stomach turned and she felt as if the plakous from earlier may make a second appearance.

The prickling feeling in her arms continued to strengthen and the heat in her face spread, igniting her body in an inferno.

With a loud crack, the Cyclops's mouth slowly cranked open, and a thick, lush vine with black leaves crept in and wrapped around Kore's waist, pulling her free of the monstrous jaws. The Cyclops fell to its knees with agonizing cries, shaking the realm with its fury.

The vines set her on the top of the cliff where she could watch as they shot out from the ground, wrapping tightly around the creature and yanking the Cyclops down. Snaking around its legs and arms, binding them tight while other vines slipped around its neck and eye.

The creature fought and pulled at the vines that engulfed him, causing them to tighten with each thrash. Its hands dug and clawed at the vegetation, which only agitated them all the more. The vines constricted around it, tightening their grip until a few pops and cracks filled the air.

"Stop," Kore whispered, and they paused.

A lush, soft vine reached up from the ground and grazed across her cheek. She had not seen them so full and lively. They were different here, bigger and thicker. Holding more life now than in the mortal realm, where they were shriveled and looked of death.

Kore grazed her fingertips over the vine. "Hello, dear friend," she greeted before turning back to the Cyclops, who lay tangled and ensnared in her vengeful friends. Its one eye was wide and ready to pop free.

"I warned you." She flicked her wrist, and the vines responded quickly by constricting the Cyclops once more. It yelped for help from the other, but its friend did not move.

"You had one chance, Arges," Polyphemus muttered. The heartless creature turned his back to its friend and departed through the opening from which they came.

Kore flicked her wrist again, and this time, the vines released the beast.

"I do not like being unkind, but you left me no choice. Go now, with your friend!" Again, this voice that left her lips was unfamiliar and cold.

The Cyclops gasped for air as it looked up to her with his bloodshot eye, anger and fear coating its hard, leathery skin. Its nostrils flared as it grunted angrily but stood and turned to follow the other.

The heat left Kore in dwindling waves, starting from the top of her crown and ending in the tips of her fingers and toes. Her head felt light again, but this time it was not due to an indescribable stench. She was exhausted, having exerted too much of her divine power.

The false sun had gone and was replaced by an equally false moon. She turned back to the wall that blocked the valley and river. The blockade she had been tricked into.

She walked over, stopping a few feet from the ledge, and leaned out just enough to get a view of what was below. There was no path that she could see, no door that led to any hall. Only fog and darkness. The nymph had directed her into a trap.

It was a trick, Kore thought, turning back to the safest path she knew to get to the palace. Only to be paused by another delight she never thought she'd see.

Her eyes lit up at the sight. The fields that had been empty upon her arrival were now filled with various glowing shops and temples that extended across the entire field, from the palace to the opposite mountains. She stood on what looked to be the main street that held a clear path forward.

Shades walked around and chatted amongst themselves as if nothing had ever changed for them.

Over the chatter, Kore heard the fluttering again. She spun around, seeing only the darkness of the realm. A slight shiver ran down her spine, urging her to move on. Sucking in a deep breath, she turned one final time to face the ghostly village and headed through.

Some shades drifted around while some appeared busy, walking from hut to hut. They did not appear to notice her as she made her way up, pausing at a temple that was constructed just as the mortals usually had them, with several columns surrounding the inside altars and statues of gods. She stepped closer, peeking into the *cella*, the main chamber of the small temple.

A black, carved statue of Aidoneus stood centered in the middle with several dark marble benches placed around it. Three shades stood around the statue with their hands at their sides and palms facing down. Hanging their heads low as they spoke in soft murmurs. Praying.

They were . . . worshiping him. Something she knew not to be an event for the mortals who were living. She smiled softly and exited the temple.

When she stepped back onto the main path, several shades took notice of her. Their glowing blue eyes gaped as she walked by. She smiled softly but did not stay to speak. She did not want to bring too much attention to herself as she adventured.

An odd peace circled the air around her, bringing with it comfort and a sense of security. No longer feeling the need to rush or hurry, she took her time walking from hut to hut and temple to temple, finding comfort in the shades that prayed and worshiped at Aidoneus's altars. She found they lived near the same as they had before, chatting and telling stories along the path. Trading and bartering at the huts, most of which only offered cotton and wool. Very few held fruit or anything worth eating. Kore laughed to herself.

Of course they wouldn't need food.

Before she realized it, she found herself at the end of the path, staring up at the gargantuan mountains. She gazed up at the red, burning lava seeping from the tops and sliding rapidly down, coming to a screaming hiss as it flooded into the river that flowed past, spitting steam and boiling water high into the air behind the temples.

A few shades had gathered behind her, watching curiously as she made her way. Stopping as she did, to admire the view.

Some patches of rouge asphodel plants along the path reached for her, their vibrations intense and rapid.

"It may take some time, but we will become very close friends. I am sure of it," she whispered. It was reassuring to know she would have plants to speak with, to share secrets and tales and sing to.

You'd be surprised what grows in the Underworld, she remembered Aidoneus saying, thinking he had only meant vegetation and plants. Not whole villages with happy souls to keep them busy.

She looked back up to the great mountains, curiosity washing over her, a calling that drew her in. Despite her pain, and hunger, her foot moved forward in a mindless compulsion. She took step after step into warmer soil. The shades watched silently, no longer following behind.

The soil turned to rock and then to brimstone that was blistering against her bare feet. The sweet scent of asphodels fell away and was soon replaced by a rotten egg odor. But this did not deter her as the power of the mountain pulled her in, like a fish caught on a string.

She skipped, hopped, and jumped up the stone so as not to burn her feet. She knew by now they were blistered, but she had come too far up to turn around and hobble back. She could not stop herself even if she wanted. Her legs moved of their own accord, pushing her farther and farther up the mountain until she reached a flat plateau.

A large black door, guarded by two colossal shades, awaited her. They wore ancient Greek armor, with the Underworld crest just at their shoulder and a dark helmet that hid their faces.

She took a deep breath, realizing how far she had wandered. She was no longer just in the cluster of mountains but had found her way to Tartarus, where the most heinous of mortals were sent to spend eternity in torment and fire. A horrid place, her mother had said, but she had said the Underworld itself was horrible too.

For a location so terrible, Kore thought it would be more heavily guarded, protected inside and out.

Her heart began its wild dance once more, and she sucked in another deep breath. The intense pull of the mountain tugged at her as she slowly made her way to the guards. The whites of their eyes became clearer the closer she brought herself.

They watched her with caution but made no other movement to halt her. She took a step toward the shade on the right, with her crystals in hand.

"Hello?" Her soft voice was like smooth honey against the rough gurgling and spitting of the lava that spewed from the mountain.

The shade did not answer; instead, his head tilted from one side to the other as he eyed her up and down before stopping on the crystal Aidoneus had gifted her.

He quickly straightened up and looked to his partner. With one stiff nod, the ebony door creaked open, slowly making its way to its widest point. A gust of hot air blew past her, warming her exposed skin until it grew red.

With another deep breath, Kore crossed over the threshold, an electric pulse coating her. The moment she was in, the air around her shifted—no longer warm but *scorching*. The quiet of the night was replaced by ear-piercing screams and cries for help. She took a step forward on the ridge and found herself overlooking the endless ocean of brimstone, boiling lava, and fleeing shades.

Souls ran begging for forgiveness, screaming for aid, and crying for sanctuary. The open space seemed larger than the fields she had just left, with cliffs and peaks just as far out and distant.

Farther in raged a firepit angrily spitting into a river of flame and torment.

She hadn't the slightest clue what she was looking for. But still, her eyes scanned the chaos.

She could make out several different trails that led high up into the caverns above, and several that went down leading to lower levels. Right below her, on the main cavern floor, sat a shade who wore the same armor as the two at the entrance, but this one sat upon a bright white creature with four long, thick tails.

She took a step forward, leaning far over to get a better view, when her foot slipped from beneath her. She slammed onto her back before sliding down the hot stone, pushing her palms hard against the jagged wall, clawing at the rock to no avail. The shards dug into her palms and deep into her thighs as she tumbled down. Crying out against the pain, she slid to an excruciating stop.

She lay there for a moment, her gaze up at the cavern ceiling.

If you do not look for a way out now, you will be stuck here, a voice echoed in her mind. Repeating itself over and over.

Stuck here.

Stuck here.

Stuck here.

The voice taunted. Kore closed her eyes, envisioning the meadow, the clear skies, and the fresh, sweet smell of the garden. The new smells of the Underworld she was experiencing. There was so much more for her to see and smell. Aidoneus still had no knowledge of her even being in his realm.

No, she thought, she would not allow herself to be stuck. Her eyes shot open, and she struggled to climb to her feet, dusting off her hands and legs from the small rocks embedded into her skin.

The screaming and crying carried on, but the shade and his creature turned to Kore. His mouth hung open, but he said nothing as his creature stepped closer to her, its eyes a blazing red, glowing bright against its white fur. Kore looked up to the shade again. His face was twisted in confusion as he swept the goddess over, his hands clenching a rope around the creature's neck.

"Excuse me, would you happen to know the way out of here?" she called over the wailing.

He cocked his head to the side, his brows pulling down deep over his eyes, and after a silent moment, a low rumble followed by a loud snap filled the air. With a flash, the shade was replaced by a black mist that dissipated around her.

"Hello?" she called, but there was no response. She waited for a minute, waving her hand through the smoke, but all she managed to do was move it about the space.

That was rude. She took a step forward, and the chaos that surrounded her grew agonizing and draining. Howls bounced off the hard brimstone, sending echoes of the screams through the air. Shades raced past her, screaming and carrying on with their torments.

She took another weak step onto the burning, hard stone floor. This adventure had gone on long enough; she needed to find a guard to escort her out, and fast. Or, at the very least, find a way out herself.

She scanned the slope she had slid down, trying to find any leverage to use to climb back up. The fire that raced through her feet was searing as she attempted to find a place to start. It was not long before she realized the cliff was too steep for her to manage up on her own.

Energy pooled in her hands, and she tried to reach out to her plants. But they fell silent with no answer, unable to feel her calls through the stone. She groaned in frustration and turned back to the flat surface. This time she noticed the shades around her had stopped moving, their eyes locked on her.

Here, they were solid masses. Still bearing the skin and wounds from their mortal life. Their eyes were dark and lifeless but still somehow filled with such fury and rage as they gazed upon her.

The thick air caught in her throat, weighing her down and numbing her limbs. She inched her foot forward, and the shades reacted like magnets, their heads moving as she did. She took a full step. The shades followed again.

She managed to slowly inch her way past two when a wet, gurgling sound erupted from behind her, pausing her in her tracks.

Instinctively, she turned on her heels and was met with a pale man who had long, deep gashes all over his body. The most fatal was the one across his neck, exposing muscle and bone. Chunks of flesh clung to his exposed larynx. Crimson blood glistened against his chewed skin from the flashing flames.

Her stomach turned.

He reached his bloodstained arm out and ran his fingers loosely through her hair, making a deep, guttural moan.

“Goddess! Please, mercy!” he begged.

Kore shivered away from the touch and held her hands up to the shade.

“I’m sorry, I cannot—”

“Please grant me my request, Goddess!” another shrieked.

Suddenly, Kore was flooded with cries and prayers. Something she had never experienced as a divine, and sadly, wouldn’t know what to do if she did. Hands began to swarm her, grabbing her arms, hair, and the fabric of what little robes she had left. She was yanked one way and then the other. The cries and screams grew desperate and angry as more and more shades gathered.

“I can’t!” she urged, pushing the shades from her. But for every one shade who fell back, two more took its place.

Her arms burned as she called out to her vines, but there was no soil beneath her feet, only hard stone. She attempted to pull forth the vines from within the shades, but they lacked the proper energy force to feed the vines to life.

One of the shades grabbed her arm and yanked her back. Its grip tightened in aggravation at the goddess. He was the biggest of the shades near her and had no wounds other than a gaping hole where his left eye would have been. It oozed black and yellow pus that emitted a foul, sour odor.

He grabbed Kore’s other arm and lifted her into the air, the sea of dead closing in around her. Their screams and cries echoing in her head.

This is it, she thought. *My journey is over*.

She wasn’t sure what would come to happen, but she felt the tight squeeze of the shade around her arms, and without her divine powers to protect her, she figured she may not make it through the attack.

He pulled her up and, with little effort, heaved her across the cavern. Her back slammed into several shades on the way before she crashed hard into the serrated wall. There was a loud snap and flash of white. Her vision fell fuzzy, but she could still feel the heat against her hands and legs. She tilted her head to the side and allowed it to rock back until she fell over onto a stone step.

The heat of the brimstone pressing against her cheek jerked her up to attention. The space, spinning. Pain throbbed in her back, but she had no time. Her eyes scanned the area she fell through: a narrow stairway with the door swinging open from her fall.

She rushed to slam it shut before the shades could crowd her again. Their loud cries and pleas for help were muffled by the thick wood, their banging growing more agitated with each hit. She thought the door would come free of the hinges.

Kore pressed against the door until the banging steadied and the pounding didn't send thunderous vibrations through the rock. Until she figured the shades had forgotten her and moved on, back to their regular business.

Her head fell back against the wood as darkness consumed her vision.

A sudden shriek near the door woke her. Memories of the day flooded her mind, and she attempted to jump to her feet but was met with weak knees and a throbbing head. Still groggy from the hit, she stumbled forward on the steps, bracing herself clumsily against the wall.

Small, flamed torches illuminated the narrow corridor. The wooden door did a decent job of muffling out most of the screams. A few shades still mourned loudly by it, scratching their fingers weakly against the wood.

Her heart ached for them. Their pain and torment would be endless, and all they could do was cry for help unheard from outside the walls of Tartarus. Unheard by the king of the realm. And the only one to hear them was a goddess no mortal knew existed.

A goddess who had no business helping them.

A goddess who had no business being in Tartarus in the first place.

CHAPTER XIII

THE MISTAKE, THE CHASE, AND THE DOOR

Kore should have never listened to the strange nymph when everything in her had warned her not to. She was safer with Hermes, safer going back into the fields to search for him and the remaining shades. He told her there were dangerous creatures. She did not need the warning to avoid Tartarus, yet she still willingly ventured into the caverns.

A small sob rose in her throat as tears pooled in her eyes. Where was she to go now? She could not go the way she came. She had little energy to move, to heal herself, to even keep her eyes open. She shifted her weight, letting her arm fall to the side in search of her satchel. Her hand found nothing but ripped and torn cloth from her robes. The satchel gone, the little food she may have had somewhere in the chaos of the main cavern floor.

Her mouth grew sticky and dry, and her stomach burned with hunger. Her head stung from the earlier blow, and her spine throbbed.

This was a mistake. The thought gripped her heart tightly. She had come so far and risked so much, and for what? To trap herself in the walls of Tartarus.

No, get up.

You will get up, and you will find another guard, and you will demand they take you to Aidoneus.

Pressing her palm to the wall for support, she slowly guided herself to her feet. Her head throbbed, sending a wave of pain down her back, shaking her legs as she struggled to keep her place against the wall.

She took a wobbly step, stumbling forward and catching herself on a rough-edged rock. Slicing her already scraped palm in the process. She ignored the sharp sting as she pushed on down the stone steps, taking her time and using the wall for support. Pausing briefly here and there to catch her breath and rest from the stiffness that grew in her back from her posture.

Once she reached the bottom, her legs could no longer carry her, and she collapsed on the brimstone and accepted the heat that pressed against her numb skin—a faint burning pain, but her body was cold and welcomed the warmth happily.

The cavern fell quiet, the sound of the distant screams just a low hum in the stone. It smelled of bad eggs and ash. Fire and tears and salt filled the air. Not the most relaxing or comforting space to dare sleep, but Kore could not fight the call any longer. Her eyes pulled shut once more as the exhaustion overtook her.

A jolting yank at her arm tugged her a few feet from the entrance she had stumbled in. She jerked up, her eyes struggling to focus on the lightless cavern. Low flames did nothing to help illuminate the space. She saw blackness through clouded eyes, but the hair on the back of her neck stood on end. She did not see anything, but she could sense something was nearby.

She drew her legs to her chest, rubbing each eye to force her focus, waiting for them to adjust to the absence of light. When she felt ready, she shuffled to her feet. Ignoring the stiffness of her back and legs, she suppressed a low moan as she righted herself and struggled to scan the dark area.

Her search stopped at an opening in the wall furthest to her left, one that held dancing flames and flickering lights. An exit from one Hell to another.

The dark presence did not leave her as she made her way through the opening, finding herself in yet another cavern.

It was the smell that hit her first, nearly knocking her back. Heavy and thick with death and rot, blood, and other bodily fluids. She gagged, covering her nose with her hands.

Kore stood on a ledge overlooking the lower level, viewing a cavern unlike the last. Not low-lit with subtle flames, but bright with large black basins that housed angry fires.

There was no floor to be seen under the thick layer of muck. Chunks of flesh lay freshly scraped about the mess, draped like cloth over bone. Liquid crimson sprayed across the broken column before her. The smell of fresh death was becoming more common. It was rotten and sour, thick and choking as it clung to the back of her throat and filled her nose. She could taste it on her tongue.

Her stomach flipped and twisted as she held back the need to vomit. Across from her sat another ledge with another opening—most likely to another horrifying cavern.

She looked about the floor, finding stone steps that led to the bottom along the right side of the wall, and made her way to it. Keeping closely pressed against the rock as she descended.

Her chest felt heavy, as if she were breathing in water. The stench only grew stronger, thick with death. Fresh and old. She figured the creature that lived there must not be far, and she knew she would need to hurry, being as quiet as possible in doing so.

She searched for an opening amongst the bones and carnage. Wiggling maggots lay clustered over rotting chunks of meat. Kore sucked in a deep, ragged breath, clutched her crystals, and stepped forward. Her bare foot landed in a thick slosh that seeped between her toes. It was cold and hot, slick and slimy, and it burned her open wounds. She closed her eyes, imagining berries and jams.

It is only jam.

It is only jam.

It is only jam.

She took another step. This time the mess her foot entered was thicker, with chunks and slime.

It is jam!

It is jam!

It is jam!

She kept her eyes on the steps across the way, moving as quickly as she could. Avoiding the bones to keep quiet. The closer she got, the faster her heart raced, pounding wildly against her chest. She was close. She would make it out.

Kore had just taken another step when the sound of snapping and crunching bones halted her.

Her heart squeezed, draining the ichor from her face. Air caught in her chest. As fearful as she was, she turned her head just slightly to peek at what was with her. The heavy energy pushed against her back. Hot and suffocating.

Powerful.

A low, feral growl and foul, hot air brushed against her cheek. Her heart sank, but her feet moved, ignoring the bones and bodies that slowed her. She frantically searched for any cover she could take, but her foot caught in the sludge, sending her body down. Crashing into bones and blood.

A rough, leathery hand wrapped around her arm and yanked her into the air, sending her body flying a few feet before crashing into piles of sharp, splintered bones.

A shard pierced through her calf, sending a tearing pain through the muscle. Ichor poured around it, dripping into the dark mess at her feet.

She cried out in agony as the creature stomped closer without remorse. Her hand fumbling around the bone protruding from her leg, she grasped it firmly. The sharp pain that raced through her ripped a scream from her lungs. Tears spilled down her cheeks, but she had little time. The creature hovered above, its chest heaving violently as it blew snot at her with each huff.

She held her breath and pulled, ripping the bone spear from her flesh. Ichor poured from the wound rapidly. Searing pain and electric burns scorched her calf. With no time to aid the open wound, she swung the shard up as the creature brought his massive hand down, spearing its palm.

A deep, inhuman howl escaped it. It cocked its arm back and swung with the other, smacking Kore in the chest and knocking her back. She stumbled against the wall, falling into a narrow space that rested between two boulders.

The beast charged her, striking the wall and managing to smash its large, bloodied arm through the slight opening. Its hand clawed and swung for her, the tips of its fingers barely taking hold of the shreds of her robes.

The creature let out another monstrous howl and pounded its fist on the stone. She was stuck, face-to-face with it.

The sour rot from it filled the small area. It was not a creature Kore had known from any tale of her mother's. It was not a creature Kore had known from anything.

Matted strands of hair lay plastered to its face. Its bruised skin glistened from the light—skin that looked mortal, but the mass before her was anything but.

She pressed her back against the stone as best she could. The creature reached in further and swatted about its man-like hand. Missing each attempt at grabbing her. The thick, muscular arm had extremely prominent tendons protruding from it. Blood and other unknown fluids and substances were smeared up to its shoulder.

It withdrew its arm and replaced it with its massive face.

Kore let out a scream and pressed her back even further to the rock, ignoring the sting as it cut into her skin. It was a small irritation compared to the burning pain in her leg.

The creature bared its black-covered teeth. Chunks of rotten flesh and old blood dripped from its mouth. Its nose was misshapen and matched that of a bull. Long and wide. Its eyes sat far apart on either side of its head, just under two cracked and contorted horns.

A wet, gargled growl rushed from its chest. "I have never tasted goddess before!"

Why does everything want to eat me? she thought as her mind fogged over. The fear washed away, replaced with an untamed anger.

The creature reached back in, this time with the arm she had originally struck with the bone, which was still lodged deep in its thick skin.

Her hand shot forward, yanking the shard free and thrusting it down once more, slashing the same wound. Blood spilled at her feet. The creature drew back with a snarl but returned even more vengeful as it reached in for her.

She cried out, slamming the shard down on the creature's arm again, and it jerked away with a howl.

She hissed at the pain in her palm and legs, the movement pulling at her exposed muscle. The creature turned back to her without much pause. Its eyes grew even darker with a monstrous hunger.

"I will pick my teeth clean with your bones, Goddess!" Its voice, thick and wet. It choked on spit and blood and whatever else sloshed about its mouth.

Her face grew hot with anger. Her arms and hands ignited in flames, and ripples of energy raced, her divine power tasting the energy that lived deep within the creature. She felt the life. It was not a shade. Not a soul. It was not dead.

She drew her hands up and felt the energy like electricity zapping from finger to finger. Feeling the life the creature held. A smile spread across her face as she looked at the beast with hazed eyes.

"You will be too busy picking your teeth from the

floor!" she growled.

The energy raced from her arms like a rushing river. Pouring into the creature. She could feel her vines creeping around each bone and organ.

The monster froze, its eyes wide and mouth open. A wet, gargling noise rumbled its way up the creature's chest. His growls morphed into choking cries as vines snaked from his lips. They wrapped around, covering its eyes and blinding it.

The creature fell back onto the bones, gagging and choking and gasping for air. It struggled, pulling and clawing at the vines that ensnared it.

Kore exited the small crack and made her way to it, stepping over the shattered and smashed bones. She lowered herself beside the beast that wiggled and thrashed against her presence. Fisting its hands, it attempted to swing at her. She called forth a vine that quickly restrained each arm, yanking them down to the creature's sides. Wrapping around its body and constricting its wild thrashing.

"Now, now." Again, the voice that left her was not her own. It was the same one she had heard while in the grasp of the Cyclops. Calm but angry. Thick with a vengeance she had not felt before.

"What was that you said you were going to do with my bones?" She leaned over, the beast's eyes still blinded by the vines that choked it.

"Oh, that's right. You said you were going to pick your teeth—" she reached her hand over the creature's open mouth and tightly grasped a tooth, "with my bones."

She snapped the tooth with such ease, even she was surprised. The creature's mouth struggled to clamp down, and muffled screams and cries bubbled around the vines.

She held up the tooth, examining the size and shape. Not one known to be mortal—human or animal. A creature created—perhaps for guard, perhaps for torture.

She focused past the tooth, to the flickering light above. The way out, or at the very least, a cavern less riddled with death. She could only hope. She stood from the creature, who still wiggled and struggled against the vines that invaded his body. She would call them back, but not until she had cleared the door.

Her hand gripped the tooth as she rose. Ichor still spilled from the open hole in her calf, trailing gold down her leg into the pool of red-and-black mush at her feet. The rancid smell of it all burned the back of her throat.

Her stomach churned and she heaved, releasing what little food she had left within her. When that was gone, it was yellow bile that she spat up. She shook with chills with each convulsion, and her throat burned from the acid.

When her stomach could release no more, she shuddered, wiping her mouth with the back of her hand. She felt cold, even with the constant heat of Tartarus.

She righted herself, steady in the center of the muck. Once she was ready, she limped her way to the stone steps. Her head bobbed to the side, weak and dizzy. She had pushed her energy, her power with little replenishment or aid, with little rest and no divine food. Her stomach hardened at the thought.

Food.

She struggled to climb the steps, proving more of a challenge than wading through the sea of bones, flesh, and blood. Her leg screamed at her with every step. Every moment she put weight on it.

At the top, she rested against the wall, catching her breath from the fight and chase before scuffling to the wooden door that rested open against the rock wall. She gingerly wrapped her hand around the iron handle, using it for support as she ducked into the narrow hall.

Another dimly lit corridor with very few torches, which held low flames. Black, shining rock walls surrounded her.

Despite the dim light, Kore could make out a second wooden door at the opposite end. Closed, blocking her view from what lay on the other side.

She pulled the handle behind her, closing the door. Sliding her palms against the cool iron in search of a lock, but found nothing. She sighed. No way to block it.

Her power was quickly draining, her hold on the creature growing weaker by the second. The sooner she could get to the other door, the sooner she could drop her hold.

She turned back, limping to the opposite end, each step eliciting a yelp from her throat. Each second, her hold on her vines weakened. She could feel it slipping from her grasp like water through her fingers.

She felt a tug at her stomach. She was anxious to reach the opposite end before her hold on the vines completely fell free. Her raw and blistered feet stung against the coolness of the stone. But she kept her eyes on the door before her. A line of light illuminated from the thin opening at the bottom. Hopefully, there would be a guard to help her out of this Hell.

She leaned into the wall, nearing the door as her hold on her vines completely fell free from her. She paused for a moment to try to call them back with no luck. She couldn't feel them, she couldn't sense them, she could not call out to them as they released the creature.

A loud, gurgling roar echoed through the cavern, dropping Kore's heart to her stomach. She swallowed the lump in her throat and pushed from the wall. Her feet stung as she quickened her pace. It was as if she was walking through water, pushing as hard as she could but moving no faster than she had been.

A loud cracking sound followed by a bang flooded the corridor. Light spilled into the narrow space, signaling the release of the dreaded creature. Kore dare not turn to look as she heard the beast speeding toward her with vengeance.

She hobbled as fast as she could until she collapsed against the wood. Low voices could be heard from the other side. Her hands frantically clawed at the latch, pulling and tugging with no luck. It did not budge or free from the wall. She looked back, the creature nearing.

Air left her body all at once, leaving her cold and empty. She fisted her hands and began pounding on the wood.

"Please! Open the door!" she cried, her voice cracking with fear. She turned again and saw the creature was closing the distance fast.

"Please! Please! Let me in! Open the door!" Her voice grew frantic as she continued to bang and pound on the wood, grasping and tugging at the latch.

The creature's heat was suffocating now; he was right on top of her. He huffed, and the rotten odor fogged her head. She could do nothing but press her body into the wood. Her heart sank.

The hot, moist breath fanned across the nape of her neck. Chunks of a wet, unknown substance landed on her skin. Her body froze against the wood, and her breath caught in her throat. All she could do was squeeze her eyes shut and hope that whoever stood on the other side was kind.

"I'm sorry, Mama," she whispered.

The creature released another guttural growl as it slammed its fist against the door.

"Was Pyrros given shades?" a voice boomed from behind the wood.

"No!" another shouted.

The creature slammed its fists against the door again, with another growl. Kore felt its large nose press against her. Wet and sticky and warm. Her body rumbled, her skin crawled, and a high-pitched scream ripped through her. The creature drew back, its hands still pressed against the wood, caging her in. Her broken sobbing echoed through the hall, but the creature did not pause. It drove its head down, mouth open, teeth bared.

Everything happened in an instant. She closed her eyes, accepting the sudden fate, but then she felt an intense fire burn into her skin as the door swung open. She fell hard on the floor. Her eyes shot open just as the wooden door slammed on the creature's arm, releasing an even deeper, chilling cry from it.

“Damn you, Pyrros!” a woman’s voice snarled, shoving the arm back and slamming the door, latching it with a lock.

CHAPTER XIV

THE ERINYES, THE INTRODUCTION, AND THE KING WHO PLAYED ZEUS

Kore looked around, finding herself in a smaller cavern surrounded by blistering fire. Bright, warm, with air that smelled of cinnamon and cloves. The floor was slick with blood that glistened from the flickering flames that surrounded them. Her hand slipped as she struggled to push herself to her feet, only managing to prop herself up in the slippery mess.

"You are not a shade!" one voice cried.

Kore shot her head up and met the gazes of three women who hovered over her. They were beautiful, with the same dark skin tone and dark, curly hair. Kore did not know much about the creatures of the Underworld, but she knew of three sisters her mother referred to as the Erinyes, who lived in Tartarus.

"Nor are you wicked!" another added.

This one had white paint dotted under her eye in a unified pattern. Another, who was slightly taller than the last and graceful in her movements, slowly circled Kore. Her shoulder-length curls bounced with each step, falling forward as she leaned over to examine the goddess.

"How did you get so far?" she asked, her lips pulled

down. She reached her hand out to Kore's cheek.

"Enough, Megara. Leave her be!" The third one finally spoke. Her bright blue-green eyes stood out against her skin. Compared to the others, her curls fell longer, stretching down the length of her back.

"We do not have to be cruel to everyone," the one named Megara said, pouting out her bottom lip as she rejoined the others. "She has not earned a place here. She does not deserve the torment. Perhaps she has been through enough."

The women gathered close together and whispered amongst each other.

Kore attempted to rise again, the throbbing in her legs and feet and hands never fading, never dulling. The blood on the floor provided little traction to steady herself. She gave up, too exhausted to fight against it all.

"Come," the tall, graceful one instructed, looping her arm under Kore's.

Megara joined on the opposite side, mimicking her sister's motions. Together they assisted Kore to her feet, taking most of her weight in their arms. The sister with the patterned paint waved her hand in a circular motion, creating a black, fluffy cloud. From it appeared a dark wooden seat.

The two set Kore in it, making sure she was steady before taking their place in front of her with questioning eyes.

"Would you mind telling us why you are this deep within Tartarus?" the tallest inquired first.

Kore tried to think back through the pain. Back to the beginning of her entering Tartarus, when she was looking up at it from the calm path of the village. She hadn't been sure then, just as she was not sure now. She felt it was something she could do. Something she had to do, but it wasn't until she had gone too far that she realized what a mistake it truly was.

"Who even let you in?" the other shot.

"Alecto!" the tall one snapped.

"I . . . I am not sure why I came. I—just remember—feeling that I—had—to," Kore said between labored breaths.

She looked to the one with the face paint. "And the guards—they—they let me in."

"Why would they do that?" Alecto whispered.

"They saw this." Kore reached up for her crystal and pulled it free to show them. Their eyes grew round as they gaped at the rock in her hand.

"How did you come by that?" Alecto inquired.

"Aidoneus gifted it to me," Kore answered.

Their eyes widened as they shared glances before turning their attention back to Kore.

"He told me it was common."

"It is. Not many come by it, though. Nor use it to access the depths of Tartarus. You must be either highly brave or highly daft!" the second sister interjected.

"Hush now, Alecto." The nameless Erinys waved, her eyes still locked with Kore's. "Tell me, what is your name?"

"Kore." Her voice was softer than she had meant it to be, but she wasn't ready to be examined so intently by Erinyes, in their domain.

Megara's face lit up brightly, and a large, toothy smile stretched across her lips. She broke away from her sisters and skipped to Kore's side, cupping the goddess's hands in hers.

"Kore? It is lovely to meet you! My name is Megara. That is Tisiphone and the other is Alecto. Have you heard of us?" the Erinys introduced, jumping in front of the sister she had called Tisiphone.

"Megara, give her space," Tisiphone ordered.

"Only what my mother has told me. That you are the torturers of Tartarus," Kore answered softly, her breathing weary and weak.

Megara scrunched her nose and pursed her lips to the response. "They think us so cruel out there, in the mortal realm." Her brows folded as she dropped her head.

"Now, now. It is as expected," Tisiphone consoled her sister.

Her words did little to comfort her, though. Megara

scowled once more before turning back to Kore with a light smile.

"We are cruel, Megara. To the deserving." Alecto cackled with a wicked smile.

Megara looked at her with a crinkled nose.

Tisiphone gently cupped Kore's hands in hers as she looked over the goddess. "Dear, would you mind telling us what happened? Why you are here, in the Underworld," she asked softly.

Her face was warm and welcoming. An odd trait for goddesses described as vengeful and unforgiving. Kore had always expected them to have wings of bats and fangs. Creatures more than divines as her mother's stories claimed, but they were beautiful, as most goddesses often were.

Kore explained to them how Hermes had helped her leave her mother's meadow. Leaving out the main reason she had left, she explained that they had gotten as far as the fields when they were attacked and split up and of the nymph who led her into a den of Cyclopes.

"A nymph?" Megara hissed.

"In the river," Kore sighed, "a naiad."

"There is only one naiad nymph here," Alecto seethed.

"Minthe," Tisiphone sighed, and Megara added a deep grunt.

"Minthe?" Kore repeated.

She knew the name very well—the cousin Lotus had stayed with before arriving at the meadow. Kore remembered little about their first meeting and what Demeter had told her of the day. She simply remembered her mother leaving for the village and coming back with a nymph at her side.

"She's just an unhappy nymph is all." Megara shook her head and eyed Alecto, who was visibly irritated by the nymph's name.

"Lord Hades won't be too kind to her when he finds out," Alecto muttered.

Kore hadn't had time to think on the nymph since

leaving the Cyclopes, and now that she did, she wanted to feel angry. She knew that she should. But in the end—Kore had survived the Cyclopes; she had only needed to return to the path that led to the palace. Adventuring into Tartarus had been her idea.

"Lord Hades will not be pleased with a lot this evening." Tisiphone sighed.

"Do you know how I can get to the palace from here? I—I do not think I would like to go the way I came." Kore looked back at the door she had fallen through and shuddered.

The creature, the one they had called Pyrros, was still a threat, waiting at the door for her exit. When she looked back, the Erinyes were sweeping their gaze over her from head to toe, their eyes filled with pain and questions.

"Yes, dear. But, first, you look like you might want something to eat," Tisiphone offered.

"A bath, maybe," Alecto added.

"And a change of robes! Not to be rude, but these are a bit torn," Megara joined.

Kore followed their gaze to her robes or lack thereof. Worse off than she expected, once white, they were now covered in soot, blood, and ichor. Bloodied handprints were scattered across her body, her own hands and arms scraped and coated in her ichor, blood, ash, and dirt. Her body was painted with red, pink, and black, faded gold mixed with odd colors smeared across her skin. She could not see the faint glow of her divinity; instead, she saw pale gray.

Lifeless.

Powerless.

Her feet were raw, chewed, and blistered; burned, scraped, and blackened. But they were numb. Looking much worse than they felt.

"She should rest here for the night," Tisiphone offered.

Kore couldn't deny she was tired, and the offer of food set rocks in her stomach.

"Tisiphone! Do you think that wise? I do not

think *he* will be too happy with her down here so long," Alecto protested.

Tisiphone held her hand out to Kore. "She can't see the king like this. It is hardly presentable. The moon must be at its highest point by now."

A cool wind blew past them, and the light from the fire grew dark and shifted out of sight, replaced by a shimmering blue. The smoke drifted, and Kore found herself in a slightly bigger cavern; less fire raged around.

In the far back sat a basin carved from obsidian, with crystal spheres Kore had not seen before. It was bigger than the one back at her mother's cottage, which could only fit a single person at a time. This one looked to fit, at most, five.

To the left of the crystal basin sat a line of klines. A variety of different-colored furs covered their tops, and to the right was an opening in the rock wall that held a crackling firepit with a green-and-blue flame.

"The palace and its lord have gone to sleep," Tisiphone finally added. She guided Kore to the crystal basin and twisted the odd sphere until steaming water began pouring from the spigot.

"There is water here?" Kore blurted, surprised the mountain could obtain the liquid without boiling it away into mist.

"Of course!" Megara laughed and retrieved a golden amphora from a small table by the nearest kline and poured the bright liquid into a dark crystal kantharos.

"Before you get in and torment your body any more," she held the liquid out to Kore, "here. It's nectar. From the bees in your mother's meadow."

A flame ripped through Kore's throat, her stomach ached, and her mouth began to water, begging for the restoring liquid. It felt as if days had passed since she last ate, and she knew it had been some time since she last drank. Even longer since she had nectar and ambrosia. She reached out and snatched the kantharos, lifting it to her lips, and gulped the thick elixir down.

There were many things she hated about the drink. It was overly sweet, and she could feel it coat her insides as she swallowed. Normally, this would bother her. But today she felt the energy coat her, and her divine powers, the ability to heal, flooded her veins, igniting every inch, like warm water washing over her.

The throbbing pain in her legs and palms calmed. The open wound in her calf closed and smoothed over, leaving a faint pink hue. The slices in her palms and fingers sealed, the scrapes on her knees, arms, and legs cleared, and the divine glow returned to her fair skin.

She was still covered in dirt and blood and grime, but she felt stronger and more alert of her surroundings.

"See now? Much better," Megara cheered as she took the kantharos from the goddess and assisted her with stepping free of her tattered robes. After gathering them into a pile in her arms, she helped the goddess into the basin and left an array of oils along the side. Ensuring Kore was settled, the three Erinyes gathered around a small table on the wall that sat opposite the line of klines, giving her privacy.

Kore was finally able to be with her thoughts. She hadn't much time to take in and appreciate how far she had truly made it. Though without Hermes, she would not have gotten where she was in the first place, she took pride in the fact it was she who survived the Cyclopes and she who traveled to Tartarus.

Despite the many moments when she felt that she was done, that it was her end, she somehow had the luck to make it through. It was by the Fates that she had made it this far.

Just one more night and she could see him. She could only hope he would not be sore with her for coming and causing such a commotion already. She was sure he had heard word of the Cyclopes, and if not them, then the guard from Tartarus who had vanished on her.

Tilting her head back, Kore let the water soak into her hair. The steam droplets swept across her skin, allowing the slight draft to blow a cool breeze over her cheeks and forehead. She cupped water in her hands and poured it over her face, washing the sweat and dirt away.

Rinsing the rest of her body, she watched as the water grew murky from the soot, blood, and dirt that had clung to her. She ran her hands across the floor of the basin, searching for the spigot to drain the water, but she found nothing other than a smooth bottom.

"Are you done, dear?" Tisiphone cooed from the table. Kore nodded.

The Erinys stood from her spot and made her way to the basin. She shuffled around the outside, along the bottom of it for a moment, until she spotted what she was in search of.

Pop.

The water quickly rushed through a hidden drain and out onto the firepit, hissing and sending puffs of steam into the air around them, but never extinguishing the fire itself. The air filled with the calming scent of lavender from the oils that drifted up in the mist.

Kore exited the basin, dried herself, and dressed in the black robes that Megara had left for her. She twisted her hair free of the remaining water and then joined the others around the table as they laughed and spoke of their day of torments.

"What was that creature you saved me from?" she finally asked. Now that she felt clean and replenished, with a clear mind, she felt well enough to relive the attack.

"Pyrros? He is just a mortal we transformed. In his mortal life he used to—well—he would have—um," Tisiphone struggled.

"He would *fuck* the bulls of the village," Alecto shot, with a matter-of-fact tone. Megara suppressed a laugh, and Tisiphone cleared her throat uncomfortably. Kore's eyes rounded as she waited for more.

"Yes—*relations*. He was not a good mortal. He grew a different kind of hunger after the change, and we thought we could put him to good use in the end. Terribly sorry you had to deal with him, dear," Tisiphone apologized with comforting eyes.

"Well, enough of this seriousness! I am going to find us some entertainment!" Megara cheered, jumping to her feet. Alecto rolled her eyes and Tisiphone shook her head.

"Just because he is entertainment for you does not mean he is for anyone else," Alecto scoffed, but Megara just shrugged and danced off to the flaming pit. Kore watched with curious eyes as the Erinys carelessly stepped closer to the fire.

"Where is she going?" Kore asked.

"Fetching her favorite shade to *torment,*" Alecto responded.

"What did he do to be sent here?" Kore inquired again.

"He likened himself to Zeus and convinced his people to worship him as a god. Nothing too horrific, but by order of Zeus himself, Lord Hades had to send him here. This is quite the unsuitable punishment, and lucky for him, Megara took a liking to him; his *torment* is far less severe," Tisiphone informed.

"What does she do?"

"She makes him play the lyre; he is surprisingly good at it."

The Erinyes turned their eyes back to their sister as she took a step into the pit, allowing the flames to consume her. After a few moments, the quiet space filled with high-pitched screams and howls that erupted from the fire.

Megara soon emerged with a bright smile splitting her face. Trailing behind her was a bony, grotesque hand with bloodied, burnt skin dripping from it. Following was an equally sickening forearm, then an upper arm until a full skeleton stood before them.

Meat and burnt skin dripped from the frame as it struggled to balance. The air filled with a foul coppery scent that burned the back of Kore's throat. Popping and crackling of the bubbly, burning skin could be heard over the bellowing howls that escaped the shade.

They watched the skeleton slowly regenerate in what appeared to be a very painful manner. His body was on fire, but instead of his flesh burning off, it regenerated, building him back into the man he was before.

Kore covered her mouth and nose as the smell intensified. Organs fizzled; muscle tissue and tendons grew in a slow and gruesome way. The partially developed figure threw its head back and let out a blood-curdling cry as more of his muscle and fatty tissues appeared.

He threw himself forward onto the ground and heaved violently for a long while. His agonized cries and screams echoed off the hard stone walls around them.

Kore felt her stomach turn, but she could not pull herself to look away. All her senses had been involved, and closing her eyes would only cause his screams to intensify and the smells to strengthen. The Erinyes, however, stood over him, unmoved. Staring at the mass as if the sight bored them.

"Grab him the chiton and lyre, Alecto," Tisiphone ordered coldly when the screams died down to whimpers.

Without pause, Alecto hurried to a small chest in the corner and threw the lid open. She shuffled through some cloths before returning with a dark black chiton and wooden lyre and threw them down next to the convulsing body.

Kore watched the naked man twitch; he did not look like the shades she had seen before. His body was coated in sweat and dirt, with skin perfectly unharmed from wounds and bright eyes colored in deep green.

"Stand," Megara ordered in a soft voice. It was not a harsh demand, but he stood immediately, snatching the chiton from the floor as he rose.

A large, muscular man with dark brown hair streaked with gray. He wrapped the chiton around his hips with his eyes on Megara.

Kore looked to the other sisters who stood behind him, their vision obstructed by their angle. But Kore caught the small smile he gave Megara; after the pain he had suffered, he looked at her as if she had eased it all away.

The Erinys offered a small smile in return before she quickly bent down to pick up the lyre, shoving it into his arms.

"We demand you play for us," she ordered again, looking back to Kore with a welcoming grin. "We shall dance! Salmoneus plays the lyre almost as wondrously as Apollo," Megara cooed as she skipped back to Kore's side.

Kore thought it funny how easily she compared him to a god, though that was the reason for him being there.

The shade, Salmoneus, walked to the nearby wall and leaned against it, pulling the lyre up to his chest.

"Do you need any more nectar, dear?" Tisiphone leaned close to Kore as she spoke low.

"No, I am fine. Thank you," Kore assured.

"All right." Tisiphone smiled and then straightened in her seat. She looked to the man and lifted her hand. "You may begin."

He strummed the strings and released the first tune that swirled around the cavern. Soft and sweet, misplaced for the location, but comforting to hear after a day of screams.

The music moved across the space, slowly growing to an uplifting beat that Kore couldn't help but sway along to. She closed her eyes as her body drifted softly from side to side in tune with the melody. Megara moved near and took the young goddess by the hands.

"Let us dance!" She pulled a reluctant Kore into the center of the cavern where they had more space to move about.

The music continued to pick up in tempo, eliciting quicker movements from them as they kept pace in their dance, drawing Alecto and Tisiphone from their seats to join in the fun.

The four danced until their feet grew sore before calling it a night. Alecto was the first to retire, having drunk half an *oinochoe* of wine during the fun. She was the toughest of the three, the one who took little interest in small talk but would rather get right to the point. Her tough exterior, however, seemed to melt in her rest, giving way to an innocent glow.

"Megara, we have a guest tonight. Please see to it that Salmoneus does not stay out of the flames long, as he did the last time," Tisiphone said in a stern tone. She turned to Kore and bowed slightly. "I bid you good night, dear. Get some rest. You will have a long trek in the morning." She turned to her kline for the night as well.

"You can sleep in my kline, Kore. I have other means," Megara whispered through a smile.

Kore wasted no time; she felt as if it had been days since she last slept under furs. She hopped up and tucked herself in, allowing her body to melt into the softness. She lifted her head to thank Megara but saw no one. She and the shade had vanished.

She must have taken him back to the pit, Kore thought, resting her head back, welcoming the sleep that called to her. She felt her eyelids fall heavy, and her body sank deeper into the furs. It was when her breathing grew steady that sleep reached her and pulled her into its comforting embrace.

Kore woke to the sound of soft, breathless gasps. Unaware of how long she had been asleep or of the time, she looked to Alecto and Tisiphone, who slept peacefully in their klines; it hadn't felt like long. Another soft moan filled the air, and Kore realized what secret meeting she had awoken to. Why Alecto and Tisiphone made particular statements toward their sister and the shade throughout the evening.

Megara did not torment Salmoneus; she loved him. Kore could not be sure if he loved her back, but the idea fascinated her.

It was not an act she had considered with Aidoneus. Their relationship had always seemed platonic. When she had kissed him, he had not forced himself on her any more than she had done him. When she had run from him, he had let her.

He did not pursue her as she was now pursuing him.

She hoped that meant he felt the same for her. The very thought brought the heat to her lips. She could still feel the warmth of his pressed softly against hers. She smiled to herself as she closed her eyes and drifted back to sleep.

CHAPTER XV

THE GOD OF DEATH, THE DIVINE POWER, AND THE FALL

Megara offered Kore a slice of bread with smeared cheese. From where she got it, Kore was unsure, but she took it with a smile. She looked no different than the day before, her smile a bit wider perhaps, but nothing that gave away her secret meeting. Though, Kore had a feeling Tisiphone and Alecto knew.

A skyphos full of ambrosia sat waiting for the goddess on the stone table. It was no different than the ambrosia she ate in the meadow. It tasted and looked the same. Megara had mentioned the nectar was from the bees in Demeter's meadow—perhaps so was the fruit used for the ambrosia.

Once they had all finished their meal and nectar, Megara assisted Kore with her hair, pulling it back and tying it at the top so that it was out of her face.

"Would you like a pair of sandals, dear?" Tisiphone asked as she pulled a pair of dark leather sandals with leather tie straps from the trunk.

Kore did not care for footwear, but the brimstone was blistering, and she could not bear to burn her feet again. She nodded and Tisiphone brought them over to her side, slipping them on and helping lace them up around her calves.

"Are you ready?" Megara asked.

"We should be getting you out now, for you have a long journey ahead," Tisiphone added.

"Could we not just shift as we did before?" Kore asked.

"We cannot leave Tartarus, dear. We can only take you as far as the tunnel out."

"Where must I head from there?"

"There is a narrow trail leading down the side of this mountain. It will take you straight to the palace. You mustn't wander from that path," Megara added, Kore noted how the last part was a warning. A warning Kore would not ignore.

Tisiphone took Kore by the hand. The cavern around them faded to black with thick smoke. The smell of fire and ash clung heavily to Kore's nose as the air around her swirled to a gentle, warm breeze with a soft whistle to follow.

When the smoke cleared, Kore found that they had all arrived in a deep cavern that led out to the rest of the Underworld. The rocky wall curved up, catching the breeze from outside, creating a small cyclone within the tunnel.

Kore turned to the Erinyes with a soft smile. "You are sure you cannot join me?" she pushed once more.

Megara threw her arms around the goddess in a deep embrace. "Oh, Kore! You would not recognize us if we did," she informed with a small laugh before pulling away with a faint smile and glossy eyes.

"It was nice meeting all of you. I do hope to be seeing you again." Kore felt the slight pressure of tears behind her eyes. It was too dangerous for her to return, and if they could not leave, this was to be their last encounter.

"Do not worry on it, dear," Tisiphone cooed. The Erinyes wrapped their arms around the goddess as they bid her farewell.

With their help, Kore was able to rest and regain her strength for her journey ahead. The Underworld was full of surprises, and she would prefer not to run into any more from here on out.

She took a deep breath, smiled one last time, and turned from the ancient goddesses, making her way to the exit for the final stretch of her travels.

Once at the opening, she took pause again, the vast land a breathtaking view in her mind. The sky was cloudy and gray. Early morning light peeked just at the tips of the far-off trees.

The moist air kissed at the tip of her nose but was sadly riddled with the smell of ash and rotten eggs.

The light breeze picked up, whipping loose strands of hair across her cheeks, leaving a slight sting where they struck. She ignored it and stepped from the tunnel, searching the ground before spotting the narrow and steep path Megara had described.

She turned back to the Erinyes one last time, their faint silhouettes deep in the cave. She waved with a smile and watched as three hands waved back before vanishing into a mist.

Turning to the small path, Kore pressed her hand against the rough rockface wall. Taking slow and steady steps, she inched her way down. Loose rubble beneath her sandals caused her to slip, and she dug her nails into the rock to keep from sliding the rest of the way. She hissed at the stinging pain in her fingers as she surveyed the distance before her.

This could go faster. She was out of Tartarus, off the hard brimstone and above the soft soil. She could reach out to her plants and vines now.

The heat began in her shoulders and ran down her arms, hands, and fingers. She felt the energy as it hit the earth.

As she called to them, their life force radiated back, steady and strong. The energy rushed through her, racing down her spine, sending wave after wave and call after call until she felt the earth begin to rumble at her feet. Her body ignited and her vision glazed over as her divine power took control.

The ground quaked and buckled beneath her, splitting

the earth with a loud crack, and from the wound crept a thick black vine that reached out and grabbed her by the waist. It was thornless, with soft leaves and moss covering it, keeping her from further harm. As it brought Kore down from the mountainside, she could see the enormous hole it had carved into the earth.

The vine set Kore a few feet from the opening it had slithered through. Once released, she watched as it slipped back and the wound cranked itself shut, leaving a small patch of asphodels to cover the scar.

Now at the base of Tartarus, she was finally on the path that led directly to the palace. Her eyes scaled the side of the mountain where she once stood. It was a good distance, one that would have taken most of her day to descend if it weren't for her vines.

A shift in the smoke caught her eye, and she could see a black mass standing along the path she had been. The same mass that had appeared at the beach.

She took a step back, keeping her eyes on the figure. It jumped from the ledge, air catching its large wings as they stretched out.

She held her breath as she watched, her chipped and broken nails digging deep into her palms.

The mysterious mass fluttered its wings before coming to rest in front of Kore. Its chest flexed as its wings moved, tucking behind its back. Dark curly hair sat wildly around its face, and its thick brows hung heavy over its eyes. This was not a creature. This was a god.

The hair on her arms stood straight, and her legs refused to move.

"You are a long way from Olympus, little goddess," the god hissed.

Kore attempted to speak, but her voice was caught in her throat.

"Speak, girl!" he spat. "What business have you in Tartarus?" His face grew gold from the rush of ichor that flooded his cheeks.

His nostrils flared and his chest heaved. He looked her over until his gaze came to rest at her neck, and his eyes popped when he realized what was there, locking on the crystal. He bared his teeth with a curled lip. Like a wolf that had found its prey.

He lunged forward, an unnatural snarl ripping through him. His hands gripped her robes as he yanked her high into the air. Passing the path where she had once stood. Passing the false clouds of the Underworld. Passing the top of Tartarus.

The air was ripped from her as she clutched at the god's wrists. He pulled her closer to his face. Tendons popped from his neck, and veins protruded from his forehead as he spoke through clenched teeth.

"Where did you get that?" He ripped a hand free from her grasp, and her arm swung back as she clawed for his wrist again, gripping both hands around the hand that still clung to her robes. His other hand grabbed at the crystal around her neck, ripping it free with one tug. The leather burned her skin as it snapped.

"No!" she shrieked.

Her hand swung out to grab the crystal back, but he held it out far. A low chuckle escaped him as Kore scrambled to grab his wrist again.

"You do speak," he hissed, pulling her close. She shot out her hand again, slashing her nails across the god's face. Her other hand clamped down around his wrist, biting her nails deep into his skin.

"*Kuna*!" he snarled, dropping the crystal and wrapping his hand tightly around her neck with ease.

He quickly cut off the air to her lungs. A building pressure in her temples scattered her mind, and breathing became a struggle.

She gasped and clawed at the god's hands, but it only drew more rage from him as he tightened his grip around her small neck. He jerked her in the air from one side to the other.

His dark eyes, crazed with a vengeful hunger.

Her lungs grew raw as she struggled to pull in air. The darkness crept in around her vision, and the pressure in her head grew heavy. The heat began slowly, growing in the pit of her stomach and radiating out. It grew as the darkness did, and once everything was black, her body fell limp. Her hands slipped free from around the god's wrists.

"You will put me down or suffer an unfortunate fate. Even for a deathless god such as yourself, Thanatos!" a voice thundered.

She wasn't sure who it was, but they knew the god that held her. She thought it weird. She was numb and had time to think without the pain pressing into her neck. Thanatos was the God of Peaceful Death. But this was anything but peaceful. This was aggressive and angry.

The voice sounded just as angry. In all its unfamiliarity, and all its anger, Kore felt safe behind it.

"It is not your king you need to fear!" the voice bellowed.

An ear-piercing crack split the space. The god loosened his grip and muffled a scream. Air raced to fill Kore's lungs, burning as it went, and her vision cleared in enough time to see the look on Thanatos's face. He gaped at her with wide, frightened eyes. A gold-coated, thorny vine slipped from his mouth and wrapped around his neck.

He shot his hands up to remove the parasitic vine, releasing Kore and dropping her from the great distance he had taken her. The world around her slowed as she cut through the air. She was highly aware of how fast her heart felt against her chest and the rush of air that was again ripped from her lungs. Her eyes stayed on Thanatos as he struggled in the air above her before flying from view, still grabbing at the vine around his neck.

She pushed out to her plants, feeling their energy radiate back to her as she fell. The ground rumbled again, and vines shot out to catch her. But she was too late in her call, slipping through their grasp before they could wrap around her. Her head smashed hard against a protruding boulder that shifted as the vines emerged. A loud crunch filled her ears.

Her back popped, sending a cool chill down her legs before the feeling faded. Pressure began to build in her head once more, clouding her vision with darkness.

She blinked. Failed attempts at focusing her eyes on the clouds above. Drifting in and out of consciousness. The pain in her head was excruciating, throbbing against her. She struggled to pull in air, and each exhale sent an unfathomable stabbing pain through her spine.

The sky faded to black and then gray, and each time the clouds above shifted in shape.

Breathing became painful, and she ignored it, inhaling deeply to cry for help. But her calls were faint, silent, and unheard. Her head rocked to one side, landing in a warm, sticky substance that shimmered in the false sun. It smelled of honey and gold. Her eyes rolled, watching as the liquid pooled into the dirt beneath her. It wasn't until another gush poured out, gold in color and warm against her cheek, that she realized what it was. Ichor.

The sky faded again and when it came back, Kore was met with two beady eyes just inches from her face. An odd yet beautiful creature, with a face of a woman framed by thick black feathers and a harshly pointed beak replacing a mouth and nose.

She tried to cry out once more, but again, silent screams escaped her. The darkness crept back. She tried to fight it, watching as the creature threw its head back and called out to the sky with a loud caw.

Everything faded to black again. The space around her fell quiet, and she struggled to pull her eyes open. The pain in her skull and spine were crying for her attention.

Kore's eyes fluttered open to find two more of the creatures standing over her and one in the air fighting with something out of view. She could feel sleep creep up on her again as her focus fell out. The creatures above her cawed and squawked at whatever they had been fighting with.

Shooting pain in her neck jerked her eyes open. The creature that leaned over her had a look of concern while she frantically tried to collect Kore. She did not appear to mean any harm as she slid her wing-like arms under the goddess.

The other creature moved out of view, clearing the sky above them for Kore to see. The one that had been working over the goddess lifted her and cradled her against her feathers. The jarring pain sent a shriek from Kore's lungs—the first sound she could make, and it only ripped forth another jarring shock.

"Find Hades! I cannot move her further," the creature shrieked to another. She stood steady, clutching the goddess to her chest.

They will get him, Kore thought. *They will bring him to me, and I can finally say I made it to him.* Through all the fights and monsters, she had made it, and he would be able to help her.

Her eyes felt heavy, and everything faded to black once more.

She was cold. She was tired. Not the tired she had been. She was tired of fighting and tired of running. She wanted to rest under thick furs. She wanted to bathe, and she wanted to eat more than ambrosia and bread. She wanted to sleep, to dream. Night terrors or not—anything was better than the throbbing pain that consumed her.

The air shifted and she was warm again. The smell of spice and cypress filled her nose. She fought to open her eyes, to see him above her. But it was only darkness.

Faint, muffled voices rattled around her in heavy, angry tones. Her body moved from one set of hands to another. The warmth wrapped around her like furs, and she felt a heated hand press into her back, sending a cool wave down her spine, relaxing her instantly.

This time it was his voice that roused her.

"Ready my chambers!" he ordered.

"Yes, my lord," a soft, female voice replied.

"Have Chryseis grab water and wraps!"

Kore felt no movement, but she knew they were no longer at the base of Tartarus. Despite the fight against sleep that raged within her, she could sense the location shift. Moving her to a calmer, quieter location than that of the fields. The voices were low and muffled as she lost her battle with sleep. She was too exhausted to fight and open her eyes. Too exhausted to try to listen to the world that swirled around her.

She felt sleep and welcomed it as it took her peacefully, dulling the pain in her skull and spine to nothing more than an annoying ache. Her breathing, no longer heavy and painful, was calm and steady, just as her heart settled into a slow rhythm.

She was at peace. Her journey was over, and she was comfortable in that thought. The bravery and strength that she never knew lived within her.

If she had the strength now, she would smile, the ash and cypress a reassuring fragrance to her success.

CHAPTER XVI

THE HEALING, THE BLACK FIGURE, AND THE SMELL OF CYPRESS AND SPICE

The soft, soothing sound of water washing over rocks gently woke her. The damp air brought condensation to her hair and seeped into her peplos. She shifted, surprised at how freely she could move. The memories of the events flooded her mind, and she struggled to her feet, running her hand along the back of her head. She felt no pain, no pressure, and no indention in her skull—no evidence left of her far fall and impact.

Her mind reeled back to when she had seen the fallen boy that day, the day she had met Aidoneus. She thought it silly now to compare; he was no divine and hadn't a chance of survival, but she couldn't help but wonder if someone had watched her fall just as she did him. With eyes full of wonder and amusement.

Flat water surrounded her as far as she could see, the small patch of land just big enough for a few bodies, and vacant of anything other than tiny river rocks. Thick white fog loomed around, showing the faint hint of what Kore could only assume to be trees across the way.

She leaned over the surface, gazing down at her reflection. Everything appeared normal, but there was something slightly off that Kore couldn't quite put her finger on.

Her hair was braided and rested over her left shoulder as it always had. Her deep blue eyes, their usual intensity. It wasn't until Kore pulled her lips down that she realized the difference.

This reflection didn't mimic her reactions; instead, it continued to smile softly back at her, as it had been the entire time. Kore tilted her head to one side and the reflection did as well, but when Kore pulled her lips into a big smile, the reflection did not follow.

"Hello?" Kore whispered.

The reflection's lips did not move when hers did. She pulled back, rocking on her heels and falling back onto her butt, her back hitting something hard.

"You finally made it!" a familiar voice called.

Kore craned her neck back, meeting the gaze of the figure, the one who haunted her dreams. Only this time, the features of its face were visible and clear. They were *Kore's* features, with fire-red hair, just like Kore's, only the braid it was pulled into was longer and adorned with tiny crystal skulls that rested over her right shoulder. Her lips were a bright red against her pale skin. Freckles splashed across the bridge of her nose and along her cheeks. Just as Kore's had.

It was like looking into the reflective metal back at the cottage, a dual version of herself, only the reflection that looked back now was adorned in black linen robes. Black vines twisted around her head with deep red petals sprouting from them in a unique pattern.

The dual reached down and grabbed Kore under her arm to assist her up. She was steady in her stance on the small bit of land they occupied; her shoulders relaxed as her eyes swept over Kore.

"Made it? Where?" Kore asked.

She had never spoken to the figure before and was surprised at how calm and easy it seemed to be after so long. As if she was speaking with an old friend again.

The dual adjusted Kore's robes before offering another soft smile.

"Proavlio tis Kolaseos," she informed.

"Proavlio tis Kolaseos? Is this where divines go when they enter the eternal sleep?"

"Oh, no!" She laughed. "This is where I have been kept. Until the proper time has come." She turned to Kore with a soft smile.

"How do you mean?"

"You have never wondered why it is you can bring life and take it away, have you? Our draw to the King of the Dead and what called you to enter Tartarus?" The double lifted her hands and wiggled her fingers, drawing forth a coneflower in her palm.

She examined it closely for a moment before presenting it to Kore. Before their eyes, the flower's petals turned black and began to shrink and curl in on themselves, wilting to a dark, dry, and crinkled mess in the figure's hand.

"*We* have dual divinity of the highest form. The darkness calls to us, as we do to it," she added.

Kore noted the emphasis on the word *we*.

"What do you mean *we*?"

The dual's lips curled up into a twisted smile. "I mean, I am the you that you fear to let Mother see. I am the you that you hid away, only allowing me small moments to free my vines to the world." Her voice grew raw as she spoke. The hurt that laced each word struck Kore like a blade to the heart.

"The vines are from you?" Kore managed.

"All death and destruction you have caused was me."

"I have not caused destruction," Kore snapped.

She could not say she had not caused death. She had taken many lives from plants during her practices.

"No? Need I remind you of the Trojan soldiers *we* stuck

to that tree?" she reminded.

Kore thought back on the memories of that dream she had before her first meeting in Mt. Olympus. She had thought it to be just a dream but remembered quickly that Aidoneus had mentioned the Greek soldiers doing the very same thing to Trojans that night.

Kore swallowed loudly; her heart felt like a rock in her throat. She opened her mouth to protest but struggled to get the words out.

"The trees and vines spoke that night of a plan heard by vegetation in the distance. Their cries for help as the Trojans burned their branches carried to Mother's forest." She paused and looked over Kore briefly, and lips twitching before she began again. "The Trojans trapped the village with the fires, killing the mortals who resided there. That very fate was to befall the cypress trees of Mother's forest. It was the only way."

Kore closed her mouth as she thought on the reasoning. She could not deny that devastation was best avoided, but she couldn't help but feel there was a better way that possibly didn't involve her.

"You were not there," the figure added. Kore was ready to question her, but the figure tapped her finger to her temple.

They were one. She knew Kore inside and out, every thought and feeling, yet Kore felt as if she knew absolutely nothing about the mysterious figure.

"Where was I?"

"Asleep, in Mother's cottage. Cozy under your furs. It wasn't a task that needed you there physically. Your being unconscious makes it easier for me to take control; it just has stipulations."

"How so?"

"You saw it all, did you not?" The figure sighed.

She was right, Kore had seen everything as if she were there. She sensed every bit of the night, from the heat of the fire on her skin to the smell of burning flesh and rotting blood.

The smell still stung her nose at the thought. The figure shifted at the edge of the water, the rocks crunching beneath her feet.

"Where are we?" Kore asked.

"I told you."

"Yes, but is this inside my head? Are you in my head?" Kore waved her hands in the air around her.

"Yes and no. We are in an untapped consciousness, so you could say we are in your head. For me, I call it home," the figure explained.

"Well, why am I here?"

"Because we were injured. Here we will heal, rest, and regain our strength. Then you will wake when the time comes for that." The figure turned to look out into the black water.

"You say this is your home? Who are you?"

"It is as I have said. I am you, an untapped consciousness that you have kept hidden away. I have always been here, just—*dormant*."

"After all this time, why now do you choose to speak?" Kore spat.

"I am not sure, really. I suppose it's this place; it is quite refreshing and energizing. I think it—I think it feeds us." The figure pondered over what she had said, as if hearing it aloud uncovered a new meaning.

Kore watched her, the figure she thought haunted her dreams as it lurked in the shadows of her consistent night terrors as a young child. Looking back, all she had ever done was stand by and watch. Never saying anything, never engaging in the events that unfolded, Kore only lingered near the back.

Kore joined the figure, gazing over the still water, into the fog. The air suddenly felt warm and comforting, and a soft hint of cypress and spice filled the space around them. The figure intertwined her fingers with Kore's, and a soft smile teased at the corners of her lips.

"You set me free, though. It was liberating!"

"I am not even sure how I did. But it looks to me like I

won't be getting the opportunity again anytime soon."

"Nonsense! If you listen closely, you can hear the outer world chatter! That means you are just sleeping. Healing, as I have said. I do apologize. I would have helped sooner but you woke up."

"Woke up?" Kore questioned.

"Yes, when Thanatos tightened his grip around us, you fainted. Quite fast actually, I was surprised you did not hold out longer . . ." Her voice trailed.

"All right!"

"Right, well. I took control for that time, and the energy out there is invigorating. I can't wait to feel it once more." The figure looked back to Kore with a smile.

"But, when I wake up, won't your control be gone?"

"I do not suppose so. We have unleashed something powerful here. I have never felt such energy before." Her eyes grew wide with wonder, and a smile pulled at her lips. "I believe whenever you wake, it will be us—I do not suppose you would feel much different. More open to all your powers, I would guess. Death and destruction included. But you have unlocked something, that I am sure of."

A loud crash rang through the sky, not one known to Kore. It wasn't the sound of thunder, and no lightning struck around them, but the noise grew louder, and the figure's hand tightened around Kore's.

"Oh, you will soon wake! Something is happening!" She gasped. A loud bang cut through the sky again, and everything faded to black.

The burning radiated from the center of her spine to her skull and back again. The pain had dulled quite a bit from what she had remembered, which was a good sign that she was healing.

Someone was healing her, feeding her nectar and ambrosia to keep her divinity high enough for her body to do its work.

She tried to open her eyes, but they fought her, only

allowing a very fuzzy outline through slit lids. Still, this offered little in helping to examine the area around her. The one thing she could make out was the dancing flames of a fire nearby.

"Alena!" Aidoneus's voice rang through the air.

"Yes, my lord?" a small voice cooed.

He muttered hushed words to her quickly before two blurry bodies entered the chamber. Kore could feel her skin ignite in flame.

"Please see to it that Kore's bandages are addressed today. I assigned it to Elpida, but her conversations with herself worry me," he said in a wary and tight tone.

"I will see to it that they are dressed, my lord. I will also have a word with Elpida about those conversations," the soft voice responded.

"Have you heard anything on Thanatos? I have a few words for him."

"No, my lord."

"Well, when he is found, you let him know he has been summoned."

"No need for the summons, my lord," a third called.

Kore felt her eyes grow heavy, and she fought to try to make out the figure that entered, but it was just one large mass.

"That will be all for now, Alena. I'll call for you when you are needed." Aidoneus's voice was low and hard now.

The one named Alena did not speak, but the small figure vanished quickly, leaving only Aidoneus and the enormous mass.

"Explain," he growled.

"I had sensed a divine unfamiliar to me. I noticed Hermes was assisting her a few days back. I assumed the Olympians were up to something. I was only doing my service to the Underworld. If you ask me, you should be thanking me." The god's voice was far too relaxed for having been through the vines Kore, or her figure, had sent him.

"Thanking you? How so?" Aidoneus barked; the sound

rattled the space around her.

"Stopping this goddess from retrieving a soul and returning it to the mortal realm."

"Did she have a soul when you found her leaving Tartarus?" Aidoneus snapped quickly.

"No, but—"

"Enough," he thundered. "There is no excuse for putting your hands on a goddess. She should have been brought to me the moment she stepped foot into my realm. I will have my words with Hermes, but as for you, stay away from her."

"I would much prefer that, my lord," Thanatos said, and Kore could hear the smile in his voice.

Her eyes felt heavy, and she gave up the fight, feeling she had heard enough for now. She needed to rest again.

The sooner she was able to slip back into unconsciousness, the sooner she would wake—healthy and ready to tell Aidoneus of her journey. He was the first person she had shown her power to, when she had wilted the flowers before him all those years ago. She was excited to share with him what she had unlocked within herself along the way.

Sleep took her, but she was highly aware of what waited for her when she woke, and her body grew warm at the thought. The pain in her back was becoming a distant feeling the deeper she slipped until it was nothing more than a nagging tug in the back of her mind.

The figure waited for her on the small plot of rocky land. A smile still sat perfectly on her face. "So?" she inquired quickly.

"Aidoneus is not happy with Thanatos."

"I thought not." She smirked, turning back to the water. Her demeanor still calm, unlike the feeling Kore had in the dream that night. She had been angry then, and vengeful, whispering a single word into Kore's ear before she woke.

"Persephone," Kore whispered, recalling the word.

The figure turned; her lips pressed. "Hm?"

"Persephone. I heard it that night at the tree. What is it?"

"It is a word." The figure shrugged. "It means 'bringer of destruction.'"

"Bringer of destruction?"

"Yes. We destroyed a village."

"*You* destroyed a village," Kore corrected.

"If you say so." The figure shrugged again, turning back to the fog.

She seemed to be waiting for something unseen. Kore sat and slipped her bare feet into the cool water, waiting for whatever it was.

The figure took the spot beside her, and they quietly gazed out over the water together. Kore was growing a slight understanding of the shadow that had haunted her. A shadow that wasn't truly a shadow—it was her—Kore. The darkness she had kept away, just as the figure claimed.

Kore drifted between sitting on the small land of rocks, speaking with the figure about her dual divinity, and brief moments of wakefulness when she was able to hear Aidoneus's voice and get blurry glimpses of him. There were times when he sat on the kline beside her and apologized, others when he asked her why she would be so careless to venture to his realm. No matter what he spoke of, Kore only wanted to hear his voice.

She yearned to press her palm to his cheek and reassure him that she was all right. She was healing and she was happy. Despite the fight, the fall, and the injuries, she had so much to be proud of. Her happiness wasn't from just making it to the Underworld.

For so long she'd lived under her mother's guidance, told what to do and where to go, though that was never very far. She had always feared needing someone for the rest of her life. She didn't want to *need* anyone, and she had to prove to herself she didn't *need* anyone.

She had traveled the Underworld alone; she had been without her mother at her side, and she survived.

Her body shuddered and a responding shock of pain shot through her. It was cold. Wherever she was, they must have let the fire die. Or the one called Alena was redressing her wraps again. She didn't have long to think of the reason before the warmth returned, wrapping around her like a cocoon. The familiar scent of burning cypress and spice filled her nose.

She could feel him all around her, but she couldn't see him, couldn't reach out and touch him with her hand. Her body shuddered in frustration, and a soft, gentle sigh escaped her lips.

The cracking and popping of burning logs filled her ears. Her body weighed down by thick, warm furs. The smell of cypress, spice, and burning wood danced around her in its now familiar way.

She started slow, creeping one eye open and then the other, allowing her vision to focus.

She found herself in a spacious, round chamber with several openings circling her that looked over vast darkness.

The kline that cradled her was bigger than any she had ever seen, with thick black furs scattered over it. To the left of her sat a roaring firepit with flames licking at the dark, carved crystal that housed it. The floor, columns, and even the stone around the kline were all black with slivers of gold stain running through them.

Golden accents twisted along the marble wall. A sizable portrait of Aidoneus hung above an obsidian-carved throne. Two crystal-carved hounds sat on either side; each had a paw resting on a black, carved skull.

Ichor flooded her cheeks as she observed the painting of the king. He sat on the same throne that sat below the portrait. His face was hard, with dark hooded eyes, an expression she had seen a few times from the king. He wore nothing; only a thin black cloth lay a mess over his lap, covering very little, and a black vine crown sat atop his head. Limp black petals were scattered around it.

She felt a tug at her heart as she stared up at the crown, the one she had made him upon their first meeting. Before she knew who he was, when she had requested he tell his king *hello* for her. Her cheeks warmed at the sight, the thought he had kept it all this time, was painted while wearing it. It wasn't her best work at the time, but now—it would forever be one of her favorites. After all, Aidoneus didn't see a problem with it.

Despite the stiffness in her neck, she lifted her head as best she could. Shifting under the furs to free her hand, she felt them rub against the bare skin of her stomach and breasts. She was naked. Exposed. Having only the furs to cover her in this unfamiliar place.

"Oh! You're up!" the soft, now familiar voice echoed.

Turning her gaze, Kore found a small nymph with thick, curly hair and deep brown skin. Her fingertips were covered with soot just like the nymph at the front gates, and her eyes were a burning red that Kore could see even with the distance between them.

She held a platter with a kantharos and skyphos, most likely of ambrosia and nectar for Kore to consume. The nymph briskly walked to Kore's side and set the platter on the kline, looking over the goddess with cautious eyes.

"How do you feel?" she pressed.

Kore wasn't sure how to respond; she felt fine, a little confused, but otherwise all right. She lifted, propping herself on her elbows to get a better view of her new surroundings.

"Where am I?" she asked in a dry, raspy voice.

"You are in the king's chambers. He did take the liberty of sleeping on a different kline—just over there—to give you space." She pointed to the right where a small kline sat. It was nothing fancy. Not something a king would be known to turn to.

Kore did not want space from him. She rubbed her eyes as they still adjusted to the light.

"Is he near?" she asked.

The nymph released a soft, musical giggle before she spoke. "Yes, let me get him."

She sprang up from her spot and skipped from the chamber. She was oddly pleasant and happy for a nymph in the Underworld. But, after everything else, Kore had learned to expect the unexpected.

Her mother's stories were no more than that—stories. Stories were not often taken literally or pulled from the truth, and the ones her mother strung together of Aidoneus and his realm were no different.

Kore adjusted the furs around her, reached for the platter, and pulled it to her as she waited. She brought the kantharos to her lips and took a deep sip, welcoming the sweet, thick drink happily, not realizing how parched she truly was.

"Goddess?" His words were hard and unsettling, but that didn't matter to her. She swallowed with a smile.

"Lord Hades."

CHAPTER XVII

THE GOD OF THE DEAD, THE BATH, AND THE FIRST DINNER

He sat at the edge of the kline, his chin in his hand as he watched her finish the ambrosia the nymph had brought.

"Kore?" he finally asked. She looked up and there was a long pause before he spoke again. "Are you well?"

With him finally in view, close enough to touch, she was much better. The pain in her head and back dulled to just an annoyance in her mind.

"I am better now that I am awake." She smiled, but he did not return the gesture.

He looked over her with concern and a hint of a look she was familiar with from her mother, one she got when her mother disapproved of her actions. And like she did with her mother, Kore dropped her head in response.

"I am just a bit sore in some spots," she added with her eyes on the skyphos of ambrosia.

"You should rest."

"I think I have rested enough." It dawned on Kore that she hadn't the slightest clue how long she had been sleeping. She would have guessed a few days; she knew her healing process wasn't as fast as her mother's, and given her wounds, she guessed that it would take a bit longer than normal.

"How long have I been sleeping?" she asked.

"Two moons."

"*Two moons*? Does my mother know?" Her eyes shot up to him.

"She knows." He turned to look out from the chamber, into the darkness of his realm.

"She must be coming for me."

"Hermes informed her that you needed to heal. He gave his word that you were in good hands." Aidoneus turned to look at her; the look of disappointment faded and was replaced with worry. "Kore, why are you here? Why were you in Tartarus?"

He folded his brows down, creating a small dimple between them. Kore's hand twitched, begging to move, to lift and press her thumb to it and smooth it free, but they only pulled down further as he waited.

She wasn't sure how she should answer. There were a handful of reasons she was there. To flee an arranged marriage, to come and say goodbye if that was what was to be, to tell him she wanted nothing more than to be with him. She found his realm beautiful from what she did see, despite the creatures that chased her. She remembered the busy village and the shades that walked it. Something she would have to ask him of later.

Watching his eyes, she could tell he was growing impatient waiting for a response, but she still couldn't settle on one, not at the moment.

"I—" she began, her eyes locked in his. The memory of his last visit flashed before her. "I *fancied* a walk."

She smiled at him, repeating the same reason he had given her. He pressed his lips together, his brows falling even deeper over his eyes.

"You *fancied* a walk? Through *Tartarus*?" Confusion twisted his face.

"I do my best thinking when I walk, and I thought, why not through Hell," she joked, but he was unamused.

"You broke your back," he said flatly.

"Yes. But it is only a little sore this day," she argued.

"You smashed your skull."

"Yes, and that is but just a slight headache now." She smiled softly once more at him, but he was unmoved, only looking over her with concern painting his face. After a long moment, he finally spoke.

"Can you stand?" he asked, rising to his feet, "I have arranged for my nymphs, Alena and Callisto, to prepare you a bath."

Holding the furs to her chest, she slid her feet from the kline and placed them on the cool marble floor.

He held out his hand to assist, and she took it happily, pulling herself up, but her legs were weaker than she had anticipated. She crashed forward, the fur slipping free and landing at her feet.

Aidoneus stumbled back, smacking hard against the floor, Kore landing on top of him. He groaned.

The fall sent a sharp pain down Kore's spine, and she hissed in response.

An immense heat pressed against her bare skin. Her eyes grew wide, realizing her position. With a leg on either side of the king, his body flexed beneath her.

"Oh!" Kore gasped.

He froze. The heat grew even stronger between them. He made a noise in the back of his throat and rolled her to the side, reaching around and grabbing the furs that had fallen.

"Here!" he huffed, pulling them over Kore's naked body. He hurried to his feet, his face and chest a bright gold from the ichor that flushed his skin. Kore had never seen such emotion from him.

"The bathing hall is just down that walkway there—" He pointed to a path between two columns behind him. "Alena left oils and fresh robes for you." He then turned on his heels to rush away.

"Aidoneus! I cannot stand on my own!" she cried out, gripping the furs.

He stopped at the entrance, his body tense and rigid as he turned, looking back to her over his shoulder. It was quiet, and after a few moments, he returned to her side and gently scooped her into his arms.

He carried her across the main chamber and out onto the stone step path that led to a much smaller one. Black marble and obsidian with the same accent of gold mixed in. The black columns were lined with the same flickering torches and open walls to view the realm. In the center sat a deep bathing pool that was carved into the floor, filled with steamy water.

Next to the pool sat a variety of lekythoi of all sizes, a basket of dark red rose petals, and fresh black linen robes.

He walked over to the edge where there were clear steps to enter. Pausing again, he looked around for a moment as a realization started to form.

"I will get someone to assist you." Clearing his throat, he placed Kore at the edge of the pool. "Can you get in on your own?" He was already making his way back to the entrance they had come through.

"I can manage," she said softly as she removed the furs from around her shoulders and slowly lowered herself into the steaming, hot water, allowing it to creep over her stiff muscles and joints. A small groan of pleasure escaped her as she tilted her head back.

"Alena!" Aidoneus called, his bellowing voice bouncing and rattling the columns and pillars. He waited patiently with his arms folded across his chest. A black cloud appeared before him and from it manifested the small nymph from earlier.

"My lord?" she inquired with a bow.

"Please see to it that Kore is well tended. She may require assistance," he instructed before leaving the chamber.

Alena skipped to the side of the pool with a bright,

welcoming smile.

"I did not get a chance before. I am Alena. I will be your head handmaid while you are here."

"Oh, I do not think—"

"By order of the king. I do not mind; it is not often he has guests." She smiled again as she offered Kore the basket of petals. With a nod, Kore reached in and grabbed a handful and tossed them in the water.

Kore watched the flowers float around her, twirling and spinning and leaving a burgundy trail in their dance. The lekythoi clicked together as Alena moved them around in search of something particular. Her soot-covered fingers spun each until they were evenly spaced and lined up along the edge of the pool.

"These are body and hair oils. There is Rosmarinus oil in this one; that one has equisetum oil. Those are for your hair." She tilted each lekythos as she spoke. "This is Valeriana oil, and this is Verbascum oil. Those are for your body," she added, pointing to the second set at the end. "Is there anything I can help you with?" Alena smiled down at her.

Kore felt an anxiousness she hadn't before. She didn't like how Aidoneus had said so little and how he left her, though it was in the hands of a sweet nymph. She'd much rather have his aid.

"Thank you. There is one thing I may ask. Do you think, possibly, Aidoneus—I mean, Lord Hades can assist me? I hope he does not mind, but I do have words for him," Kore asked politely.

"I can check with him if you'd like." Alena smiled, and Kore quickly responded with an enthusiastic nod. "Very well, one moment." The nymph giggled as she jumped to her feet and headed to the front of the chamber.

She peeked around the deep red tapestry that was tied up against the entrance column. Kore took the time to take in the view from the pool that looked over the realm. The way the chamber was positioned made Tartarus the center viewpoint.

Its glowing red lava trailing down the side in a blistering river.

Sprinkled in the sea of darkness were the gleaming lights from the village tucked at the base of the raging mountain. Glowing blue shades floated amongst themselves, living as if they had never left the mortal realm—from what Kore could see.

Glittering stars sprayed the night sky, more than she had ever known on the mortal realm. Shades of greens, blues, and purples lightly tinted the sky just as the petals tinted the water around her.

"You summoned me?" His deep voice startled her, and she turned to find him standing at the edge of the pool.

"A summon? Of the king? I would never. But an invitation." She drifted to the end where he stood, letting the buoyancy of the water help her move. She looked up to him. "An invitation I would give most happily!" she finished, watching as the golden color brightened his face once more. He closed his eyes and inhaled deeply.

"Does my nudity bother you?" The words fell freely from her mouth without her meaning to speak them aloud. He opened his eyes and gazed down at her with a lifted brow and clenched jaw.

"No," he said flatly.

"Well, as long as it does not bother you, would you mind helping me with my hair?" She pulled her curls over her shoulder and ran her wet fingers through them. Without a word, he took one step into the water and sat on the edge.

A smile split her face as she spun around and pushed her hair back to him. He cupped the water in his hands and gently poured it over her head, allowing it to saturate every strand. Repeating this process a few more times until her hair grew heavy.

"Did Alena inform you of the oils?" he finally asked.

"Yes."

"Did you pick one?"

Kore turned to the row of oils and picked the one she

was sure Alena stated was the Rosmarinus oil. When she came back, she placed herself between Aidoneus's legs, his chiton just barely touching the water's surface. His chest flexed as he gazed down at her. His lips pressed flat, and he placed his hands on her shoulders.

She held her breath, ready for whatever was to come, but Aidoneus only turned her around to face away from him. She was not sure what she was expecting, but the nagging feeling of rejection toyed with her.

He took the oil and poured it into her hair until every strand was slick with it. The relaxing feel of his hands in her curls sent chills over her skin.

"Did I cause much trouble being here?" she asked after a moment.

He paused briefly as he thought on her question. "The Cyclopes aren't too happy about being outwitted by a goddess. Thanatos is—well, you just keep your distance from him."

"I am sorry if I caused him any injury."

"Don't be, he knew not to attack a goddess. One of this realm or not." He paused for a long moment while he rinsed her hair. "I apologize for the injuries you've sustained while here, in my realm."

"You did not cause me harm." She giggled.

"No. But every soul in my realm is my responsibility. Thanatos should have brought you to me." His voice grew cold as he spoke.

"I am much better now," she reassured.

"Yes. I can see," he said tautly, which made Kore nervous about what was next for her.

Was he going to clean her up, feed her, and hand her to Demeter?

"Will you be sending me back to my mother?"

His hands fell from her hair as he stood, stepping from the pool to stand above her.

"I cannot give you back to Demeter in any condition other than that in which you left her meadow, and you cannot walk." He paused to look over her. "Would you like to be returned to your mother?"

"I would not. I was hoping to view more of your realm."

"Is that what you came all this way for?" He raised a brow.

She shook her head with a smile. "No, but I have found your realm to be incredibly beautiful, and interesting. Like the shades over there!" She pointed to the small village that lit the dark fields with blue lights. "I am curious to see what they have done in this life."

"Will you tell me why you journeyed all this way?" He sighed, but Kore did not plan on answering just yet. There were bound to be better moments to tell him but now was not one of them. Keeping her eyes on the water's surface, she twisted her hair to squeeze out the remaining liquid.

"I think I am ready to eat now," she sighed, ignoring his question and making her way to the step.

She lifted herself and sat with her legs still in the water. Aidoneus handed her a strigil to dry with before turning to look out over his realm, giving her privacy to scrape the remaining oil and water from her and dress in the robes Alena had provided.

She struggled to lift her leg free from the pool, but before she could say anything, Aidoneus was pulling her back into his arms and adjusting the robes over her. Burning cypress and spice cocooned her in his warm fragrance. She leaned into him, feeling his arms flex around her.

"Is my nudity that horrible?" She sighed. His chest hardened as he sucked in a sharp breath.

Nudity had never been an issue back at the meadow; the nymphs and Kore usually spent hot days in the spring nude. She thought it was a normal thing, for the gods anyway.

"No," he said stiffly. "You are a guest in my realm. I do not wish to cause you discomfort more than you already have endured." He made his way from the bathing chambers, heading a different direction than they had come.

They traveled down an open stairway with the stars shining above them. Sizable golden basins holding flickering mounds of fire lined the path and lit the way. Once at the bottom, Aidoneus proceeded to walk down a long, covered corridor.

The darkness of the night did nothing but shade the details from her, and the false moon was not as bright as the one Selene toted.

A small light appeared in the distance, growing as they drew near. The closer they got the more she could make out the outline of a small woman. Another lampades nymph, she guessed.

"Lord Hades," the nymph greeted in a singsong voice, her hair as red as the fire she held in the torch, standing out against her pale ivory skin.

"Chryseis. Was the dining hall set as instructed?"

The deep tenor of his voice rumbled through his chest. Kore felt a warm feeling sink deep within her; it was a strange warmth and one she had not felt before. It heated the pit of her stomach, and she pressed her thighs together in response.

"Yes, my lord. We made quite the spread!" she cheered.

The nymph didn't seem at all fazed by Kore in his arms, as if the sight was normal for her, but Alena had stated Aidoneus didn't keep guests, and there was no known time when he had let another living mortal or divine into his realm without consequence.

"Thank you, Chryseis. You may tell the others that you are relieved for the evening." His voice rumbled again, causing the odd warmth to reignite.

"Thank you." She bowed once more before quickly departing into a puff of smoke.

"They are fast," Kore commented softly.

"They are good at what they do."

"And what is it that they do?"

"They serve me. As all the creatures of the Underworld do. The nymphs are just more—willing." He continued with their walk to the hall, turning down another split-off corridor.

"Oh?" she breathed, wondering what else the nymphs were more willing to do for him. A small tinge of jealousy rose in her chest.

"I gave them a hall of their own, one I do not know the location of. It shelters them from the creatures that wish to do them harm," he explained.

They entered a round chamber, just like the others, but far larger and more extravagant with walls and columns lined with black and gold accents that twisted and framed the ceiling in such mesmerizing ways. A long, obsidian table sat at the center, covered in a vast assortment of wines, bread, cheeses, fruits, and meats. In the middle sat two chairs identical to the chair she saw at Mt. Olympus, with the same dark crystal carved to throne.

Kore looked up to Aidoneus as they came to the table. He was eyeing the spread and looking pleased with what was available.

He set her down in a chair and grabbed a platter from the center.

"What do you like?" he asked, placing two skyphoi of ambrosia onto the platter. Kore hadn't much else in her life besides bread, cheeses, fruits, and vegetables. Her mother didn't allow them meat, and she honestly wasn't too sure how she would feel, but she had always wanted to try it.

"What animal?" she questioned but trailed off as she looked over the odd shapes and colors. The smells watered her mouth, and she fought the urge to wildly grab everything in her reach. She hadn't realized her hunger until it was presented to her, the smells and sights taunting her stomach.

"Lamb." He pointed to a slab of meat that was cooked until the outer skin was charred and blackened. "Roasted chicken," he added, pointing to a golden-colored pile of meat.

"I will try the lamb," she offered with a puzzled look.

A quick smile flashed across his face as he plated the chunk of meat and walked around to gather more food.

"Wine?" He held up an amphora to her.

"Mother never allowed wine," she informed innocently.

"Yes, well—you are in my realm now, and you may do as you desire." He poured the deep red liquid and added the kantharoi to the tray as he continued around the table, plucking odd fruits and cheeses. He placed the platter before her and took his spot on the throne.

Kore looked over the pile of food he had collected for her. A mix of bright colors splattered the tray. The meat, the cheese, the fruit, and wine. She didn't know where to start, but she figured starting with the things she had never had before would be a good place to begin.

"Have you never had meat before?" he asked, watching her as she examined the slab.

"No, Mother—"

"Did not allow it," he finished. "I will assume your mother did not grant you many experiences, but as I have said, as long as you are here, you may do as you please."

"Is there a limit on how long I may stay?"

"That is your choice. You are free to leave when you like." He plucked a grape from the table and popped it in his mouth.

"I would very much like to stay. If you do not mind, of course." She smiled.

His face scrunched in confusion at her response.

"Why?" He shifted quickly after the words left his mouth and cleared his throat. "What interests do you find here?" he corrected.

Kore knew all the reasons she wanted to stay, why she needed to stay. But just like her reasons for traveling so far from home, she felt this was information that had a proper time to be addressed.

"As I said, *Lord Hades*, I find your realm beautiful. The

fields, the flowers, the rolling hills, and mountains. It is more stimulating than the meadow and forests my mother crafted. Hermes said Hecate created the sky!" Her heart sank, remembering the words she heard Aidoneus hiss when she had first woken to his and Thanatos's conversation. The words he would have with the God of Messages.

"You weren't too hard on him, were you? Hermes? He was only helping." She rushed the words from her lips.

Aidoneus kept his eyes on the table as he spoke. "I have had my words with Hermes."

His response left an emptiness in Kore. She did not want anyone to get punished for her requests. She hoped Hermes wouldn't be too sore with her, but knowing the God of Messages, he had probably already forgiven her.

"You should eat," he said, pointing to the platter.

Kore began picking at the fruit and nibbled on the lamb, which she found to be tasty; it melted in her mouth with a salty, gamey, yet robust flavor. It was mild but sweet.

Before she knew it, she had finished the lamb and was ready to move on to the next. She tried, tasted, and nibbled on everything in front of her as if she had never tasted food of any sort before. She sipped on the wine, slowly at first, but once she was past the dry bitterness of it, she was able to drink it more smoothly.

She did not see the draw to the liquid; it was something both man and gods seemed to enjoy. It wasn't sweet or refreshing, and it left her throat dry and craving a more satisfying potion to quench the thirst. After each drink, she followed it quickly with the nectar, giving it a sweetness that helped her take it down.

When her kantharos ran dry, she tilted it to Aidoneus in a request for more.

"You think it wise?" he asked stiffly with a raised brow.

"You said I may do as I please," she slurred.

"That was before I learned of your low tolerance of it. Perhaps for tonight, that will do."

"Well," she sighed, "what are we to do now?"

"It is late, you should rest."

"I am not too tired." She laughed, leaning back in her chair, excited to hear his plans.

"I suppose you wouldn't be. I am not so tired either." He stood, stretching his arms over his head. His muscles flexed from his shoulders to his chest and abs, inviting that strange new warmth to build once more.

"If you want to view my realm, you must learn to walk again."

CHAPTER XVIII

THE HARPIES, THE PRACTICE, AND THE MONSTER

Aidoneus waited patiently by a polished obsidian slab. It was reflective like that of the metal plates Kore was used to, only black—with a clearer reflection. He wore just a dark chiton at his waist, leaving his chest bare and golden. His eyes fixed on Kore while Alena slowly guided her from one end of the chamber to the other. Her legs were wobbly and weak as she struggled to hold steady. But the sweet nymph was gentle, kind, and slow, and she held her hands gingerly under Kore's elbows.

It had only been two days since Kore had woken from what was a long slumber. Her muscles and joints were weak from lying so long, her legs just regaining feeling after being motionless, sensation slowly winding through them.

Kore steadily placed one foot in front of the other and leaned her weight over. She did this with the other leg, moving just as slowly until she and Alena had neared the crystal-carved vanity that held the polished obsidian.

Aidoneus's eyes swept over Kore as she braced herself against the vanity.

"That will be all for today, Alena. Thank you," he said

softly with his eyes still on Kore.

Alena made sure the goddess was steady before bowing and disappearing into her cloud of smoke. She had only just begun her therapy for the day, and he was already cutting it short.

His eyes followed the length of her body before coming to rest on her face. She watched as his jaw tightened and his lips pressed.

"Was something wrong?" she breathed.

He slipped his arm around her waist, and with his free hand, he twined his fingers in hers. He pulled her closer so that her weight was rested on his side. A trail of fire ignited along her skin where he brushed against her. He was warm and soft and hard all at once. Her heart raced, pulling her stomach up to her chest. An odd feeling. She inhaled deeply, resting her chin on his chest, gazing up at him.

"Not at all. I just thought I would assist you today. It appeared that Alena was—" He paused, searching for his words, "in need of a break."

Kore's eyes rested on his lips. He turned his gaze down, his arm tightening around her waist.

Alena had been helping Kore and running most of Aidoneus's requests. She had hardly seen any other nymphs the last few days except for Chryseis.

"I thought it be best you walk greater distances than that of the chamber." His chest rumbled against her chin.

"Where will we go?" she cooed.

"Where would you like to go?"

Kore pressed her lips together as she thought about where she would like to be. She had been cooped up in the chamber the last two days, only leaving to the bathing pool and the dining hall. Fresh air would be nice.

"Could you show me the fields of asphodel?"

"Is that truly where you would like to be?" He lifted a brow and smiled.

Kore nodded in response, and without another word,

they were surrounded by smoke. It smelled of cypress and spice and ash, just like Aidoneus, and it was just as intoxicating.

She hadn't ever really taken notice of the scent of the clouds and smoke the gods made. Having never been so engulfed in their shift to register it. Their divine energy was just as they were, with the same scent drifting in the air about them and colors of smoke that matched their divine auras.

When the smoke cleared, tall, overgrown asphodel plants and long blades of wild grass surrounded them in all directions, blocking out her view of the palace and Tartarus. Fresh air filled with the sweet scent of the untouched asphodels calmed her mind. Her skin grew warm under the bright light of the false sun, heating away the cool chill of the chamber.

She shot her eyes up to him, his lips in a half smile. "Where are we?"

"Asphodel fields."

"But these are—"

"Overgrown. Yes. This part of the realm has not been filled or accessed yet. We will have more privacy here." He pulled her in closer and guided her forward. Moving slower than she had in the chamber, she found that having to move around grass and plants made it a bit more challenging. Aidoneus was patient, holding her hand and guiding her gently by the waist. She could feel the heat of his hand pressed against her hip.

"I suppose you still are not willing to tell me why you are here," he said suddenly.

Kore shot her eyes back up to him. It was not a question she had prepared for, though she knew she needed to give him an answer soon. He did not appear to be aware of her mother's and Zeus's arrangement for her and Ares.

Would he send her back if he knew that Zeus was involved? Zeus usually had say over everything, even the King of the Dead. Would Aidoneus want to risk a war over her? A full-on uproar between brothers and the God of War on her fate? What reason would Aidoneus have?

"Is the reason so important?" she asked.

He raised his brow, stepping slowly with her and carrying most of her weight in his arm.

"The living do not normally venture down to my realm without cause." He sighed.

"Cause?"

"Love, power, fortune. You would be surprised." His hand pressed against her, his warmth seeping through the fabric. She sucked in a deep breath as the heat raced through her, stopping at her center. Her hand squeezed his, and she swallowed thickly.

"I did not come for power or fortune or any of that," she offered, hoping he noted her avoidance in saying the word love. He looked at her with questioning eyes.

"Then what are you here for?" he pressed, not catching her last statement.

She suppressed a low groan.

"Sanctuary," she lied.

The hand at her waist twisted in the fabric, brushing against her soft skin and leaving a burning fire against her. His brows pulled down over his eyes, folding the skin in the center.

"Sanctuary?" he echoed, his voice deep with concern. "From who?"

"My mother," she lied, but this was an answer he seemed to accept.

Her mother was not known to be unkind, but most still did not want to cross her, a fact Kore had always wondered about her mother. The only stories she did not share with Kore were those of her own sorrows and sins.

"I will not ask what she did. But I must ask why you went to Tartarus. Hermes said he was taking you up the path to the palace." He pulled her close again, taking all her weight in his arms.

She hadn't noticed when, but they had stopped walking.

His hand twisted in the fabric at her side. The feel of him sent heat and chills about her skin all at once. Her eyes dropped to his lips, causing a thick lump to grow in her throat. They looked soft, kissable.

Kore had never thought of lips in such a way. What were kissable lips? She had no experience other than with him in the spring. But if she had to say, Aidoneus's lips were kissable, since she had already kissed them.

Kore released a soft breath, her eyes still locked on him. He flattened his hand on her, his thumb moving in a circular motion over the fabric. His breath fanning across her face. Cypress and fire and ash. She blinked, his question coming back to her fogged mind.

"I had gotten lost. I walked through the village, and when I got to the end, I am not sure, I just had a feeling that told me to go in. It was the most peaceful decision I had felt at the time." She thought back to the moment when she decided to scale the side of Tartarus and enter its gates.

"*Peaceful*?" he echoed again.

She nodded. He seemed to chew over that word for a moment but said nothing else on the matter. He released some of his hold on her, allowing her to carry some of her weight as they began walking again.

"How did you get in?" he pushed.

"The guards at the front, they saw the—" She reached her hand up to grab the crystal, but only felt the smaller quartz her mother had given her. "Oh!" she gasped, shooting her gaze down.

"Oh, that's right." Aidoneus chuckled softly. "Here. The Harpies found it when they found you."

He pulled forth the black shard crystal, wrapped in leather, and slipped it over Kore's head.

"Thank you." She sighed with relief. "The guards at the entrance saw this and opened the doors. Then there was another guard, but he disappeared on me," she added.

"He did not tell you to wait?" His voice grew dark, and

annoyance coated it.

Kore shook her head. "No, he did not speak. He just vanished." She proceeded to tell him the rest of her horrible adventure through Tartarus. Noting how his body and arms flexed around her and how his eyes softened and darkened at every turn of her story. He was angry, and sad, and amused at her adventure. Apologizing every time she mentioned she was wounded.

"'Tis not your fault," she reassured him, but the deep crease between his brows did not lift.

"Tartarus is a dangerous place. I am surprised you made it out," he said darkly. "I know I said you may do as you please here. But promise me you will not step foot into Tartarus again." He looked down to her, his eyes dark.

"I do not plan to be tormented by the shades any further," she promised with a smile.

Fighting the shades and unknown monsters really was the last thing she would want to do again.

He searched her face, stopping on her lips. She thought he would move. To kiss her, to speak, to walk. To do anything, but he just fixed his eyes on her for a few more silent moments. The heat between them grew, burning her where their skin touched.

Her breathing hiked, pulling his attention. He blinked a few times, his focus falling back on their current surroundings, and he loosened his grip around her waist. He fixed his eyes forward and shifted them, taking a slow and steady step.

They continued walking through the tall grass and wild-grown asphodels. No sound other than the faint breeze blowing past and their feet upon the soil could be heard.

Aidoneus loosened his hold on Kore every few feet, allowing her to slowly put her weight on her legs. They were more mobile now, less stiff and achy, her joints more flexible than they had been that morning.

It was close to dark, and the false sun was moving behind the hills as the false moon began peeking from the high peaks of the mountain. She noticed Aidoneus's arm around her waist had become nothing more than a hand on her back, gently guiding her forward.

She looked up to the god with a smile. Overjoyed, she rose on the tips of her toes and wrapped her arms around his neck, molding her body to his. For a moment she could feel his hands hover above her waist, frozen, and she wanted him to just wrap them around her. To pull her closer and surround her in his warmth.

Finally, the warm roughness of his hands smoothed over her bare shoulder. The heat of his breath fanned across the crook of her neck, and she fought the shudder that raced through her.

"You should still take things slow," he muffled, his lips grazing the skin just under her ear, obliterating the internal battle she held with herself.

She wanted to kiss him, to feel his lips against hers. She pulled back until their cheeks connected. Her stomach hardened and her palms felt clammy.

Why is this so hard now? she thought, having done it so easily before. She parted her lips slightly, sucking in a small amount of air. Her head felt fuzzy and light, and she shut her eyes.

"Are you well?" he asked, pulling away from her.

She did not respond; she only kept her eyes shut. Feeling silly having missed her chance due to nerves. She hadn't been so shy in her spring; she shouldn't be so now. Not after all she had endured getting here. In this spot, in his arms.

The air around them swirled, and the faint hint of cypress and fire filled her nose. The soft feel of the soil between her toes vanished and was replaced with the coolness of smooth marble. Her eyes popped open to see that they were surrounded by the now familiar black columns of Aidoneus's chambers with a spitting fire already lit, warming the space for them.

"I will have Chryseis bring up your meal." He guided

Kore to his large throne and helped her into the seat.

He smoothed the wild strands from her face, the heat of his palm searing into her cheek. She thought back to the night she spent in Tartarus. The soft, breathless moans that drifted in the air while Megara and Salmoneus spent their time together. The whispers of their lovemaking filled Kore's ears.

It wasn't until he wet his lips that she realized she had been staring. She exhaled and he straightened, walking back toward the opening of the chamber that led out into a long corridor. He called to the nymph by name. Loud and abrupt.

A cloud formed, wasting no time between his calls, and cleared just as instantly. Chryseis appeared with a half-smile on her full pink lips.

"My lord?"

"We will be dining here tonight," he informed her.

Saying nothing else the nymph bowed and vanished. Aidoneus made his way back to Kore, pausing for just a moment as their eyes locked. His muscular chest and sculpted abs were tight, shining in the light of the fire.

Would she ever get used to his beauty?

She kept her gaze on him as he stepped up to her side, leaning over and resting his arms on the armrest of the throne. His eyes locked on her just as securely. He clenched his jaw, flexing the muscle there.

His mouth twitched as if he was going to speak but instead, he dropped his eyes to the black Underworld pin at her shoulder. They then trailed along her collarbone, and he swallowed hard before speaking.

"I hope you do not mind black," he finally said, his eyes hovering around her neckline.

An odd statement: she had been wearing the robes since she had woken. It was a bit late to wonder if she enjoyed them.

She did—she found them to be fitting and loved how the linen hugged her curves and how the black looked against her skin. Making her freckles and hair pop and glow. She also enjoyed the fact that she did not have to worry as much about them getting dirty wherever she sat, as she had with her white robes.

"I much prefer them over my other ones, thank you." She smiled, tilting her chin to him. Even with him leaning, he towered over her. A great mountain.

"My lord," a small voice announced from the corridor opening.

Chryseis stood with a loaded platter in her hands. Alena joined her with a second platter holding an amphora and two kantharoi. The wine most likely. Aidoneus did not look back to them; instead, he waved his hand for them to enter but kept his eyes fixed on Kore.

The two nymphs set the platters on top of the furs of the kline before turning to exit. Soft giggles escaped them as they disappeared into the corridor.

"Are you hungry?" he inquired, holding his hand out to her.

She took it instantly, ignoring the tingling shock that raced through her. She would never tire of his touch, his skin connecting with hers. The heat and electric shock it sent through her. It was charging in some ways and others, giving her warmth deep at the pit of her stomach. She rose from the chair, and he guided her to the kline, lifting her legs onto the furs before taking his spot beside her.

Kore looked over the meal on the golden platter before her. Meats, cheeses, and bread lay scattered. Aidoneus poured the wine into the two kantharoi. Light and golden in color, it smelled heavily of honey. He passed her a kantharos before taking a deep drink from his own. He emptied it quickly and refilled it before picking at small bits of food.

Kore took a sip of her wine before pulling shreds of meat from the slab before her.

"What is this creature?" she quizzed, examining the bit between her fingers.

"Chicken." He pulled a piece for himself and slipped it into his mouth.

Kore had spent time with the chickens in the meadow, raising them from chicks until their time came to an end by natural causes. They were certainly never thought of as food.

She tossed the piece into her mouth. It wasn't unpleasant, but she did not care to think of the chickens in the meadow as she ate. She pushed the meat down and followed it with a quick sip of her wine. It was sweeter than the red wine she had drunk a few nights back, smoother too.

After they had finished, Aidoneus waved his hand in the air; the platter and kantharoi disappeared into the smoke and cleared from the kline.

"Will you show me how to do that?" she breathed, her eyes still on the spot the food had just been.

"Hm?" he hummed, following her gaze.

"Traveling and manifesting things. With smoke? My mother can travel—she never cared to, so she never taught me," she explained.

A low chuckle rumbled the kline.

"Yes, I can teach you," he said with a smile, big and bright, that presented the deep dimples in his cheeks.

Kore's heart swelled and the heat consumed her again. This was a sweet torment. The sweetest, yet most aggravatingly painful. This would be easier if he could just guess why she was here. If she didn't have to say it with her own words. Words that seemed so easy in thought, but now an impossibility.

What are you afraid of? the voice in the back of her head raged.

Myself.

Aidoneus stood off to the side again while Alena guided Kore from one end of the chamber to the other. Back to the same routine as the first two days. She had hoped the king would take her back out to the fields for fresh air and privacy, but he argued again that she should take it slow, and the fields called for more than walking.

The hills called for climbing up and running or near skipping down. The soft soil made for unsteady ground. It was a challenge, but that was what Kore wanted. She felt her progress moved faster with the natural obstacles, though it did leave her sore and stiff when she woke.

She had attempted to keep the stiffness from Aidoneus, but to her surprise, he was already dressed and sitting on his throne waiting. He had watched as she stretched and groaned in pain. Watched as she slowly climbed from the kline and furs to her feet and watched as she rubbed the soreness from each leg before her eyes met his. She could see that he saw the pain.

Now he watched as Alena slowly guided Kore back and forth. Perhaps she shouldn't rush her healing. She was up and could see him. She could feel his warmth and smell his musk.

A sudden sense of unease washed over her.

What would he do once she was well enough to walk? What if Hermes told her mother the moment he learned she was well once again? She did not want to remain weak, but now that she thought on it, it would be best not to rush it. To enjoy the time she had with him while she could.

Alena guided Kore to Aidoneus's side, letting her grab hold of the crystal table he leaned against.

"That will be all, Alena," he said.

"Would you like me to send your meal up?" the nymph asked.

Aidoneus looked to Kore, his eyes sweeping her from head to toe, and nodded stiffly.

"No meat," he added.

CHAPTER XIX

THE TOUR, THE GARDEN, AND THE PETRIFIED TREE

"You need not run, Kore!" Aidoneus called, but Kore did not care for his words.

Cooped up in the chamber, she felt stuffy and caged again, but her legs had regained their strength. Her spine and skull had healed, and she was ready to stretch her body.

She was overjoyed with the opportunity to finally be out where the false sun was warming to her skin. The strong scent of asphodels filled the air around her, bringing her a sense of peace. The freedom to walk without aid and run again.

After Aidoneus pointed out the small meadow, Kore sprinted off with the king close behind her, filling the air with laughter and joy.

"You need to take it slow," Aidoneus said when he caught up to her.

But Kore had grown tired of going slow and being careful. She felt ready to stretch her legs, smell the air in the fields, and finally look around the realm with the guidance of its king.

"Oh, but there is so much of your realm to be seen!" She looked over the vast land before her.

Some areas had rolling hills, others climbing up to great peaks. Rivers twisting and turning, connecting in one spot, and disconnecting in others. It was beautiful, and it had something she had not expected—life.

Life flourished in a realm occupied by the dead. The grass and flowers around her vibrated against her bare feet happily, welcoming her to the land for a second time.

"If you plan to stay, then there is no need to rush." He sighed.

Her heart sped at the sound of his words. He was allowing her to stay; it had been a deep worry for her over the past days as she healed. She feared he would soon turn her over to her mother the moment she could walk again.

Kore did plan on staying, and that added comfort, but it did not stop the nagging fear that her mother would storm down and drag her back to the mortal realm.

"I do not want to take you from your duties," she admitted.

He had spent most of the week with her in his chambers, listening to the stories of the time she had spent with her mother in the fields, where she helped double the harvest. She even told him how Ares had joined them during that time, but she did not speak on the arrangement made.

There had been only one day that he had gone to the Judgment Hall to cast his judgments upon the shades that had been backed up in his absence. Leaving Kore to spend the day with Alena and Callisto, another lampades nymph who was quieter and more reserved than Alena.

Her innocent, childlike face was framed by long brown waves, reminding Kore of Hebe in many ways. Incredibly young in appearance but wise beyond her years, she was sweet and soft just as the other nymphs in the realm were and was happy to show Kore the main halls and chambers while she and Alena helped her regain her strength and ability to walk.

"My duties are handled with or without my presence." The wide grin Kore had come to love appeared across his normally stone-set face. "You are free to question me till your heart's desire," he teased with a deep laugh.

Kore felt lucky to hear the beautiful sound. His laugh was like music, and it caused warmth to gather within her, a warmth she gladly welcomed.

They continued along their path, stopping at new flowers that Kore did not see in the mortal realm. She mentally logged the information Aidoneus provided, new plants to study, craft, and care for. As much as she thought she wouldn't, she could not deny that she missed her practice, she missed her garden, and she missed her bees, goats, and chickens.

Kore plucked a purple flower and held it in her left hand. It was an oddly shaped floret, with petals that looked to be a butterfly from the side, and from the front, it resembled the helmet Aidoneus wore upon their first meeting.

Closing her fingers around the flower's head, she focused her energy through the petals and back into her body—her way of processing the plant, studying it. She pushed the energy out into her right palm, and a bright, glowing light flashed briefly before an identical purple flower head manifested.

Aidoneus kept his eyes on her as she worked, observing in silence. She lifted the clone until it was eye level and examined it briefly. The color was slightly lighter, and its petals were soft and flimsy, making the flower look . . . sad. Its energy, faint and inconsistent in pattern.

Kore pulled her lips down at the creation, unpleased with the turnout. She had spent three years practicing cloning and she had thought she had mastered it, but down here, it wasn't just their language and vibrations she had to learn.

She felt a tinge of disappointment as she gazed down on the weak clone, watching as the ends slowly blackened and curled in. The words from her dream suddenly replayed in her head.

I suppose it's this place. It is quite refreshing and

energizing—it feeds us.

The blackness spread quicker as if the thought powered her darkness, engulfing the flower. Soon, the flower sizzled, and a small stream of smoke drifted from the petals, leaving them dry and brittle to the touch.

"Did the flower wrong you?" Aidoneus suddenly asked, breaking the silence.

She considered telling him it had, since it had not come out how she intended. A bad injury and two moons of sleep had weakened her powers, or the simple fact the plant was new to her. Either way, it did not form as she planned.

"No, it did not wrong me. It was just a bit soft looking."

"Are flowers not soft?" Curiosity with a mix of confusion lined his face.

She giggled softly to herself, forgetting that the topic of density was something she and her mother had discussed. It had only just dawned on her that not many others would understand such things.

"Well, yes. They are to some degree or another. But petals that are too soft are often too weak to withstand the weather. Helios and Apollo usually see to it that they suffer a horrible fate . . . " Her voice trailed off as she continued to study the dried crumbs in her hand.

"I do not think your fate was any more forgiving." He leaned over to study the pile in her palm. "But if you would prefer your own torture chamber for the plants, I can supply one." Though his words were grim, he offered a pleasant smile.

Kore was not sure if he had meant to joke with her or if he truly intended on gifting her such a chamber.

"Come with me." He chuckled, shaking his head as he turned and offered his arm to her.

She took it hesitantly, unsure that she wanted such a chamber—torture chambers were usually down in the dungeon. Gloomier than Kore would care for.

His lips pulled up into a wide, beautiful smile. Small

laugh lines appeared at the corners, and his body shook from the booming laughter that escaped him.

"Come." He chuckled again and tugged her through the various fields that led up to the bridge.

"Do you honestly have a chamber of torment—in the palace?"

"Yes. Several. I can spare a few."

"I do not think I will be needing such a chamber." Kore pouted; she had not considered her actions to be along the lines of torment. It was a mutual transaction between them. Her and the plants.

"We shall see." He sighed.

They continued down a low, rolling hill where the asphodels reached up to Kore's waist.

"The asphodel fields?" she began, reaching her hand out to lightly graze the petals as they passed.

"Yes?"

"Are they full of the night villages?" Kore had spent most of her evenings in the bath, watching the small glowing village below. The shades moved about their life as if it had not stopped, but only during the night when the shadows gobbled up the realm.

"Yes. All parts of the asphodel fields have villages—as you call them. They live an average life as they did in the mortal realm," he explained.

"Can we walk through the one between the palace and Tartarus? This night? I walked through it the night I came, but I did not stop to look around." She gazed up at him, watching as he chewed over the idea.

"I see no harm in it."

The two made their way to the entrance of a large, ominous, obsidian-carved bridge. Golden basins lined the path, and though Kore could not see the raging flames, she heard them as they passed by.

Beneath them was a drop that Kore could not put a distance to, the bottom masked by a thick, stagnant fog. She thought it was endless, but quickly remembered the valley that ended with a wall and monstrous Cyclopes.

Once they stepped from the bridge, Aidoneus guided Kore to the left and up a new path of steps that led to a small alley between two temples. One, Aidoneus pointed out as the Hall of Judges, where Aeacus, Minos, and Rhadamanthys stayed. Though, Aeacus and Rhadamanthys did most of their work there, while Minos was said to assist Aidoneus in the Judgment Hall.

The other temple, Kore was sure, wasn't occupied. But she didn't have time to investigate long as Aidoneus led her down a second alley until they came to a mountain of steps that appeared to be endless from her position.

"This leads up to the torture chamber I spoke of," he teased with a smile, leading her up.

She reluctantly followed, curious to see the chamber Aidoneus was so happily gifting to her.

By the time they had made it to the top, Kore's legs felt as if they may give out beneath her. She put her hands on her knees and paused for a moment to catch her breath. It was a bit more work than her legs were ready for.

"How much further?" she asked breathlessly.

"We are here," he said with a deep chuckle.

Kore looked up to find a courtyard full of empty marble pots and garden beds. The black pillars, which reached high, held low-hanging vines that had seen better days. Every inch of the court was flooded by the light that was free to spill in. An ideal location for a soon-to-be flourishing oasis.

"'Tis a garden!" Kore shot happily, pushing herself up to get a better view.

"It was built in with the palace, but I have had no use for it. I hoped you could bring life back to it?"

"Back?" she repeated.

"It was a flourishing garden in the beginning. I have more than neglected it. I was hoping you wouldn't be as cruel as I have."

"Aidoneus, you are not cruel." She sighed, turning to face him. "This is beautiful. Your realm is breathtaking. I do not know of one cruel person who could create such beauty."

She intertwined her fingers with his and walked along the path to see more of her new space.

"You can grow anything you would like. If you do not like it, you can do what you must. I thought you would enjoy a place to practice your dual divinity in peace," he informed.

Kore's eyes rounded; she had only heard the term from her dream. She hadn't figured it was a known phrase.

"You mentioned Demeter did not know you had that ability, so I assume she never mentioned dual divinity to you?"

Kore nodded in agreement. "What does it mean?"

"A dual divine is something that most other divines would consider a powerful being. More so than Zeus. There is only one other god with such a power. I do not think it can be compared to your gifts, however," he explained.

"Who?"

Aidoneus's body went rigid as he thought on the answer. Then he turned to her with a smile and continued. "I think that would be a good conversation for another time. For now, you have the freedom to practice all you wish." He held the smile on his face as he guided Kore forward.

She was curious about this new term and the other divine who held the power and why Aidoneus did not want to speak on it any further. It seemed a good topic of discussion given the circumstances.

They walked and looked over the empty pots, a silent stillness resting in them. There was no life growing, but Kore could see that the soil in the beds were dark in color and looked to still be rich with the minerals needed to sustain a garden.

They came up to a series of pillars placed in a circular formation around a stone-guarded pond. The murky green water was filled with algae and tiny, ghostly fish that feasted upon it.

The deeper into the courtyard they walked, the more Kore's heart filled with joy. Aidoneus planned for her to stay, and this gift was more than proof. Her heart felt as if it were ready to burst free from her chest. The tingling radiated through her arms, leaving the familiar burn in its trail.

A soft smell of lavender filled the air, and tiny bits of purple florets began to drift around her, landing in her hair and about her feet and falling into the folds of her robes.

"What is that you are doing?" His handsome smile returned, doing little to help, sending another wave of petals to rain down.

"I am not sure. I think I am just—happy!"

His smile was even bigger than before as he reached his hand up to her but paused and drew back, his smile fading. "I am happy to make your time here as pleasant as possible." There was a slight sadness in his words, and Kore wasn't sure what there was to be sad about. She pushed up on her tiptoes, pressing her lips gently against his cheek.

"Thank you, Aidoneus. I adore all of your gifts," she whispered before pulling away. He warmed beneath her, his face lighting up a dazzling gold.

They made their way around the garden once more, stopping at a bed that was located far in the back, practically hidden by fallen marble and broken columns. The only bed to have something other than soil.

A white, brittle tree with branches that stuck out every which way, with not one leaf to be seen, sat in the center of the dried dirt. The bark cried for water and nourishment; its chalky white texture was not something new to Kore. It had been petrified.

"What is that?" Kore pointed to the bed, feeling Aidoneus tense beside her.

"Do not worry yourself with that one," he responded stiffly.

She waited for more, but he only pressed his lips together as he glared at the bed and the tree within it.

He does not like this tree, she thought, the realization only feeding her interest in it even more.

When he relaxed, they headed into the palace. Kore had a lot of work ahead of her when it came to the garden. The soil was rich enough to plant, but she was concerned with the false sun and its power to give the plants what they needed from it.

They made their way to Aidoneus's chambers, where he called upon Alena and Callisto.

"We will be taking a walk through the villages tonight. See that Kore is dressed for the trip," he ordered.

The nymphs shared a glance before bowing to him and leading Kore off to the bath chambers.

They gave her time to bathe and cleanse herself in private. Returning soon after to dress her in black linen peplos adorned with the Underworld's pin to keep it up at her right shoulder, leaving the other bare.

Callisto combed out Kore's hair and tied it up on top, letting a few curls fall free around her face. The two nymphs looked over her closely before sharing another smile.

"Wonderful!" Callisto cheered with a bright grin.

They guided her out and back into the main chamber, where Aidoneus stood. He wore his regular black chiton with a dark, thin fur tied at his waist. His hair was pulled back from his face and tied at the nape of his neck.

"Would you like your crown?" Alena offered, holding up a black-and-gold crown with thorns and spikes protruding from it.

"That will not be necessary for this trip," he said with a wave of his hand.

He turned to face Kore, his gaze trailing her from head to toe before locking on her face.

He cleared his throat. "You look lovely."

"Thank you." She looked down over her attire and back to him. "You look lovely as well."

He smiled softly and held his arm out to her just as he did in the fields, and she gladly wrapped herself around it.

"You two are relieved for the evening. You may tell the others," Aidoneus said with a snap of his fingers.

In an instant the world around Kore shifted, consuming her in a cloud of smoke. A gust of cool air blew past, sending the smog away, and when it cleared, she found them outside, back in Asphodel Fields just between Tartarus and the palace.

"How come you hadn't done that earlier?" she gasped, catching her breath from the transition.

"I enjoy walking." He chuckled softly.

Her body warmed at the sound, and she couldn't help but laugh along with him.

The sun touched behind the far-off mountains, casting shadows that crawled over the land until they consumed the realm and giving sight to the blue glow of the shades that slowly began to illuminate the field as ghostly temples and huts appeared all around them.

Shades of all sizes and intensities passed by, chatting and greeting each other as mortals normally did. It was only a moment before they took notice of the two divines in their presence, and the few shades nearest quickly bowed.

"My lord, what a surprise!" one said with his head to the ground. He looked up to them, his eyes no longer a mortal hue but a glowing white, his skin a translucent blue. His chest held a glowing orb where his mortal heart used to be.

"Good evening, Othello," Aidoneus greeted pleasantly.

The shade named Othello looked to Kore and quickly bowed again. "My lady!"

Kore wasn't sure what to make of the gesture; the people at the village had never greeted her as they did her mother, mostly because they saw Demeter as a divine, with her glowing skin and ageless face. She had walked that village for years. But Kore had only just gained her divine glow. Nobody saw her as a goddess because nobody knew her as one.

Then again, she wasn't sure if she enjoyed the affection.

She had only just arrived in the Underworld and had no claim to it or its souls and creatures. She looked up to Aidoneus, who seemed content with the shade's gesture.

"Othello, this is Kore. Please see to it that she is treated with the same respect as you show me," he instructed.

Othello bowed once more to the two and carried along on his way. More shades came to greet them, and just as Othello did before, they greeted Kore with a bow and a welcoming smile. Aidoneus greeted each one by name, explained that Kore would be staying, and checked in with their activities for the night.

They walked through the village, watching as the shades traded off goods and chatted amongst themselves as if they hadn't entered the realm of the dead. They didn't fear the king as they did in the mortal realm. They were at peace, happy even, greeting the divines with a smile and a bow as they passed.

Kore stopped at a few stands that had a variety of fabrics and wool. She ran her hand over a bundle of black wool, half expecting for her hand to fall through, but was pleasantly surprised to feel the soft, plush fibers beneath her fingers. She picked it up to examine it more closely. It was merino wool, one of the finest and hardest to obtain.

"This is hard to come by in the mortal realm," she thought aloud.

"If you like it, it would mean a lot to me if you took it, my lady," the shade offered with a smile. She was a small woman with high-set cheeks and a pointy nose.

"Do you spin?" Aidoneus inquired.

"I had started some time ago to take my mind from the plant work. I am not great at it, but it was relaxing." She laughed to herself, placing the bundle of wool down.

"Take it," he ordered.

"I haven't a wheel to spin."

"It is as I have said, while you are here, you are welcome to have what you like." He picked up the bundle and thanked the shade kindly, placing two small, round disks on the table before her. They looked to be coins, but they were black and resembled much of the obsidian throughout the realm.

When the shade caught sight of them, she graciously bowed with heavy thanks.

"What were those?" Kore inquired as they stepped away to the next ghostly stand.

"Obsidian coins. They are similar to obols but harder to come by than this wool. I am not sure what the shades use them for, but I know the coins are highly valued amongst them. They may barter with the other creatures of this place or trade them amongst themselves for other goods. It makes them happy and gives them the sense of normalcy they so long for," he explained.

"You are kind to your people."

"Is that not how a king should be?" He smiled down at her.

"I would like to believe so, but not many mortal kings are this way."

"Not many mortals are this way. At least not until they are judged for those indiscretions in front of others. It is a public cleansing of the miasma they have carried through their mortal life."

Kore had grown learning Aidoneus wasn't what her mother had made him out to be. But she never thought that the quiet, reserved god she had come to know was so full of compassion and care for his people.

"Why do you allow everyone to think so poorly of you? Not just the mortals, but the gods? Have the other divines not seen this beauty?"

"It is no business of mine how the mortals think of me. It only becomes my business when they arrive on the shore of Styx. As for the other divines, they do not venture here. Just as I cannot stay long outside of this realm, they can only stay for a day within it. Only the Chthonian gods can be in here for any amount of time." He turned to her with a questioning gaze.

"Is that why my mother hasn't come for me?" she asked quickly.

He raised his brow. "Yes."

Kore thought about the gods she knew to come and go from the realm. Hermes, an Olympian, was also a Chthonian god. Kore was not—as far as she knew—a Chthonian divine. She was not sure what kind of divine she was, and she had only just learned the term dual divinity.

"Aidoneus?" she breathed.

"Yes?"

"Do you suppose that my dual divinity is why I have been able to stay so long?"

"That is a possibility I have considered." He kept his eyes forward as he spoke, and his voice seemed distant, as if he wasn't answering her question alone.

It was new to him just as it was new to her. Even if he had an idea of what dual divinity meant, he wasn't sure what it meant for those in his realm. If it was the divinity or the power of making and taking life.

They continued the night stopping at each temple and hut for Kore to look over what they offered. The shades all greeted her the same with a kind bow and welcoming smile; they gave thanks to their king and parted happily. It was peaceful, friendly, and kind. She had forgotten she was even in the Underworld until they passed the last glowing temple and made their way back toward the palace.

She wasn't sure if it was the energy of the shades drifting away or if the excitement of the evening had worn off, but her eyelids became heavy, and she fought back a yawn.

"Do you need rest?" he asked.

"Just a bit," she pushed through another deep yawn.

He pulled her into him, engulfing them in smoke. Taking them from the darkness of the fields to the dimly lit chamber as the fire began to die down.

"I will give you your time," he whispered before turning on the balls of his feet and making his way toward the bathing hall, giving her privacy to undress.

CHAPTER XX

THE HIDDEN CHAMBER, THE NYMPH HALL, AND THE HISTORY

"May I take this with me?" Kore asked with a smile, pointing to the few fresh figs on her plate.

"Of course." Aidoneus chuckled softly.

She collected her fruit and danced to his side. "What are your plans for the day?"

Aidoneus had spent most days helping Kore get around, and once she was able, he spent the days showing her his realm.

"I have some Judgments that require my immediate attention today. What of your plans?" Aidoneus wiped his mouth clean from his meal and stood. She had not thought of anything to do or any place to go without his company.

She thought about spending time in her garden, having brought some beds back to life with flourishing plants and herbs, but she hadn't yet toured the whole palace. Besides, she would prefer Aidoneus by her side in the garden, as he had been the last few days.

She wanted to start her spinning, but Aidoneus was having a wheel crafted, and he mentioned that it would take some time before it was ready. The only thing she had left *was* venturing the palace.

She had only seen the few chambers and corridors they routinely traveled, but nothing more.

"I think I may explore the palace. If that is all right?"

"Very well." He smiled before placing his thumb and index finger in his mouth, creating a high-pitched whistle that echoed off the marble around them.

After the ringing cleared, the sound of distant howls rolled through the air in an ominous symphony.

Black mist swirled around the entrance column at a speed faster than Zeus's bolts before stopping at Kore's feet. When the cloud drifted away, Pita was left in its place. His head tilted and his tongue lopped to the side in his apparent smile—if a hound could do such a thing.

Kore ruffled the thick fur between the hound's ears, and he leaned into the touch as his tail pounded against the floor.

"All that show and smoke for a lap hound," Aidoneus scoffed, reaching down and patting Pita along his back. "You've taken the fight out of him."

"Oh no, he is still a vicious war hound! See—" She giggled, bending down so that her face was level with the hound's.

Pulling one corner of her mouth up to bare her teeth, she released a playful growl. Pita jumped, his paws spread and head pulled back. His tail swung from one side to the other, responding with an equally playful grunt.

"Yes, well, this vicious war hound will accompany you. The palace is big and has many halls. Pita is well acquainted with it, should you find yourself lost."

He offered her his arm, and she took it with a grin as he guided her from the hall into a great, long corridor.

Aidoneus bowed to the goddess. "Please call for me if you need. I will hear you." He smiled before turning and walking from the corridor into a side chamber.

"Well, Pita, it is just us now. Where should we go first?"

Her voice was soft as she spoke, but the great hall still echoed her words back.

The hound bumped her hand with his muzzle and walked a few feet in front of her. He paused, turning his head back and waiting for her to join him. A soft giggle escaped her lips as she skipped to his side. She ruffled his ears once more before they walked down the long corridor, Pita leading the way.

Her eyes traveled along the columns, up into their frieze and pediments. Unlike Mt. Olympus, these did not show the Olympians, but the many creatures of the realm. There were winged, four-legged creatures with the head of a man in a crouched stance. One featured a familiar bird-like creature with a woman's face; she, too, was crouched as if ready to pounce on an unsuspecting guest.

They traveled through a few different corridors, some long and wide, while others were short. Some had painted amphoras and pithoi lining the walls, balanced delicately on short black columns, while most were lined with basins of fire.

Kore kept her hand in Pita's fur as she examined the high-up friezes, hardly taking notice of the path they walked as the hound guided her. They turned between two pillars, entering a break-off corridor, one much shorter and darker than the last, with fewer torches along the columns and walls. It led to an enclosed chamber shielded in a deep burgundy tapestry. She examined the fabric, thick and covered in dust.

A cover for something unseen, and she felt she needed to see it. Her hands found an opening between the cloth and the column it hung from.

She pushed the heavy tapestry away and stepped into a low-lit chamber. Pita followed close behind with his nose to the floor as he huffed and sneezed.

Dust that had clung to the tapestry fell free from the movements, tickling her nose and stirring a few sneezes from her as well. She wheezed in the chalky air and looked around the dark area. Possibly one of the only ones she had seen that had no flames cupped in torches and basins. She could make out a kline that looked to be identical to the one in Aidoneus's chamber. Large but covered in white furs that held a thick layer of dust.

Across from it sat a table carved of a shiny black crystal with tiny white spots scattered about it. A dust-covered slab of polished obsidian sat atop the table with various aryballoi and alabastra scattered around.

She slid her finger across the smooth surface, leaving a trail in the dust and creating a small pile at the end. The chamber was not one used often—most likely for guests who had never visited, nor planned to. She found it strange Aidoneus had not mentioned or given her this chamber in the beginning, instead, allowing her to take up his kline while he slept in another only a few feet away.

A soft flutter swarmed her stomach at the thought of him wanting her closer than this chamber would allow.

Pita sniffed around another part of the tapestry, ears erect as he focused on something on the other side. He whined and whimpered before ducking his head under the thick fabric and crawling free from the chamber. Kore ran after, smoothing the fabric out with her hands in search of an opening she wasn't finding.

The hound popped his head under the tapestry once again, puffed out air through his nose, and pulled his head back under. Kore ducked down, lifting the tapestry with one hand and following close behind.

Pita sat patiently waiting with his tail thumping hard against the marble floor, sending more dust into the air. He tilted his head to her and let his tongue lop out once again. The dust tickled her nose, releasing another small fit of sneezes. She wheezed in the dry air in an attempt to collect herself.

"What did you find here?" she huffed between breaths. The area they entered was slim, wide enough for one, with a low-hanging ceiling. Aidoneus was much too tall and wide set to fit in such a narrow space, but Kore and Pita fit perfectly.

She allowed Pita to take the lead, giving her a quick and easy way out if she needed to turn and run for any reason. The hound seemed to know where he was headed and trotted along, his tail swaying from one side to the other. He seemed to have picked up the smell of something and began to quicken his stride.

"Pita, wait!" She shot after him, but he continued to gain speed before darting around a corner. Kore followed, now at a run to keep up, turning down the same corridor and crashing into the hound, stumbling into a marble wall.

A dead end.

The goddess struggled to her feet—groaning at the pain—but Pita seemed unfazed by the collision as he licked at her hand. She giggled, looking at the wall that halted them.

The hound sniffed and huffed along the base of it, pawing and digging at something unseen. Kore leaned over to get a better look, pressing her hand against its cool surface. She knocked loose a piece of sheet marble from the wall, causing it to fall flat on the floor with a loud shatter as it broke into tiny pieces. The hole it left allowed bright light to flood into the small, dark space.

A pleasant mixture of honey and rose filled the air. It was sweet, warm, and smelled of women. A lovely reminder of her nymphs back at the meadow.

Pita shot through the hole, leaving Kore in the small, dark space.

"Pita!" she cried out, crawling through after him.

She entered a short but wide corridor, with white-and-gold marble floors. The columns that surrounded them were also white with shimmering gold streaks twining through. Much different than that of the rest of the palace and even the realm. With whites, pinks, and golds, it looked more open and livelier.

She turned to look at one end and found a beautiful golden door. A black basin sat to the left with a low fire that wasn't needed. The space was already brightly lit despite the lack of torches or fires to illuminate it.

Pita made a deep, rumbling growl, his teeth bared as he took steps to the opposite side. The door on that end was far less wonderous than the last, having been damaged at some point, broken down, and torn to pieces. Parts of the white marble were blackened with soot from a mighty fire that burned some time ago. The door was blocked by planks of wood, large bits of broken marble sculptures, and chunks of enormous obsidian rock—and more lay piled against the mess.

Kore remembered the Cyclopes and the crafted wall that blocked the river. The hall the nymph had spoken of was real. She had been truthful about at least that; she just neglected to mention the creatures that were blocked from it, and for great reason. The thought of the lampades nymphs having to battle the Cyclopes sent a chill down Kore's spine.

"Come on, Pita, let us go," she said, patting the hound, and they turned back to the golden doors.

Musical laughter rang from inside as the nymphs enjoyed their time. Kore lifted her hand and pounded against the gold.

"Oh! Who could that be?" a soft voice called, quickly followed by a wave of frantic shushing.

"It is Kore," she called back to them.

"Kore!" a familiar voice echoed. The door clicked before slowly creaking open, and Kore was greeted by two flickering red eyes.

"Hello, Kore! Pleasant surprise seeing you," Alena greeted.

Pita squeezed through and bounded into the chamber, causing a wave of harmonic giggles from the other nymphs. Alena welcomed Kore with a hug and following bow. She pulled her into the hall, shutting the door behind them. There was a second click as she locked the door once more.

Kore looked around the chamber, which was round like the others but less spacious, with several klines lined up along the marble walls on either side. The wall across from the door had been carved out, opening it up to the calm waters at the mouth of Acheron.

At the center of it all sat a raging blue flame that danced in a large stone pit. Around it were several small stools carved from rock and crystal, and upon them sat several nymphs. Some Kore had already met, and some were new to her, but they all smiled and bowed their heads kindly.

Chryseis sat closest to Kore, her cheeks and nose tinted red against her pale skin. Next to her sat Eleni, sister to Alena. They looked nearly identical, but Alena was shorter, and Eleni had longer hair. Kore had only spoken with her one time over the week, a quick passing as Aidoneus walked her through the palace.

"Kore, you know Chryseis and Eleni here. Callisto is fetching drinks at the moment, but she will be along. These two, however, have been busy with their work—haven't you, ladies?" Alena chided.

"Yes! Oh, yes!" one chirped, dancing around to their side. Her creamy white hair framed her face with large ringlet curls. Just like the other lampades nymphs, she had flickering fire red burning in her eye, but the other was a deep watery blue.

"Kore this is Elpida. She is a Gemini nymph," Alena introduced.

"A Gemini nymph?"

"She is of two different nymphs put into one. A lampades and a nereid powering one vessel," the second unnamed nymph informed in a flat tone.

A lampades nymph who looked much different than the others. Elpida's hair was snow white and stuck out in every direction, with leaves and twigs tangled and twisted in her strands. The others seemed more cleaned up.

Kore noted that the other nymphs had only soot-coated fingers, but this one had soot-stained fingers, hands, and wrists, fading further up her arms and onto her chest.

"And this is Agatha. She spends a lot of time with our

fair Lady Hecate. When she is not busy in the Judgment Hall." Alena looked at Agatha and then Elpida and lastly Eleni. "In fact, are you not all needed?"

"Oh! We are going to be late!" Elpida cried. "Lord Hades won't be happy," she said but in a lower, less cheerful-sounding voice.

"Hush now, Gemini. Let us be on our way. Quickly," Agatha said as she walked to the door and waited for the two other nymphs to join her. Elpida and Eleni said their goodbyes to Kore and dashed up to join Agatha.

"Where must they go?" Kore asked Alena. She watched as Agatha snapped her blackened fingers, and the three nymphs vanished from sight.

"They have shades to escort to their places here in the Underworld. They help bring them peace on their crossing to their final phase," Alena explained.

She took Kore by the hand and guided her to the pit to sit. Kore's attention was on Pita, who ran playfully through the sand outside the opening on a small beach. Marble stones led from the hall out where lapping waves from Acheron played.

"Do you all have duties?" Kore inquired as they both took seats on the cool stone. She was surprised at how cool the area felt despite the fire blazing before them.

"Oh no. Only if we choose to. Those who do not are free to go about their days."

"You choose to work?" Kore hadn't meant for her words to sound as harsh as they did, but they didn't seem to affect Alena. She simply smiled and looked at Chryseis, who followed with a soft giggle.

They were soon interrupted as the fire began to crack and pop wildly; the flames rose and turned an intense blue shade. The fire hissed and crackled again, spitting flames and ash their way.

A shape formed, pushing through the flames like a thin barrier until a small woman emerged in a thick flare that disconnected from the main fire. She walked a few feet from the pit, her flaming body shaking and rippling away to reveal sweet Callisto with two amphoras in each arm and a smile upon her bright face.

"*Kalimera sta Archaia*!" Callisto sang when she caught sight of Kore.

She walked to a low table near the opening in the far wall and began pouring the liquid from the amphora into four kantharoi.

"Hello," Kore greeted with a smile. She soon turned back to Alena and waited for the conversation to continue.

"Um—oh yes. Some of us choose to work because of all that our king has granted us. Before him, our ancestors were left to tend these barren and frightful lands. Facing cruel and senseless creatures daily. He gave them this hall in the beginning," Alena explained.

"The beginning?" Kore echoed.

"Before he was king. Before the palace and fields, it was only Tartarus, the rivers, nymphs, and creatures. But then he drew this lot, and when he created his palace, he created this hall to keep us safe."

"Could you imagine if the draw had been fair, and we got Poseidon or worse—Zeus as our king?" Chryseis laughed, and Alena shot her a fixed look.

"Fair?" Kore echoed again.

Alena cleared her throat and shot Chryseis another vengeful look before turning back to Kore with a soft smile. "Some of the other gods, specifically Hecate, think that Zeus and Poseidon set up the draw so that Lord Hades would get the Underworld."

"Purely out of jealousy and pride, if you ask me," Chryseis added.

"How do you mean?" Kore asked.

Callisto joined them with the kantharoi and passed them around.

Chryseis leaned closer to Kore. "Lord Hades is the oldest of The Six Greats. But he was the last to be reborn from

Cronus. Some think that is the reason he stopped aging long before his brothers, leaving them a great deal older in appearance," she said, her voice just above a whisper.

"It has been rumored that they grew drunk with jealousy. Rage even. So, they sent him here, gave him very little time in the mortal realm, and allowed the mortals to craft their own depiction of him."

"When *did* he stop aging?" Kore pushed.

"Hm, I *think* it was around the twenty-sixth, possibly twenty-seventh year. Nobody is sure. He isn't too open about it."

"Nobody knows if that is all true, Chryseis. It is not kind to spread possible lies on our king," Alena warned.

"*Possible* lies. However, Hecate can see things the Fates cannot, and I believe in her premonitions," Chryseis said in a matter-of-fact tone.

"Even so, if that were true, would we have wanted a fair draw and risked getting one of the other brothers? We are extremely fortunate for all we have." Alena shrugged. Chryseis and Callisto nodded their heads in agreeance.

"We would not be given the same privileges, possibly would have been made to leave the palace grounds, or gods know what," Alena finished.

"Leave palace grounds?" Kore repeated.

The nymph pressed her lips flat as she thought of what to say.

"We do not leave the grounds because it is not safe. Only Agatha ever ventures off the grounds—but that is because she shifts to Hecate's cavern; she does not walk the fields. We are safe here," Chryseis interjected.

Kore remembered the nymph from the river, the one who had led her into a trap. She had not been bound by this rule. "What about the nymph in the river of Acheron? Minthe?"

CHAPTER XXI

THE STORY, THE ELIXIR, AND THE NYMPH NO ONE LIKES

"Minthe?" Alena shot. Chryseis hissed, and Callisto choked on her wine. They gaped at the goddess with wide eyes.

"How do you know of her?" Alena's voice was desperate.

"She led me to the Cyclopes."

"Of course she did!" Chryseis hissed again.

"Hush now!" Alena snapped.

Kore had not heard Alena sound negative or angry before. She had not seen any nymph angry before, and this was a first. However, this was not the first time she had seen negative reactions to the nymph's name.

"Did she wrong you in some way?" Kore pressed.

The nymph had undoubtedly wronged Kore, but why did everyone else feel so much hatred toward her?

"She just is not—a very nice nymph." Alena sighed, releasing her anger and calming herself in one deep exhale.

"Try vile and cruel," Callisto added. "She'd do anything to keep anybody away from Lord Hades."

A deep hissing noise came from the back of Alena's throat. It was frightening, feral as if Callisto had been prey. Her eyes narrowed on the nymph, and Callisto dropped her head.

Alena cleared her throat and looked back to Kore with softer eyes. "Perhaps you would want to ask Lord Hades about Minthe. It is not our place to say." The gentle nymph sighed, patting Kore's hand.

There was a twist in her stomach, and Kore felt she may have already guessed why she needed to ask Aidoneus about the nymph—why Minthe would keep anyone from him and why everyone seemed to know of her.

Just because there had not been word of Aidoneus having a partner didn't mean he hadn't had one. That he had never been with a woman. Who would even know when they hardly spoke of him?

Kore felt silly. She hadn't thought he would have endured so long without. Who would? Kore was having a hard time herself, and she had never even experienced such feelings.

Of course Aidoneus had been with women. He had lived lifetimes before Kore had even been born.

"Has he ever taken a wife?" She breathed softly.

Alena looked at the others and slightly shook her head to keep them from speaking—and that was answer enough. Kore dropped her eyes, not sure why she felt upset. She had no right to him or to be upset at what he did with his existence before her.

Perhaps she was hurt that he had not told her when she asked back at the meadow. Now that she thought on it, he hadn't said no—but she had only focused on the fact he had not said yes. Her stomach knotted again, and she felt the bile rise in her throat.

"Do not think too much on it, my lady." Alena cupped her hand over Kore's again. She offered a soft, reassuring smile before taking a sip from the kantharos in her hand, scrunching her face at it. “Callisto! We said the light wine!”

Chryseis was already finishing hers off without a care. “I brought both! I only poured this one for fun. Are you ready?”

“We are going to brew moon milk. It is a special elixir we like to drink on nights of the full moon,” Alena explained, swiftly changing the topic.

Kore did not mind. She had heard enough for now and wanted to take her mind from it. The familiar drink seemed to be a good distraction.

Her mother had made moon milk when she was younger. They would warm goat’s milk with lavender or chamomile and a drizzle of honey. It had been one of her childhood favorites when she needed help sleeping. It was something she had enjoyed doing with her mother that did not involve plants. However, she had never heard of it being made with wine.

“Does wine mix well with goat’s milk?” she asked innocently.

The three nymphs shared glances before falling into a fit of laughter.

“Sorry, Lady Kore,” said Alena. “We do not mean to laugh. Forgive us. We do not add milk of the goat or the cow to our mix. It is milk of the poppy that we add, a powerful relaxant. Would you like us to show you how to craft it?” Kore had not learned much about the poppy plant while with her mother. She did know it was often used to dull pain among the mortals, but its effects on the divine were still a topic to master.

“I would be pleased if you did!” she answered.

They made their way to a table that was lined with tools and ingredients.

“Agatha taught us how to make it; the only upsetting part is we must let it sit until nightfall. She claims it makes it stronger, and who am I to argue?” Chryseis gathered a mortar and pestle and a handful of poppy flowers. She handed them to Callisto before taking her place with Alena.

Callisto joined Kore and filled the bottom of the mortar

with a few of the poppy flower heads, mashing them with the pestle. She worked until the heads were nothing more than a small amount of powder and then added more heads and repeated the process until the mortar was full. She dumped it into a pile and handed the set and a few more flower heads to Kore. Meanwhile, Alena and Chryseis were busy pouring the second liquid into an iron pot.

Kore finished her task and handed off the powder to Callisto, who was working away and mixing the powder she had ground with a small amount of water. She took the powder from Kore and dumped it into her mix and continued stirring. When it reached a thick consistency, she moved it over to the iron pot, and Chryseis began to stir it all together.

Alena and Callisto took a place on each side of the pot and lifted it from the table. Sidestepping their way to the pit, they set it on the hot rocks at its center. The fire licked at their legs and arms, but the nymphs were unbothered.

Chryseis stirred the mixture until the milk was boiling and thick, and the faint whiff of citrus drifted in the air around them. When it was time to remove it from the heat, they carried it back to the table to cool and rest.

The nymphs then set an alternating schedule of who would stir the pot and when, as the mixture needed to be stirred frequently.

"It will solidify and spoil if we do not," Alena explained.

They passed time on the steps leading out to the sand and water. Kore watched as Pita ran and splashed near the shore that was concealed by the high climbing rocks.

The nymphs shared stories of their day, during their time aiding Kore when she slept off her injuries. A lot of sponge baths and bandage dressing. The screaming match between Aidoneus and Thanatos. Alena ended up having to escort Thanatos from the palace because it had gotten so bad.

"I thought he might rip him in two. We know all too well what happens when Thanatos is gone. Probably the most unorganized the Underworld had ever been, backed up on shade judgments and all."

"What happened to him?" Kore gasped.

"He had been tricked and imprisoned. Serves him right, really. He always thinks he is so bright. But he is not, and because of his hubris, our king had to roam the mortal realm and help collect and gather souls. Leaving judgments for the late evenings."

"It was awful!" Callisto cried.

They shared more stories of the true Underworld history Kore had longed for since she was just a child learning of Aidoneus. About the kind and caring king who elicited an unwarranted amount of fear from the mortals. She asked why he did not try harder to change their views, but Alena said that Aidoneus hadn't the time to prove to the mortals that he was a good god, when he was busy being a caring king to his people. It was an understandable answer.

When she thought of it that way, it made sense. He did not seem much interested in changing the minds of the divine who already had their set views as well. A view Kore never had when it came to Aidoneus.

The sun began to kiss the tips of the distant mountains, and Callisto took that as a sign to try the moon milk. They gathered around the pot, and Alena spooned the drink into each vessel until they near overflowed. Kore sipped the excess; the sweet liquid warmed her from the inside out. Her face grew hot and tingly, glowing a bright gold from the flooded ichor under her cheeks.

"Oh!" Chryseis panted. She had taken a few small, slow sips before gulping it down as quickly as she could.

Alena had mentioned it was a monthly drink to be consumed under a full moon, but no other information, leaving Kore unsure of the desired intent. All she was sure of was that the liquid was a relaxant, and it did just that.

As the warmth of the drink radiated through Kore's body, she felt a numbness trickle down to the tips of her fingers and toes. She pulled her hand up to her face, struggling a bit with the sudden amount of weight pressing down on it.

She wiggled each finger one by one, opening and closing her hand and pressing her fingers together. All of which she could not feel, not entirely anyway. She could see them move about, giving her the feeling that they were there, but they were numb. She rolled her head back, light from the elixir. Her foot slid forward, just enough feeling in it for her to walk. She gathered herself, holding her hands out, and hesitantly made her way to the stools by the pit.

She sat with her hands pressed hard into the stone for support as the world spun around her.

"Are you well, Kore?" Callisto asked, walking to Kore's side. The nymph waited patiently, taking her spot on the seat next to the goddess.

"I—I cannot feel my fingers," Kore whispered, placing her focus back on her hand.

"That is normal. The first time is always very sensational. Once the feeling comes back, that is."

"When will that be?"

"Hm, not too long, I suppose. It is different for everyone." Callisto shrugged.

Kore dropped her hand and looked out onto the ocean. Darkness cast out around them, the stars reflecting off the calm, watery surface of Acheron.

Nothing could be heard but the soft waves washing against the stones and the loud popping from the fire beside them.

Even Pita rested peacefully on the cool marble floor, taking in the warmth from the fire and the brisk ocean breeze. Salty mist collected in Kore's hair, weighing her already heavy locks down, and dampening her robes, causing them to cling to her skin.

The moon made her way into the sky above them—a

bright, white, glowing ball near identical to that of Selene's, only Kore noticed this one was white no matter its phase. Selene had always tinted her moon in different shades of white, reds, and creams. She was fond of red most often. But this false moon remained white, only changing its phase as the real moon did.

A loud crackling filled the chamber, breaking the peaceful sound of waves and quiet. Three streams of black mist swirled into the chamber, two landing by the iron pot of moon milk and one landing in front of Kore and Callisto.

"No fair! You three always start the ritual without us!" a voice cried before the smoke cleared, leaving the three nymphs from earlier in their traces.

Elpida and Eleni appeared by the pot, and Agatha morphed from the smoke before Kore and Callisto.

"There is still plenty left," Chryseis huffed, rolling her eyes and grabbing three more kantharoi from the small wooden box.

"Lady Kore! You are still here!" Eleni cheered, filling up her kantharos and quickly taking the first sip.

"Lord Hades will want her back soon," Agatha said in a flat tone. "He appeared distracted today."

Kore wobbled to her feet. "Is it late?" she slurred.

"I see you were generous with the moon milk." Agatha sighed.

The three nymphs smiled unapologetically.

"I will take her back," Agatha said, extending her hand to Kore.

Pita quickly woke from his slumber and bounded to Kore's side. He leaned against her, head tilted, tongue out and ready to depart the chamber.

"Ready?" the nymph asked as Kore took her hand.

"Ready," Kore slurred, prepared for the shifting of the hall, but unprepared for the sickening feeling in her stomach as it flipped and turned. She stumbled forward, bracing herself against the kline.

"What is this?" Aidoneus's thunderous voice rumbled.

Kore wasn't sure if he was angry or concerned, but he wasn't happy.

"It would appear that the others have shown her the delights of moon milk," Agatha informed.

"I—I asked," Kore slurred with a soft giggle.

"That will be all, Agatha."

Agatha bowed and disappeared into a cloud of smoke.

"Pita." His voice was still rigid, and the hound snapped to attention. "Be gone with you."

Pita immediately vanished, racing from the chambers.

Aidoneus walked over to Kore's side, looking her over for a moment. He pulled his brows together, pinching the skin between them.

"You had a bit more excitement than I expected," he said in a flat tone.

"I stumbled upon—on the nymphs hall."

"Did you?"

"Yes," she chirped; her mind reeled with the whole day's events.

She had many questions, from the unused chamber to the nymph named Minthe. Was that chamber hers at one point? Was it his wife's?

"Who is—is Minthe?" The words slurred together and fell from her mouth just as quickly as the thought sprang to her mind.

Aidoneus's body flexed and his jaw set hard. His eyes locked with hers and his nostrils flared, but he did not speak.

"She was the one who—who put me on the trail to the Cyclopes. The Erinyes know of her and . . ." Her voice trailed off. She did not want to get the lampades in trouble.

His breathing grew deeper, moving his shoulders with each breath as he waited, but she was silent.

"And?" he hissed through his teeth.

Whoever this nymph was, she stirred an emotion in him. He was angry.

"I was told that I should ask you of her?"

He exhaled, fanning his heated breath across her face. Fire and cypress and ash.

"She is nothing to be concerned with. If she sent you to the Cyclopes, she will be punished." His voice fell low and heated.

"You—you would punish your old lovers?"

His brows pulled down more, his eyes dark. "She was not a *lover*."

"A hetaira then," she slurred again.

His lips pulled down. "What?"

"Or was she your consort?" Kore tilted her head to the side as she watched him through hooded lids.

"I see the nymphs shared more than moon milk with you."

"Will you not tell me? I feel I have—have a right to know. Being she tried to kill me."

"Right now is not the proper time to have such a talk. You are not in the right state," he began. "I will deal with the nymph that tricked you. You need not worry."

"How—how so?"

"How do you mean?"

"How are you going to deal with her? How—how you used to deal with her—"

His eyes were on her as she sat, her hand sliding up the fabric of his chiton until her fingers brushed against the skin at his hip.

"Would it be so wrong if you dealt with me—in the same manner?" she whispered.

"Kore," he groaned, grabbing her wrist and pulling it free from him. "You do not know what you are asking."

He dropped her hand and marched from the chamber.

"You should sleep," he called back without a second glance as he vanished from view. Leaving Kore alone with her racing thoughts.

CHAPTER XXII

THE NYMPH NAMED MINTHE, THE NYMPH NAMED LEUCE, AND THE LONELY GOD

Kore hovered over the empty plot of soil in the furthest part of her garden. She had skipped breakfast, still angry with Aidoneus from the night before. The moon milk allowed her to remember every bit of the evening despite it feeling like she had been drunk from wine. She did not like how he refused to answer her questions, nor that he left her alone in the chamber all night, never returning to his separate kline.

She violently moved her hands in the soil, gripping and yanking at any dead roots she felt. Clearing the spot for her vines. His words replayed in her mind. If the nymph had not been a lover, then why would she attempt to keep Kore from him? How did she already know of Kore to begin with?

Her energy raged like a flame, ripping down her arm and flooding into the soil at the thought. Calling to her vines.

Why could he not just tell her of the nymph? It hurt her to think about him with another, but she could not allow herself to believe he went without for so long.

She tore her hands free, sending soil into the air. The bed began to rumble as the vibrations from the vines came on strong and erratic. They crept slowly at first, snaking from the dirt and climbing up the shattered column that sat just behind the plot. They twitched and jerked around the broken bits of marble, squeezing a chunk until cracks filled the air and it burst with a loud pop. Small bits of debris and dust fell to the ground around her feet.

She held her hand out to graze the thick of the vine, and it moved into her touch. The warmth of the energy pulsated through it like a heartbeat.

"I see you have been practicing with them." His voice was low, withdrawn in a way. Kore didn't turn to him. She drew the vines back until they were out no more than a foot from the soil.

"Are you not hungry?" he inquired, joining her at her side.

She could feel his eyes on her, but she still did not turn. Unsure if it was from anger or her embarrassment, or both. She moved to the next bed, one she had filled with yellow coneflowers.

She brushed her fingers across the petals. Their colors brightened and the petals grew full at her touch.

She was angry he had not been honest with her. She had not been completely honest in her reason for coming, but being wed and fleeing marriage were two different things to hide.

She moved on to the next bed without a word. Aidoneus followed along, his eyes still on her.

"She is a nymph I used to have in the palace for—entertainment," he began.

Though she knew what form of entertainment he had meant, she did not like being spoken to in riddles as if she were still too young to understand.

"Please, Aidoneus. I am not a child, no need for fancy words." She motioned her hands over the flower heads, drawing forth the same magic as before. Brightening their colors and growing their petals.

"If she was your lover, you can say that. I do not expect

you to not have had a lover. I cannot expect you to not have a lover even now. I just—" She paused, her eyes falling to her hands.

Did she even want to know if Minthe was his lover—did she need to hear him say it? The thought of him lying with the nymph in the same kline he allowed Kore to stay in sent her belly into flips.

No. She did not need to hear him say it. "You need not explain yourself," she finished with a half-smile.

She moved down to the next bed, sweeping her hands over the poppy flowers.

"That may be so. But I may be the reason she sent you to the Cyclopes. So, you see, I am afraid I do have to explain." He dropped his shoulders, defeated. Kore waited, moving her hands over the stems and leaves of the poppy flowers.

"Minthe lived in the palace in her own chamber for a while. Providing me with . . . comforts I was unable to find elsewhere." He paused, looking over Kore and her reaction, but she kept her eyes on her hands, her stomach feeling as if it were being torn from her as he spoke.

"I had her leave some time ago," he finished.

The chamber covered in dust came to mind, and she finally turned to him.

"Was that her chamber? The one that is not lit by flames and closed off by tapestry." She watched as his arms tensed and his chest stilled. She waited, but he gave no verbal answer. She turned to the next bed.

"That was Leuce's," he said softly.

Kore spun around, locking eyes with him. She opened her mouth to ask who Leuce was, but words did not come.

"She was my wife," he said, dropping his head.

Kore felt her heart drop to the pit of her stomach. "*Wife?*"

His lips twisted and his eyes cast down. "It was not long. Which was best."

"Did you love her?"

He shook his head. "Do you recall the trade I told you of during our last visit? The mortal who had traded her soul for her love?"

"Yes."

"I didn't give you the truth then. The mortal was a nymph. She did offer her soul for a mortal's; that part was true. But there was more to it. I had to agree to the trade—her life for his, but with the condition that if he did not love her in return, she would be my wife."

Kore gasped, her eyes wide as she watched and waited.

"I needed a queen, Kore. At the time it did not matter if we had love for one another or not."

"So, you trapped her?"

"I did not. She agreed to the terms. She knew the consequences of the arrangement. Though, she did not expect to find the mortal with another woman. Being wife to the God of the Underworld was not what she wanted and—" He paused, swallowing thickly. "A week after, Minthe found her in Acheron."

"She took her own life because of the agreement?" Kore spat.

In a way, she felt sympathy for Leuce, a sort of common ground and understanding. An arranged marriage she wanted no part of, and sadly it ended in her untimely death. Aidoneus fisted his hands and his brows pulled down low over his eyes but said nothing.

Perhaps he was no different than his brothers after all. He read the scrolls of each mortal; he said so himself. Every past sin, every future path they had before they passed on and their string was cut.

"You knew," she whispered.

"What?"

"You knew. You knew what he would do once returned," she accused.

His face twisted, bringing back his deep scowl and cold, hard expression.

"Souls cannot be brought back without dealing with the Fates," he said flatly.

She felt the air squeeze from her. He had known the mortal would run to another. He had tricked the nymph, as most gods were known to do.

As his brothers were known to do.

"You are cruel." She spun on her heels, shielding her eyes as the pressure of tears poured through.

She moved forward, but his fingers slipped around her wrist and pulled her back to him. He wrapped his arm securely around her waist, anchoring her to him. She gasped out against it and attempted to pull away with no success.

"I am cruel?" he growled. "Have I been so cruel to you?"

"No," she breathed, "but how can you say you are any different than my father or Poseidon when you treat women just the same?" She pulled at her arm in an attempt to free herself, but his hand tightened around her wrist.

"I have given you the freedom to leave whenever you choose. You may leave if you feel I am so cruel," he offered, his face set hard—like stone. She squeezed her eyes shut, the tears spilling freely as she pushed against him.

"Do you want to leave?" he pushed again.

She shook her head.

"No? You choose to stay with someone so cruel?" he barked. She shook her head again, unsure how to answer. "No? Then what do you want, Kore? Why are you here?"

She couldn't lie anymore; she couldn't keep it a secret, not now.

The tears poured down her face as she struggled to form the words, but when her eyes met his, she felt a heavy pull in her chest that rose to her throat and from her lips.

"I was to be Ares's bride. His gift from Zeus . . . and my mother." She sobbed, tears still trailing down her cheeks.

"I thought if I came down here, my mother would not follow, and Ares would not know. At the time, when I heard of the engagement—I thought, even death would be a better fate."

His eyes widened as he listened, and she continued.

"Divines cannot die. So, I thought of the next best thing. I enjoyed our visits, looked forward to the next time you would appear in my mother's meadow. The day I learned of their arrangement was the day I learned I was a tradeable good to them."

He was silent for a moment, his eyes searching hers. He pulled her up to his chest. His warmth wrapping around her like thick furs.

"You asked if I loved her." The air around them shifted, growing dark as her plants and flowers disappeared and were replaced by tall, wild trees.

"And my answer is *no*. That is the truth—but I did not lie when I said I am responsible for every soul in my realm." He tugged Kore along the base of the trees on a fine narrow path, one that looked to be often walked. The trees were unfamiliar to her. Their thin white trunks led up to a branch of webs sprouting green leaves. Small white flowers floated above, some sweeping down to the ground and dancing with the leaves and twigs.

They climbed a small hill until stopping at the largest tree she had seen in the area.

"Where are we?" She huffed, struggling to catch her breath after the climb.

"Leuce Island." He pulled Kore in front of him, placing her between him and the great tree. His lips were just at her ear as he spoke.

"Leuce's death is one I carry with me. I did not feel anything for her, but when she died, there was . . . guilt. Guilt that kept me up for days. So I crafted her this—a memorial to her life. An apology." He paused; his hand slid down Kore's arm until it met her hand.

He extended them forward and grazed Kore's fingers against the low-hanging leaves. "I do not wish that for you. That is why you are free to go." The heat of his breath against her ear sent a shudder down her back.

"As for Minthe, she was cruel—that is why I sent her away. I would have cast her from this realm had I known she would have meant to harm you," he said, dropping their hands.

The air around them shifted again, filling the space with blackness. The sweet pine smell soon changed to the heavy mix of flowers from the garden.

"Your mother and Ares cannot touch you here. Zeus cannot touch you here. You are free to stay as long as you please—as I have said, you are no prisoner." He turned her so that she was facing him, his eyes distant. "I have some business to attend to at the moment; however, you may carry on with your practice. We will speak on this matter later." He released Kore's hand and quickly vanished into a dark cloud.

Kore stared at the smoke, her eyes locked on the space even after it cleared. The dry air finally rushing free from her.

I did not love her. His words repeated in her head. He may have said he did not love her, though Kore did not care if he did one way or another. If he had, that only meant he was capable of it. He could love again if he wanted.

He had crafted a whole island of trees for her. Though Kore still wasn't sure of the tree type or its significance to Leuce, she felt it only right to learn more of it. To spend time in the space and speak with the trees.

She turned back to the small, empty bed, and for once since being gifted the garden, she hadn't any idea what to grow.

CHAPTER XXIII

THE GARDEN, THE THRONE, AND THE SCROLLS

Aidoneus had kept his distance the last few days, staying mainly in the Judgment Hall. Kore felt it was because he was unsure of how she felt. She had had time to think about their discussion of Minthe and his wife, and she had moved on. It was a past before he had known she existed—it did not feel just in her heart to hold it against him. After all, he did not kill Leuce, and from the looks of it, whether he did love her or not, he cared deeply for her and felt responsible for her death. Not a sign of a cruel individual.

Perhaps the time he gave her was needed. She had no reason to call him cruel, especially after all he had done for her.

She swallowed thickly at the thought.

With him providing time, it left Kore to her pleasures and practices, spending more and more days in her garden.

Which also gave her more time to plan. If she could get the plants thick enough, she could disguise her work with the petrified tree. She wanted time to study it and had been ignoring it while she plumped up the rest of the plants and flowers.

After her morning rounds, she made her way to the lifeless tree. It sat unchanged and unmoved. She had tried only once to push energy into it, but with no success. She pressed her palm against it, and dry, splintered pieces fell into the soil. There was no life to absorb, no energy to harness or reform. She couldn't even force it to wilt or break down and clear the space.

A stubborn tree, but Kore felt that the remains were no match for her regardless.

"What were you?" she whispered, circling the bed as she inspected every inch.

"Lady Kore?" Callisto entered the garden from the side stone path; in her hands, she had a kantharos of nectar and a platter of sliced figs.

"Lord Hades sends his apologies about this morning. He wanted to start the Judgments early today. He asked that I bring these to you," she said softly as she placed the kantharos and platter on the edge of the garden bed.

As Kore had figured, she rolled her eyes with a smile.

"Thank you, Callisto," she muttered, locking her eyes on the tree again. Callisto followed her gaze, her lips turning down instantly.

"Do you know of this tree?" Kore quizzed.

"Me? No, I do not. It has been here since I was born. I do believe Agatha would know of it," the small nymph offered.

Kore flashed her a bright smile. "Please bring her for me. Let Lord Hades know I will send her back."

Callisto said nothing more as she vanished into her cloud.

Kore walked over to the kantharos and platter, plucking a fig slice and mindlessly nibbling at it as she thought on the tree before her. She took a deep sip of the nectar and proceeded around the bed.

After some time, two black clouds drifted near, stopping

at her side. Once the clouds cleared, the two highly different nymphs appeared. Callisto held a sweet smile on her lips, while Agatha remained emotionless.

Callisto was always a joy to be near, with a soft, sweet grin constantly present upon her lips. But Agatha always looked to be in a bad mood, far more serious about her tasks than the others.

"Yes?" her cold voice droned.

"Good morning, Agatha!" Kore greeted. "I was just wondering if you would happen to know of this tree here?" She lifted her hand to the petrified wood beside them. Agatha inhaled deeply, her eyes shooting from the tree to Kore and back again.

She nodded once.

"Can you tell me of it? What—well, what is it exactly?"

"It was a flourishing pomegranate tree," Agatha said slowly.

"Pomegranate?" Kore echoed.

"'Tis a fruit that only grows here."

"Are there no other trees like it?"

"Yes, dear," a light voice sang from behind her.

Kore spun on her heels to find another divine standing just a few feet away from them.

Her skin glowed a deep gold in the shadows. She held her hands, palm to palm, across her chest with long, draping sleeves. Her jet-black hair fell in waves down her back.

The divine pulled her lips up into a lovely smile as she bowed to the group.

"Hello, Lady Hecate!" Callisto cheered with a returning smile and bow.

"Good morning, sweet Callisto!" Hecate greeted.

Kore had heard very few stories about the goddess Hecate. She knew she worked a great deal with spirits, but that was the most Demeter gave. Any stories involving any divine of the Underworld were always cut short.

"Lady Hecate," Agatha greeted with a low bow. Hecate

made her way to the three, her smile never fading.

"I must be heading back now," Agatha informed before quickly disappearing into her smoke and drifting away.

"H-Hello," Kore greeted shyly.

"Hello, Lady Kore. I am sorry I am so late to introduce myself. I have had a busy few weeks in the mortal realm. I do hope you can forgive me!" Hecate said warmly.

"'Tis fine, Lady Hecate," Kore assured.

"Oh, please call me Hecate." She looked back to the bed. "I hear you have inquiries about this pomegranate tree?"

"Yes, I wanted to bring it back. But it seems to have no life left and will not allow me to wilt it down." Kore pouted in frustration, then gazed back at the ornery tree.

"You say you cannot wilt it?" Hecate questioned.

"I have the ability to draw the life from the plants, which wilts them, and I can harness that energy and recreate it. I have not been successful with this one because it lacks a life force I need."

"That would make sense. What was it you wanted to know about it?"

"I was wondering if there was another tree just like it that I may draw from. You mentioned that there is," Kore said.

"There is a tree that sisters this one, yes, but are you so sure you want to bring *this* tree back?" Hecate asked.

Kore tilted her head to the side with a questioning look.

"This tree bears fruit not many would find appealing. Not amongst the living, that is," Hecate explained.

Kore and Callisto sat on the wall, listening intently as Hecate continued.

"The fruit is a binding fruit crafted by the Fates. Lord Hades was obligated to consume it upon accepting his place as king. It ties him to this realm, and anyone else who eats it."

"What happens if someone eats it and leaves?" Kore quizzed.

"The calls of the dead will draw them back." Hecate's voice was distant as if she was taken back to a far-off memory.

"And they will just come back?" Callisto asked.

"Well, the souls can be very persuasive," Hecate said, blinking her eyes as she focused back on the present. Her voice was low when she continued. "I cannot stop you from giving the tree life. But you should know its powers and the consequences that come with it, along with the dangers of retrieving the second tree."

"Dangers?" Kore echoed.

"Yes, the tree you seek is located within Tartarus. I hear you have had experience with such a journey." Hecate paused, indifference carved in her face.

Kore did not see the consequences of eating the fruit to be as horrible as Hecate made it sound. She did not plan to leave anytime soon, and even if she did, she would not need the souls' call to return. She would always return to the Underworld and its king. A bit of fruit was not needed. But if her mother were to come down and demand her return, Kore felt it best to have a stronger reason to stay. She would need quick access to the fruit, not a full journey away. She would need the tree to grow again. She would need to draw life from its sister.

She would need to return to Tartarus.

The thought of going back through the treacherous caverns sent a hard shiver down her spine. She hadn't seen any trees or felt any sort of life when she was last there. Which could only mean the tree was further into the bowels of its trenches, hidden deep and difficult to find.

"How can one flourish in Tartarus?" Kore asked.

"It sits by a river. Hades uses it as punishment for some shades. Some souls eat it, forever binding them here," the goddess explained.

"I thought they had no choice but to stay?"

"Oh, they do not, dear. Our lord thought it a joyous idea to taunt the souls he punished with temptation without satisfaction. They will never grasp it, but if by the Fates one in the river does, they will still be bound in this realm. Breaking the torment does not free or absolve them of their crimes, as they think it does."

"Are the souls who are there dangerous?"

"They are too weak and starved to notice anything but what is directly before them." Hecate began picking through the soil and dried leaves that lay free in the bed, and said nothing more.

Kore needed time to think. A second journey through Tartarus would be dangerous, but at least she had an idea of what lay ahead.

She finished with a few other plants that sat around the chalky trunk, making the leaves as big as she was to shield her upcoming work.

The rest of the morning moved by quickly, and the divines and nymph walked the newly flourishing garden. They questioned Kore on plants and vines that grew in the mortal realm, the ones that she had enjoyed. She showed them the edible plants and which flowers made the best jams and which ones did well in honey.

Hecate showed interest in Kore's herb garden, pointing to a few with inquiries about their name and benefits. When she had asked to take a few with her, Kore happily offered Hecate the freedom to roam the garden and pick what she liked, promising to leave some wax tablets near the herb bed that had a sketch and brief description of the herbs. Allowing Hecate a chance to learn the mortal herbs that grew.

Early in the afternoon, the women decided to take a walk to the Judgment Hall. Kore had yet to see it or the king doing his daily duties, dressed in his royal judgment chiton. She often forgot he was a king, never having the pleasure of seeing him in his crown, and she would very much enjoy seeing him on his throne.

They left from the garden, headed down the same stone

steps Aidoneus had brought Kore up when he first brought her to the courtyard. They traveled only a few flights before turning into the round hall in the middle of the palace. The columns were open to view the entire Underworld, black and gold like all the rest. On the pediments were different depictions of Aidoneus in various poses.

Upon each column hung different skulls—from mortal to Cyclopes and other frightening beasts. Each of them cradled a raging flame.

The bustling crowd of shades filled the small space, their blue glow lighting up the hall. Their chatter and surprise a roar echoing from the columns.

Kore's eyes fell to Aidoneus, who was already looking in her direction. His royal garments were much different than what he had worn to the village. His thick chiton was its customary black, draping heavy over his legs. Leather straps crossed over his chest, adorned with spikes that stuck out and golden buckles that kept them tightly wrapped around him.

He held his bident in hand, black with a leather strap wrapped around the neck. Her eyes traveled until they locked with his, air catching in her chest. He shifted slightly in his place and broke their gaze to look upon the shade who stood before him.

His throne was unpretentious, even for him, with a high, solid stone backrest. Kore was surprised it hadn't any carvings in it, just a solid, smooth back, reflecting all who sat before it. More skulls lay piled, one atop the other, holding the flat marble slab up where his arm rested. Despite being a large god, the throne made him look just a little smaller with ample space that surrounded him.

Pita, Nyx, and Cerus sat at attention at his side, their eyes focused on the crowd before them. They were undistracted by the raging noise around them, and it was the first time Kore had seen them all look so serious.

She tried to listen in on what words were being shared at the throne, but all she heard was the conversation of the two shades who stood just a few feet in front of her.

One shade, frail and hunched forward with his shoulders caving in, shivered and moaned, "He will not be kind to us for what we did."

"Lie! You weak coward. Offer up another soul in place of yours. He's a god of bargaining; he will like a good trade," the other shade whispered. He stood more erect with his chest puffed out. As if he, a mere mortal, could deceive the God of the Dead during judgment.

Kore looked to Hecate, to see if she had also heard the shade's words, but the ancient goddess kept her focus up front. Listening intently to the topic by the throne.

She switched her gaze to Callisto, who also seemed unaware of the shade's misleading plans. No matter, Kore would continue to listen to his words until it was his turn to be judged. She wanted to find out what it was he truly had done before she heard the lies that would taint his tongue before the king.

She felt her ichor boil at the attempted deception. She wanted to grab him, scold him for his planned lies, but she knew her hands and her powers—divine or not—would not be able to harm a shade.

The hair on the back of her neck rose as she stood there, stewing in her anger.

Aidoneus was quick in his work, reading a scroll, giving his judgment, and they were on their way with either Agatha, Eleni, or Elpida. Very few tried to plead their case at life, and Aidoneus struck no deals or bargains. He read their moral wrongdoings and sent them on their way.

When they were finally near the throne, he called out the name of the shade before her, the timid one. He shuffled to the front before the king and bowed. His body quaked under the god's gaze.

"Fotios Heli!" Aidoneus bellowed, holding his free hand out, waiting. An older man wobbled up and handed a thin scroll to the king.

He looked over it for only a moment before looking back to the shade.

"You have done nothing heroic, it would seem. Up until the last bit even, you hadn't done anything incredibly vile. But you did not think for yourself at the end, and that was your deciding fate. You will be placed in Tartarus for your dying crimes," he ordered, lifting his hand in the air and snapping his wrist to one side.

The shade vanished. There was no smoke, no mist of darkness. He was just gone. The shade had not even tried to plead his case. Whatever Aidoneus had read in the scrolls made for a quick and easy decision.

Kore watched as the older man walked back up to Aidoneus with another scroll; this one was much thicker than all the ones she had seen. He bent down and whispered something in Aidoneus's ear, creating a twisted expression of rage and pleasure upon the king's face.

Had the man known of the shade's plans all along?

Hecate leaned over and whispered, "What angers you, Kore?"

"This shade, he plans to lie," Kore whispered back. Rage boiled up again as she waited for his name.

"I see." Hecate righted herself and continued to watch the judgments, a soft smile teasing her lips.

"Deimos Gorgophone. Step forward," Aidoneus ordered, and the shade did as told, bowing before his king.

"My lord," Deimos hissed through clenched teeth.

Kore balled her hands into fists, fighting herself to stay in her spot and not make a scene, but Aidoneus appeared to take notice. He stood from his throne, making his way to where she waited, and held out his hand.

"Come, I would like to hear what you have to say," he whispered.

She blinked at him for a moment, hesitating before placing her hand in his. He guided her up to his throne and allowed her to sit first before taking his spot beside her.

The throne was just big enough for them to fit comfortably.

He leaned down, close enough she could feel the heat of his breath brush against her ear. "I have watched you all evening, Goddess. Did this shade do something to upset you?"

His words sent a fierce shiver across her skin. She turned to him, his face just inches from hers. The strong smell of burning cypress, wood, and fire flooded her mind.

"Uh—" She blinked. "'Tis not what he has done to me, but what he plans to say to you."

Aidoneus looked at the shade, who stood motionless and confused. When he leaned back to Kore, he swept her hair away from her ear. The tips of his fingers brushed across her skin and left burning trails in their wake.

"And what may that be?" His voice had a coldness to it, but his eyes were warm as he looked down at her.

She shivered once more, struggling to control it. Her gaze moved to the shade for the first time since sitting on the throne. He and the few remaining souls stood motionless with their ghostly oculars fixed on her.

Hecate and Callisto made their way to Minos. An approving smile sat on the ancient goddess's lips while Callisto held a beaming grin. They passed without a word and took their place with the other divines and nymphs.

Kore turned her gaze back to the king, pressing her hand on his thigh and lifting herself until their cheeks met. "He plans to lie, and bargain for his life," she whispered in his ear.

Aidoneus smiled lightly at her before turning hard, dark eyes to the shade.

"Deimos Gorgophone, I have been told you would like to plead your life's case. However, you will not plead to me. You will plead to this goddess, here. I advise you to speak with her as you would with me." His voice fell as thunder in the hall, rattling Kore where she sat. He leaned back, resting against the smooth stone, and waited for the shade to speak.

Kore wanted to hear his lie, but even more, she wanted

to know his crime. What would he try to cover in his attempt at a second chance?

Deimos rounded his eyes, speechless before the unknown goddess. He looked to Aidoneus and then back to Kore, unable to speak as much as he had just moments before.

"What were your crimes?" she probed in a voice not her own.

She was patient and calm while waiting for the shade to find the right words, ready for his lie and eager to hear it. But Aidoneus was not as patient.

"Deimos, I have here your scroll of life. Come now, lie or truth, I have matters to attend to after I send you on your way." Irritation coated his voice, but when he looked down to Kore, he flashed her a mischievous smile. An action that stirred her soul and brought heat to her lower belly. She shifted in her spot, crossing her ankles to fight the feeling—but the heat only extended up her body.

She had missed his smell, his touch, his very presence. Her body reacted so easily to him, in a traitorous way.

"My lord—"

Aidoneus held up his hand to stop the shade. "I said you will speak to the goddess."

Deimos looked back to Kore, his eyes still wide with fear.

"My lady, I beg you, I thought the temple had been emptied. I had meant to steal from the temple, but I had not meant to kill anyone," he prattled, but Kore knew deep down he had meant to kill. He had already admitted to enjoying his crime. She turned to Hades, waiting to see if he would answer, but he had already started reading over the scroll of Deimos's life charges.

His hands tightened over the roll, his knuckles became white, and his skin pulled tight, showing every tendon and vein. Kore leaned over to get a glance as well. Her eyes skimmed across the parchment until she saw the words *young maidens* a few dozen times throughout each passage. She felt the ichor boil under her skin as she read more and more about his life atrocities.

"What do you think?" he whispered to her.

She knew he already had a placement, but she enjoyed that he wanted her opinion.

"Tartarus." Her tone was flat and cold, not a tone she was accustomed to leaving her lips.

Aidoneus turned back to the shade. The muscles in his jaw flexed and his nostrils flared.

"Deimos, we have heard enough from you. You will be granted no more time to plead." He stood and held out his hand for Kore to rise and join him. She gladly took it, twining her fingers with his. "What say you, Goddess?" he boomed.

Kore looked to the shade, his lies lost on his tongue. He shook rapidly at her gaze, dropping his head to avoid her eyes. She enjoyed his fear; it gave her a taste of what it meant to be a goddess and have the power that she was never able to experience.

"Tartarus." Her usually soft voice projected loud in the hall, echoing off the columns and marble.

"I agree," Aidoneus boasted, lifting his hand high in the air, preparing to wave the shade away.

"Wait! Your Majesties, please! I beg—"

"Beg?" Kore shot, stopping the shade from spewing any more lies. "You seek to beg for a better judgment, but you sought to lie to the king to get it." She stepped toward the shade, releasing her grasp from Aidoneus.

"No, I—"

"Enough! I heard your plans of deception earlier this evening." Kore felt a hand wrap gently around her arm, giving her a light tug.

Aidoneus stepped between them, his body big enough to shield her from the shade.

"Lady Kore has made her judgment on you. Tartarus," he thundered again, lifting his hand once more and waving the shade away to his new dwelling.

The burning fire in the pit of her stomach quickly melted, as if the very presence of the shade had caused the outrage that boiled in her.

Aidoneus turned, his face bright with a smile that displayed the glorious dimples she loved so much.

"You do this well. I may have you join me more often." His laugh shook the hall as he turned to the older gentleman from before, who wobbled to their side and bowed to them. His smoky gray hair fell around his face in thick curls. He looked to Aidoneus and then to Kore with a soft smile.

"Yes, my lord?"

"Kore, this is a dear friend of mine, Minos," he introduced.

The man bowed once more. "Pleased to meet you, Lady Kore."

"I have an important matter to attend to with Lady Kore. I will need you to finish out the last of the judgments," Aidoneus ordered.

Minos smiled to the divines and bowed before turning and calling the next shade.

Aidoneus grabbed Kore and tugged her into the corridor. His hand gripped her tightly.

"I apologize! Had I done too much?" she shot quickly, dropping her eyes to her hands.

"No, no. You were magnificent." He chuckled. "A bit too magnificent actually. I will admit, you struck a bit of fear in me."

"You? The Lord of Darkness? The absolute power." When she looked up, she found his bright blue eyes just inches from her. Her body felt a pull to him, to close the short distance between their lips. She was close enough to take every bit of his scent in, and she wanted more.

He squeezed her hand gently, pulling her free from her mind and back to the present moment.

"Um. What was that matter we need to attend to?" she asked breathlessly.

"Uh—" He sighed, straightening his stance but never dropping her hand. "Hermes brings word of your mother."

Kore had not seen Hermes much since she had arrived. He had been by a few times her first week up but had since been busy with his godly duties in all realms. He hadn't much word on her mother then, just that she was aware Kore had been injured and was receiving aid.

She hoped her mother was doing well on the meadow, taking care of her goats and hens, making sure Lotus wasn't worked too hard by Morea. Above all, she hoped her mother wasn't spending her days worrying about Kore and instead was enjoying the light and the nymphs. Kore wanted to be in the Underworld; she wanted to be with Aidoneus. She was happy and she did not plan on leaving. But she would be lying if she said she did not miss her mother or her dear nymph friends.

Hearing what she had been up to these last few moons was something Kore needed. She hoped she could convince Aidoneus to let Hermes stay for dinner a few evenings and she could hear and share stories with her mother, through letters and gifts, whatever way she could to let her mother know she was well and happy.

"I do hope she is faring well! I cannot wait. When will he be here?" she prattled.

"I thought you would enjoy his company for dinner this evening," he offered.

Kore could hardly contain her excitement. Her body wiggled happily while they made their way to Aidoneus's main chambers.

"Since you dealt with shades new to the realm, you will be needing to cleanse differently," he instructed.

"How do you mean?"

"You will need to cleanse yourself of the miasma new souls carry. Alena had already set the chamber for me, but you may go first."

They entered the main chamber, where Aidoneus

stripped his head of the jagged crown.

"First?" The word didn't sit right with her; she didn't want to go first. Though she didn't want to go after him either. The strange new heat began to rise in her again.

"I figured you'd enjoy your time alone," he said.

"I think I have had enough time alone, thank you," she countered. "I have never cleansed miasma." The lie fell from her lips in a whisper, and her heart thumped its way into her throat. "Would you mind showing me?"

Aidoneus gazed down at her, his brows drawn together. Ichor flooded his skin, turning his chest and cheeks a bright golden color.

"You do not have to," she added quickly. Turning on the balls of her feet, she made her way to the bath chamber.

Heat teased her cheeks as she entered. The steaming water sat with a variety of oils along the edge. Various sized candles were placed around the pool, and scattered bay leaves floated in the water—something that was not normal for her bathing.

"Kore, why did you walk off?" Aidoneus's voice echoed from the entryway of the chamber. She jumped in response, the sudden sound startling her. She turned to find him leaning against the column with his arms folded over his chest.

"Your silence is, at times, intimidating," she admitted sheepishly. It was also the strong nagging feeling of his silence ending in rejection.

"Sometimes, Goddess, your inquiries are intimidating," he said with a smile and made his way to her side, his eyes holding hers all the while.

She could feel the heavy pounding of her heart. His eyes trailed down from hers to her neck and then to the pin that held her robes. His hand reached up, fingers grazing over the obsidian.

"You surprised me today. I had not realized your vengeance spilled over all life," he teased and worked at the pin until it fell free from the cloth. The linen dropped from her shoulder, exposing her bare chest to him. He brought his eyes back to hers, holding them as he moved. A half smile danced on his lips.

She inhaled deeply, holding it in her chest as she watched him. His eyes held a different hunger.

She had been nude in front of him before, and he hadn't seemed so welcoming to it then. Now, it seemed as though he craved it. His hand slid from her shoulder, finding her breast and teasing her nipple until it came to a point. She shivered under his touch, causing small bumps to lift across her skin.

His hand slid further down, slipping his fingers under the fabrics that fell at her waist. He pushed them down, letting them fall about her feet and leaving her naked before him.

With his eyes still locked on hers, he unstrapped the leather belts around his chest and let them fall to the floor with a loud thud. Kore's hands inched up to his chiton, but he grabbed her, pausing her motions.

With his free hand, he pulled at a strap attached to his chiton, and it fell free from his hips, landing in the pile at their feet. He found her hand once again and brought it to his lips, placing a gentle kiss upon it.

Her heart felt as if it would burst through her chest, fire growing at her core. She fought the urge to glance down, even for a second. Aidoneus had not looked away from her eyes as he removed her robes, and she did not want to be the first to break this little game. Though she did not need to look, either way; she could feel him pressed hard against her stomach.

He pulled her hand free from his lips and guided her into the pool with him, his eyes still holding hers as they submerged themselves. Once the water covered them, he allowed his gaze to break free from their hold, only for it to fall to her lips next.

"What is different in miasma between shades and the living?" she whispered.

"Not much, more bothersome if left on the skin. It is cleansed the same way." He laughed softly.

They moved near the assortment of oils, and Aidoneus grabbed one at random—a clear lekythos with a yellow-tinted oil, and more bay leaves inside.

He twisted the cork free. "Lean your head back."

She did as told, letting her hair fall into the water. Aidoneus poured the oil mix over her strands, allowing it to saturate her roots. It smelled of strong bay and olive, a mix her mother had told her was an excellent cleanser.

His fingers worked to massage the mix into her scalp and hair until they were thickly coated. Kore turned and took the lekythos and poured some oil in her hand.

She reached up, smoothing it into his hair. His height proved challenging. A wicked smile flashed across his face as his hands gripped her thighs and pulled her up to his chest. He sat on the pool bench and leaned against the edge. With a leg on either side of him, her body molded to his.

His hands pressed into her hips as she smoothed the oil over his hair. She tried to stay focused on the task, but his heat pressed against hers, and every slight movement sent an electric shock through her.

He took her hands in his, and she froze as he pulled her closer until his lips grazed over hers. She inhaled, taking in his scent, his breath—hot against her lips, clouding her mind.

A low growl came from the back of his throat, and his arms wrapped around her waist. He anchored her body to his and spun, pressing her back against the pool wall.

His lips crashed into hers, hard and urgent. She inhaled deeply, parting her lips and inviting him in. He was frantic, his hands grabbing at her thigh, hips, and breast wildly. He broke free from her and traveled down to her neck. His hand found its way between her legs. The blazing fire in that spot grew to an inferno as his fingertips moved against her.

Kore let out a soft yelp that he quickly covered with his mouth, tasting her moans.

"My lord?" a soft voice called from the entrance. A deep growl rolled through him as he reluctantly pulled free, leaving her lips raw and swollen.

"Yes, Alena?" he bit through his teeth.

"I know you informed me not to bother you during your bath." Fear tainted her voice. Something Kore was not familiar with.

His fingers moved against her as he spoke again. "So why are you here?"

"Well. You also told me to inform you when Hermes was here, to—to inform you the moment he arrived. I apologize! I will let him know you will be just a bit longer." Her voice shook with a clear anxiousness coating it.

"Oh!" He growled again. "Tell him we will be right down!"

"Yes, my lord."

His eyes grew soft as he looked over Kore. The corners of his lips fell, and he dropped his hands from her.

"I apologize, I should not have . . ." He sighed, pushing away from her. "We shouldn't keep Hermes waiting."

Kore wasn't sure how to respond. Her body ached for his touch, for him to come back and continue what he had started.

"It is for the best," he added.

"I do not think it so," she said breathlessly.

"You say this now."

"I will say this always," she argued softly, with a smile.

He pulled his brows down, an internal fight raging within him, clear on his face.

"That be the case or not, we should hurry to see what news Hermes brings of your mother."

CHAPTER XXIV

THE DINNER, THE NEWS, AND THE REASON

"Sweet sister!" Hermes cheered, lifting Kore in a deep embrace. "I have missed your bright face!"

His blond hair stuck out wildly in all directions, the flush of his golden cheeks just as bright as she remembered. Though it hadn't been all that long, it was the longest she had gone without seeing him.

"I have missed you dearly, Hermes! Please, sit, tell me of this news!" Kore cheered.

Overjoyed to hear word of her mother, she didn't feel the need to run through all the pleasantries of casual conversation. Aidoneus pulled a chair out for her and got to work putting together her platter as she waited on Hermes to right himself.

He grabbed a platter as well and began picking at the various fruits and cheeses available.

"No honey bread, Hades?" he shot with a smile. Aidoneus did not bother looking up.

"I am sure I can make some for your next visit, Hermes," Kore offered sweetly.

"I would love that! I haven't had any in some time now."

"Hasn't my mother made any?"

It was not like Demeter to not bake; if anything, Kore would have suspected her mother would overbake in her absence.

Hermes's smile fell as he cast his eyes back down to the table.

"Oh, well, you see . . . That brings me to my visit, I suppose." He took a seat with his platter of fruit and inhaled deeply, keeping his eyes focused on his hands. "The last I heard, Demeter had found shelter in Eleusis. Disguised as a crone, no less. She was living among the mortals. But that was near two moons past."

"Is she not in the village?" Aidoneus inquired.

"The village was destroyed with all its people. I would ask if Thanatos spoke with you on that group, but I can understand why he hasn't." He shot a quick look at Kore.

"Is she well?" Kore pushed.

Hermes shrugged with a heavy sigh. "I have been told she was looking decently happy during her time there, but she was not found amongst them when Thanatos collected. I suppose she had moved on before the slaughter. I highly doubt she would have allowed it if she were there."

"Who told you this?" Aidoneus requested as he placed Kore's platter down in front of her.

"Helios of course!" Hermes laughed.

Helios should be renamed the God of Scandal, Kore thought and rolled her eyes.

"But is she well?" she repeated.

Hermes gave her a despairing glance. "We cannot be sure."

"How do you mean?"

"Helios had not seen her since the days before the slaughter. We suppose she has transformed again, but not sure what to." He popped a grape into his mouth and chewed.

"Is Zeus looking for her?" Aidoneus inquired.

"Zeus is most preoccupied with a new budding war.

Hestia and Artemis have been searching diligently, though."

"What of the nymphs at the meadow?" Kore asked.

"They are well. Hestia stays with them when she is not searching for your mother. She has even taken on the deliveries and management of the animals," he said with a half-smile.

There was silence as Hermes popped a bit of cheese into his mouth. Kore had lost her appetite, her stomach feeling as if it were in knots.

How were they unable to locate her? Divine energy was heavy and strong. Even with shapeshifting, the divines' glow was much too powerful for them to look like mortals.

She nervously picked at a bit of bread, her mind on her mother.

"She will be found, though; the sun and moon divines have been on the lookout for her. She is probably out in disguise again, enjoying a mortal life. She seemed to be doing as much in Eleusis with that family and their babe," Hermes prattled.

"A babe?" Kore blurted out.

"Yes, she seemed to be fond of him from what Helios and Apollo saw. I am really surprised how well she took your leaving, Kore. Honestly—she just found another creature to care for. But I cannot say the same for Ares!"

Aidoneus shot Kore a glance before taking a deep drink of wine. She straightened her back, curious by what he meant but too nervous to ask. Her mouth twitched as she thought of a response, a question—but she only had one.

"Does he know I am here?"

"He does not. But he is searching," Hermes said, his eyes on Aidoneus. He cleared his throat nervously before speaking once again. "I think I will see if beautiful Alena happens to know where the wine is!" He rushed to his feet and darted from the hall.

Kore shifted in her seat. If Ares was looking for her, it wouldn't be long before he found her. If he went to Helios, he may just get what he was asking for. At first, the Titan was annoying, but now—he was a danger.

"You are safe here," Aidoneus assured.

"Helios already knows so much. Who is to say he won't tell Ares?" The pressure of tears felt heavy, weighing down on her chest.

A small smirk flashed across his face. "The Sun gods are not fond of him. Just as he is not very fond of them. Even so, Ares is not welcome here. You will be safe." His eyes met hers and he offered a reassuring smile.

"I did not think he would care so much. I thought my mother would be the one out looking," she said softly.

"Are you upset she is not?"

Kore couldn't say she was upset with her mother—she would prefer her not to look—but Kore couldn't help but feel a slight sting that her mother did not even try to send word with Hermes. She simply moved on to another village. What about the nymphs? The goats, the chickens? What of them?

She was not upset, she was hurt. She shook her head, letting the tears slowly roll free. Aidoneus's warm palm pressed against her cheek, wiping them away with his thumb.

"It is normal to be," he said softly.

She smiled back, her hand reaching up to his when Hermes's joyous voice echoed down the corridor. Aidoneus paused, his hand still resting on her cheek, his eyes on the entry where Hermes was to come through.

He dropped his hand and leaned back in his chair, the fold between his brows dug deep.

"Surprise me, Alena! You know best!" the cheery god sang.

He took his seat back at the table and picked at the fruit again. "So? Kore and Ares! Wouldn't that have been a sight?"

"Did you want to end your evening in Tartarus, Hermes?" Aidoneus spat.

The God of Mischief laughed, throwing up his hands and shaking his head. "Alena is still picking out the wine!"

Kore tried to suppress her laughter.

"Very well," Aidoneus scoffed.

He cleared the space between them, allowing room for the drinks to come. After a short while, Alena appeared beside Hermes, balancing three crystal kantharoi in one hand and a black oinochoe in the other.

"What have you brought us?" Hermes quizzed joyously, batting his eyes at the poor nymph.

He had always had a way with the creatures, captivating them with his charm and whatever else he thought to do. Kore never meddled in his affairs; she just enjoyed his stories. He seemed to have a favorite wherever he wandered. In the meadow, it was Ampelos he lusted after. Here, it would seem Alena was his favorite, possibly even over Ampelos.

"I brought a white wine, with the grapes from Elysium. We do have red if you prefer?" Her soft voice had a hint of honey to it as she spoke directly to the Messenger of the Gods.

"That will be all for now, Alena," Aidoneus ordered.

The sweet, innocent nymph reluctantly pulled her gaze from Hermes and back to Aidoneus.

"Yes, my lord," she said apologetically.

After she placed the oinochoe in the space Aidoneus made and passed out each kantharoi, she bowed to the divines and vanished just as quickly as she came.

"Hermes, must you taunt my nymphs?" the king asked.

"Only Alena. I fancy her. She always smells of honey! It is quite enjoyable!"

"She does smell sweet," Kore admitted with a giggle. Happy to have a distraction from the news of the evening.

Aidoneus hid a smile as he stood to pour the wine for the evening. The three divines drank until the oinochoe was empty and called for Alena to bring another, but with red wine instead. Kore did not care for the bitterness and dryness of the red wines; she found the white wine to be sweeter and easier to drink. Perhaps a bit too easy as she began seeing double.

They spoke of many things, including how much Kore

enjoyed the Underworld, about her time in the Nymph Hall, and her moment passing judgments. Hermes listened intently, wide-eyed with a bright smile.

"She brought life to the courtyard again," Aidoneus added.

"Did she? I really must see it!" Hermes slurred, drunk from the wine. He looked to Aidoneus, who offered only a single nod. "Come, come, Kore!" Hermes urged.

He made wobbly movements as he rose to his feet and danced to Kore's side. She stood slowly to steady the spinning chamber around her. When everything stilled, she turned to Aidoneus and held out her hand.

"It is all right, you show Hermes your work," he suggested, sipping his wine once more. "I must speak with Minos about those final shades."

Kore parted the king with a smile and a soft bow before turning with Hermes and heading off to the courtyard. As much as she would have liked Aidoneus's company through the garden, she wanted a moment alone with Hermes. His mention of Ares was a call for concern. She expected her mother to move the mountains and seas to get her back, but instead, her mother found new happiness in the mortal realm. That comforted Kore, in a sense. However, she did not expect Ares to be upset, let alone more upset than her mother. That did not comfort her.

"Hermes?" she whispered. The bright and cheery god turned to her with a smile and glazed eyes. "What did you mean when you said you were surprised how well my mother took my leaving, but not Ares? What has he done?" she asked, locking arms with Hermes for support.

"Uh—well—being the god he is, he took your departure rather personally. You know, leaving the day of the announcement was basically telling him *no*," he slurred.

"Well, that is what it was," Kore pointed out.

"Yes, well. He doesn't like being told *no*."

"I don't like being forced into marriage," Kore slurred

with a shrug.

"That may be so, but you handled it better, I feel. Running away. Now, Ares. He took his rage out on the Greeks for a few moons but has been very feral lately, attending Zeus's calls when he pleases. Normally, a usual response but not during times of war. It's his most favorite time to be involved!"

They turned out from the corridor and made their way up the steps that led to the courtyard above.

"Honestly, I think you just hurt his pride. Something Aphrodite has no issue stroking for him." He snickered.

Kore was not knowledgeable about the divines' relationships, but she did know Aphrodite was wed to Hephaestus and that they had a lot of problems. Ares being one of them.

"If he has her, why is my hurting his pride such an issue?" she asked.

Hermes side-eyed her just as they came up to the plateau that held the courtyard.

"You do not know the God of War well, sister." He chuckled.

They crossed the stone arch that led into the garden, and Hermes's eyes popped wide as a dramatic gasp flew from his lips. Their previous conversation was forgotten amongst the beauty of the garden and wear of the wine.

"Wow, Kore! Lovely work!"

"Thank you! It is a very lively garden!"

The two stumbled around some of the beds that housed purple-and-white flowers with petals that formed a cupped star.

"What are these?" Hermes inquired, reaching down to smooth his fingers over one of the petals.

"These are crocus flowers," she informed.

"They are beautiful!"

They continued around the upper half of the court, and Kore explained the name of each vibrant flower they passed until they reached the bed with the white, brittle, petrified pomegranate tree.

"Ew! What is this?" he sneered.

"'Tis a pomegranate tree."

"Oh? I have seen the great and beautiful pomegranate tree, Kore, and this is not it."

"It is just petrified—and how do you mean you have seen it? I hear this one has been this way for some time, and the other is in Tartarus."

He examined the area a bit more, struggling through the blurred vision.

"Well, I have not been to Tartarus. That is one thing you can have over me. But if I do remember correctly, this was the spot of the old tree. If there is one in Tartarus as you say, what does it have to do with this nasty one?"

"Do not be so rude to my plants!" she ordered, reaching out to place her hand upon the dry bark apologetically. "I am sorry, my friend; he did not mean his harsh words," she soothed.

"Oh! My apologies!"

When she turned back to him, he had his familiar wicked smile, the smile he had before asking an insanely inappropriate question.

"What is it, Hermes?" She sighed.

"I brought you all this way for you to confess your love. Have you?"

"Not exactly. I have not found the right time to tell him much of anything."

"Haven't had much time, or just have not done so?"

She snapped her eyes to meet his. She wanted to be upset with him, but she found herself furious at his words, furious with herself. Because he was right. She'd had time, more than enough time to tell Aidoneus how she felt. She just wasn't sure how he felt; at least she wasn't all that sure until this evening.

She was enjoying her time with him as it was, and she did not want to ruin that with heartbreak. Having to drop her head and return to the mortal realm, face her mother, and marry Ares. That was her true fear.

"I just do not wish to hear he does not feel for me what I feel for him. I can be content with what we have now if it means staying close with him," she admitted.

She took a seat on the stone floor, resting her back against the marble bed, and Hermes was quick to join her.

"If you don't mind, may I draw attention to a few small details?" he offered, and she nodded. "Lord Hades, as you have seen, is not normally this kind. He does not let anyone, mortal or divine, into his realm. You have been here four moons now, and it looks like he has accommodated everything for an extended *guest*. I mean, he has you in his chamber, and not the one that's halls away from him." He looked down at her with a smile. "I think it is safe to say he feels the same. But you did not hear that from me, of course."

His words warmed her heart and gave her hope. Perhaps Hermes was right; it was time to tell Aidoneus her feelings.

The only question she had now was how to present it.

She leaned her head against Hermes's shoulder with a soft giggle. "I heard nothing of the sort."

"So, what do you plan to do with this here pom-pom tree?"

They struggled back to their feet to look over the trunk of the barren tree.

"I plan to bring it back. Hecate knows of its sister's location in Tartarus. I have a few more questions for her about it before I go, but I am not sure I want to make the trip again. It was—"

"Do you know what the fruit of this tree does?" Hermes interjected.

"Yes. Hecate gave the warning already. I am aware."

She did not see the problem with the repercussions of the fruit. She hoped it would ensure Ares did not steal her away. Nor could he make Zeus return her.

"Well, if Hecate said so." He shrugged. "She knows

best."

They looked over the tree and soil a bit more before Hermes grew sluggish and his sentences became riddled with yawning.

"Well, dear sister, I must be on my way. I have some matters to attend to."

"Will you be all right headed back?"

"Oh yes! My chargers have gotten me where I need be even in the worst of conditions," he assured her with an embrace and a soft kiss atop her head. "Be patient with the king. He has even less of an idea of what he's doing than you."

They entered the corridor, stumbling their way back to the dining hall, laughing along the way. Hermes had told her of new ideas and phrases he wanted to pass down to the mortals for fun. He thought it would be a silly little joke to play on them. Anything for a slight laugh with him.

"You are truly the worst, Hermes." Kore giggled as they entered the hall. Aidoneus was gathering more fruit on a platter that was already occupied by two kantharoi and a smaller oinochoe.

"Don't give up on him," Hermes whispered with a wink. He lifted his hand to Aidoneus. "I shall be taking my leave, my lord!" His words slurred together with a light laugh. He shot Kore one last glance before wobbling from the hall and down the path to the bridge.

Kore made her way to Aidoneus, who was already on his way to meet her with the platter in hand.

"Did he enjoy your work?" His voice was smooth and low, a sound that melted her at her knees.

"He did."

"Good. I thought we would enjoy the rest of this in my chambers. I have a few questions of my own this night."

She nodded reluctantly as a rock formed in the pit of her stomach. She could not think of any questions left to ask, not that there were many. At least not ones she could answer herself. She only knew as much as she had already told him.

Unless his questions were not of Ares or her escape. Perhaps they were of some other matter.

The rock in her stomach grew, and she felt the wine begin to make a quick exit.

"Oh! Here." Aidoneus grabbed her hand as he spoke, shifting the corridor around them. The dizziness did not help, and she leaned into Aidoneus for support, burrowing her face in his arm.

"How are you well?" She sighed when she realized that he was immune to the effects she suffered.

"You had more wine than I." He moved from under her, and she opened her eyes.

The chamber shook, spinning around her, but she could tell they had arrived just beside the kline.

Aidoneus set the platter on the furs. Taking Kore's hand, he guided her to sit and leaned her head against the stone headrest of the kline.

"Perhaps I will drink this wine myself." He laughed, lifting her legs and placing them beside the platter. "What would you like first?"

Kore lifted a brow, confused by his question. "Hm?"

"Food," he said with a laugh.

"Was that the question you had for me?"

"No, no. But I see you are in no condition for questions."

"Oh? What condition am I in?" Lying back made her realize just how tired the wine truly made her, but it also brought that familiar sensation to her skin.

She slid her hand across the fur, and the soft linen hairs tickled as they rubbed against her skin. When her hand found the fabric of his chiton, he caught it there, his jaw flexing.

"Kore." He exhaled deeply, closing his eyes. "We should not."

"And why not?"

"To start, you are not well," he said stiffly.

"Would that be so wrong?" she quizzed, lifting her head from the stone.

He squeezed his eyes shut and inhaled deeply through his nose. "Yes."

She did not like that answer, and she wasn't going to accept it, not after the moment in the bath or all the other moments before.

She leaned into him, tugging her robes up so that she could easily lift her leg over his lap. Straddling him once more, she slid her hands over his chest until they came to rest at his shoulders. His lids squeezed even tighter.

"Please look at me," she whispered before placing her soft lips over his. His body froze beneath her, but she did not stop. "Please," she begged again in a soft voice. She could feel his excitement grow beneath her, pressing against her and eliciting a breathless moan from her. His eyes snapped open at the sound, burning into hers.

"Do not beg me, Goddess," he groaned.

"Then, I command it," she whispered, her lips crashing into his. His hands gripped tightly at her hips. His lips parted, inviting her in, tasting her on his tongue.

Her hands found their way to his hair, twisting and pulling him closer so she could take more of him in.

He slid his hands up her back and gripped the loose fabric of her robes and pulled them down, exposing her bare chest. He pulled away from the kiss to take in the view before him. His chest heaving rapidly.

He wrapped one arm around her waist and shifted his weight until she was lying flat against the furs. His eyes trailed along the length of her body, stopping at each curve.

Her fingers found their way to the fabric of his chiton, pulling at the sides until it fell free. He leaned over her, lips colliding, his excitement throbbing against her through the robes. She moaned into his mouth, rolling her hips as she did.

Aidoneus twisted his hand in the fabric about her waist until he found her skin. The contact burned her, ripping a heavy gasp from her lungs.

He paused, his hand tight on her waist, his lips hovering

above hers. He pressed against the softness of her hip. A guttural sound rumbled from his chest.

"Kore," he exhaled, "we shouldn't. You are not well," he said again, lifting his head to look into her eyes. "I am afraid you have had too much wine."

"Would we continue had I not?" she breathed, placing her palm gently against his cheek. She pushed her hips against him once more, watching as his jaw clenched.

She took that as a yes. A low, frustrated groan rattled through him. He shifted his body again, this time maneuvering the fur over her. Breaking free from her grasp, he reached over for the platter and set it on the crystal table beside them.

Kore did not know whether she should be mad or upset. She did not feel the same rejection as she had before; instead, she felt frustration as the heat grew between her legs.

Aidoneus climbed into the space next to her. Keeping the furs between them, he wrapped an arm around her and brought her closer to his chest, tucking his face into the curve of her neck, his lips soft against her skin.

"As much as I appreciate your enthusiasm, I am afraid I cannot give you what you want," he whispered.

"And what do you know of what I want?"

"I know it cannot be this."

"Then you know nothing of what I want." She sighed. Hermes was right, Aidoneus was just as lost when it came to all of this as she was.

"You may be right," he said softly, trailing his fingers gently along her arm.

She shook under the touch. "I will not stop."

The feeling of sleep finally came, pulling her eyelids down like heavy weights.

"I know."

CHAPTER XXV

THE GODDESS OF WITCHCRAFT, THE NYMPH (AGATHA), AND THE TEA

Kore sat across from Aidoneus as they ate their breakfast, though she enjoyed being close to him. She felt she always missed his most beautiful expressions when she sat beside him. His smile, the way his dimples sat on his cheeks when he laughed, all the little things she had realized she missed. Though, she enjoyed being close to him as well.

He kept his eyes on her while they spoke, discussing their plans for the day. He had work to do in the Judgment Halls. Kore, however, had plans to visit Hecate in her cavern. The herbs the goddess had requested had finished drying, and Kore thought it would be nice to deliver them herself since the ancient goddess had been busy with her spell work for the last few days.

She had requested Kore gather them, and Kore had a few more questions she wanted to ask about the pomegranate tree in Tartarus. Despite not having the slightest clue where Hecate's cavern was, she did know of one nymph who did.

"So, you mean to deliver those herbs this day," Aidoneus confirmed. His voice had a hint of sadness pulling at it.

"Yes, I will be going to Hecate's cavern."

"Hecate's cavern? Would you like Pita to join you?" he offered.

"No, as much as I enjoy his company, I would like to request a different companion."

He raised a brow and waited.

"I was wondering if I could borrow Agatha for the day?"

"Agatha has work in the Judgment Halls," he said stiffly, but he hadn't given her a no.

"I know, but I was hoping she'd guide me. Seeing how she spends a deal of time with Hecate," Kore pointed out.

She watched as he chewed over the thought in his mind, contemplating sending her off without a guide, an incompetent guide, or a guide who knew of the location she sought. He took a deep sip from his kantharos.

"Very well. I am sure she could use the time away. The shades have been more consistent."

"The war?" she guessed.

"It would appear that way." He paused, his eyes falling on a slice of wheat bread along the table. "Hermes has been asking about the bread you promised him. He will be joining us for dinner this evening."

"Oh, I did not know you invited him." A smile spread across her face. She had enjoyed the visits with Hermes the past few weeks. He had been dropping by the palace more often after departing shades at the Judgment Hall.

"I hadn't. He took it upon himself and stated he would be bringing all of the supplies," Aidoneus said flatly.

She tilted her head as she watched him. He didn't seem so happy to have Hermes by, but he did not turn him away. He raised his brow, ready to answer her unspoken question.

"I wanted to learn as well." His lips turned up into that smile that melted her heart. It was something she would never tire of.

Hermes had brought honey with him during his last visit,

and she promised a lesson the next time she saw him. The God of Mischief was not one to forget a promise. Certainly not when it came to honey bread.

"I will be sure to be back before the sun touches land." She giggled.

"Very well." He wiped his mouth with a cloth and stood. "Agatha!" he called out, walking around to Kore's side. He held out his hand to her and assisted her to her feet.

The eccentric nymph appeared at the end of the table. "My lord." She bowed to him, then turned to Kore. "Lady Kore."

"Good morning, Agatha. It would seem your assistance in the Judgment Hall will not be needed this day; however, Kore will require your aid. You will see that she is well assisted."

Agatha nodded, and a faint smile appeared at the gifted day.

"Be safe," he said to Kore before dissolving into a cloud of smoke.

"How may I help?"

"Good morning, Agatha," Kore greeted. "I must bring a few herbs to Hecate. I was hoping you would show me the way."

"I can do that."

"Wonderful! I have lessons to give this evening, it would seem, so it will be a short trip," Kore cheered.

The two walked from the dining hall and made their way to the courtyard so Kore could garble and pouch the herbs Hecate had requested. Agatha was always quiet, a nymph of very few words, which wasn't the case for most of the sweet creatures. But then again, the lampades nymphs were much different than the hamadryad nymphs.

Kore and Agatha entered the vibrant and lively garden. A stone table sat near the arch that led out to the fields below, upon which Kore had laid out all the herbs Hecate requested.

Artemisia, piperita, rosa, and rosa canina. Hecate had

written the names on a small parchment on the table for Kore to gather.

Agatha examined some colorful flowers in a bed near the table while Kore removed the dried blooms and petals from the stems. She pouched each herb, tied them off, and placed them in the satchel that she used for gathering.

"I believe that is everything. Are you ready?" The goddess grinned.

"Yes." Agatha held out her hand for Kore, and she took it, watching as they became engulfed in darkness. The air around them grew cold then blisteringly hot and only faded to a comfortable temperature when the smoke dissipated.

A small fire in the center of the cavern warmed the small space. Spices and floral notes invaded Kore's nose, pleasantly overwhelming. Bones and odd-shaped skulls were balanced on the ledges of the rocky walls that surrounded them. Against the left wall sat a long stone table with various pouches of herbs, small dinos, and kraters for mixing along with lekythoi.

On the right wall sat a smaller stone table with several black candles. Their wax dripped down the side, drying over old wax. Kore noted the various crystals that lay scattered about the table and saw the two she was already well familiar with, but there were new ones amongst those. Pink ones, some orange, green, and purple.

Kore hadn't known there to be more crystals than the few her mother had worked with. Then she learned of the crystal that was most common in this realm.

Looking around the rest of the cavern, Kore could not make sight of Hecate, at least not from the light provided by the small fire.

"Is she here?" Kore whispered.

"I am here, Lady Kore." Hecate's musical voice came from the shadows in the back.

"Have we interrupted you, Lady Hecate?" Agatha asked with a bow.

"Not at all, dear," she assured, stepping into the light.

Her hair was pulled up high into a small puff at the top of her head, a soot handprint covering her face.

"Hexing mortals again, I see," Agatha smirked.

"Oh, only a little." Hecate tossed a fine black powder into the fire, turning the flame a bright green.

"What had this one done?" Agatha asked.

"Disrespected the dead." Hecate walked around to meet Kore and took her by the hands. "And what brings you all this way?"

"The herbs you requested are ready, so I thought I'd bring them by. I also had a few questions I wanted to ask of you." Kore pulled the pouches from the satchel and handed them to Hecate.

"Wonderful! I do thank you dearly!" Hecate took the pouches over to the larger table and set them with the rest, taking a pinch of herb from each new pouch and sprinkling them inside a small mortar.

"You are most welcome. If you do not mind, what are your plans with them?" Kore inquired.

"Just a tea." Hecate smiled as she crushed the herbs together.

Agatha joined them to watch as Hecate placed a black pot of water over the firepit and went back to prepping the space. Spreading a thin cloth over the mouth of a small amphora, she then put the herb mix in the center of the cloth, holding its place with her free hand.

"Agatha, would you be so kind?" She tilted her head to the pot on the fire, and Agatha quickly retrieved it. She poured the boiling water over the herbs and cloth while Hecate held them in place at the mouth. Once all the water was in, Hecate tied the cloth together by the corners so that it held the herbs like a pouch. When she was sure it was secure, she dropped it into the water and covered the amphora with a flat dish.

"Agatha, since you are here, you can practice your shadowing spells," the goddess offered.

Agatha bowed to the divines and crept into the shadows,

quickly disappearing from their sight.

"Shadowing spells?" Kore echoed.

Hecate looked at the goddess from the corner of her eyes. "It is to help me with my mortal workings. She is the only one I trust to take the power more seriously."

"She does seem to be most authoritative."

"Oh, because she is! She is like a mama to the other nymphs. The only elder nymph left from the beginning." Hecate's voice trailed, locked in a distant memory of the past.

"The only one? What happened to the others?" Kore gasped. She remembered the tales Alena had told her back at the hall, about how Aidoneus created it to shelter them from the creatures that lurked.

"Murdered. Eaten. Raped by the other gods or turned to flames to flee all of those outcomes." She shrugged.

Kore's eyes widened at the words.

Hecate's face fell. "Has Hades not told you?"

"Not him. The nymphs had informed me he built a hall as shelter from creatures like the Cyclopes."

"The creatures and the other gods of this realm. Not all are as kind as Hermes or myself. As I hear you have learned," Hecate added.

Kore's body shuddered at the thought of Thanatos and their fight. She swallowed hard and pushed the memories back.

"Agatha remembers the horror they had faced, so she tends to see things in a different light. The others were just little ones when it all happened, so they do not grasp the dangers as she does. She will take the practice seriously, where I fear they will not." Hecate sighed, pouring the tea into two kantharoi. She took Kore over to the firepit and guided her to sit on the floor beside it.

"He has done a great deal for them," Kore said.

"He is a kind and giving king," Hecate noted.

Kore had always seen him as kind, not as a king or a god, but as a person. It was warming to see the divines of his realm, the nymphs, and shades all saw him how she had. She just wished her mother would see it. Perhaps she had. Perhaps that day long ago, on Mt. Olympus, Demeter saw how kind he truly was, and maybe that was the reason she had not ordered Kore's return just yet.

She hoped her mother found him to be a better match for her than Ares, and by her leaving Kore with the God of the Dead, she hoped that was her mother's way of letting her know.

Kore took a sip of the tea; bitter yet it tingled her tongue and lips with every sip.

"This is delicious tea, Hecate. What do you call it?" Kore gushed, finishing the last of it.

"Divination Tsai. It is the reason I asked for that pairing of herbs. I know you still hope to seek the pomegranate tree in Tartarus. It is hard to explain the location of it, so you will have to see it for yourself."

"How does it work?"

"First, we close our eyes."

Kore lowered her eyelids, closing her eyes and waiting for the next instruction.

"Next, we breathe. Deep inhale." Hecate paused and took a deep breath. "Then—exhale." She let out the air she had gathered in a steady exhalation.

"We do this quietly until the tree presents itself to us," Hecate informed.

Kore was familiar with the breathing technique. It was one of the first things her mother taught her for grounding before she used her power to draw the energy and life from the earth to create. Kore had used this technique until she learned of another way to draw the life force out.

She was not, however, familiar with waiting for visions. But she did as told, taking in a deep breath and slowly exhaling it out. At first, her mind just ran through the events in her day that had already occurred.

Inhale. Exhale.

Memories of Aidoneus's hands at her waist flashed across her mind's eye. The burning feeling of his palms seared her skin.

Inhale. Exhale.

Visions of Thanatos, angry and covered in ichor, her vines snaking around him.

Inhale. Exhale.

"Open your eyes, Kore," a voice ordered.

It was not a friendly tone, but it was a familiar voice. One she'd rather never hear again. She opened her eyes and found herself in a dark space. Hecate, the fire, the skulls, and the table of herbs had all vanished and left her alone.

"You know you belong to me," the voice growled from behind.

She closed her eyes tight and held her breath; the only sound she could hear was her heart pounding against her chest.

"You hear me, little goddess?" the voice growled again.

"I do not," Kore whispered.

She could feel the pressure build behind her eyes as she fought back tears.

"You are mine!" His voice grew louder.

"I am not!" she cracked, cupping her hands over her ears, but his voice only grew in intensity.

"I am coming for you, my little goddess!" he boomed, his enormous hand gripped around her wrist. The fire she felt was different. It was painful. It was scalding. She cried out against it, yanking her hand away and falling back.

She landed on hard, burning brimstone. The sound of wailing screams filled the air with the smell she still had not found a name for. The smoke from the nearby blaze circled her, choking her and drying her throat.

She looked ahead beyond the flames and found a brightly lit grove in the far distance. She struggled to push herself up, but once on her feet, she slowly made her way to it, wincing at the pain the scalding floor began ripping from her feet. Air tore from her lungs, pulling pressure at her heart.

The further she stepped from the fire, the more the smoke drifted from her. The sound of rushing water began to climb over the sound of screams. From a small trail in the moss, she came near a shallow river with crystal-blue water spilling over the jagged rocks and brimstone. It wound down and around the grove, creating a small, lush patch in the barren rock of Tartarus.

The water came to a rushing swirl around a small hill of stone, moss, and patches of wild grass. Clinging to the hill of rock with thick roots sat a flourishing tree with bright green and yellow leaves. The low-hanging branches held large, round red fruits, which dangled just above a few chained shades at its base.

Their bodies were half submerged in the rushing water, and their weak and shriveled arms reached up to the branches, desperately grasping for the fruits just out of reach. They had their backs to her, all scraped and bloodied from the jagged rocks.

Inhale. Exhale.

The rotten odor and thick, heated air became light with the hint of spice and fire. The burning beneath her feet grew cold, and the screaming around her fell quiet and was replaced by the soft crackling of burning wood.

She gasped for air, fighting against tightened lungs. She could still feel every vision from Aidoneus's hands at her waist to Ares's hand at her wrist and even the hot brimstone beneath her feet.

Her eyes shot open and quickly sought out her wrist to examine. It appeared normal, no redness or burn in any way, unlike how it had felt. Her unharmed hand reached up and grasped her crystal to ensure she was out of the visions.

"Did you not see the location?" Hecate asked with wide eyes.

"I did, I just think I—I got a bit more than that." Kore was not sure what to make of the vision of Ares. It could very well have been her fear of him.

"What did you see?" Hecate inquired.

Kore did not want to mention Ares; if it was nothing, it would remain so. The vision of the tree could be wrong as well, but she would soon find out.

"I saw the pomegranate tree, surrounded by shades and water," she explained breathlessly.

"I see!" Hecate said softly, shifting in her spot. "What all did you see?"

"The cavern had a blazing fire in the middle and a river rushing alongside it. In the far distance, I could see the tree and shades." She shuddered at the thought of their torn and shredded backs.

"Sounds? Smells? Did you do anything?" Hecate pressed again.

Kore thought over the vision, pulling every detail to the front of her mind and closing her eyes for a clearer recollection.

"The air was of a rotten odor, and the smoke from the fire was suffocating. I could hear the screams of the tormented souls around me but only saw the ones chained to the jagged rocks at the tree's base," Kore explained.

"Hm, more helpful than the information I gave you, was it not?" Hecate stood, walking back to the table of herbs and pouring herself more tea. She was right. It was more than what she had given, but only by a little. Kore still had no idea where that cavern was.

Perhaps another elder being could assist, and Agatha was the next oldest one Kore knew besides Hecate and Aidoneus. Kore hoped she had more insight to share.

"Would Agatha know?" Kore asked when Hecate returned with her tea.

"I have never asked her, but I am sure she would have a better idea. She should be along shortly. You were out for some time, and she mentioned you saying you wanted to be back before the sun touched the land," Hecate said, sipping her tea.

Kore stretched her arms above her before climbing to her feet. Her body was stiff and sore from sitting. "How long have I been out?"

"A few hours I would say. Four or five." Hecate shrugged.

Kore's eyes widened; it had all felt like a few minutes.

"You are back," Agatha's low voice droned as she slowly emerged from the shadows.

"Yes. It was an adventure all over again." Kore forced a smile and turned back to Hecate with a bow. "I do apologize. I did not mean for the visit to seem so short."

"It is fine, Lady Kore. It did not seem so short to me."

"I do hope I can come again; I enjoyed the parts I was conscious for," Kore added, bowing a final time before Hecate drifted back into the shadows and out of sight. "Agatha, before we go back to the palace, I wanted to ask you something," Kore began, and Agatha waited. "Do you happen to know the location of the pomegranate tree? The one in Tartarus?"

Agatha's eyes fell to the black crystal around Kore's neck and then slowly climbed their way back to the goddess's face.

"I do." Her tone was low and flat.

"Could you take me?"

"We do not venture from the palace," she reminded.

"Could you tell me where?" Kore offered, remembering the story Alena had told.

Agatha looked her over for a moment, her lips pressed and brows pulled down.

"If that is what you wish." It wasn't exactly a yes, but it was good enough.

"I would appreciate it, Agatha, and if it isn't too much more, please do not tell Aidoneus."

Agatha nodded once. Kore joined her with a smile and took her by the hands.

"All right then, I am ready!"

CHAPTER XXVI

THE JUDGMENTS, THE CROWN, AND THE THRONE

Kore was awakened from the bright rays of the false sun beaming in through the columns. She stretched and reached her arm back, her hand finding the furs beside her. She rolled over with a groan, in search of his warmth, but all she found was more fur.

She had grown used to waking up with Aidoneus beside her over the last few mornings. After the night in the bathing pool, she had made it a point to request his company alongside her in his kline. Though, he had also made it a point to place the furs between them.

The mornings she woke to him already risen for the day meant they were to be days full of judgments, which had become more frequent now that the mortals were at war again. Sending more and more shades to his realm, busying the king. Keeping his mind occupied with scroll after scroll and life after life.

She yawned and rubbed her eyes, allowing them to focus on the bright light that flooded in.

"Finally awake I see." The sudden sound of Aidoneus's

deep voice startled her up from her spot. “My apologies, I had not meant to frighten you.” He chuckled with a half-smile, dressed in his judgment robes and ready for the long day ahead.

“You didn’t frighten me.” She smiled sheepishly. “Just unprepared. Are there to be a lot of judgments this day?”

“I am afraid so. Which brings me to my request of you.” He sighed.

Kore propped herself up on her elbow, holding the furs to her chest with her free hand, so as to not start something she knew he would inevitably end.

“There have been a lot of shades to judge by myself. It would please me if you sat by my side in this day’s judgments,” he said with his eyes on the furs in her hands.

Kore hadn’t anything planned for the day, and spending it with Aidoneus was more appealing than wandering about the palace as she had been doing the last few weeks. She also wanted to learn of this war and how many souls it sent to Aidoneus’s realm.

“I would love to!” she cheered happily.

“Does judging and punishing souls excite you, Goddess?”

Kore only smiled in return.

“Callisto and Alena will be in with proper robes and judgment attire,” he informed, rising to his feet. “I shall be seeing you in the hall.”

He bowed with a smile and departed, leaving only the remnant of his smoke lofting about.

It wasn’t long after his departure that two trails of smog drifted to her side and the nymphs appeared with more than just smiles to offer. Callisto held a bundle of linen robes in a deep, dark shade of red. Resting on top of the fabrics were two round, obsidian crests with a carving of a three-headed dog. Cerberus.

Alena held a pointed object draped in a dark, sheer fabric. She placed it on the end of the kline and assisted

Callisto in laying out the robes.

"What is all this?" Kore quizzed.

"Royal robes. Lord Hades wants the shades to respect your word as they do his. Being a divine isn't enough when it comes to judgments," Alena informed.

"They have never seen you, and since the mortals hardly speak Lord Hades's name, they wouldn't know the difference. Just like the beauty of the realm, you will be a surprise. You will be like a queen to them," Callisto gushed.

"She *will* be a queen to them," Alena corrected. "They will see her as queen when they enter."

They finished assisting Kore into the many layers of the royal robes. Callisto pinned everything up at each shoulder with the crests while Alena fiddled with her hair, braiding it down her back and laying it across her right shoulder.

Finally, Alena pulled the sheer fabric from the hidden object she had placed on the kline, revealing a black-and-gold crown. The band consisted of what appeared to be vines but was made of the hard obsidian of the realm. The vines twisted up into several points. Clear, sparkling gems lay scattered through the piece, giving it a dazzling glimmer when it reflected the light at just the right angle.

Alena placed it atop Kore's head and stepped back with Callisto to admire their work. Their lips pulled across their faces, displaying two beautifully bright smiles. They glanced at each other, their joy quickly intensifying.

"Magnificent," Callisto whispered.

They walked her over to the dark polished obsidian to see for herself.

Kore had never seen her divinity glow so bright; the deep red from the robes added a beautiful balance of light and dark. Her hair was a brighter red than she had ever seen it, and even the way the free strands fell around her face looked as if she was perfectly sculpted. She felt beautiful, she felt powerful, and she felt—seductive.

"We should get you down to the Judgment Hall!"

Callisto said.

The nymphs grabbed Kore's hand and off they were, a speeding cloud through the corridors and down the steps until they were just outside the halls. Shifting and moving through the chambers were two vastly different feelings for Kore. While one almost robbed her of her breath, the other was a freeing feeling as she flew through space around her.

"Wait right here. I will go inform our lord of your arrival; he will want you to enter alongside him," Alena announced. She made her way into the hall and around the front of the throne where Aidoneus sat. The hall was already crowded with shades, and some even spilled out into the front court.

Alena spoke quickly in hushed tones as she informed the king of Kore's arrival. He rose from the throne and headed out to the corridor where Kore stood. Her chest stilled and her heart throbbed when she took in his royal judgment robes.

When he turned the column and caught sight of her, he took pause. Her breath caught as his eyes trailed her body, taking in the view.

"Yperochos. Queen Kore." He bowed; his lips turned up at his words. He took her by the hand and leaned close so that his lips were just near her ear.

"Are you ready for the real judgments?" he whispered.

The heat of his breath grazing across her skin was charged with his scent of cypress and fire. Before she had a chance to answer, he wrapped his arm around her waist and pulled her close. Taking her hand in his, they walked back to the throne.

The murmur of soft chatter from the shades came to a quick halt as they all gaped up at the king and his unnamed queen. After a few silent moments, a wave of hushed whispers circled the hall once more.

Aidoneus did well to ignore the shift as he guided Kore to his large throne, big enough for two. The shades' cloudy eyes locked on their intertwined hands.

Once the two divines sat, Minos entered with a large basket of scrolls. Alena came by Kore's side and leaned into her with a voice just above a whisper.

"We will be back with a fruit platter," she informed as she looked back to the shades. "There are no breaks during judgment."

Kore nodded and leaned back into Aidoneus, who was already occupied with a white-handled scroll in his free hand. He read through it quickly, presenting a small passage to her. The name scribbled at the top read *Ocnus Bianor,* and what she read of him indicated he'd had no ordinary life.

"What a way to begin the day," he whispered.

From what Kore had read, Ocnus had spent his mortal life making elaborate dealings with those less fortunate than he. Feeding promises of golds, riches, and the favor of the divines, so long as they labored to build him a palace "fit for a god." However, once the palace was finished, he released the servants without so much as a grain of wheat, making their labors frivolous in the end.

She searched his eyes for a hint of what he was thinking, but they were fixed and focused. She looked through a few more passages, learning most of these dealings ended in the death of the poor worker or the worker's family. Including young children and the elderly.

She lifted her head to speak into Aidoneus's ear. "These actions were senseless and wasteful. Even if these lives had not ended, what came of the work they did? He wasted hope, time, and life."

Aidoneus did not speak, but his lips pulled up in an approving smile.

"When we send souls to Tartarus, do they just go and wander? May I give him a punishment?" she inquired.

"Did you have something in mind?"

"Yes, I would like him to feel as they did."

Aidoneus nodded once, closed the scroll, and turned to the shades before them.

"You may read him his punishment," he offered with a smile.

She knew exactly what she wanted the shade to do, but she had never dealt out an eternal punishment. What if her punishment was not severe enough? What if it was too severe?

She took a deep breath and straightened up as the shade approached them. He bowed slowly, his eyes locked on the two divines' intertwined hands, but never on their eyes.

"Ocnus, you are aware of your mortal crimes, yes?" she began, and Ocnus quickly nodded, his eyes still down. "Then it should be no surprise to you that you will be going to Tartarus, but I have a task for you."

She stood and took a slow step toward the shade. "You will look up to me," she demanded.

The shade hesitantly obeyed, his eyes finding and locking with hers.

"You will weave me a rope of straw, long and beautiful. Fifty meters in length."

The shade's face twisted, a slight smile tugging at his lips.

"Be forewarned, Ocnus, there are hungry beasts about. We wouldn't want one to eat up all your work, now would we?" A wicked smile danced across her face as she glared down at the shade.

When he finally broke free of her gaze, dropping his head, Kore walked back to Aidoneus's side and sat.

"A mule will eat his work as fast as he can weave it. But I do wish him an inability to see the creature," she said softly.

A low rattle erupted from Aidoneus's chest as he fought a chuckle. "As you command." He lifted his hand and flipped his wrist as he had before, and the shade was gone.

He handed the scroll off to Minos, who had another empty basket beside him where he would place the completed ones after the shade had departed.

Alena and Callisto returned with the platter of fruits and nectar and placed it on the wide armrest of the throne. The two bowed quickly and took their spots next to Elpida, Agatha, and Eleni, who all stood behind Minos.

Aidoneus reached into the basket at his feet and pulled forth a scroll with a golden pole. He opened it between them, allowing Kore a view of the parchment as well.

This shade was far different than the first one, his life full of nobility in every way one could think of. Devoted to the Theos, a caring, loving husband and father, he was a war hero from previous wars Kore had not yet learned of. He was not just noble; he was heroic and spent his life earning his spot in Elysium.

In the top right of the scroll next to the shade's mortal name of *Euthymius Irene* sat a small etched-in *II*. She looked up to Aidoneus.

"What is this here?" she questioned, pointing to the numeral.

"That is the number of lives he has already lived. He will be granted one more if he chooses, and if he lives that life as pure as the last two, he will be sent to the Isles of the Blessed. It is an honorable place to be for one so pure," he explained.

"So, he goes to Elysium?"

"If he so wishes. He still has the option to be reincarnated once more. He may choose that, or he may choose Elysium. We will have to see." Aidoneus righted himself to scan the sea of shades.

"Euthymius Irene!" he called.

The shade made his way to the throne, his head held high. Aidoneus took Kore's hand and guided her to her feet to approach the shade. They met him at the steps. His eyes were on Aidoneus as he bowed to the divines; he was not fearful of looking at them as the other had been.

"It is good to see you again, Euthymius. I see you followed through with your promise," the king said to him.

"I have and I would be pleased to do it once more."

"Very well." Aidoneus nodded, held out his hand, and grasped Euthymius's ghostly arm. "Once again, good luck."

A light emitted from the grasp between the god and the shade. Growing brighter, engulfing him until the hall was illuminated by it in a blinding flash. It flickered a few times and then faded away, Euthymius fading with it. Aidoneus turned to Kore with a soft grin before leading her back to reclaim their seats on the throne.

"Where did he go?" Kore whispered.

"To be reborn. Hopefully, he takes the righteous path with this one as well," he explained.

They took their seats and readied for the next scroll.

The rest of the day carried on in that fashion. The souls who were sent to the Asphodel Fields were escorted off by Eleni, the ones who chose Elysium were escorted by Elpida, and the ones who were subject to the mourning fields went along with Agatha. Any shade sent to Tartarus was sent at the hands of Aidoneus, and any who were granted reincarnation were sent with his blessing.

Kore had made several judgments and punishments to those sentenced to Tartarus, and they all went with great approval from Aidoneus. He held her close to him most of the day, his arm around her waist, caressing the softness of her skin through the fabric. He brushed his fingers across her arm, teasing her skin as he whispered in her ear.

He whispered of how he enjoyed her vengeance when she placed her punishment, of how she surprised him. The feel of his lips lightly brushing against her ear, mixed with the heat of his breath always stirred the same reaction in her core.

Every touch brought forth a heated flush to her face and knotted her stomach in the most pleasant ways, offering her distraction between each shade's judgment.

It wasn't until the false sun had retired for the day and the moon made her appearance known that Aidoneus called Minos over to the throne.

"Minos, we will be taking our leave for the eve. You will finish up here," he ordered.

"Yes, my lord." Minos bowed and proceeded to grab a scroll from the basket. Taking his spot in front of the throne, he called out the next name.

The divines stood and made their way from the hall into the main corridor.

"You did wonderfully, yet again. I hope it was not too boring for you. I would like you to join me for more."

Kore had not found the judgments as terribly boring as Aidoneus made them sound. In fact, she quite enjoyed them.

"I would enjoy that." She smiled.

"I am happy to hear." His lips split across his face, displaying his laugh lines. He paused for a moment, his eyes sweeping over her. "Come, let us cleanse before we eat."

He shifted them to the bathing chamber, where candles lay scattered about the entire chamber floor. Several lekythoi lined the edge of the bath and were accompanied by a small basket filled with white asphodel petals.

"You get in. I will grab you fresh robes. It appears those were left in the main chamber," he said, turning on his heels and making his way toward the steps.

Kore turned back to the steamy pool and removed the pin from her shoulder, allowing the linen robes to slip free from her and land about her feet. The chamber was a bit cooler than it usually was, and it sent a quick shiver down her spine and caused little bumps to rise on her skin.

Pulling the crown free from her head, she set it on the bundle of robes at her feet and walked into the warm water.

She let the heat slowly overtake her body and relax her sore muscles. Looking out to the opening before her, she swam to the front end of the pool. As with most evenings, she rested her arms on the edge and gazed out at the glowing village in a sea of darkness.

The deep night sky melted into the blackness of the fields, cut in half by the flooding red river of Tartarus, glowing brightly as it raced down the side of the hellish mountain.

It was his footsteps she heard first, pausing at the edge of the pool.

"Do you enjoy the view?" His voice was low and dark, a sound that shook her in the most pleasurable way.

"I do." She sighed, swimming back to the row of oils.

He held a bundle of fabric in his hand that he set down at his feet, his eyes locked on hers. He pulled at the leather binding at his waist, dropping his chiton to the floor before removing the leather straps around his chest and letting them drop to join the rest of the pile at his feet.

She tried to keep her eyes on his, but when he lifted his arms to remove his crown, she could not control their quick descent.

Her face grew warm as she continued to watch while Aidoneus entered the pool and made his way to her side.

"Would you like me to cleanse your hair, Lord Hades?"

"Allow me." He smiled, grabbing a lekythos.

Kore spun around, placing her back to him. The heat of his body pressed against hers. He poured the oil in her locks and began smoothing it through her hair, massaging her scalp as he went. Her body melted back under his touch, her eyes closed, and as she leaned her head against his chest, a soft moan escaped her lips. She felt his hands freeze in her hair, and his body became rigid.

For a moment, Kore thought he was going to withdraw his hands and back away, but then she felt them slip to the hollow of her neck. Her body shivered at the touch, her eyes opened, and she tilted her head just enough to catch his gaze. His eyes were dark as they looked over her, full of hunger and longing. Something she had only seen one other time.

She turned, her body pressed against his as she ran her hands up his chest and paused at his neck, causing his body to tense once more under her touch. He leaned back against the pool's edge, allowing her to straddle his lap as she had done the first time, and she gasped.

His hands found the crease of her waist and pulled her close. Their lips crashed together. He inhaled deeply, parting her with his tongue.

His fingers gripped her waist, eliciting a soft yelp, and his lips fell from hers and found their way to the curve of her neck. She cried out softly again, moving her hips into him, feeling his length pressed against her.

His hands traveled up, taking her breast. Her lips fell to his ear, where she kissed and sucked and licked at his skin. A deep groan ripped through his chest, and his hands moved back to her waist.

"Aidoneus," she whispered.

A sound that pulled another ragged groan from him.

"I love you."

Just as soon as the words left her mouth, his body froze.

"You should not say such things," he growled, tightening his grip.

"Why do you deny my love for you?" Her voice still a whisper.

"The Underworld is no place for love." He repeated the same words he spoke to her the last time they met in her mother's meadow. She pulled her head up so that she was looking into his eyes—eyes that were now filled with hurt.

"I do not believe it so, as I feel it in my heart, and I think you do as well. Why deny it?"

He stared at her for a long while, his hands still anchored to her soft skin, refusing to let go.

"You will tire of this," he said flatly.

The words enraged her deeply, but she took a shallow breath and chose her words carefully before she spoke again.

"Why are you so positive that I will grow tired of this? Of you? Have I not shown you that I care? I lied to my mother, ran away from the only home I knew, and paid a fine price to cross on the ferryman's boat. I pounded at the doors of Tartarus. I was chased, attacked, and broken just to be here. To be with you. Why would I tire of it?"

He was quiet for a long while, unable to find the words to protest with.

"You called me *a* queen, so let me be *your* queen," she demanded, pressing her lips against his again with more passion than she knew she was capable of.

He did not stop her, and he did not pull away. He welcomed her, pulling her closer and kissing her back with an equally matched passion. His intoxicating scent flooded her senses, pulling free a side to her she had only wished to have known.

Her hands found their way to his hair where they twisted and pulled at him. He gripped her wherever he could, kissing her urgently, his body shaking every time she pushed her hips down on him.

Another ragged groan ripped through his chest as he pulled her to him and rose from the pool. The oils still slick in their hair.

He carried her from the bathing pool to his chambers, his lips never breaking from her skin as he walked to the kline and set her over the furs, leaning over her naked body and taking in every inch.

His hands traveled from the curve of her hip to the center between her legs. A smile spread across his lips when her body shook at the touch, catching her moan in his mouth.

Fingers grazed against her soft, sensitive skin, and her hips bucked in response. A low chuckle rose from his chest as he swept his fingers over her slit once more, tasting each moan and gasp that escaped her.

She rolled her hips into him again, and this time, he caught her thigh in his hand and pushed it to the side, allowing him to easily fit between her legs, his head resting against hers.

Kore's mind became a haze, fogged by his smell, touch, and taste. She was surrounded by him, and she still felt it was not enough.

"You are sure?" he inquired breathlessly.

She nodded, tilting her head back and taking his lips

once more. In one motion, he slid into her, coaxing a gasp from her lips.

Her fingers dug into his shoulder, and the pressure of tears began to build as he worked, slowly rolling his hips. He ran his thumb over her cheek, clearing the tears that had collected there, and replaced them with soft kisses.

Her hands clung to his back, pulling him closer and deeper, and his lips made their way to the hollow of her neck, where he groaned against her.

His body shook as he ground deeper, and pressure started to build at the pit of her stomach. It was euphoria. It was ecstasy. It was a new taste of power.

Her hands found their way to his hair, twisting and tangling in the strands as she was hit with wave after wave of pure pleasure. She cried out and her body shook, her labored panting edging Aidoneus on, his thrusts driving into her faster and deeper until a ragged groan ripped from his chest and his body shivered. He collapsed on top of her, breathing deeply and kissing her neck.

"Is this not better?" she whispered.

"Is what?" he moaned against her soft skin.

"Not having to fight yourself."

She shifted—rolling her hips against him again, teasing him, begging him for more. A deep growl rumbled in his chest as he grew hard again, his body reacting to her movements and thrusting into her hungrily, as if this were the first time.

She wrapped her legs around his waist to pull him in deeper. Each breathless moan that escaped her stirred a feral and savage look in his eyes, but she did not fear it. She welcomed it, thirsted for it. He took her mouth in his, parting her lips with his tongue and invading her mouth with soft, gentle movements. Tasting her, teaching her, coaxing her.

The pressure within her began to build for the second time, her head flooding and her mind going blank. She cried out against him, her body convulsing as the waves of ecstasy rippled through her. But he did not slow. His hand gripped her waist tightly while the other found its place, wrapped securely around her neck. His lips left hers, trailing down until he found her nipples. He licked and sucked until they grew hard and taut.

A heavy and labored groan viciously ripped through him as he came, his body collapsing once more on top of hers. His skin was sticky and damp, slick with sweat from their lovemaking.

"I would have to say that it is better," he finally answered, combing his hand through her hair.

Kore wrapped her arms around him, tucking her head against his chest, and a smile curved her lips at his words.

"Kore?" he whispered.

"Hm?" Kore's body relaxed into him, molding to his as if they had been made for each other.

A vanilla scent filled the air, and yellow-and-white flowers began falling around them. Aidoneus picked one up, twirling it between his fingers before tucking it into her hair.

"I love you too."

CHAPTER XXVII

THE TRIP TO TARTARUS, THE SECOND JOURNEY, AND THE GROVE

Kore leaned into Aidoneus as they sat up in the kline, after he had demonstrated his work. She had not seen the small yellow-and-white flowers in the mortal realm, nor had she seen them in the garden of Olympus or the fields in the Underworld. Its flat, white, star-shaped petals cupped around a golden bell, and its sweet smell lofted around them.

"You can create life," she mused.

"Only this." His voice was apathetic.

"Only this? What do you call it?"

"I call it a narcissus. It *was* the only thing I could touch that had beauty and life."

"Was?" she repeated.

He gently smoothed his thumb across the curve of her jaw.

"I get to touch something far more beautiful now," he whispered, hooking her chin with his index finger and thumb, tilting her head so that she was looking him in the eyes. "Are you happy?"

Kore inhaled deeply. Happy was not the word she would use to describe how she felt. She shifted, closing the distance between them, and pressed her lips against his.

"*Enthousiasmos*," she breathed after pulling away.

Her body relaxed into his, and he kissed her once more, with passion, with heat, burning and tingling the soft, delicate skin he touched. He pulled her leg over him so that she was straddling his lap. She quite enjoyed the position, having the ability to see and kiss his face and the way his hands pressed against her back.

He moved from her lips to the hollow of her neck and then to the curve of her breast. Taking her in his mouth, licking and sucking her nipple until it was erect, then doing the same to the other. His hands worked about her hips, moving her close against him as he filled her.

Kore cried out against the waves of pressure that carried her to her climax. Her nails dug into his shoulders. His hooded eyes met hers, burning her with his hunger and need.

"*Panémorfi Vasílissa mou*," he moaned.

Kore pressed her palm to his cheek, and he held her hips as he moved into her faster. Her head rolled back, and the spasms peaked with another climax. Aidoneus followed close behind with a ragged, breathless groan.

She fell against him, exhausted, her body still riding out the small shudders that rang through her. Aidoneus ran his hands along her back and through her hair.

Kore could lie with him all day, not just in this way. In any way. She felt free with him, a sense of power she had longed for without knowing. A power that was fueled by the energy of the realm. This was her home; this was where she belonged. With the King of the Underworld.

He withdrew from her, pausing for a moment before fully exiting. His jaw clenched and Kore wasn't sure if he would dive back in or fully part from her.

She felt him twitch, and her body reacted in response, but this time she was quick to regain control over her emotions. Despite his arms wrapped securely around her she pushed herself up until he fell free from her.

A deep-chested groan rattled within him as his brows pinched together and he accepted the small defeat.

"We should eat." She sighed.

"Have I not satisfied you yet?"

"You have, but I am afraid I need food too."

"Very well." He smiled, rising from the kline with her still in his arms. He set her on her feet, the cool marble sending a slight chill down her spine.

"Shall we bathe first?" he asked with a wicked smile. The heat flushed Kore's face once more as she nodded.

They ate their ambrosia and nectar rather quickly. The thickness was better washed down with fruit and wine in the later part of the meal. Aidoneus had explained to her that it helped to not feel weighed down by the choking mixtures.

She could feel his eyes on her, watching her every movement.

"Yes?" She giggled.

"I can have Minos handle the judgments for today if you'd like company," he offered with a mischievous tone.

They had spent the last week keeping busy in the kline or pool. Learning, teaching, and worshipping one another, leaving the judgments to Minos for the time, but they had backed up to an uncontrollable number in the king's absence. The judges of the realm worked day and night in the hall, placing the shades. But still, many spilled out onto the court and even to the bridge.

Aidoneus felt it was time he returned to get the shades down to a reasonable number and gave Kore the option of returning as well, but she had asked for just one day to herself.

She only needed one.

She smiled softly. "I was thinking of going to see Hecate again."

"Will you require Agatha?"

"Not to join me, but I do have a question on how to get there from the fire in the Nymph Hall. They had mentioned shifting through it," Kore fabricated.

He stood, holding his hand out, and she took it as they made their way from the dining hall, stopping in the corridor.

He pulled her hand to his lips and placed a kiss on each knuckle. "I shall see you tonight, *Vasílissa mou*."

Kore's body shook at the sound, how the words fell on her ears. She would never tire of it. It was a power he gave her. One she felt deep in her stomach.

"Call for Agatha," he said before vanishing into his cloud and disappearing.

She cleared her throat, having not attempted a call to the nymphs before.

"Agatha!" She waited but received no answer. "Agatha?" she called out louder.

"Yes?" Her cold voice droned from behind Kore, causing the goddess to jump.

She spun around to find Agatha standing a few feet from her. "Oh! Were you there that entire time?"

"I had only just arrived," she said flatly. "You required my assistance?"

"Yes, were you able to write out the location?" Kore inquired.

Normally she would give a morning greeting, but she was in a hurry, and Agatha was not known to greet with average pleasantries either. The nymph reached into her robes, pulling forth a folded piece of parchment that she handed to the goddess as she bowed before her.

"If I may," Agatha began, "take one of the hounds."

She vanished without waiting for a response, leaving Kore alone in the hall.

Take one of the hounds. She had not called for any of the hounds before either, but she recalled how Aidoneus did the first time Pita joined her on an exploration. Placing her forefinger and thumb along the sides of her cheeks, she blew through the slit in her teeth—releasing a high-pitched whistle. It echoed through the corridor and bounced from the columns.

Once the ringing stopped, the symphony of howls filled the air as it had before. A speeding cloud rushed to her side, presenting the adorable hound with his lopped tongue and tilted head.

"Will you be joining me on another adventure?" Kore giggled. The hound thumped his tail hard against the floor in response. "I will take that as a yes."

She tucked the paper into her robes, and they headed out, walking past the Judgment Hall and out onto the steps that led to the bridge.

Kore hadn't had much practice with her shifting, which would probably have been useful for today. Instead, they would need to walk, and quickly.

Once they had crossed the bridge, she took a seat on a nearby boulder to put on the sandals she had tucked away that morning and looked over the parchment Agatha had given her.

At the top, in small writing, was a description of the journey, while in the bottom half, Agatha had sketched a map. Kore read the written explanation first.

"Avoid stepping foot on the main cavern floor and stick to the ledges and walls as much as possible. The cavern you seek is on the opposite side. It is a brightly lit cavern closest to the great fire. By sticking to the ledge and heading right, you will wrap around and find yourself at the open mouth of the cave where water spills in."

After looking over the sketch, she folded the parchment and placed it back in the folds of her robes. She looked down at Pita with a hopeful smile.

She had promised Aidoneus she would not return to Tartarus, and at the time she had meant it; she would still prefer not to go back. But the threat of Ares was all too real, and with the vision burning in her memory, there was only one way to determine if it was worth anything at all. She had to go for the tree, to test the theory.

Pita pressed his nose into her hand, and she exhaled the breath she had been holding. "Let's go."

She led the way through the fields, Pita bounding and pouncing through the sweet-smelling asphodels. His dark fur popped up now and then through the light-colored stalks. Kore, however, kept her head low under the tops of the flowers, moving quickly through the field to make better time. It wasn't the journey to Tartarus that worried her; she was out in the open and hoped Aidoneus would be too busy with his eyes on scrolls and shades to look out over the fields long enough to catch her.

She had the aid of the plants, folding them over her a bit more for cover as she went, and the trail up to Tartarus's entrance was riddled with enough rock cover to keep her out of view. The only way the rocks could help her from there.

She looked back to the palace; the walk didn't seem to measure up to the actual distance she traveled. The false sun was at its highest point, giving her more time than she thought.

She shrugged. At least she would get this done before nightfall. If she stayed along the wall as Agatha suggested, it wouldn't be too long until she was at the tree, and if her vision was correct, it should only be a small hop over to the rockface the tree clung to.

Searching the rocks in front of her, Kore felt it best to keep low and out of sight. Ducking behind the boulders as she moved from the soft soil and onto the hard, lifeless brimstone and its loose, shifting rocks. The heat quickly warmed the soles of her sandals, but Pita did not seem to mind it as he sniffed around the path.

They moved quickly, not pausing despite the dry burning Kore felt with each breath. The strong stench clung to her nose, adding an extra layer of difficulty to her breathing.

When they reached the same plateau Kore had found during her first visit, Pita calmly walked ahead, marching toward the guards with his ears erect.

"Pita!" Kore struggled to her feet, ignoring the pain in

her throat as she followed behind.

Pita came to a stop once he had reached the entrance and was only a few feet in front of the unmoved shades, the same serious two Kore had greeted before. She walked up, taking her place alongside Pita, and sucked in a breath, grabbing her crystal in hand.

"I would like to enter," she said sternly.

The shades looked to each other before bowing and opening the door—just as they had the last time. The hot air blew past her like a raging fire in the wind.

Kore sucked in another deep breath, preparing for the ear-splitting noise to come as she stepped forward and crossed the threshold into Tartarus.

The screams swirled around her; the cries struck her. Pita moved against her as he passed, guiding her to the dark shadows near the wall. She followed quickly, not taking a moment to look over the edge and catch sight of the shades or guards. She scanned the cavern where the fire blazed, her eyes following the trail along the wall that wound around the length of the grotto Agatha wrote about.

They kept close-pressed to the wall, scooting along with the shadows. For the hound, the task appeared easy, but Kore struggled to balance along the narrow ledge.

She flattened her back against the jagged wall and sidestepped her way with her eyes on her feet, avoiding the few shades who took notice of them, their arms outstretched to her as they moaned and cried their pleas.

The heat of the fire blazed against her skin as they came near it, the shades dissipating from its rage.

Pita whined, his tail whipping from one side to the other. His ears popped up erect as he stared down a gaping burrow along the wall where they came to cross. A low, rumbling growl escaped him before he shot forward, speeding along the path and disappearing into the cavity.

"Pita!" Kore called, but she had no time to wait.

She rushed along, ducking into the opening to follow

suit. The burrow was nothing more than a corridor that led into another brightly lit cavern. The low-hanging rocks tugged and snagged her hair when she squeezed through, and the sound of echoed screams filled the small space from something deeper within.

Pita sat at attention near the opening. The cracking of a whip brought Kore to a halt. She waited until the sound shot through the air again, and this time it was followed with a piercing scream and a cackled laugh.

Kore crept closer, stopping near the opening with Pita. Her eyes searched the space until they landed on the source.

A bloodied shade, bound and tied at the wrists, was hunched over a gory mess. His back to his punisher and head low. His tangled strands clung to his face from the crimson that dripped from an open gash in his head.

The whip zipped through the air with a whistle and crashed with a loud crack. The shade jerked his head back, teeth baring as he endured the lashing. When the echo of the crack settled, the cavern was filled with a high-pitched, wicked cackle. A laugh of joy and evil and vengeance.

The whip rang through the air once again, slicing as it went, striking the shade again and again. Kore watched with wide, searching eyes, examining the ledges before her eyes found pause on the punisher. At first, she saw only the long, swinging whip, black with split ropes at the end. It swung back, ready for another blow, and Kore's eyes fell on a familiar divine.

Tisiphone pulled her weapon up, the tail of the whip cutting the air as it went back with a zipping sound. She shot her arm down with a stomach-tearing laugh, high and manic, and the air split in two. The shade cried out as flesh ripped from the bone. Chunks and thick crimson liquid landed in a streak at Kore's feet, and the sadistic laughter echoed as the whip sliced the air once more.

Kore felt the ichor rush through her—Tisiphone had seemed the sweetest of the three upon their last encounter.

More mature and understanding. Seeing her now, doing her divine duty, was like seeing a separate goddess. The goddess she had seen before had been motherly; the one before her now was a punisher, a creature that enjoyed the pain of others.

"Tisiphone!" Alecto's voice echoed through the cavern. "I think that will do for now. We have more to move through."

There was no response, just more wicked laughing as the shade burst into flames—his screams carrying through the cavern.

He burned for a moment before the flame died down and presented a new shade. This one in the same state, hands bound, facing away from the Erinys. Head bowed.

Kore took a step back as the whip pulled up.

"Come, Pita, that will be enough for us," she whispered, turning from the display.

Pita did not hesitate and followed close behind. She allowed him to take his place back in front of her as they climbed back onto the narrow ledge. The blistering fire blazed wildly, the shades screaming and crying, and a burning, rotten smell filled her nose. An attack on her senses.

"Just a little further," Kore assured aloud, more to herself than to the hound.

He knew where they were going; walking the caverns of Tartarus was natural for him since the Erinyes often used all three hounds to aid in their torments.

He shot his head back to her and lobbed his tongue out, smiling at the goddess before proceeding along the curve of the wall. She continued sidestepping the whole way, keeping her eyes on Pita or her own feet until the narrow path transitioned into a wider ledge.

"It should be around here," she breathed.

Looking to the fire, she remembered from her vision that she was not standing above it—she was standing across from it at level ground. She leaned over, ignoring the shades who gawked at her.

Below them on the main cavern floor sat the grotto

where the sound of rushing water echoed, and light moss crept along the rock that faced away from the blaze.

"We have to go down—" As she spoke, she made the mistake of looking into the crowd of shades. Most ignored her; some took notice. But her eyes locked with one she was most familiar with. The one with the missing eye.

The one who had attacked her the first visit through the cavern.

His lips turned up into a bloody smile as his hand reached for her.

CHAPTER XXVIII

THE POMEGRANATE TREE, THE CONSUMING ENERGY, AND THE TRANSFER

Pita's low growl startled her, and Kore rocked back from the ledge. The hound's bark drove the shades back as it bounced from the brimstone. All but one. He paced back and forth, his eye never leaving Kore. Her heart raced and her breathing spiked. Pita barked again, his hair standing on end and his ears erect as he homed in on the disobedient shade.

The hound reared back, slowly lowering his head. With a deep, maddened growl, he sprang forward, throwing himself from the ledge, and plunged onto the shade, sending them both crashing across the hard brimstone with a thundering crack.

"Pita!" Kore cried out.

She searched around for a way to get down to the bottom floor, but there was nothing. No slope, no path or pass to reach Pita. The drop wasn't too much of a distance; if she hung on to the ledge, she could lower herself and then fall the rest of the way.

Rocking back, she positioned herself with her back to the fire. Her hands gripped the stone as she pushed away from the ledge, lowering her body.

A violent growl tore through the air and a hand gripped her ankle, yanking her down hard. She crashed on the brimstone, her foot still caught by whatever had torn her free.

She shot her head up and found the one-eyed shade from before. The flesh at his neck was torn open, and blackened blood spilled free. A gargled groan escaped him as he yanked his arm back, dragging her across the burning stone. She yelped, kicking and twisting from the shade, but he held on with a bone-crunching grip.

Another growl ripped through the air, and Pita heaved himself onto the shade once more. They crashed down hard, the shade releasing Kore as he went. The vicious hellhound tore at his throat. Fangs sank deep, tearing flesh from bone. The sound of snapping tendons joined the horrific symphony as Pita tore violently into the shade without pause.

The nearby souls took notice of the ruckus. Some fell back at the sight of the hound while others had their eyes on Kore.

She wasted no time, scrambling to her feet and darting toward the opening of the grotto. She ducked behind a large boulder and pressed against the cool moss that grew on it. The vicious snarls mixed with wet, gargling cries continued to fill the air.

The vegetation around her vibrated with energy. She could feel their life, and her power reacted instantly. Calling forth whatever she could.

Vines lashed out, shooting themselves over the boulder and whipping at the shades who wandered nearby. The cries and screams soon fell faint under the roar of the fire. Kore peeked around the boulder, finding Pita calmly licking at his front paw. A blood-filled victory.

"Pita! Come!" Kore demanded, her vines pulling back.

The hound raced to her side. His fur was slick with blood, and chunks of flesh clung to his muzzle. She patted the top of his head, thanking him for his protection.

As she took a moment to catch her breath, the faint smell

of grass began to fill her nose. It drew her attention to a small winding path that led deeper into the grotto.

Once ready, they followed the trail, walking between the rocks and boulders. The air was light and fresh as the smell of salt and water filled the space around them. She looked back to the fire that blazed at the center of the cavern. Her heart swelled at the sight. It was just as her vision had shown.

She turned, rounding one last boulder before the sound of rushing water replaced the screams. The crystal-blue liquid rushed by, spilling over the jagged rocks and brimstone. The babbling stream wound down and around the grove, just as she had seen.

Clinging to the rock with thick roots that crept into the running water below sat the pomegranate tree.

The shades with the half-submerged bodies moved sluggishly in the river. Their weak and shriveled arms reached up to the branches, desperate for the fruit that hung above.

They stood steady, their moans and groans barely audible above the rushing current. Their backs were torn and cut from the rocks they rubbed against, and trails of blackened blood trickled into the fast-flowing stream.

Kore's veins ran cold and the air squeezed from her lungs. Every detail, every sight, every sound, every smell was just as she had envisioned.

She tried to breathe but it was cold, and she felt a prickle crawl up her spine. It stung when it reached her lungs, filling them with ice as the realization unfolded before her eyes.

If this vision was true, that meant the one of Ares had to be as well, and if that was the case, she had little time before he arrived. However he planned on doing that.

Pita shot ahead again, his nose to the ground as he sniffed out a path. Kore's legs shook but hesitantly followed. If she wanted to get the energy and transfer it, she would need to remain focused. She wasn't going to allow Ares to take her away. Not even if Aidoneus fought for her—a promise she knew he planned to keep. But there was nothing wrong with a little binding to aid in the task.

Her eyes shot back to the beautiful, flourishing tree. Just as spectacular as Hermes had described. It felt a shame Aidoneus didn't want that beauty in the garden.

When they came into view of the shades, the moans grew silent, and chains fell still. Their gazes landed on her and then to the hound. Pita lowered his head with another low, rumbling growl, fangs bared as he took a step forward. Kore took the opportunity to continue, scanning a boulder that sat a reasonable distance from one that was nearest her path.

She bunched her robes up in her hands and took a small leap onto the rock, wobbling for a moment before taking the next jump. Her foot slipped, throwing her slightly off balance before she was able to right herself, preparing for the next leap.

She bent at her knees and pushed off, but her sandals provided little traction on the slick stones, and she stumbled forward.

Her hands clawed at the roots while the current fought to push her down, splashing her face, blurring her vision, and clogging her nose. She gasped as she struggled to pull herself free, and the water that rushed by pushed at her arms more and more.

She tried calling out to Pita but choked on the invading liquid that flooded her mouth. Her hand broke free, cutting deep against a jagged rock while the river worked to push her away.

Thick fur pushed from under her arm, heaving her up onto the rocks and moss before the hound climbed free himself. He shook off the water from his fur before pressing his nose gently against Kore's cheek, licking her from chin to ear a few times before she lifted her hand.

"Thank you, Pita," she panted, running her hands through his wet fur.

She craned her neck back, gazing at the tree, bigger now that she was closer. The sweet, tart fragrance filled her nose.

She coughed up some water and waited to catch her

breath before climbing to her feet. Her chest felt raw and on fire from the attack on her throat.

Before her sat the dreaded tree with a background of fire and death. Life that had managed to grow in a sea of despair.

"Goddess, please. The fruit," one shade begged.

Yes, the fruit. A taunting smile pulled at the corner of her lips as she lifted her hand and gripped the low-hanging produce. Twisting left then right, she yanked down until the pomegranate gave way with a soft pop.

She held it up in hand, the energy like nothing she had ever felt before. Pouring into her in its own rhythmic tune. The hard, bright red flesh smelled slightly bitter with a sweetness mixed in.

She tucked her thumbs into the pit where the stem had once been and pulled at the flesh, splitting it until the deep crimson juices began to spill free, dripping along her robes, staining her fingers and hands as she worked. She pulled free several seeds from the fleshy center. The sweet aroma filled her, and her mouth burned and her throat ached for just a small taste.

The seeds vibrated wildly with energy in her palm, pulling a heavy weight down on her hand.

No. She closed her eyes, drawing the energy from the seeds deep within her. Her arm shook rapidly as she drew in the life and stored it within herself. The radiation slowed and faded to a stop. When she looked down, six shriveled, dry seeds rested in her hand.

She dropped them at her feet and placed her palm over the bark of the tree. Its vibrance shook her to her core. It flooded her mind and blurred her sight. She cried out, yanking her hand back, but the blazing burn still scorched her skin. Her arm trembled from the contact. Her legs gave out beneath her, and she dropped to the soil.

Pita paced frantically around her, whining and pressing his nose against her arm.

"Kore!" Aidoneus's voice thundered.

Pita fell back, whimpering as he did, and Kore didn't bother lifting her head; the energy that ran through her made it difficult.

When he stood over her, his eyes fell to her stained hands and the crimson drips on her dress. His hands shot out, gripping her and yanking her up so that they were nose to nose. He was not gentle or kind in the movement, and Kore yelped at the pain it caused.

"Did you eat the fruit?" he barked.

He searched around frantically until he found what he sought. He snatched it up and held it to her face.

"Did you eat this fruit?" His voice was louder, heavier, and full of anger. He threw the flesh down, his nostrils flared, and his body shook.

Kore blinked at him, his eyes piercing her with a rage she wasn't used to.

"Did you?"

"No!" she cried, her body still buzzing from the energy the tree poured into her.

"What did I tell you? Didn't I tell you not to come back here?" His voice shifted from anger to panic as he gripped her face between his hands. "What are you doing here?" he barked, crushing his lips to hers, kissing her urgently. He pulled away to look her over once more. "Didn't I tell you?"

When he tugged her back, he kissed her again. Kore hadn't a moment to speak. She only gazed up at him, taking his lips, hearing his interrogations.

"I was—I was worried!" he yelled, pulling her into his chest, wrapping them in a cocoon of smoke. The smell of salt and sweat vanished and was soon replaced with fire, cypress, and ash.

They appeared in the chambers on the kline, Aidoneus quickly fussing over the stains on her fingers and dress. Checking her for cuts or wounds, his hands like feathers as they danced over her skin, tilting her head from one side to the next. He ran his hands along the back of her head, along her neck, and down her back. The press of his warm, rough hands against her sent chills across her skin.

"Are you well?" His voice breathless and concerned.

"I am well," she lied.

From the outside, she looked well, but her body raged. Ignited with the energy that flooded her. She needed to release it, back into the petrified tree. It was not meant to stay within her, and she could feel it tearing and ripping around, attempting to claw its way out as painfully as possible. She struggled to suppress the shudders that shook her body.

"Have the judgments finished?" she quizzed.

But Aidoneus did not answer. His eyes were dark as they fixated on the crimson stain upon her hands.

"Why were you in Tartarus, Kore? Why did you go to that tree?"

Kore looked up to him, her heart beating wildly in her chest. She could not hide it any longer. It was dangerous to not say anything. It was time to speak of her vision.

"I needed to make sure of something," she began, dropping her eyes to her hands. "The last visit I had with Hecate, she had brewed a tea that was as magical as it was delicious." She paused and looked over him for any hint of displeasure. He nodded once.

"Agatha has made mention of Hecate's teas," he said slowly. "And what did this tea cause?"

"Visions," she whispered, "one of the tree, and one of . . . Ares."

"Ares?"

"At first, I did not think it meant anything. Some of the visions were just memories." She continued to explain the vision of the tree in Tartarus, not mentioning the fact that it was the reason she had gone to see Hecate in the first place. She spoke of the dark vision with Ares, of his threat to take her and how she felt the war was a distraction of sorts.

Aidoneus pressed his lips flat as he thought on the possibility, his brows falling deep over his eyes as his jaw clenched.

"I need to speak with the judges. You should get cleaned up and meet me in the Judgment Hall," he said flatly, rising to his feet. Nothing more was said as he vanished into his cloud.

Kore exhaled, a labored groan following. Her body shook in the intense heat. The energy crawled about her skin like a creeping spider. It twisted her stomach and set fire to the ichor in her veins.

She jumped up and rushed from the chambers, down the small flight of steps, and into the courtyard. Her mind became numb, blinding her to the light from the false sun. With her hand up shielding her eyes, she crossed the length of the garden until she found the bed with the petrified tree.

She threw herself onto the stone and shoved her hands deep into the dry soil. The energy ripped through her fingertips as if someone was pulling her bones from her skin. The splitting pain tore through her and she cried out, throwing her head back as an agonizing scream squeezed from her lungs. The energy shredded down her arms, pulling more and more screams from her as it escaped.

The only other sound she could hear apart from her cries was the cracking and popping of the tree before her. The dry, brittle bits falling free, replaced with a deep brown trunk. The soil grew damp and dark as small worms and beetles wiggled to life.

Her arms turned to fire as the last of the energy drained from her just as violently. She broke free from the soil and her body rocked back. Her vision darkened, and she slammed down on the ground and cracked her head against the stone bed behind her. A blinding pain left her dazed and dizzy.

A gentle tug from a thin branch at her wrist stirred her up until her eyes opened, trailing the branch up to the lovely honeysuckle that sat in the bed she had fallen against. She rolled her head to one side, her eyes falling on the once-petrified tree.

To her amazement, it had taken the energy, the power,

and it shed its chalky coating to reveal a brown bark. Its branches were slowly stretching out in preparation for the leaves and heavy fruit it would soon carry.

She smiled to herself. Her work was complete and the hardest part out of the way. Now she only needed to wait for the tree to heal and for the fruit to blossom.

Her head grew heavy as she struggled to climb to her feet. Her vision fared no better, blurring and doubling her sight. She leaned against the beds for support and shuffled to the steps that led to the bathing chamber.

The stairs were no easy feat. She clawed her way up them, throwing herself on the marble floor and crawling to the pool.

Flickering candles danced across the dark columns. She noticed only a few lekythoi of oil and a basket of lavender flowers by the pool. Next to them, folded neatly, sat her black linen night robes.

She submerged her hands in the water, watching as the crimson juice dissipated from her skin. The warm water was soothing and calming to her still buzzing body.

She slipped from the soiled peplos and quickly sunk into the steaming water. She did not hurry to the oils but instead let the heated water consume her, dunking her head back to soak her hair, rinsing the sweat and dirt from her face. Relaxing the tremors from her body.

When she was ready, she picked the oil that smelled of lavender and poured it over her hair and skin, smoothing it in and massaging it into her sore muscles.

Her body slowly returned to normal, and the shaking slowed and the remnants of the energy faded away.

She rinsed her hair until it was no longer slick and climbed free from the pool, running her fingers through her strands, twisting them to release the excess water before swiftly braiding her hair and resting the braid on her right shoulder.

Kore slipped on the linen robes, the fabric sliding across

her freshly cleaned skin. It clung to parts of her that still held moisture, but she headed out anyway, her legs feeling much more energized, to the Judgment Hall, where Aidoneus had asked her to meet. She kept to the inner corridors where she could look in on the judgments without being noticed.

A loud rumble of noise grew as she approached the hall. It wasn't the average shade chatter.

This was rowdy, uncontrolled, and frantic.

When she reached the bottom steps, Aidoneus, Hermes, Minos, and two other divines stepped from the hall shouting and arguing with one another about something Kore was not yet clear of. She waited where she was and listened to see what all the fuss was about.

"Where did you collect all of them, Hermes?" Minos questioned; his voice was shaky.

"As I have said, along the shorelines of Attica to Thessaly. Thanatos took inland shades, Macedonia to Epirus. They have come from all over Greece, Minos," Hermes said.

"Was there war?" Aidoneus thundered.

"I mean, yeah. But not anything that would cause this number of casualties," Hermes informed.

"There are too many young ones, Lord Hades," a tall, bearded man said.

Aidoneus's face set hard like stone, and his hands fisted when he caught sight of Kore. Wasting no time, he made his way to her, his expression never relaxed. He looked over her, his eyes falling to her hands. "Are you well?"

Kore nodded as her attention drifted to Hermes and the three other men.

"I have called for council. About the vision you had of Ares," he began. "The judges would like to have a word with you about what you have seen. If anything incriminates him as the cause. It would appear not all of them think this can be of his doing."

"What if—"

"He knows better than to cross me." He took her hand,

and they were surrounded by darkness.

CHAPTER XXIX

THE COUNCIL CHAMBERS, THE GOD OF WAR, AND THE VISION

Kore had not yet been in the Underworld council chambers; it was in a part of the palace that was deeper into the brimstone of the mountain the palace was carved from. Hidden because it was rarely used for council amongst the gods, not when all meetings were held on Mt. Olympus.

Despite it being rarely seen, the torches and golden basins of fire still burned bright, lighting the black marble and flickering against the gold streaks that swirled through the floor.

In the center sat a long, obsidian-carved table, smooth on the top, reflecting the dancing flames that clung to the column walls. Around it sat twelve thrones that matched the ones in the Olympus chamber. Colors, creatures, and all. Only, unlike the one in Mt. Olympus, it was Aidoneus's throne that sat at the head of the table.

He pulled one of the smaller thrones near his, keeping Kore closest to him and furthest from Thanatos, who was summoned to the council for his insight. He sat at the far end of the table with Hecate on his left and Hermes beside her.

Next to Kore sat the three judges: Minos, Aeacus, and Rhadamanthys.

Kore had not met Aeacus and Rhadamanthys, but she knew they passed judgments on the shades before they shuffled off to their final judgment and placing.

The three of them all held the same stoic face, their eyes cloudy with age and wear, their skin worn from the years both from their mortal and their divine life.

"Thanatos? What have you seen of the war?" Aidoneus inquired.

Thanatos straightened in his seat, careful to keep his eyes only on Aidoneus. "War does not require my attention. War is not peaceful," he began.

Kore suppressed a laugh. She found it slightly ironic that the god who had attacked her, dropped her from a great distance, and broke her back was sitting here, discussing peace.

"I have collected too many souls away from war grounds for this increase to be the act of war. If Ares means to distract you, I do not think this is how," Thanatos offered.

"What have you seen?" Aidoneus asked.

"Not much. Some snow—illnesses amongst the mortals peak during this time. That, and the war, possibly," Thanatos suggested with a shrug.

"We will have to speak with the Nosoi to see what they have been up to. If either of you see them out, send them back to me," Aidoneus ordered Thanatos and Hermes.

They both nodded in acceptance. Kore knew of the Nosoi as some of the spirits that were freed from Pandora's box so many years ago. Creatures of illness and diseases. It was a story her mother shared frequently.

"What of Ares?" Kore whispered to him. Even if Thanatos had not taken any souls lost at war, she still felt Ares had a play in it and the increase in shades. A distraction was what he wanted, and calling for the Nosoi was just that.

"Hecate, please place protections at the entrance

temple," Aidoneus ordered, taking Kore by the hand.

Hecate nodded once with a ghosted smile.

"Would Cerberus not be enough? Surely nobody can pass the creature," Aeacus asked.

"It would appear a few can." Aidoneus sighed, shooting a glance to Kore.

He was right. In fact, Kore was not the only one Cerberus had let pass, according to her mother's stories. Mortals had ventured past the creature to gain audience with Aidoneus a few times before. He had let Kore pass with just the offer of some bread and the crystal Aidoneus gave her. He was a good guard but not an exceptionally great one.

"I would prefer to take extra precautions until this is all sorted out. Hecate, what can you say on the vision Kore has seen?" He pulled his attention to the Goddess of Craft and waited.

Her eyes flickered from Kore to Aidoneus, her voice low but firm as she spoke. "Visions of the tea are very subjective when it is only visual. Kore stated that in this vision, she only *heard* Ares. Words are more solid. Ares does plan to come for Kore, that much is clear. If I had to say, given the timing of war and increase in shades, it does not seem entirely impossible for the God of War to incite a distraction."

"Very well. Please see to it that that temple is well protected and sealed from those who should not be here," he ordered.

Hecate swiftly rose from her throne, bowed, and departed from the chamber.

"Hermes, I want you to keep an eye on the souls you collect, and watch for Ares. If you come to pass him, please inform me. Thanatos, that goes for you as well," he ordered again, dismissing the two gods from the chamber. Leaving only the three judges left to consult with.

"Aeacus, Rhadamanthys, I want you two to start asking the shades about their passing. Perhaps if we have a better understanding of how they are departing the mortal realm, we can pinpoint the cause of the increase," he instructed before turning to Minos. "If you notice anything strange or any patterns from what Aeacus and Rhadamanthys hand off to you, bring it to me immediately."

The three judges nodded and departed the chambers as well, leaving only Aidoneus and Kore. The basins and several torches had died down, casting the light of only two dancing flames in the now dimly lit chamber. Kore looked up to Aidoneus. His face was set hard, his eyes dark, looming over the table before him.

She slipped her hand over his arm and leaned into him. "I am sorry to have caused so much trouble."

He placed a finger under her chin and tilted her head up to his, the hardness of his face falling into the softness she had grown so fond of.

"You have nothing to apologize for. I am only glad you are safe," he whispered, taking her lips to his.

The scorching softness of his touch consumed her, every thought that had brought her to this chamber suddenly gone.

He pulled away with a wicked smile. "Shall we eat in the dining hall? Or in our chambers?" His voice fell low and smooth. She liked the sound of *our chambers*. The tickling warmth started to rise in her core from his words, but she could not deny she was hungry.

"If I say *our chambers*, will we truly *eat*?" she quizzed with a raised brow.

His smile widened as he shifted them.

When his smoke cleared, Kore found that a platter had already been sent up and placed on the table beside the kline. An oinochoe of wine and two kantharoi sat beside it.

"Wine?" he offered as he poured it into both kantharoi.

"Will you deprive me of your love if I do?"

He raised a brow to her with a half-smile. "Only if you wish it."

"I do not."

"As you command," he teased, handing her the

kantharos and placing the platter on the fur before them. He searched her eyes, the bright blue like a deep ocean.

"I would like you to stay close to me for now. Just until we know what Ares plans."

A request she could happily agree to. "I do not mind that," she assured.

She felt better being by his side, safer, protected. She also felt as if her time with Aidoneus was never enough and she always craved more. She enjoyed sitting beside him during the judgments, and contrary to what he said, Kore did not feel they dragged on endlessly. She enjoyed reading the different life stories of the mortals, how they lived, how they worshiped, how they committed acts of sin. It was all very vibrant how they worked.

"How were the judgments today?" she inquired, interested to hear of the many engrossing lives of the day.

"Long and tedious without you to assist, really. That is, until Hecate came looking for you and a guard made mention of Pita attacking a shade." He sighed. "I will admit, it was the most stimulating part of the day, but I would prefer you at my side. I enjoy your vengeful nature—your punishments are always so . . . intricate."

At times she had thought she may have been a bit harsh on some shades she had sent to Tartarus, but he never stopped or scolded her for her decisions. He agreed happily and proudly with all of them.

She smiled up at him. "I promise to make tomorrow more entertaining."

They ate through the meal and drank down the whole oinochoe. The tingling sensation washed over her skin, making it sensitive even to the fabric that brushed against her. She giggled at the feeling, mesmerized by the pleasure it offered. Her head rolled back, leaning against the stone, feeling the coolness press against her bare shoulder.

"Are you well?" Aidoneus leaned in, brushing his fingers across her cheek and tucking a loose strand of hair behind her ear. His breath fanned across her face, stirring the air with his scent. She watched him, his warm eyes sweeping her face and finding rest at her lips. She lifted her chin until she came up to his ear.

"I do not wish for you to be gentle with me." Her voice a breathless whisper.

She pulled back slightly, her lips searching for his, finding their warm softness. He kissed her slowly at first, the taste of wine still on him. She wiggled her way under him, slipping one leg on either side of his waist as she pulled the loose fabrics of the robes up past her hips, allowing the burning heat of his skin to press against hers.

Aidoneus took both her wrists in a single hand and pinned her arms up above her head. With his free hand, he removed his chiton before sliding his hand up and gripping the thickness of her thigh. He positioned himself at her entrance, sliding the tip of his head along her slit, drawing a soft cry from her.

He worked his lips to the curve of her jaw and then up to her ear.

"Tell me you want me," he ordered breathlessly, his heat still sliding along her entrance. She arched her back and bucked her hips against him, begging to take him in, but he kept his place.

"No. First, tell me you want me," he ordered again. She felt the frustration rise from his hesitation.

"I want you," she groaned.

"Louder," he ordered again.

"I want you!" she cried out, lifting her hips against him. But still, he taunted her with her wants. Sweeping his lips across her jaw, his warm breath growing heavy against her skin as he teased her with his length.

"Tell me you love me," he growled.

"I love you!" she cried out again. He plunged deep within her without warning, a deep-chested groan ripping from him. Her nails dug into her palms, and she cried out from the mix of pain and pleasure. He filled her in the most perfect way, splitting her as he moved deeper.

His hand released hers and made its way down until it cupped around her neck, his thumb pressed gently against the hollow of it. She gasped in response but still pushed herself into his grasp, welcoming the light pressure building up in her head.

"*O Vasiliás mou*!"

His body stilled and he turned his face into her neck, the heat of his breath fanning across her skin.

"Say it again," he panted, thrusting forward.

"*O Vasiliás mou*!" she repeated, and a deep growl rumbled in his chest. He pulled near free of her before pausing again.

"I love that," he breathed, moving his lips over hers and kissing her, deeply and with an urgency she could not grasp. He dove back into her, harder and faster, and she felt her breath catch in her chest, hard and raw. Her hands clung to his back, nails digging deep into his skin. She felt the pressure and heat build as she came to her peak. He kept his motion, kissing and licking at her neck.

She cried out as the waves of her release rippled through her, shaking her body against his. The movement edged him closer and closer to his own release until a loud, guttural groan ripped through him, and he came to a violent finish.

He wrapped his arms around her and rolled to the side. Keeping her pressed to his chest, he ran his fingers gingerly down her back.

"My love. *Vasílissa mou*," he said breathlessly.

Her body shuddered at his words. She enjoyed how they fell so freely from his lips. It wasn't something she had considered when she ventured down. But if he was pleased with giving her the title, then that meant he truly planned for her to stay, to be with him. A thought that warmed her heart.

She was at peace, she was content, and she was satisfied with everything in her life in the moment. She had fallen in love with the God of the Dead, and despite all of the horrors she had been told and all she had put him through, he loved her just as much. And that was more than she could have asked for.

Resting her head against his chest, she closed her eyes and listened to the sound of his heart's steady beating, the slow rise and fall of his chest allowing her to drift into a dreamless sleep.

The next few days had passed by in a blur. Kore and Aidoneus passed their judgments during the day with no word yet on Ares or the war. Every moment that had gone by without a sign, Kore grew less worried of the possibility of his unwanted arrival.

Along with the protection on the entrance temple, Aidoneus had also ordered Pita, Nyx, and Cerus to stand watch with Cerberus.

Kore shifted in her spot next to him on the throne as they looked over the mundane life of Maia Pavlos. She hadn't done anything entirely interesting, good or bad. She followed the divine regularly, worked with her mother and father in the fields, and grew up to marry and have children—an average life for a mortal.

Aidoneus read her scroll carefully, looking for any hint of any health-related issues to cause her death. He had been very thorough with every life, but still found no sign of illnesses in most of the shades as Thanatos had suggested. Closing the scroll, Aidoneus looked over the small shade and then back to Kore with questioning eyes.

"She will do nicely in the villages of Asphodel," Kore said softly.

"I do believe you are right." He smiled to her. "Eleni, please escort Maia to Asphodel."

The slender nymph gracefully skipped to the shade's side and held out her hand. The instant the shade grasped Eleni, the two flashed from sight, off to the fields to settle into her new life.

Aidoneus held out the scroll for Minos to take, and Kore could tell from the set look on his face that he had news. The crease between his brows and the slump of his lips told her that it was not good.

"My lord, my lady," he bowed, "I have word from Aeacus and Rhadamanthys on the probable cause of this increase of shades."

"Inform them to meet in the council chamber immediately. I will have these shades guided to the temples to wait for their judgment," he ordered, rising from his throne.

"Elpida and Eleni, find Hermes and Thanatos. Tell them they are needed in the council chambers. Agatha, take these shades to the temples."

He took Kore by the hand as he spoke, directing everyone to their new tasks. Once they had all left to carry out their orders, Aidoneus and Kore made their way down to the council chambers.

Aidoneus did not shift, but instead walked through the corridors and halls, down the many flights of stone steps, and through the dark, carved dungeon halls until they found themselves in the bright, round chamber.

"Have a seat, my love," Aidoneus instructed, pulling her throne from the table.

As he took his place beside her, the three judges appeared behind their respective thrones. They greeted the divines with a bow and took their spots without a word. The silence sped Kore's heart and hardened her stomach.

Aidoneus looked to the two empty chairs where Hermes and Thanatos had sat last council; his eyes grew dark as irritation built on his face.

"What news do you carry?" he asked in a deep rumble.

"We have questioned every shade over the last few days of what brought them here. There were not many who died at the hands of war," Aeacus began.

"However," Rhadamanthys added, "the majority of the shades claim there hasn't been any sustainable harvest in over four moons. No harvest of grain, fruit, vegetables. No grass to feed the cattle, no grain to feed the hens. They have called it the Great Famine."

"Have the crops been destroyed by war again?" Aidoneus inquired.

"Not likely. The famine is not just in Greece, my lord. It covers the whole globe," Aeacus stressed.

Hermes appeared from a white, fluffy cloud, landing gracefully in his chair.

"I was told I was needed. So here I am. I have arrived," he said brightly, but the energy in the room was anything but bright. He looked around, his smile slowly fading. "Not that type of council, I see."

"Have you seen Thanatos?" Aidoneus asked in a flat tone.

"I have not," Hermes chirped.

"And Ares?"

"He did visit Mt. Olympus yesterday. Grabbing a great deal of ambrosia and nectar. More than I feel he needs, but leave it to him to be greedy during a time of war."

"And what of this famine—have you not seen anything strange?" Aidoneus pressed.

"What famine?"

"You mean you haven't noticed the crops haven't grown?" Kore pushed this time.

"I pay little attention to the mortal world and the issues they have. That is Zeus's job. But still, he has not mentioned anything such as a famine. He has been too focused on the war and trying to get Ares to care about more than just himself."

"It is time you start paying attention to the mortals and

their troubles, my friend," Aidoneus scoffed.

Another black cloud appeared, lofting over Thanatos's spot. Once it dissolved, he appeared in his seat.

"You summoned me, my lord?" His voice was low and unmoved.

"Yes. We have news on the increase." Aidoneus growled.

"Oh?"

"It would appear there is a famine circling the globe. Hermes has been of no help since he does not mind much other than himself."

"Excuse me?" Hermes chirped, but Aidoneus continued. "What have you seen?"

"It has been hard to tell since the colder days have begun."

"What of the last harvest?" Kore interjected quickly. Aidoneus looked to her, but then brought his focus back to Thanatos, who kept his eyes only on the king. As instructed.

"I do not recall seeing a last harvest on my travels, but then again, I was far too busy collecting souls to take notice of their habits," he droned.

"It would be helpful." Minos finally spoke. His voice not as weak and frail as it normally was. "It would help you as the God of Death to understand why it is you are visiting mortals. Even more when you see consistencies or inconsistencies in their passing."

"It would be wise of you to be aware of your work, Thanatos," Aeacus added.

The God of Death glared at the judges but did not speak, though it was clear he had much to say.

"What of Limos then?" Rhadamanthys offered, and Aidoneus raised a brow, a thought he had not considered.

"Thanatos, find Limos and bring him to me. Quickly," Aidoneus ordered, and just as soon as the words left his mouth, Thanatos was gone. Not even the remnant of his cloud could be seen.

"Minos, Rhadamanthys, Aeacus. That will be all for now. Thank you."

The judges bowed graciously and departed as they usually did.

Kore turned to Hermes. If there was a famine, surely her mother could help. And as much as she did not want to leave, she would if it meant helping slow the flow of shades spilling in. She would do what must be done. "Has my mother not returned?"

Hermes turned to her with downturned brows and pale cheeks.

"No one has seen Demeter for some moons now. I have asked the sun gods and the moon goddesses, but they have all said the same. They have lost sight of Demeter after the village. Wherever she is, she isn't in her divine form."

"Could she be behind this?" Aidoneus suggested.

Kore knew her mother. It was not in her power to take life, and she loved her creations too dearly to destroy them. If she was in hiding, she was probably as unaware as the rest of them had been.

"She hasn't the power to wilt her work," Kore assured.

"But she can stop a harvest from sprouting," Aidoneus corrected.

Kore looked up to him, her eyes wide.

He was right, she could stop a harvest if she wanted. But Kore did not feel her mother would do such an act. Demeter had been aware of Kore's location and reasoning for being there. Not the whole reason, but that Kore had been injured, and according to Hermes, she had been fine with it at the time.

She would have just retrieved Kore if her being there was an issue. Kore knew her mother loved the mortals and her work far too much.

Aidoneus held her eyes with his, as if he were reading her thoughts and questions as they spun through her head. He opened his mouth to speak, but two ominous clouds appeared at the opposite end of the table. Once the smoke cleared,

Thanatos and another god came to view.

The new god looked to be younger than Kore. His wild, curly hair swept over his tired eyes. His bronze skin was heavily splashed with freckles about his face and chest. He hunched over the throne before him, exhausted from his travels, and his eyes began to close.

Thanatos shoved his shoulder, rousing him once again.

"Huh?" He yawned, looking around. His face held a bit of confusion as he squinted about the area. "Where am I?"

"Limos?" Aidoneus stood and walked around the table.

"Oh!" Limos gasped, and his eyes grew wide as he bowed briskly. "My lord!"

"Limos?" Aidoneus began. "You have seen better days, my friend. Are you well?"

"Oh, I have been everywhere the past few moons." He paused to yawn again.

"Tell me of your travels," Aidoneus ordered.

Limos rubbed his eyes and squinted for a moment at the king, thinking on where to start.

"At first, I wandered Greece, the farms and the animals. The villages too . . ." His voice trailed as he broke into another yawn. "Then I traveled to Europe because I was called upon. From there to Asia, and it has just been this way. Going where I am called. So many mortals and creatures cried to me," he explained in a drowsy voice.

His eyes began to close, and again, Thanatos shoved his shoulder to stir him awake.

"Ow! You do not have to be so rough. You may be peaceful in death, but you are an aggressive ass!" the young god shot. He looked back to Aidoneus, his eyes low and drowsy. "Was there something needed of me, my lord?"

"You have given all I need for now. But I do have a task for you. While on your travels, I want you to look for Demeter. You know of her, yes?"

"Oh yes, my lord. The Goddess of Harvest." He nodded lazily.

"Good. I want you, Thanatos, and Hermes to keep an eye out for her on your travels. If you see her, come straight back to me," Aidoneus ordered.

The three divines bowed to the king.

"Bye, Kore!" Hermes cheered happily before turning into his white, shimmering cloud and evaporating from sight.

Thanatos moved forward, his arm ready to grab Limos, but the tired god stepped to the side at the last minute, his face still swollen with exhaustion.

"I am perfectly able to leave myself. Thank you," he scoffed.

He turned to Kore and Aidoneus with a sleepy smile and bowed, departing into his grayish, low-lofting cloud.

Thanatos was next, bowing silently to only Aidoneus before taking his leave as well. Once there was only the two of them, Aidoneus finally looked down to Kore, his eyes set.

"Do you really think my mother stopped the harvest?" Kore questioned softly.

His lips pulled up at the corners in a hopeful smile.

"She is the Goddess of Harvest; it would not hurt to see what she knows." He sighed. Placing his hand under her chin, he lifted her head to him. "Demeter has never been vengeful. I do not see her taking out her anger on her plants and the mortals. But she may have some knowledge on the matter."

It was comforting for Kore to know he did not believe her mother could commit such acts. Murderous, vengeful acts that were punishable by Zeus. Something Demeter would never take part in.

She had promised her only daughter to Ares by Zeus's word; if she wanted to cause a famine, that would have been a more foreseeable reason.

Kore did not like Thanatos, but she hoped he and the other gods would find her mother soon.

CHAPTER XXX

THE GOD OF HUNGER, THE GOD OF MESSAGES, THE GOD OF DEATH, AND THE GODDESS OF HARVEST

Kore leaned far over the ledge of the garden bed, pulling the invasive weeds free from the roots. The tree had been easy to hide over the last few moons since she transferred the energy. But over the last few days, the fruits had blossomed, grown, and ripened quicker than she had anticipated. She hadn't an idea yet of what to do after picking them, so she settled with tucking the branches up in an attempt to hide the bright red fruits.

She pulled her robes up and climbed into the stone bed, her bare feet sinking into the soft soil. She managed to find two thick, peaking roots that she used to balance herself.

Reaching up and pressing her palms against the first branch, she pushed her energy into it, weaving it up and over a fruitless offshoot that hung just above. She repeated this with a few more of the lower hanging fruit-bearing branches.

"I can still see them," Callisto whispered to Alena.

"Shh." Alena giggled. "You can always deliver them to

the Erinyes. I hear they love them."

That would be an easy way to hide the fruit but meant Kore would need to go back to Tartarus, and she did not want to risk that journey a third go.

"Who would deliver them?" Kore thought aloud.

The nymphs did not answer as they continued to watch her work her way around the tree, tucking and weaving the branches together until the low-hanging fruit became very visible, high-hanging fruit instead.

"That did nothing at all," Kore huffed, hopping down from the soil.

"Perhaps if you grew tall flowers here, surrounding the tree," Callisto suggested.

The goddess tilted her head; the idea was not a bad one. The bed was big enough and held enough soil to support thinner roots without obstructing the tree's nourishment.

She lifted her arms and pushed the pulsating energy through her fingertips, her eyes clouding over as she called forth tall stalks from the soil. She pulled them up until the tops reached the lowest branch of the tree. An electric charge surged from finger to finger.

From the tops of the stalks sprouted large red petals. The flowers blended into the leaves of the tree, creating the illusion of a rosebush from afar.

"Oh! How lovely," Callisto cooed.

"That should do nicely for now. At least until I find a way to tell him that I returned life to it once more," Kore said.

Kore and the nymphs made their way to the small stone table she used to dry her herbs. Piles of flower trimmings lay scattered flat about the top, taking in the false sun's rays and releasing their moisture to the air. She grazed her fingers against the brittle leaves of a drying mugwort plant.

"Does Hecate plan on making another tea?" Callisto guessed.

"She does. Hopefully one that can help us locate my mother." Kore took a bundle of the dry mugwort and began garbling the flower tops from the stems.

She broke off the roots and leaves and tossed the stems into the gardening pot beside her. The three piles found their way into three separate pouches as she moved on to the next herb in line.

She separated the flower heads, leaves, and roots from the stems and stalks, piling the three and tossing the rest into the pot next to her, working until they were all separated and pouched.

"Are you traveling to deliver them to her this day?" Alena inquired next.

"Not this day. She will be by to get them on her own time," Kore informed.

"Well then, what are your plans for the remainder of the day?"

"Aidoneus wishes me to stay nearby. So, I haven't much planned other than this." Kore sighed.

She had enjoyed her freedom, and though it was for her safety, she wanted nothing more than to run through the fields and visit the villages at nightfall.

They had kept to the palace while Hermes, Limos, and Thanatos searched for her mother, and kept an eye out for Ares. There had not been any motion forward on that front, and the gods had not come any closer to finding her mother than they had to finding out the cause of the famine.

Every day that had passed, Kore felt more and more that her mother could possibly be the cause, but the reasons remained unclear no matter how hard she thought.

"I suppose I can sneak down to the halls and listen in on the judgments," Kore thought aloud.

"Lady Kore, Lord Hades has requested we keep you from—"

"He can keep me in the palace for my safety, but he cannot keep me from my fun," she interjected with a smile, and Callisto giggled softly. "Besides, it should be nearing its end," Kore added, looking to the sky, the sun on its way to meet the land.

Alena followed her gaze and turned back to her with a soft smile. "Very well."

They left the garden through the corridor that led straight into the palace, following the path from one long corridor to the next, until they came to the stone steps that met outside of the hall.

Kore and the nymphs tiptoed to the nearest column and peered around it.

The throne sat with its back to them as Aidoneus read off the fate of the shade before him, his voice hard and steady. Kore could see Minos off to the right, prepping another scroll for the king to look over. Behind him were the three escort nymphs waiting patiently to take the next soul.

The hall was full again with an odd number of souls that spilled out onto the courtyard. Shades of all sizes and ages chatted softly amongst themselves as they waited their turn. A twinge hit her heart at the thought of this all being due to her own mother. The meaningless and senseless murders just did not seem like Demeter, but she had been finding it harder and harder to continue believing that.

Aidoneus ordered off the shade, who went along with Agatha, and Minos was already handing off the next scroll. He began reading the first passage without pause.

"Melita Nephele," he called out, and the shade made her way forward.

Kore spotted Hermes and the young god Limos enter the hall.

Limos looked no different in his face, still exhausted with deep bags under his eyes and pale skin, but Hermes had a look she had never seen on him before.

His lips were pulled far down into a scowl, his brows pinched in the center, and his usually soft, honey-colored eyes looked almost black from where she stood. His face held no excitement or victory. He had news, and the news was not good.

Kore felt her lungs tighten, squeezing the air from her as she watched. Her heart raced, pounding against her chest and stirring her ichor to a boil. A shiver ran down her spine when the realization rained down on her.

It was her mother. For whatever reason, it had been her mother all along.

The two divines stepped to the throne with a deep bow before Hermes leaned in and spoke soft, quick words to the king. Hermes paused for just a moment before he and Limos disappeared into their clouds and zoomed through the hall, passing Kore and the nymphs as they sped down the corridor that led to the council chamber.

Kore glanced at Alena and Callisto, who had no words to share. She straightened and swiftly turned down the corridor after Hermes and Limos, the nymphs close behind.

Once she made it to the stairs that led to the dungeons, she began to run. Skipping a few steps, she leaped down, taking a small pause when she reached the bottom to catch her breath. Once the nymphs caught up, she began sprinting down the corridors once more. She ignored the raw breath that ripped through her lungs. Ignored the weight in her feet as she struggled to move faster.

"Lady Kore, please wait!" Alena called as the two ran along behind her, but Kore did not pause or slow. She made the quick left into the chambers where Hermes and Limos waited. The gloom still carved hard on their faces.

"Hermes!" she cried breathlessly.

Her vision became blurry as the pressure of tears began to build behind her eyes.

"Hermes, what is it?" she cried again, walking to the table. "Please tell me it is not her."

Hermes only looked down without saying a word. The air rushed from her lungs, and her knees buckled, weakened by the run, and collapsed beneath her. Hermes stood to help, but the nymphs were at her side before he could make it. They assisted her up and into her throne before taking their place on either side of her.

"We should wait for Lord Hades," Hermes said softly.

Kore shot her tear-filled eyes to him. "Hermes, please! She is my mother!" she begged.

The bright god pulled his eyes from hers and dropped them to the table as he took his seat once more.

"She came to Olympus this morning," he began hesitantly. "She was very clear, Kore. Either you be returned, or the harvest won't be."

The last of the air in her lungs was pushed free from her, her body felt numb, and her mind was brimming with thoughts too scattered to form a coherent sentence. A dry, burning sensation inflamed her eyes as she stared at the god.

"No," she cracked.

Alena and Callisto looked down to her quickly and back to Hermes.

"It is not up to you. Zeus has already ordered I deliver you back to Olympus this day. I am only waiting to speak with Lord Hades to allow you a proper goodbye." His voice was dark and heavy, not anything she was used to from the god.

They waited for a few more moments before a dark cloud of smoke appeared in Aidoneus's throne, revealing him slowly. His jaw was clenched tight, his hands fisted, and his eyes fixed on Hermes.

"Speak," he barked.

"Demeter has returned to Mt. Olympus early this morning. She made an offer with Zeus, offering the return of the harvest for the return of her daughter," Hermes stated again.

Aidoneus's arms flexed, and his jaw tightened even harder.

"Kore must be returned?"

Hermes nodded stiffly, his eyes shooting from Kore and back to the king.

"They are waiting for her on Mt. Olympus now."

"No!" Kore shot again and finally Aidoneus looked at

her, his eyes angry and dark.

"There is no discussing it. If Zeus *orders* your return, you must go back!" he growled.

"And you would let me leave so easily?" she shouted, jumping from her throne. Her body ignited in an intense blaze as she vibrated from head to toe. "It is my choice!" Her voice thundered and her body was consumed by a bright, burning flame. The chamber around her melted away, smoke and cinder swirling. An ear-shattering scream broke out as the lights around the chamber fell dark and her flames grew tall above her head.

The air around her shifted when the fires died down and the smoke cleared. She looked about her to find she had shifted to Aidoneus's chambers, where a fresh platter of food sat waiting for them on the table beside the kline, but she gave it little mind. Her eyes burned from the tears that pushed at them.

The scream ripped through her violently, and she fell onto the furs. She gasped for air but all that came was the exhale of her cries. A weight lay heavy on her chest, crushing her and pulling more cries and gasps for air. Tears spilled over the furs before her, soaking them in her anguish as she sobbed.

Her mind raced with thoughts about all that had happened over the last twelve moons. How Hermes had stated that Demeter had been fine with Kore's staying there to heal.

Why would she not just tell Hermes that she wanted Kore back, rather than start a whole famine? Why would she hide away for so long? None of her actions linked to this point.

Kore released her pain through tears and screams for what seemed like hours before the intoxicating scent of cypress and ash filled the air and tingled her nose.

"Kore." His voice was deep and demanding, but Kore did not turn to him.

"Kore," he said louder.

She turned to glare at him from over her shoulder. "My mother cannot make me leave."

"Not your mother. Zeus," he growled, wrapping his

hands around her wrist, but she quickly yanked it back.

"My father cannot command me either!" she barked, her voice echoing in the chamber.

Aidoneus looked at her round-eyed with an open mouth, words lost on his tongue. She stood from the kline to face him, her chest heaving from the anger. She stepped toward him, and he stepped back.

"I am not a gift to be traded or promised. I am a goddess and I demand more for my life than that of what others have planned out!" Her face a bright gold, her nostrils flared, and her body rose until she was eye to eye with him.

Heat radiated from her toes to the top of her head. She moved forward again, and this time, the King of the Underworld stumbled back until his back met a column.

"I will not leave my home," she bellowed.

Aidoneus's fingers slipped around her wrists, gently holding her in place.

"You must," he whispered.

His hands tightened around her as he guided her back down until her feet touched the floor. Pain flashed in his eyes, but he held firm to her.

"Your mother has caused a lot of trouble, for Zeus and for me. You must return. Zeus will punish her—he will send her to Tartarus, Kore. Is that what you want for her?"

"No, but there must be a way I can stay and have her end this."

"You cannot stay."

"Aidoneus, I love you. I do not want to leave," she begged, grabbing his face between her hands.

His eyes gazed down at her, glossy with tears. The deep fold between his brow appeared as his eyes swept over her.

"Please do not send me away," she whispered.

His brows pressed deeper together.

"Don't send me away," she whispered again.

A heavy, ragged breath escaped him before his lips crashed into hers. He kissed her urgently, voraciously.

Her body fell limp under the burning of his skin on hers, her mind fogged by his scent, his taste. He wrapped her arms around his neck and dropped his hands to her waist, pulling her up to his chest and kissing her even deeper. She wrapped her legs around his waist, and he spun them around, pinning her against the column, the marble digging into her back. She hissed at the pain but did not stop taking him in. His hands fumbled around the fabric at her waist as he struggled to move it free.

She pressed her hips against him, enticing a deep groan. His hands became frantic as he pulled at her robes and ripped them free from her.

She cried out against him when his fingers finally slid along her warmth.

Aidoneus pushed his chiton down, letting it fall around his feet, and guided himself into her in one smooth motion. His thrusts were deep and rough, and the sounds that left his chest were almost feral as he worked. His hands found their way to her chest, and his mouth consumed every inch of her neck. He ripped the robes at her shoulders, pushing them free and exposing her breasts.

The moans and cries that left her only stirred him deeper, harder. Her hands tangled in his hair, pulling and clawing at whatever she could. Her nails dug into his back, leaving deep scratches down his skin as the building pressure overpowered her. Her body began to spasm, and she reached her release, pulsating waves of ecstasy ripping through her.

She cried out again, clutching his hair and skin. But he did not stop. He pulled his lips from her and locked their eyes as he thrust into her harder. She tried to pull away, but he held her tightly in place against the column.

She buried her face in his neck, crying out with each wave of pleasure that crashed through her. She gasped for air as her body slumped against him. But he was not finished with her.

Taking her lips in his once more, he kissed her deeply,

parting her lips and invading her mouth with his tongue. A guttural groan ripped through him again when his body spasmed with the power of his release. He broke away from her lips as another vicious growl tore through him, and he fell against her with a heaving chest.

He withdrew, loosening her legs from his waist and placing her back on her feet. Keeping his eyes away from her as he pulled his chiton up around his waist. Kore moved forward to press her hand against his shoulder, but he pulled away.

A hard rock formed in her stomach. She had never felt ashamed of being exposed to him before, but the feeling washed over her like a strong wave.

She pulled up the ripped fabrics and held them to her chest.

"Aidoneus?"

"You should gather your things," he said flatly, still avoiding her.

She felt the rock drop at his words. Her eyes widened as she stared at him. The air in her lungs ripped from her, but he did not look up at her gasp.

"Aidoneus, what do you—"

"You need to leave with Hermes and go back to your mother. You cannot stay here any longer." His words were forced and cold.

"I thought—"

"You thought wrong." He walked from her and stood near the firepit. Her heart thundered in her chest, throbbing with pain. She inhaled deeply but could not sort her thoughts out.

"What?" Her voice was soft and shaky.

"You thought wrong. You cannot stay," he repeated.

"But we just made love," she cracked as she fought the onset of tears.

"No. You know nothing of love. I told you I could not give you what you wanted." His words were like venom to her, but still, she pushed.

"What shall you call it then?"

"Something for me to remember you by," he growled.

His words broke her worse than the fall that had shattered her skull and snapped her back. Her lungs grew tight and made it even harder for her to breathe. A hard sting pressed against her eyes as tears clouded her vision.

Her mind scattered thoughts before her, their times together, his touch, his kiss. His very words telling her of his love for her. He had called her his queen on more than one occasion, and according to every divine and nymph in the realm, that was a kindness he did not extend.

No. She would not accept his words. She pushed herself forward and looked at him, his eyes still cast on the fire.

"No. We made love because you love me," she argued.

His body went rigid before his eyes finally shot up to hers.

"I do not love you," he said flatly.

Making the rock in her stomach fall once again, this time pulling her heart down with it. She rocked back on her heels.

"You do; you said you do."

"I told you the Underworld was no place for love. Yet you came in search of it anyway."

"I came in search of you," she corrected with a broken voice. The tears choking her words.

"I was never lost or in need of finding, Kore."

She blinked at him, her mind now reeling with questions.

"What about all those moments you told me of your love? Or all those times we made love, because no matter what you say, that is what it was."

"I gave you what you wanted."

"And you did not?"

Aidoneus's jaw flexed as he looked over her, his lips pressed in a flat line and his brows pulled together.

"I did not," he finally breathed.

The words struck Kore like a blade to the heart, water flowing over her eyes as tears flooded down her cheeks.

"You do not want me?" she gasped softly.

His eyes closed and his jaw flexed once more. He inhaled deeply before fixing his gaze back on Kore. He leaned over her slowly, sweeping her body from head to toe and back before coming to rest at her eyes. His were cold and unwelcoming, something she had never seen in them before. She shrunk back from him.

"I do not," he hissed.

Her heart caught in her throat, yet somehow still felt like it was being ripped from her chest all at once. She gazed at him with wide, tear-filled eyes, unable to speak, unable to move. It wasn't until her jaw grew sore that she realized she had been clenching it to fight back tears. Tears that had already begun pouring from her eyes.

He looked down on her, his gaze clouded and angry. He was cold and for the first time since meeting him, since knowing him, she saw the cold, heartless god everyone had warned her he was. Her eyes widened as she fought back more tears.

"I know you love me. I feel it," she gasped.

"I do not love you," he pushed, his brows pinched together tightly as he looked down upon her.

Her breath caught again at his words, cutting her deep.

"I do not understand."

"Kore." For a second, she thought she saw pain flash in his dark eyes—just a moment before they returned to the cold, vacant glare. "Do not make this harder than it has to be."

He took her face between his hands and leaned in until his nose just lightly touched hers.

"You were just something to do." He sighed, releasing her face.

His words impaled her. Stealing her air and cutting her heart free. She stumbled, catching herself on the hot stone beside the pit. But he did not help her, and the tears that ran down her face did not sway him to her comfort. He only turned on his heels and made his way from the chamber.

"You can gather your things. Hermes will be in his chariot by the Judgment Hall, waiting for you there," he called, leaving her alone in the chambers.

Her heart felt as though it had shattered. She leaned against the hot stones, not caring about the scalding pain that seared into her arm. It was nothing compared to the pain his words had just caused her.

The absolute slaughter of her heart and soul laid out before her. Her chest fought against each ragged breath she drew in. More tears formed trails down her cheeks as she silently sobbed into her torn robes.

His words hurt her, but still she felt there was more. The way he had touched her, kissed her, spoken to her, the way he made love to her. The nymphs of the palace claimed these to be acts he had never shown another. Why would he show her if she had meant so little to him?

She wiped the tears free from her face as her thoughts finally started to reorganize themselves.

There must be more to his words.

She would have to go with Hermes, for her mother's sake. But the issue was not going. It was how she would get back down. Making a deal with Zeus seemed common enough; he always seemed to like any sort of deal that benefited him. She would just have to make him see reason in her staying.

Or give him no choice in the matter.

When she felt she was able to move her legs, she made her way to the trunk that sat at the end of the kline. It held all the robes and peplos that she had acquired over her time in the Underworld.

She searched for the deep red peplos and chiton set that she wore to judgments. Once she found them, she quickly changed, adjusting the folds in the chiton to create a deep pocket.

She walked over to the polished obsidian to view

herself. If she wanted to be taken seriously when she made an offer to Zeus, she wanted to look the part, and nothing made her look or feel more powerful than her judgment robes.

Her hands worked in her hair, braiding it and resting the braid over her right shoulder.

"Lady Kore?" Alena's soft voice called from the back chamber. Kore spun on her heels to find all the nymphs, their eyes just as full of tears as hers.

When their faces met, they ran to embrace her in one big hug. Even Agatha joined in with tear-filled eyes.

"We will miss you dearly!" Elpida cried.

Kore hugged each of them deeply for a few moments, leaving Alena for last. "Come with me to my garden," she requested softly as she hugged the nymph. Alena pulled away with soft, watery eyes and bowed. A silent acknowledgment to her request.

She turned back to the rest of the nymphs and said her goodbyes to each of them once more, thanking them for their kindness and all they had shown her. She was forever grateful for them, and though she did not plan on this being her final farewell, she still grieved with them.

Elpida and Eleni helped gather the rest of Kore's robes and garments while Agatha gathered a few of the small trinkets and crystals Kore had collected. They placed everything in her satchel, each embracing her one last time with watery eyes before departing off to their hall.

Once the chamber was clear, Kore and Alena made their way down to the garden.

"I will miss you, Lady Kore," Alena said with a sigh as they entered the courtyard.

Her plants and flowers welcomed her but did not seem as enthusiastic as they normally did. She could feel their low energy pulsating through the air around her. They knew she was to be off, and they were sad. Their vibrant color was just a bit duller, their lively blossoms and leaves just a bit droopier. They were in mourning of her, and their sad vibrations pained her soul.

"I do not plan on being gone long," Kore finally said.

She made her way around to the hidden pomegranate tree where she had been but a few hours before. Its bright red fruits were hidden well with the bright roses.

She lifted her robes and climbed into the bed, grazing her fingers along the thorny rosebush before her.

The branches snapped and recoiled from her touch, creating a clearing for her to walk to the tree. Reaching up, she grasped the plumpest pomegranate before tugging it from the branch with a loud snap.

"Thank you, my friend," she whispered softly, pressing her palm against its trunk.

The tree vibrated against her happily, forever thankful for her reviving it. She patted the bark, hopped from the bed, and walked back to Alena's side with a soft smile. The nymph's eyes grew wide, and she gaped at the fruit in the goddess's hands. She watched silently as Kore tucked it into the pocket she had crafted in her chiton and moved her peplos over it to conceal the lump it created.

"You plan to eat it?" Alena gasped, her eyes still on the pocket.

"I do. They cannot keep me if I am bound to this realm," Kore answered.

Alena shook her head nervously, her eyes finally meeting Kore's.

"I suppose they cannot," the nymph said with a soft, nervous smile.

Kore took her by the hands. "Can you take me to Hermes? I don't think it wise I walk through the palace."

A helpful smile spread across Alena's face.

"Of course," she said.

They let the garden shift away from them and transform to the front entrance of the Judgment Halls.

Kore scanned around until she saw the white-and-golden chariot that belonged to Hermes. He stood by his chargers, patting them with a half-hearted smile as he waited to steal her away. Kore turned back to Alena and embraced her.

"I will be seeing you soon, my friend," she whispered, breaking away with a smile.

The nymph watched as Kore walked to the God of Messages and stood by his side. He looked down at her, his eyes sweeping her robes.

"Yes, that is exactly what your mother wants to see." He sighed. "You do look nice, Kore, very powerful, very dangerous, very—Queen of the Underworld. Do you really think it wise with your mom and her temperament?"

"I think—I will be taken seriously."

"Who am I to tell you no? I am only here to take you back."

"Please do not remind me."

They turned from the chargers and stepped into the chariot.

"I do not want to take you from your love, Kore. After council with Hades, I had to inform Zeus, and when we went and looked, I guess you could say it's horribly dire. Worse than I recall, but then again, I haven't been inlands near fields for a while," Hermes thought aloud. "Thanatos said he would worry about those mortals. I enjoy the beachside anyway, so I agreed." He shrugged, whipping the reins and starting his chargers off. Guiding them over the bridge and down the long, winding hill that led to the asphodel fields.

Kore held on to the bar, watching the beauty of the realm—of her realm—pass by. If her plan did fail, she would miss this view, the realm, and its king.

Despite the hurtful things he had said, she still longed for him, for his touch and his kiss. She chose not to remember their last moments, but all the moments before. The ones when she felt most happy and loved. She wanted to remember it all how it was.

She turned to look back at the palace, a dark cloud lofting low above it. After all the time she had spent there, admiring the beauty of the realm, she now found it unrecognizable. It looked dark and frightening—gloomy, just as her mother's tales described.

Her eyes scanned up to the top where Aidoneus's chamber sat, and through the thickness of the cloud, she thought she could see the small outline of his frame, standing in the opening. Watching her leave.

Her heart ached again at the thought of it being because he was making sure she left, but a part of her hoped it was something more. She turned back as Hermes raced through the fields and passed the entrance temple.

"Hermes?" Kore called over the wind.

"There is a route made only for chariots, dear sister!" he called back, gripping the reins even tighter. He cracked them against his chargers once more.

She looked before them to find a thick row of trees lined along the riverbank. There was no clearing or bridge for the chargers to pass, but Hermes made no attempt at slowing.

"Hermes!" Kore called again, her hands gripping the railing of the chariot.

Hermes shifted behind Kore, placing his arms on either side of her. "Hold tight, *sis*!"

"What did I say about calling me things I don't know?" The words ripped from her mouth as the chargers took flight into the air, galloping over the water and treetops.

Kore's nails dug into the metal of the rail, and she hissed at the pain it caused.

Hermes kept his place behind her, keeping her steady as the chariot descended back onto flat grounds. It landed gracefully and without pause, and the chargers galloped through the low-cut fields and over the Styx River.

How they could see past the thick fog was beyond Kore, but they proceeded without losing their speed.

The air grew thick with the smell of war and death. Cold from the weather and quiet from the lack of animals around.

Once the fog finally began to clear, Kore saw only the

desolate, dry land of the new mortal world. There was no harvest; there was no life. This was more than a winter break in vegetation. This was the destruction and death of all things her mother held dear. The once-green, grassy plains were now dry, flat lands of dirt. Kore gasped, and the rough, dry air tore through her throat and lungs.

She could not fathom why her mother would commit such an act of vengeance without cause. And her daughter being cared for in the Underworld did not warrant such a misuse of her power. Only to bring Kore back, and then what? Marry her off still? Keep her trapped in the meadow? She would prefer the meadow, where at least she would be with people she loved and cared for.

She was unsure of her mother's intentions, but Demeter would have to find a way to bring the harvest back and live with the fact that Kore would be staying in the Underworld.

Kore turned around, looking over the back of the chariot at the dead grass bits that flew behind them. She leaned down and held her arm out to graze the dry blades that raced past her, cutting her fingers as they went.

"Kore, what are you doing?" Hermes shot, slowing the chargers to a stop.

She hopped off the chariot without a word, the brown, dry grass slicing at her feet. She hissed at the pain but walked a few feet from their stop, trying to locate a viable patch.

She bent down and placed her hand on the grass, pushing her energy into it, but the grass did not wake. She called out to it and heard nothing back. Its life force had been drained for far too long for her to help.

"I am sorry, my friends," she murmured before rising to her feet and making her way back to the chariot to rejoin Hermes.

He looked at her with questioning eyes, but she did not speak. Her mind played over her mother's every lesson, her every word on how she cared for the plants. How she cared for even the tiniest blades of grass. She loved trading with the mortals, seeing how they enjoyed her work. She would not think to torment them in place of another.

Demeter had been upset that morning Kore decided to leave. She had been worried about telling her daughter of an engagement she knew would not work. She was content with knowing she had been safe and cared for in the Underworld.

None of it made sense. Kore knew her mother—this was not her—and as much as she wanted to stay in the Underworld, she needed to see why Demeter had caused this.

Hermes snapped the reins, and the chargers took off once again, kicking up dirt and dust. The barren land blurred past them once more.

"What happened?" she whispered.

CHAPTER XXXI

THE POMEGRANATE, THE SEEDS, AND THE DUAL

"What happened is your mother has a horrible time maintaining her emotions," Hermes said, whipping his reins once more the moment Kore had stepped back into the chariot. With the echoing crack, the chargers sped off.

"I thought you said she was handling it well?" Kore pushed.

Hermes shrugged, keeping his eyes on the trail ahead. "I did, but I guess she had a change of heart. Perhaps the destruction of the village was all she could handle. When you get up there, you can ask of it. I did not get a chance to speak with her."

Kore kept her eyes on the land that passed, and her heart sank with each reminder of her mother's wrath. The dirt was dry and lifeless. No birds flew above, and no creatures ran alongside them. It was a barren, empty land. Even the Underworld held more life within it.

Kore felt a heavy pull at her heart at the very thought of the realm she was leaving behind. The words that still stung her ears. From the ones of love and admiration to the hateful ones Aidoneus had just spoken. They both brought tears to spill from her eyes as she silently sobbed.

"Kore," Hermes said softly, wrapping his arm around her shoulder and pulling her close. "Whatever Hades said to you, I am sure he did not mean it. He is just as hurt as you. But you do not understand what is to become of your mother if you do not return and she continues this. What is to become of you, of all this. Your travel, me helping you, all the mortals dead—it would all be for naught."

"What would have become of us if I had not returned? What is to become of us now that I have?" Kore inquired.

Hermes pressed his lips in a flat line as he looked back to the path ahead.

"Zeus said your mother will be sent to Tartarus for her crimes. You *will* be exiled to the mortal realm to marry Ares and uphold your duty as both the Goddess of Spring and the Harvest," he said dryly.

He is lying to us, a voice thundered in her head. It didn't match that of her dual or one she had ever heard before. But it was one she found an odd feeling of comfort hearing, protective and guarded as she knew she would need to be.

Kore dropped her hand to her side and gripped the pomegranate she had tucked away.

That is what you all assume, the voice pushed again, and it was something she could agree with. In her heart, she knew Aidoneus did not mean his parting words, and Hermes informing her of the threat at hand only fueled her plan. She just needed to figure out how to get her mother to safety and how to present the idea to Zeus that it was best that Kore stayed in the Underworld.

Hermes cracked the reins against the chargers three times, and they took off at lightning speed, blurring the land around them. Wind smacked Kore in the face, sending her back, and she threw out her hands to clutch the railing of the chariot.

"Sorry!" Hermes called as they sped off, racing up to the

steep climb to Olympus. Kore could hear him struggling to suppress his joy from the ride. She knew he felt for her, her mother, and possibly even Aidoneus, but he found joy where joy was not often found—most annoyingly at the wrong times.

The two divines sped up the side of Mt. Olympus with haste to meet the King of Gods and Demeter, to settle this dispute and find out why Demeter would cause such a fuss after being indifferent about it in the beginning.

By the time Hermes had tied his chargers up at the stables, Kore had more questions on her mind than she had when they left the Underworld.

"Are you ready?" He stepped to her side.

Kore's eyes scaled the stretch of mountain all the way up to where the council chamber sat.

She inhaled deeply, ignoring the twisting in her stomach as she looked back to her half-brother. "I am ready."

Kore placed her hand on the pomegranate once more as they headed up, reluctantly taking each step one by one up the long stairway. The energy slowly weighed on her shoulders the further they went. Overpowering and suffocating.

"They are waiting for us in the council chamber." Hermes sighed as he placed his hand on the golden handle. He waited a moment, watching as Kore steadied herself, preparing her mind for what lay on the other side.

He pulled the handle, opening the door with a loud creak that echoed through the empty halls.

"I thought you said they were waiting?" Kore argued as they stepped into the vacant council chamber. The thrones and table lay bare without any hint of the other divines. Even the energy around Kore felt stagnant against her skin.

"I did. I mean, they were," Hermes pondered to himself.

Kore didn't focus on him long, as the vibrations from the garden began to push against her. During her first visit, they had been calm and happy to greet the Goddess of Spring. Now they seemed anxious to get her attention. Calling and crying out to her. Her mother's vengeance had affected even them.

While Hermes wandered about the chamber, looking under objects not meant for hiding, Kore made her way to the garden to console the plants. Their worries were just as heavy of a weight on her as the mortals. She stopped before the grass, preparing the wave of emotions that would wash through her the moment she entered.

"I am sorry, my dear friends," she whispered to them. With a deep breath, she took a step in.

The shock wave that ripped through her was less agonizing than that of the pomegranate, but still pulled her to her knees. She gasped, pressing her hands into the ground as their words filled her.

Their cries were not due to pain from her mother, but from the pain her mother was enduring. Kore could feel Demeter's energy through them, seeping up from the soil and blooming out from the blossoms. The undeniable scent of fresh baked bread lofted all around her.

Her hands ripped free from the dirt, and she fell back onto the marble floor, colliding into Hermes as she did.

"Do you really think right now is the time to play with your plant friends, Kore?" he asked her.

The vibrations of the grass, the garden, and the flowers filled her ears with what they had witnessed. Fear, pain, agony—all filled her chest with a heavy rock. She looked up to Hermes with rounded eyes.

"She's hurt!" Kore blurted.

Before the god could question her, she was up, running from the chamber in the direction the garden had warned. She raced into the corridor, and her mother's energy fell on her instantly, pulling her like a fish on a string until Kore was faced with a second set of golden doors bearing another depiction of a battle. Only, this one focused on the God of War himself. The sound of muffled sobbing fought to break through the thick gold.

Kore gritted her teeth and pushed against it with no luck.

She grasped the handle with both hands and attempted pulling, but that, as well, offered her little. With no time to think and a scattered mind, she pushed her energy into the door, calling for her vines from the very earth beneath the marble under her feet.

"Mama!" Kore called out.

"Kore! What are you doing?" Hermes probed as he walked up.

"She's in there!" Kore called out to her vines once more, feeling their vibrations as they began to push through the marble. The silly god looked around the door frantically but didn't ask her how she would know. He only offered more assistance.

"I'll find the key." Hermes flew down the hall and out of sight as Kore pulled the vines free of the marble with a loud crack.

"I'm coming, Mama!" Kore guided her vines around the handles of the door.

The hall filled with a thunderous boom as the door busted free of its hinges and crashed to the ground. Darkness and the scent of burning wheat spilled out when Kore peered in, waiting for the dust to clear before rushing in for fear Ares was waiting. Using her mother to lure her into a trap somehow.

The vines raced in first, whipping about the walls beside the door for any waiting god. They smashed the nearby columns and felt for any sign of life, finding nothing but the cold marble and stone.

From deep within the chamber, in a weak, frail voice, a sound sent chills through the goddess's heart.

"Kore?"

BONUS

HERMES

Hello. Welcome, it is I! Hermes—the one and only of course. Now, I know what you are probably thinking—*Hermes! You were hardly in this story, and Ambrosia clearly states your book isn't a part of this series!* And you would be correct, but, as correct as that may be, I thought I would share my side of things—or at least a particular little bit that I had a hand in. I am actually quite proud of my work—thank you.

That is not all I have to share; I am sure you are also wondering, *Hermes, how do you know modern words like* sis *and* hang*?* Well, that is where this story begins. Now grab some wine, some sweet honey wheat bread, and a nice comfy seat, because I am about to give you a bit of the behind-the-scenes—which was me! I am the behind-the-scenes!

To start this tale off right, I must remind you that I am the God of Messages, and being as such, I have come across a lot of secrets and actions. From hidden affairs to secret divine-mortal unions, I have seen it all. A lot of my tasks take me far and wide. So, I am sure you can imagine the things I have collected.

Anyway, it was upon one request from Zeus to the Fates that I stumbled upon the most curious of discussions between the creepy ancient ones and the Goddess of Witchcraft. I will say, my vocabulary is all due to this particular day as well, as I like to browse the Fabrics of Time. It is safe to say I had quite the day in their cavern, but the information that was shared between them and Hecate was of most interest.

This was before Demeter had conceived Kore, so I hadn't known all too well of whom they spoke at the time.

I had tried tricking the information out of Hecate the following day—but she was not having any of my antics. She did, however, manage to track me down a moon later, stating I would be beneficial to the Fates' plans. And thus she informed me of the imbalance that had begun to rise within the Underworld. The Fates need balance, and so they crafted a divine into the golden tapestry that held all the gods' and goddesses' threads of destiny.

A divine who was to be the Queen of the Underworld.

But there was a catch to this plan, as with most of the Fates' plans: Hades and this new divine had to come together naturally and without knowing this destiny was crafted for them. Elsewise, the imbalance would only grow stronger and out of divine control.

So, keep all that information in mind. A new divine is to be Queen of the Underworld, and Hades is not to know.

But I know, Hecate knows, and the Fates know.

I also may or may not have slipped it up to my sweet Alena one night after a few too many kantharoi of wine. And Hecate had to inform the Erinyes for one reason or another, but she would not share that with me.

All in all, those of us who helped Kore did so because we knew she was to be our queen. Not to mention, she is my youngest half-sister, and being a Chthonian god, I can sense the darkness that creeps in all of us, the darkness that allows us to roam the Underworld.

Kore has always held a strange pulsating power, darkness hidden under her bright, cheery face. Darkness that cried to be where she was destined to be.

It *was* a nice little secret that I enjoyed holding, and it is probably worth mentioning that Hecate said she would turn me into a goat and send me to reside with the Erinyes if I was to tell anyone. Being on Hecate's bad side is not on my to-do list.

As I mentioned, she said I could not tell anyone of this—least of all Hades—but she did not say I could not give a slight shove in the right direction.

So, that is why we will now move forward, to my sweet baby sister's seventeenth year!

Now, I am no God of Love, but I do what I can, where I can, and this was a time when I could do just that.

"Hermes!" Zeus thundered, a summons, really, to the

throne room for my daily tasks. An agitating wake-up call.

I enjoy a slow rise, one that starts when Helios sweeps away the clouds from his bright sun before riding it around for the mortals. A peaceful way to wake up. Something about the beaming rays opens the flowers in the garden—their scents flooding all the chambers and halls like a washing wave of serenity.

When Zeus wakes you, you get none of that. It is abrasive and jarring.

I jerked up, white furs falling about my waist. I rubbed my eyes as I struggled to see, but it was all still so dark, and it took my eyes a moment to adjust.

"Hermes!" Zeus called again.

I groaned. It would have been nice to collect myself before starting my duties—but duties call.

I swiftly jumped to my feet, free and bare, and had half a mind to present myself as such since he wanted to wake me from such a blissful slumber. But as joyous as that would seem, it would only slow my day down.

I grabbed my white chiton and slipped it on, tied a golden belt at my waist, and slipped on my golden talaria. I walked over to the reflective metal plate to look myself over. My hair fell angelically around my face, as always—perfection. Not much needed to be done to obtain this level of beauty, really, but I ran my hands through my golden locks a few times before shifting to the dining chamber for some ambrosia and nectar. Most of the divines complained of the two, but I absolutely love them! The sweetness is everything.

I gathered my kantharos of nectar and shifted to the throne room to greet my dear father. As you can imagine, my shifting cloud is a glorious white puff with a splash of golden dust—but can you guess its smell? Now, if you guessed honey, then you know me all too well.

Anyway, I arrived right in front of Zeus, who lazed back in his large white-and-golden marble throne. The oval chamber sat flanked by high-reaching columns—as most all of our décor is. Large, golden tapestries draped from one column to the next, creating a beautiful wall of designs behind him. The tapestry would also catch Helios and his sun's rays, lighting the entire chamber in blinding chaos.

I bowed, as one must when greeting the King of Gods. His snow-streaked hair fell calmly around his face and rested on his shoulders. His beard was short-trimmed this day, but usually, it was a nest at his chin.

"You called for me?" I asked, taking another sip of nectar. My eyes on his.

"Today is Kore's birthday. Did you get her a gift?" he inquired.

He never got her a gift; that, too, was one of my duties—along with reminding him of the day. I was pleasantly surprised he had remembered on his own. However, if he remembered the day, I did not see why he had not retrieved a gift for her himself.

"They just returned from their work not two days ago. I haven't had the chance to ask what she favors," I said, finishing off my nectar and dissolving the kantharos into a mist.

"You visited them frequently during their work. Had you not asked then?" he countered.

"I suppose not."

"You know what that child likes. Just get her something you have given her once before . . ." His voice trailed off as his eyes drifted past me to the entrance. A large smile spread across his face.

"Hera! Good morning, my little peacock!" he said in a booming voice.

I turned to find the lovely but not so kind Hera—Queen of the Gods. Her red-blonde hair fell in waves over her shoulders and down to her rib cage. Her deep blue eyes studied me as she sauntered closer to us.

"Hera," I greeted with a bow.

"Hermes. Pleasant surprise to see you here, in the palace,

this early—still," she said in a condescending tone, hinting for me to get started with my duties away from Mt. Olympus.

I wish I could say she disliked me for being one of Zeus's children, but that wasn't it. She did not like that I was a Chthonian god and that I spend a great deal of time in the Underworld—a location she despised nearly as much as she despised the women Zeus went off with.

I smiled politely to her. "I was just leaving." I turned back to Zeus, who was already moving from his throne to greet his wife. "Was that all?"

He nodded quickly and took Hera by the hand; she shot one last look at me through slanted eyes before heading to the throne with her husband. I turned and left the chamber. I needed just a bit of time to think of what to get Kore.

There were few things she cared for because there were very few things she knew of. But if I had to guess, the one thing she had most definitely asked about frequently over the last three winters was Hades. Or *Aidoneus* as she called him. Cute in a sense—he hadn't used that name in centuries. I had assumed he disliked it.

I thought he would make a nice gift; my only issue was figuring out how to package him up and deliver him because he would never do so willingly—he is about as dense as a rock when it comes to romantic feelings. Where he sees curiosity, I see an odd infatuation—but at least she was a tad bit older now. Not to mention I could not just tell him to go see her. I had to plant the idea like a seed and make him think he thought of it on his own.

"Hermes!" I heard Apollo's voice echo through the corridor. I spun around to see him already bounding my way with parchments in hand.

"Apollo," I greeted cheerfully.

"I have messages for my mother if you could take them to her on Delos." He handed me the parchment and leaned closer. "And these—are from Helios. He said you would know what to do with them." His voice was low as he spoke.

He handed me a few bundles wrapped in leather and tied with twine. I nodded and took them as well, balancing the parchments for Leto and the bundles from Helios. I manifested a satchel at my side and slid them in.

"It shall be done." I clasped my hand around his forearm, and he did the same with me before he departed for Helios's Temple.

Delos was a distance from Olympus, and the bundle Helios needed me to deliver was an even further distance, plus I still had shades to guide.

I knew I would have to tell Hades something, so I thought I would let him know of my busy day—possibly toss in the fact that it was Kore's birthday. I would be busy all day anyway, might as well warn him of the late-coming shades.

I shifted to the Underworld, finding myself in the Judgment Hall, which Hades also used as his throne room. His throne, however, was not as ostentatious as Zeus's. It was rather plain actually, large even. He could lie down if he felt the need, and he is a good bit taller than I am, wider too. But he sat, leaning back with his arm resting on the flat armrest slab and resting his chin in his hand. Looking just as bored as he always did.

He didn't take much notice of my entrance, only flashing his eyes up to me and waiting.

"Careful, my lord, all that excitement to see me may hurt your back!" I toyed with a bow, but still, he was quiet, only pulling his brows down in response.

"I come bearing news. Some you might enjoy." I chuckled.

"I do not enjoy news, Hermes," he said boorishly.

I laughed again—his tone always so flat and unmoved.

"Well, I thought I would inform you of my lack of shades this day. You see, I have some distant drop-offs to make, and it is dear Kore's seventeenth year—Zeus has ordered me to drop off a gift to her. One I will have to find myself and take to her in Demeter's meadow, so I will be bringing my share of shades through a bit later than usual," I informed.

As I spoke, I watched his body and posture for any change at the sound of her name. There wasn't much movement in his body, but his eyes seemed to light up a bit. I smiled as I watched the thoughts roll around in his mind.

"Very well," he muttered.

I bowed once more before shifting to drop off the remaining messages.

I walked the group of late shades to the Judgment Halls as I said I would. Helios and the false sun of the Underworld had both long since ended their day and were replaced by their beautiful counterparts. The false moon for this realm, Selene, and Artemis for the mortal realm.

The hall was luminescent with the glow of shades; it had been some time since I had seen them spill out as they did. The last time I had witnessed such an overflow was when Thanatos had gotten himself chained up.

I left the shades with the rest of the group and tucked myself behind the dark obsidian-carved column, poking my head around. My eyes fell to the king at his throne.

He sat up straight, his brows pulled down, but I could see the ever so faint smile that ghosted across his face. For most who did not know him, he would have still appeared to be unfazed or indifferent—but I could tell he had not been attending his judgments the whole day, and I could only take one guess as to where he had spent most of it.

The only way to be sure was to speak with Helios, as per our agreement. He should have news for me on this matter.

The light and airy sensation consumed me as I shifted from sight and headed back to the sweet tips of Olympus, arriving at the exquisite, yet pretentious dining hall. The long table was carved of selenite crystal, loaded and spilling over with copious amounts of fruits and meats, cheeses and bread, and every form of ambrosia and nectar one could imagine. The air was heavy with cooked lamb and honeyed wine.

It was late, and most of the other divines had already passed through for their share. Yet still, the table remained cluttered from end to end.

I grabbed a small platter of figs and cheese. Demeter did not often bring her delightful baking, so I had to make do with Hestia's attempts—which, unfortunately for the Goddess of the Hearth, were just not up to par with Demeter's.

I had begun pouring my wine when I felt my brother's presence enter the hall. It was as loud as he was and just as bright of an energy.

"Hermes, glad to see you. How was my mother?" he asked, joining me at the table, where he began to gather his meal.

"She is well, wishes for you to see her, as always," I said, meeting his gaze.

His eyes fell dark at my words, but he did not leave. I felt there was more he needed to say.

"Have you seen the Dark One today?" he pressed.

"Only this morning. But I had deliveries to make—as you would know."

"Of course. Well, Helios has sent for me to get you and you alone for his day's discoveries."

"Perfect. I was on my way to visit him."

His lips twitched into a smile as he held out his free arm. I took it and we shifted to Helios's Temple. It sat at the highest peak, even surpassing that of Zeus's throne room.

We arrived at the front steps, surrounded by puffy white and cream-colored clouds cloaking the great ball of fire and shielding it from the mortals below. Casting shadows and night about them.

"Come, he has been waiting," Apollo urged as he ran up the steps and, with one hand, swung open the great door.

The strong scent of sunflowers and fresh summer air

drifted free with a wave of heat.

We entered the main chamber, where the ancient god rested upon his sunstone throne with one leg slung lazily over the armrest. His icy-white hair stuck out in all directions like a blazing fire. His glowing golden eyes fell upon us as we made our way to the citrine seats that surrounded a small, floating bronze table.

He nodded once and we took our seats before him.

"Helios," I greeted, and he nodded again. "You sent for me?"

His eyes closed as he nodded for the third time.

"So, you have seen Hades in the mortal realm?"

Again, he nodded.

"In Demeter's meadow?" I pressed. Perhaps I should lead with better questions.

He finally spoke, his deep voice echoing around the chamber. "Demeter's daughter is quite lovely. A vengeful child too. A darkness that seems to meet that of Lord Hades's darkness."

"How do you mean?"

He was never one to give a straight answer, always "riddle me this" and "riddle me that."

"It would seem the young goddess is far more fearless than her mother," he began. "I had never seen something so sweet and soft—certainly not with divines so dark. It brought light to the meadow. For the Dark One gifted the child a precious crystal, and to thank him, the sweet young Goddess of Spring gracefully melted her body to him, lifted on her delicate toes, and pressed her lips firmly against his. The Dark One did not halt this contact; surprisingly, he welcomed it."

He told the event as if it were some old romantic tale—so many details to describe a kiss.

"And then?"

"She ran away from him." He shrugged.

I scrunched my nose at him. "She ran away from him?"

"She did not seem frightened—but she did seem to be in

a hurry after departing from him," Apollo added.

"Did he go after her?"

"No—I believe he just shifted back to his realm or wherever it is he likes to be," Helios said.

I nodded, pleased with my work—his smile at the Judgment Hall was satisfaction enough that my plan had been a success. Though, I had not figured Kore to be so bold.

Helios shifted in his seat, moving his leg from the armrest and straightening himself so that even while sitting, he seemed to tower over me.

"I have kept my eye on the Dark One and the Goddess of Spring as you have requested. Now, what of my request of you?"

THANK YOU FOR READING!

I want to start by saying: Hades and Persephone are more than just characters to me. They are gods; they are the Theo I follow. I do consider myself Hellenic, and for me, this is more than just a retelling. It is an offering to them.

I always say this is not my story to tell. I am just putting into words the story I have been given.

When I first thought of publishing and what stories I wanted to write, dark romance was not my top pick—I tend to lean toward thriller and horror. But I am so happy that my first published piece is for Hades and Persephone.

This book alone took a total of three years. I went through writer's block, imposter syndrome, quitting my job, and starting a business, all during the pandemic of 2020, and I am ecstatic to have completed it—I got it done, and not only do I hope my family is proud, but I hope *They* are as well.

I cannot express how thankful I am that you chose to read my book until the end. You made it! I know the ending was a bit of a cliffhanger, but I promise it will all be worth the wait!

I certainly hope you enjoyed the adventure as much as I did and that you stick around for Hades's account of things.

Ambrosia

ABOUT THE AUTHOR

Ambrosia R. Harris is a dark fantasy author with a deep interest in Greek mythology. She combined that with her love of writing to create her first series, The Taking of Persephone. Her books focus on self-discovery and women's empowerment while also stirring in a bit of romance. When Ambrosia is not writing, she is spending her time studying herbalism, filming content, and chasing after her children. Ambrosia grew up in the dry desert of Las Vegas and currently still resides there with her husband, three kids, and their pets.

OTHER BOOKS BY AMBROSIA

The Dark Realms Series:
Sunflower in the Shadows

"Hi, I'm Mina Karim and I'm... Well, I'm not too sure what I am. Not anymore anyway. But what I am sure of, is never, under any circumstances, offer your soul to a demon while drunk."

After breaking every rule in the book, Mina and her friends accidentally summon an ambivalent demon, creating a domino effect of terrors they now must find a way to fix.

The problem? Nobody truly knows about the power they stumbled upon. Now, Mina finds herself working with the very demon who took her soul, to find a way to break their tether. Will they be able to break the bond? Or will the truth send them spiraling further into the endless depths of the Six Circles?

Demons and Mortals Series:
Best-Seller
Muse
Revenge
Demon King

Some mortals make deals with demons for riches or fame, but the women of the Comeaux family want none of those.

A short series of interconnecting stand-alones about three mortal sisters who want the best out of their careers, and three demon brothers they were promised to. Each story is four chapters long, so they are perfect for a quick, spicy palate cleanser.

www.ingramcontent.com/pod-product-compliance
Ingram Content Group UK Ltd.
Pitfield, Milton Keynes, MK11 3LW, UK
UKHW040741171125
9004UKWH00045B/866

9 798349 478703